Don't miss a single misadventure of the marvelous mistress of mystery—as Miss Seeton . . .

witnesses a murder at the opera in PICTURE MISS SEETON . . . investigates a local witches' coven in WITCH MISS SEETON . . . assists Scotland Yard in MISS SEETON DRAWS THE LINE . . . mixes with a gang of European counterfeiters in MISS SEETON SINGS . . . dons diamonds and furs for a game of roulette in ODDS ON MISS SEETON . . . encounters trouble at a tennis match in ADVANTAGE MISS SEETON . . . visits Buckingham Palace in MISS SEETON BY APPOINTMENT . . . takes a cruise to the Mediterranean in MISS SEETON AT THE HELM . . . foils some roadside bandits in MISS SEETON CRACKS THE CASE . . . helps to solve a series of suspicious fires in MISS SEETON PAINTS THE TOWN . . . stumbles into a nest of crime in HANDS UP, MISS SEETON . . . helps to capture an art thief in MISS SEETON BY MOONLIGHT . . . calls on her maternal instincts to solve a crime in MISS SEETON ROCKS THE CRADLE . . . attends a cricket game in MISS SEETON GOES TO BAT . . . tends to her garden—and roots out a killer—in MISS SEETON PLANTS SUSPICION . . . plays a backstage role at the Plummergen Christmas pageant in STARRING MISS SEETON . . . helps trap some murderous antique thieves in MISS SEETON UNDERCOVER . . . investigates the case of a missing princess in MISS SEETON RULES . . . crosses paths with some very dangerous characters in SOLD TO MISS SEETON . . . and takes a bite out of chocolate-covered crime in SWEET MISS SEETON.

Available from Berkley Prime Crime Books!

HERON CARVIC'S MISS SEETON

Bonjour, Miss Seeton

Hamilton Crane

BERKLEY PRIME CRIME, NEW YORK

BONJOUR, MISS SEETON

A Berkley Prime Crime Book / published by arrangement with
the author

99/04 c.2

PRINTING HISTORY
Berkley Prime Crime hardcover edition / October 1997
Berkley Prime Crime mass-market edition / September 1998
All rights reserved.
Copyright © 1997 by Sarah J. Mason.
This book may not be reproduced in whole or in part,
by mimeograph or any other means, without permission.
For information address: The Berkley Publishing Group,
a member of Penguin Putnam Inc.,
200 Madison Avenue, New York, NY 10016.

The Putnam Berkley Inc. World Wide Web site address is
http://www.penguinputnam.com

ISBN: 0-425-16534-5

Berkley Prime Crime Books are published
by The Berkley Publishing Group,
a member of Penguin Putnam Inc.,
200 Madison Avenue, New York, NY 10016.

The name BERKLEY PRIME CRIME and the BERKLEY PRIME CRIME
design are trademarks belonging to Berkley Publishing Corporation.

PRINTED IN THE UNITED STATES OF AMERICA

10 9 8 7 6 5 4 3 2 1

BONJOUR, MISS SEETON

PROLOGUE

The main—indeed almost the only—street in the Kentish village of Plummergen runs in a long, broad, gentle curve from the Brettenden fork in the north to the Royal Military Canal and across the bridge to the distant wide expanses of the marsh in the south. This north-south direction means that every morning the sun, if not obscured by cloud, shines into windows facing the eastern side of The Street (as the main thoroughfare is proudly named), while in the afternoon it shines into windows facing the west.

Plummergen's post-office-cum-general-store stood more than proud in its new livery on the eastern side of The Street. Mr. Stillman, postmaster and proprietor of the most important emporium for several miles, had recently replaced the shop's canvas awning—orange-and-brown stripes with scalloped edges—with a straight-edged version striped in black and white. Plummergen did not forget its past success in the county's Best-Kept Village contest, when archrival Murreystone had failed even to be placed, and in This Year of Grace 1974 the sturdy spirit of competition was once again abroad. Rumour held that Murreystone had secretly consulted BBC Radio's *Gardener's Question Time* team, which Plummergen (having failed to think of it first) considered unfair. Murreystone (insisted Plummergen) must not be allowed to Get Away With It. Cheats did not deserve to prosper: Plummer-

gen—having on that earlier successful occasion wiped Murreystone's collective eye without difficulty—did. The post-
office awning was only one of many schemes this year to
make a previous second best the best of all. . . .

Yet on the afternoon when our narrative begins the new
awning had come in for more brickbats than appreciative
bouquets from the post-office shoppers. The rays of the midsummer sun had proved too relentless for even the best quality canvas to bear, for though the Longest Day was five days
past, the temperature continued both steady and high.

Behind the cheese counter Emmeline Putts tossed her
head and fretted for the weight of the new white muslin cap
that crowned in milkmaid style her short dark hair. Emmy
did not dare sigh too loudly, for Elsie Stillman wore an
identical frilled confection without complaint—but Elsie
(who had made the muslin caps) was the wife of Postmaster
Stillman, and thus Emmy's employer. If the ones who paid
the wages wanted to beautify the people as well as the fabric
of the village, Emmy wasn't going to argue with them.

But they couldn't blame a girl for sighing and tossing her
head. Anything to get the air moving. "Ooh, it's so hot,"
moaned Emmy, pleating half a sheet of greaseproof paper
into a makeshift fan. "So hot . . ."

"Hot it certainly is," said Mrs. Henderson, whose brow
was bedewed with perspiration. "Like an oven in here, the
way the sun beats down. I'll take a tin of peaches, ta, Mrs.
Stillman—and one of evap as well. It's too hot to carry ice
cream home, newspaper wrapping or no."

"Visitors, Mrs. Henderson?" enquired Mrs. Skinner in
the tone of voice that suggests luxuries of the tinned-
peaches-and-evaporated-milk variety can only be justified by
a circumstance so abnormal (in one so unpopular as Mrs.
Henderson) as the necessity to feed a guest. Mrs. Skinner
had quarrelled with Mrs. Henderson some years before over
the church flower rota, since when the two ladies had never
been able to agree about anything. As it was, however, on
a day like this clearly impossible to dispute the state of the

weather, Mrs. Skinner had been forced to fall back on oblique personal insult—which might or might not prove ultimately worth the effort of invention according to Mrs. Henderson's willingness to rise to the bait.

"Hot ain't the word," interposed Mrs. Spice pacifically. Such pacifism on her part was unusual. She had never quite made up her mind which side of the Skinner-Henderson feud she supported—in the interests of lively debate she was often happy to change opinion in mid-sentence, if the mood took her—but the relentless heat had sapped her confrontational energies, and rather than struggle down from her metaphorical fence she preferred to postpone an otherwise promising argument for a later occasion.

Besides, the entire shop could be confident that Mrs. Henderson was *not* expecting visitors. The last-but-one bus of the day had already been and gone, nobody would visit as late as the last, and few of Mrs. Henderson's acquaintance, outside the village or in, owned a car.

"Flaming June!" proclaimed Mrs. Spice in the manner of recent newspaper headlines, and with an ironic twinkle in her eye. "Not," she added quickly, "that I'm sure you haven't done your best to keep the sun out of here, Mrs. Stillman—but there's really no arguing with nature when she's set on her course, is there? I'll have a pound o' mild cheddar, Emmy, and I don't want it wrapped in the top sheet, neither."

Emmy dropped her greaseproof paper fan and blushed. Mrs. Stillman shot her a warning look but said nothing as she busied herself with Mrs. Henderson's tins. Mrs. Skinner, who had wondered whether to take offence at having her limelight thus dimmed, glanced out of the window. What she saw made her decide at once that it was far too hot to care. "And July like to be worse, they say—though we'll find out for ourselves next week," she offered. It was a neutral comment signalling tacit acceptance of a truce for the rest of the day. Her quarrel with Mrs. Henderson was of long and honourable duration: she could tell that nobody was in the mood to indulge it. . . .

For there was a far more tantalising—albeit fitful—schism in Plummergen that was likely to occupy everyone's attention in about ten seconds flat.

An eager Mrs. Skinner pushed past young Mrs. Newport and her sister, the triplet-haunted Mrs. Scillicough, in order to block anyone else's view of the door of the shop. The door was propped open to allow whatever breeze there might be to struggle through it: there was, therefore, no jangle of the bell to herald the new arrival as, with a weary tread, she crossed the post-office threshold.

"Why, hello! Didn't see you on the bus coming back, Miss Nuttel," came the cheery greeting from Mrs. Skinner. Every head in the shop whipped round. Eyes gleamed, pulses quickened. Mrs. Skinner felt a warm glow inside that was less to do with ambient temperature than with satisfaction at having beaten her fellow gossips to the draw. "Thermometer's certainly got up since this morning, hasn't it?" went on Mrs. Skinner as Miss Erica Nuttel—tall, bony, equine of feature—acknowledged the salute with a silent nod.

"Hardly the weather for walking far—specially by yourself," persisted Mrs. Skinner, an upward lilt of enquiry in her voice. "And carrying so much shopping," she added, with a pointed look for the bulky canvas bags depending from Miss Nuttel's aching and elongated arms. "Why, a body could collapse with heat stroke miles from anywhere—and no one to send for help," she went on as Miss Nuttel, disdaining a second nod, tried to move past her.

"Or turn their foot on uneven ground," offered young Mrs. Newport, overanxious mother, in doom-laden accents. "You want to take care, Miss Nuttel, walking alone, never mind you're wearing a hat for once—and very handsome, too, if I may say so—but look at poor Sir George."

"It was his wrist Sir George sprained, not his ankle," said Mrs. Scillicough at once. Mrs. Scillicough's triplets were a village byword for frightfulness; their four Newport cousins were (as far as any adult of the village could tell) paragons of infant rectitude.

"Yes, and we all know how he did it, too," chipped in Mrs. Henderson. "Him and the admiral . . ."

The company (with one exception) was pleased to find this remark amusing, and a titter ran round the room.

"A—a Monica Mary hat, is it, Miss Nuttel?" enquired Mrs. Skinner. There was a noticeable element of control in her voice, and everyone—except, as before, Erica Nuttel—tittered again.

"Yes," said Miss Nuttel through clenched teeth. "Excuse me. Stamps." Squaring her shoulders as well as she could for the weight of the canvas bags, she trod grimly past the queues at the cheese and grocery counters towards the grille at the back of the shop, behind which Postmaster Stillman earned his keep.

"Any milk-bottle tops for the collection, Miss Nuttel?" This from Mrs. Skinner, with another upward lilt.

Miss Nuttel turned to face her interrogators. "Animal protein," she informed the shop through gritted teeth, "is—is anathema." With which she turned back to continue her slow progress to Mr. Stillman's grille.

"Milk's hardly an animal," observed Mrs. Henderson in a loud voice. "And when it's for the kiddies, poor crippled mites, you'd think *anyone* would want to—to do their bit."

Miss Nuttel halted her march at the grille—where she paused, reached into the pocket of her slacks, and withdrew a crumpled brown envelope on which the keener-eyed could make out the scrawl of a shopping list. From this, with a flourish missed by nobody, Miss Nuttel tore the top right-hand corner and dropped it in the grey plastic dustbin Mr. Stillman had temporarily withdrawn from sale and for which—so great had been the clamour to be allowed to purchase it later at a Shop-Soiled Discount rate—he was selling raffle tickets as a further boost to funds.

"Do their bit?" echoed Mrs. Skinner with a grin. World

War II and its associated memories had been very much to the fore in village consciousness of late. "That's more like war talk than charity, I should say."

"Charity begins at home," said Mrs. Scillicough with a sideways look at her sister. Three children of the same sex and size couldn't afford to be choosy if those more fortunate in their family structure cared to pass on any unwanted clothes, toys, or books. Which Mrs. Scillicough thought that they ought to do, blood being thicker than water. In some cases. So she had always understood.

"Yes, we've a lot to be thankful for in Plummergen," said Mrs. Newport piously. "There's people far worse off would be grateful to have a roof over their heads that didn't leak, and no money to spare, poor souls, even when it's medical."

"It's a blessing to have good health," said Mrs. Henderson with equal piety.

Mr. Stillman was busy with his files. Miss Nuttel, too weary to interrupt him, had time to glare over her shoulder at the gossips. "Start with the diet," she advised them as she waited to be served. "Purify the system. No fish, no fowl . . ." Her equine features twisted in a grimace. "No . . . flesh. Plenty of roughage—and low salt," she added as Mr. Stillman cleared his throat for her attention. "Twelve second-class stamps," said Miss Nuttel, turning back to the grille. "Please," she added as the postmaster coughed.

There was clearly no more fun to be had with Miss Nuttel until her business was concluded. "Poor little mites," said young Mrs. Newport with a loud and sentimental sigh. "Makes me rejoice in my heart that my kiddies are good as gold—in respect of their health, that is," she added after what was almost a meaningful pause during which her sister shot her a furious look, but could say nothing aloud. Natives of Plummergen have throughout the generations honed to the finest of arts the art of insult. They know to a nicety how far one may push another without overstepping the border between what might and what must be misunderstood.

"Count your blessings, that's what I always say," said Mrs. Newport. "Asked for an extra daily pint, I have—all for a good cause, ain't it." This was a statement, not a question, and her audience murmured hearty approval of the opinion expressed.

Mrs. Scillicough was not to be outdone. "Well, I'd write more letters if it wasn't that everyone I'd write to lives within walking distance, save Christmas," she informed the murmurers, somewhat irritably.

"And don't they just love soaking the stamps off in warm water?" cried Mrs. Newport, with a pitying smile for her sister. "Such a shame it can be so messy, though. Sometimes." The meaningful pause was more obvious here. Practice, in Plummergen as elsewhere, makes perfect.

Miss Nuttel, folding stamps into her purse, snapped the clasp shut, slipped the purse in the pocket of her slacks, picked up her shopping with a sigh she almost managed to stifle, and began to move away from the post-office grille. Her thin lips were pressed together, and she was doing her best to allow her eye neither to catch, nor to be caught by, the eyes of the other shoppers.

The other shoppers brightened. Here was an opportunity for something more interesting than a routine demonstration of sibling rivalry. "Off home now, Miss Nuttel?" enquired Mrs. Skinner in friendly fashion. "It's getting near teatime, of course, and I daresay you'll be looking forward to a bite to eat."

"You'll be thirsty after . . . your walk," countered Mrs. Henderson. "By the canal, was it? Even on a day such as this there's nobody could blame you for not wanting to drink out o' that water. Proper murky, it is."

"Gives you collywobbles," said Mrs. Spice, seizing her cue. "Hope that's not what's the matter with Mrs. Blaine, Miss Nuttel, you with your own well and all in the garden and that thunderstorm on Monday stirring things up. Is she very poorly? Seems funny to see the one of you out without the other, except that—"

"Migraine," said Miss Nuttel, and once more pressed her lips together.

She soon had to open them again as the sympathetic (and barely ironic) clicking of tongues was coupled with a skillfully artless surging of the post-office shoppers across her path, inviting further intelligence with the unspoken but obvious inference that if none was forthcoming, Miss Nuttel's going would continue to be hindered. Miss Nuttel perforce uttered a few taut syllables to the effect that earlier in the day her friend Mrs. Blaine had seen fit to lie down in a darkened room with cotton-wool plugs in her ears. Whether or not (Miss Nuttel's tone implied) such prophylactic self-deafening was merited, Miss Nuttel did not care to say; whether or not it was the business of anyone but Mrs. Blaine was also no subject for general discussion. Now, if they would excuse her—

"Funny to see you around on your own," said Mrs. Skinner, echoing Mrs. Spice. "Except that, well—"

"Glad you think migraine's funny," Miss Nuttel broke in. "Can't say I share your sense of humour."

"Well, no," said Mrs. Skinner, simpering. "As to funny, perhaps the word was ill-chosen—but you know what I mean, Miss Nuttel. The two of you it's always been, these dozen years or more, but now—"

"Now I'd better get back," said Miss Nuttel, squaring her elbows (as well as she could) when she saw how far away the door of the post office still was, and how many people she would have to pass to reach it.

"Things to do," said Mrs. Henderson, looking wise.

"Cooking," suggested young Mrs. Newport, efficient earth mother, with a faint titter.

"Gardening," amended her sister automatically.

"Good afternoon," said Miss Nuttel with a brisk nod as the sisters stood for one brief moment apart and she saw her way clear. With the back of her neck hot with embarrassment Miss Nuttel headed for the post-office door and passed over the threshold. If the door hadn't been propped open—

and if her hands hadn't been full—she would have taken the greatest of pleasure in slamming it shut and making the bell jangle on its spring.

As it was, she could only trudge away with her feet and arms aching, her nose in the air, and her ears resolutely deaf to the seething turmoil of speculation she knew she must be leaving behind her.

It was too hot to stay out of doors any longer than she must, cotton-wool recuperation notwithstanding. Erica Nuttel hesitated only briefly at the kerb, looking up and down The Street for approaching traffic, and then made a diagonal crossing to the other side, where the shadows of hedge and fence and front wall were beginning to form on the footpath as the sun sank lazily in the west.

"Ahem. A splendid afternoon, Miss Nuttel." From under the brim of an ancient panama hat the ginger beard of Rear Admiral Bernard "Buzzard" Leighton wagged in some embarrassment at the newcomer across the fence of Ararat Cottage, the property the Buzzard had, on making his retirement landfall in Plummergen, chosen more on account of its name than its next-door neighbours.

"And—er—a splendid hat," he ventured. Miss Nuttel looked at him in silence and nodded. "All by yourself, I see," the admiral pressed on, making desperate small talk. "Ah—everyone keeping well?"

"Thank you," said Miss Nuttel after a pause. "Yes. As well as can be expected," she added after another pause. She coughed. "Must be getting on," she said as the Buzzard seemed about to say more. "Excuse me."

Placing one canvas bag on the ground, she set her hand on the latch of the gate of Lilikot, the plate-glass-windowed home she and Mrs. Norah Blaine (known to her friend as Bunny) had shared for the past twelve years.

From Miss Nuttel's point of conversational view it was a remarkable coincidence that one of the admiral's honeybees, its leg sacs bulging with yellow pollen, should choose that particular moment to zoom wearily past on its way to the hives at the back of Ararat Cottage. Miss Nuttel's hand leaped from the latch. She snorted, flapped at the hapless insect, threw back her head, and skittered with her feet in a manner making her resemblance to the equine tribe even more pronounced. Even before a recent neighbourly contretemps, Miss Nuttel, from the day of the apiarist admiral's arrival in the village, had lived in terror of anaphylactic shock, and carried an old ballpoint pen with her wherever she went, just in case.

Nobody who was nervous of being stung could be expected to make polite conversation, and Miss Nuttel had never had any liking for bees. The incident both parties were too embarrassed to mention outright had only made matters worse. She nodded again to the admiral—who had turned almost as red as his beard—pressed her lips together in case she should accidentally inhale, opened the Lilikot gate, grabbed her canvas bag, and hurried up the front path without pausing to slip the latch behind her. Admiral Leighton removed his panama to mop his brow, waved the hat in polite farewell towards her retreating back, and returned in great relief to his flowers.

Miss Nuttel's hand was shaking as she inserted her key in the front door, and her legs trembled. The hot summer afternoon was full of buzzing, whining creatures of the air. She had to draw several deep breaths before, blinking at the contrast of sunny outside and shaded interior, she could nudge the door open and step to safety.

Having set the shopping down, she shook her cramped arms to loosen them, cursing (but quietly) at the pins and needles. On exaggerated, ill-balanced tiptoe she made her way along the hall. Nostrils flaring, she glanced only once up the stairs in the direction of that room where Mrs. Blaine must be supposed to slumber beneath her patchwork counterpane. Miss Nuttel hoped that neither linen rustlings nor outside conversation had disturbed the cotton-wool-muffled slumber, but she knew better than to go upstairs to find out. Always assuming she had the energy to climb the stairs—

which she hadn't. She was really fit for nothing after that business with the admiral and the bee, not to mention the post office and . . . everything else. She would make herself a cup of chamomile tea—just the thing on a hot day, and good for the nerves as well—but in case anyone else should happen to appear and say that a spare cup would be gratefully received . . . she would boil enough water for two. Or maybe . . .

The afternoon sun glaring through the kitchen window outlined in dazzling gold the door at the end of the hall. Miss Nuttel reached the door and pushed. Linear gold turned into a trapezoid riot of dancing dust motes as light from the kitchen spilled the length of the hall and made Miss Nuttel blink.

Above the busy hum of—Miss Nuttel held her breath—no, *not* bees, bluebottles—she heard the siren call of chamomile. She gasped, narrowed her eyes, licked her lips, and stepped forward in eager anticipation.

Sunlight filled the kitchen, casting stark dark shadows against which the bluebottles were invisible. Miss Nuttel, who did not approve of chemical sprays, made a mental note to replace the flypaper and moved on.

Miss Nuttel stopped with one foot in midair. One of those dark shadows . . .

Miss Nuttel set her foot firmly on the tiles. Shadows went with sunshine. The kitchen faced due west. The afternoon was well advanced. . . .

Miss Nuttel found, for some strange reason, that her own preference seemed to be for retreat rather than advance. Yet any idea that one of those dark shadows was even darker than summer sunshine could achieve was . . .

"Ridiculous," said Miss Nuttel in a voice unaccountably loud, despite all her previous thought for the sleeper in the upstairs room. Bunny and her migraines . . .

Bunny.

"Bunny," ventured Miss Nuttel. "Bunny?"

That one dark shadow, unlike the shadows of windowsill

flowerpots and the rim of the sink, had no sharp edges. It might rather be said to—to sprawl. . . .

And—something—moved—buzzed—about it. . . .

Without realising she did so, Miss Nuttel moved towards the shadow. Golden dust swirled about her as she forced herself near and instinctively knelt—began to kneel—beside that dark, sprawled shadow on the kitchen floor. The shadow around which bluebottles—

Miss Nuttel jerked herself away just in time. Kneeling would make her slacks . . .

"B-bloody," whispered Miss Nuttel through white lips, and then: "Bunny!" Shrill, piercing, it was a cry from the very heart—the heart that thundered in Miss Nuttel's chest and sent the blood boiling in her head until, with one last cut-off cry, she collapsed in a faint beside the sprawling shadow. . . .

And there were two dark shadows on the kitchen floor of Lilikot. One was tall, thin, angular; the other was short, plump, and seemingly without breath.

Surely without breath. What breath could come from one whose head was such a mass of red, sticky, splintered ooze?

But if this was premeditated murder, it was not the work of a moment. Motives must be established. . . .

And these take our narrative back almost four weeks—to the beginning of the month of June.

CHAPTER 1

It was the first day of June, and Plummergen was in the news. Granted, the media's initial enthusiasm had died down somewhat, and the Kentish village was no longer making headlines—but it was still in the news. The great British public's current perception of Plummergen was of a wholly admirable place where some quite remarkable people lived . . . and died.

And in the manner of their dying—or at least in its aftermath—the inhabitants of Plummergen could be even more remarkable: as the recent death of Horace Jowett had proved beyond all reasonable doubt. MISER'S MULTIPLE MILLIONS! the *Daily Negative* had screamed in letters two inches high. GENEROSITY OF A VILLAGE RECLUSE and PENNY-PINCHER LEAVES HIS POUNDS TO CHARITY were discreet variants on the same theme. Every article told the same heartwarming tale of how the young Jowett had retired from the world after the loss of his sweetheart at the outbreak of the First War. (Good-natured invention had the girl incinerated when a zeppelin was shot down over the fields where she was picking blackberries: local realists with long memories knew that she had run off to become a camp follower in France, not that anyone local would mention this fact to the press. Even less would anyone mention the rumours that one of the most respected bordellos in Paris during the Second World War had been run by a Madame Prunière. To know that bordellos existed might be one thing, but to know the name of the proprietress was to know ... well, too much.)

So Horace Jowett had made his sullen retreat behind a front door resolutely locked, barred, and bolted against intrusion. Shortsighted, he was never conscripted into His Majesty's Forces. While he continued to work on a farm for the duration, as soon as the Armistice was signed in 1918 he forfeited a week's wages in lieu of notice and went home to lock, bar, and bolt the back door, too. Apart from a repeat performance during the six years of World War II, he was never known to step outside again. The General Strike and the Depression passed him by. His views on the Abdication went unheard, for nobody thought to ask him. Nobody ever saw him. He communicated with the world (meaning the few deliverymen prepared to hack a path through the flourishing jungle of his front garden to the house) by means of handwritten notes left in the porch under a battered plaster cast of the *Venus de Milo*. This lady being, albeit armless, nude, together with the fact that the notes were written in red ink (which could only be interpreted as scarlet) was seen as indicative of Horace Jowett's mental state, and the village maidens who had originally hoped to tempt him from his fastness decided not to bother. There were so few maidens in the village that they could afford to be choosy.

Like most right-thinking persons, Plummergen delights in giving the runaround to jacks-in-office. When, after the passage of years, a meddlesome Man from the Ministry drove fifteen miles from Ashford in an attempt to Do Something about Horace Jowett and his old-age pension, the predecessor of Postmaster Stillman was more than happy to fill in the necessary forms saying he had no objection to Horace's being sent his money through the mail each week instead of having to walk all of half a mile to collect it from the post office as most people did. Baffled, the bureaucrat withdrew, muttering dark threats about Social Services and the Mental

Health Act. These threats, for various reasons not unconnected with native cunning, came to naught.

Others of the red-tape persuasion would from time to time surface in the vicinity of Horace Jowett, but they, too, were worsted. Dr. Knight maintained that whatever his personal and medical opinion might be, he knew of no law that compelled any freeborn Englishman to breathe fresh air if he had no wish to do so. An overgrown garden (said the vicar, the Reverend Arthur Treeves) was a joyous celebration of the natural world and a haven for wildlife. Sir George Colveden thought it no more than common sense if a chap chose to hoard his daily papers in bundles and use them instead of coal. Read 'em, burn 'em: twice the use at half the price. Only sensible. Wartime spirit. Make do and mend. Couldn't afford to throw money around . . .

Then Horace died, and it turned out that he could. Had he burned banknotes instead of pulped and hand-bricked newsprint, he would hardly have noticed the loss. "Nobody," said local Wise Woman Mrs. Flax in her wisest tones, "who's *mental* could ever make that much money!" The current successors to the Man from the Ministry were unable to dispute this point, and Horace had the last—admittedly muted—laugh; but the Ministry Men were quick to take their revenge by warning their colleagues from the Inland Revenue that the estate of Horace Jowett would merit very close attention.

Yet even what was likely to remain after tax had been deducted was calculated in millions, and the estate was a talking point in Plummergen from the moment the story broke. Exaggerated in the telling it might have been—but the exaggeration was to the greater glory of the village, and a matter of parochial pride. For once—and for at least a week—there was not a dissenting voice to be heard. Plummergen was in the news for a wholly admirable reason. Was not the late Horace Jowett living proof (as it were) that the village could be as generous as any in the land? And where the sons of Plummergen led, why should others not follow?

It was no more than Plummergen's duty to carry on the good work started, for the saddest of reasons but with the happiest of results, by the late Horace Jowett. . . .

And then the dissenting voices began to be heard.

"Now, I think that's a pity," murmured Lady Colveden as she came to the end of the *Beacon* feature. *The Brettenden Telegraph and Beacon (est. 1847, incorporating [1893] The Iverhurst Chronicle and Argus)* was the local newspaper, and it had done Horace Jowett proud. "Don't you, George?"

Sir George was ensconced behind *Farmers Weekly*. A swift and tactful kick from his son alerted him to the attentions of his wife. "Ugh," he said. "What's that, m'dear?"

"Mother thinks it's a pity," offered Nigel as her ladyship rattled the newspaper in a marked fashion. "I suppose it is," he added with a heartfelt sigh. "Most things are. But that's life, isn't it?" He sighed again. Nigel's life was currently bereft of all meaning, his latest romance having but recently foundered. "Life," he reiterated, and helped himself to marmalade.

"Death," amended his mother absently as she reread the *Beacon* article. "I mean *dead,*" she corrected herself as she felt the gaze of her startled menfolk upon her, Sir George having gone so far as to lower *Farmers Weekly* for a better view. "Don't be silly," said Lady Colveden. "I mean Horace Jowett, as you both know very well." She rattled the paper again. "It says here—"

"Yes, Mother, we do know old Horace is dead." Nigel was determined to be very, very kind to everyone. "He popped off two or three weeks ago, didn't he? Some time in May, anyway. And as far as I know, he hasn't changed his mind and popped back again."

Lady Colveden folded the *Beacon* with a snap and slapped it hard on the table. "Don't be silly," she said again. "I'm talking about Horace's will, of course. The *Beacon* says that what everyone's been saying is true, and all I'm saying is that I think it's a pity. That he didn't leave just a little more to the village, I mean, to stop everyone grumbling."

Nigel waved toast in an expressive manner. "Plummer-gen," he said, "can argue black's white and grey's not a damned bit of colour. They've never done anything else."

"The boy's right," said Sir George. "Think they'd be dashed grateful the old chap left anything at all—but no. Tongues'll wag no matter what. Can't change 'em."

"I knew you knew all along what I meant." Having proved her point, Lady Colveden returned in modest triumph to the paper. "Nigel, what happened to your stamps?"

Nigel spluttered on crumbs. His father leaned across and thumped him on the back. "Cup of coffee," he suggested. "Tea? Meg, you have one, too. Do you good. Need to keep up your liquid intake in weather like this."

"I'm not suffering from heatstroke, thank you, George." Her ladyship fixed the baronet with a baleful eye. "Nigel, do stop being silly. What, may I ask, is so unreasonable about wondering what happened to your old album when Candell and Inchpin are having to send Horace's collection up to Sothenhams for a specialist opinion? It says here he had . . ." She picked up the paper and began to select items of interest: "Among other rarities, two 1931 proof sheets of a previously unknown German stamp—ten five-dollar Hong Kongs with the Queen weeping blue tears because of a printer's error—a hundred one-shilling greens from the Stock Exchange forgeries of 1872—two 1847 Trinidad Lady MacLeods—and an official fake die proof of the 1840 Penny Black."

Lady Colveden frowned over the pages of the *Brettenden Beacon* at her husband and son. "It says," she concluded, "they could be worth millions. Which is why they don't want to auction them locally. And in the circumstances I would say it was only natural to wonder. . . ."

Nigel (who had stopped spluttering) and his father were gazing at her again. "Are you sure," enquired Nigel gently, "that you're feeling all right, Mother?"

"Official fake," said her husband as she drew in a deep

and exasperated breath. "Hardly sounds altogether sensible, m'dear. The *Beacon* often gets things wrong, of course," he added loyally. "Yes, that's the answer—but have some more tea, just in case."

"George," said her ladyship heavily, "I am as sensible now as I've been in my life. Nigel, if you snigger again, I'll brain you. For people who are so scathing about other people's mental state, the pair of you seem remarkably lacking in common sense—unlike the post office when they invented stamps. According to the *Beacon,* they needed to know how easy it would be to cheat the system by using forgeries, so they very sensibly found an engraver to make some. And he did, with a die. And the one old Horace had is it."

"And was it?" enquired Nigel, straight-faced. "Easy," he added quickly as his mother's hand moved towards the teapot. "Though I suppose," he went on as she eyed him again, "the only thing that really matters is that it's worth a lot of money."

"And all for charity," said Sir George, who—in common with the rest of the village—continued to be amazed that a recluse like Horace Jowett could be so successful in the matter of stocks and shares and now, apparently, postage stamps as well.

"Which is what I was saying in the first place," said Lady Colveden crossly. "That it's a pity everyone was right about his only leaving a relatively small amount to the village, because people are starting to argue about whether it's ethical to use most of it on doing up the hall when there are . . . other worthy causes. Of course, the crippled children are the most deserving, and I'm delighted the selfish old miser decided to do something useful with his life for once—and don't stare at me like that, George. You know what I mean. Anyone who hides away from the world for so long without a very good reason is selfish—or self-indulgent, anyway, which comes to the same thing."

"Might well have gone into purdah m'self if you'd been

killed in an air raid,'' said Sir George, shuddering. ''War's a nasty business. Never know how it's going to affect you.''

''Nonsense,'' was the robust retort from his devoted help-meet. ''Even if that's what happened to her, which everyone says it isn't, *you* would have waited a decent interval and then gone twirling your moustache after every blonde in sight. Nigel, if you mention Daphne Carstairs, I'll scream.''

''Some might consider that remark in rather poor taste.'' Nigel ran a reproachful hand through the wavy brown locks he had inherited from his mother, and suppressed a grin as he went on: ''Quite apart from the fact that I am currently suffering from a broken heart, I don't think it's at all fitting for a chap's son to to dwell on the many girls his father has loved and lost when—sorry!'' He ducked as her ladyship feinted towards him with the teapot.

''Broken heart or not, I think you'll live,'' his mother told him. ''If I let you,'' she added meaningfully as she put the teapot down.

''Plenty more fish in the sea,'' his father encouraged him. ''Lots of pretty girls. Need to find the right one, that's all. Don't want to rush into things.''

''But he doesn't want to leave it too late,'' said Lady Colveden, in case Nigel should start to relax. ''We don't want him ending up a—a cantankerous old misogynist like Horace Jowett.''

''He won't,'' said Sir George, sounding confident. ''Takes after his father.''

''I say,'' said Nigel. ''Steady on, you two. Son and heir all present and correct, you know. Besides, how can you say old Horace was a misogynist? Nobody ever saw him. He could have had scores of blondes popping in every night and sneaking out next day before anyone spotted them.''

Lady Colveden arched her delicate brows as Sir George stifled a snort. ''In Plummergen?'' she said, and needed to say no more.

''Point taken,'' said Nigel with a grin. ''And I'm prepared to concede without much argument that the old man was probably cantankerous—but I do resent the implication that I'm likely to go the same way. You should have more faith in your methods of child rearing.''

"Blood will tell," said Lady Colveden enigmatically. Sir George huffed behind his *Farmers Weekly*. Nigel sighed. "One can," he said, "be single and happy with one's lot. Look at Miss Seeton, for instance—''

"Yes," broke in her ladyship, "and that's another thing they're saying. I only hope there isn't any trouble—you know how poor Miss Seeton tends to . . .'' Words failed Lady Colveden. Her eyes widened in helpless appeal as she gazed from her son to the visible portions of her husband. "Have things happen to her," finished her ladyship weakly.

Sir George's shoulders shook as he huffed once more. Nigel stifled a snort. Lady Colveden rallied. "Yes, that's all very well, but you know how people gossip," she told her irreverent menfolk. "Once the word gets around that Miss Seeton has a fortune hidden in that cottage, then goodness knows who might jump to conclusions and—and burgle the poor soul. Or worse. Remember—''

"A fortune?" Sir George lowered *Farmers Weekly* to scoff. "Nonsense, m'dear.''

"I know that, George, but not everyone does.'' Lady Colveden shook her head. "Or if they do they don't believe it, because it makes a better story if they don't. Old Horace really hasn't done poor Miss Seeton any favours—or Miss Wicks, or Colonel Windup . . . well, no, perhaps not Colonel Windup—but—''

"Miss Wicks?" gasped Nigel as his father goggled. "It must be something in the water. Mother, please tell us *this minute* what has driven the village gossips demented, even if it hasn't affected you.'' Filial piety prevented the addition of *which I take leave to doubt*. "Nothing else,'' said Nigel, "could possible excuse anything so daft as thinking old Horace numbered Miss Wicks and Miss Seeton among his—his mythical conquests. Talk about bandying a maiden's name! Has this village no sense in their stupid heads?''

"They have," said his mother sternly, "more than you, Nigel. George, don't encourage him. What they are saying, as I'm sure you understood when I first said it, is that if Horace Jowett lived such a quiet life and left such a lot of money, then it's only logical people like Miss Wicks and Miss Seeton—elderly, living alone—must have lots of money as well. And—"

But this was too much for Sir George and his son. Their shoulders heaved in identical gestures of suppressed mirth—unsuccessful suppression—and identical snorts were stifled with similar lack of success.

"Quiet life?" cried Sir George with tears in his eyes.

"Miss Seeton?" gurgled Nigel, and almost choked.

"I think you're both being . . ." But her ladyship was an honest woman. The charge of being *very silly* was, in the circumstances, not a fair one. "Well," she conceded, "perhaps not Miss Seeton, but certainly Miss Wicks. And you can't say Miss Seeton doesn't—doesn't try her best to lead a quiet life. It's hardly her fault that she . . . somehow never quite manages it."

Nigel and Sir George considered this special pleading in silence for a few moments.

"And another thing," said Lady Colveden, pink with indignation. "As if it's poor Miss Seeton's fault about the glass! But they're saying because the telephone box is right outside her house—except of course that it's quite as close to the bakery—then it's bound to be something to do with her even if everyone did hear those cars on their way to Murreystone the other night. But you know how conscientious she is. If she's talked into thinking it's her fault for not taking down the numbers, she'll be off to that picture-framing place in Brettenden buying putty and knives and panes of glass when it's the post office if it's anyone, and so terribly unfair. They'll say she can easily afford it, of course, which makes it all the more unfair because I suppose she can. I'd say something myself, except they're careful not to say anything to my face—Nigel, why are you sniggering like that?''

"Stamps," said Nigel helplessly. "First Horace Jowett, now the post office and Miss Seeton. Mother, *please* have a cup of tea and try to calm down. All this—this cerebral excitement is only making things worse."

"No," said Sir George, who knew when the teasing had to stop. "Y'mother's right. Murreystone are the most likely suspects—if it was deliberate," added the Justice of the Peace with true judicial objectivity.

"A stone chucked up by a passing car," said Nigel, who could be serious when he chose, "would have smashed an outside pane, not one facing the pavement."

"It was deliberate," said his mother. "Sheer vandalism. And anyone less like a vandal than Miss Seeton . . ."

"It was Murreystone," said Nigel, and even Sir George raised no murmur of dissent. "Thank goodness the days are so long at this time of year," added the son with a speaking look for his father. "Any hint that we should reconvene the Night Watch Men on behalf of the Best-Kept Village Competition would not find favour with me, for one. Prowling up and down The Street thwarting desperadoes in the few available hours of darkness is not my idea of efficient use of time when every blessed daylight hour is spent making hay and shearing sheep and spraying the cereal for bugs."

"Umph," said Sir George, who had been wondering whether to make the suggestion and was relieved he'd been saved the bother. "Taught 'em a lesson last time," he said hopefully. "The telephone box was just . . . high spirits."

"High or low, it has nothing to do with Miss Seeton," said her ladyship firmly. "Or with Mrs. Wyght," she added. "Just because she's in the bakery and can see the wretched telephone box when she's not busy serving people . . . She says she keeps on ringing the post office, and they keep telling her they're short of manpower and will come when they can—as if anyone believes them. I'd phone them myself if I thought it would do any good," said the baronet's wife in her best ladyship voice. "But," she went on in more normal accents, "if the village improvement fund is unable to spare a few pounds for a pane of glass and some putty, then they can't be too particular about winning the competition. And I shall tell them so at the next meeting."

Nigel grinned. "If you're dropping hints, Mother dear, that someone not a million miles from this room ought to fix the blessed pane as a—as a community service, think again. It would be churlish of me to spoil everyone's fun by doing away with even one source of argument when they all enjoy themselves so much. You know how they do."

This was undeniable, and Lady Colveden did not try to deny it. Sir George, after a moment, chuckled. "Doubt if we've too much of a chance anyway," he said. "Broken glass or not. Did so well last time they'll be picking on every little thing when they judge. Hardly fair to let the same people win each time."

"Or come second," said his son with courteous accuracy.

"What's that French phrase?" murmured her ladyship. "*Pour encourager les autres,* that's it."

"Yes, well, Murreystone don't need any encouragement," said her son grimly.

"Can't really go around shooting the blighters," said Sir George with a hint of regret.

Nigel blinked. "Who wants to shoot anyone? Oh, you mean you think it was an air rifle they loosed off at our phone box, not a stone. That's a possibility."

"Admirals," said Sir George. "I think," he added.

"The Buzzard?" cried Nigel, now genuinely puzzled. The future baronet's school days were less than a decade behind him, but his interest in academic subjects had never been great. His knowledge of the French language was minimal, and of French literature, virtually nil.

"Nigel," said his mother with a sigh, "I sometimes think boarding school was wasted on you." ("I know it was," came the comment from Nigel.) Lady Colveden regarded her husband with approval. "But I had no idea you knew so much about *Candide,* George. Poor Admiral Byng.''

"French," said Sir George airily. "Chap who wrote it, I mean, not Byng. Forget his name, though," he added before Nigel could call his bluff. "Might come back to me if we could take a trip over there," he went on with a sideways look at his wife. "Educational. *La belle France* . . .''

"Don't you mean *under* there?" enquired Nigel cheerily. "Good-bye Channel ferry, hello Channel Tunnel. Chunnel. And duty-free plonk and exotic cheese and garlic bread and—and driving on the wrong side of the road when you arrive."

"There are trains," said Lady Colveden, sounding rather wistful. "And buses—as you must remember, Nigel. What about the time you and I and Julia went to Calais for the day?" She smiled as she looked into the past. "When Janie is a little older, we must go again. It makes a lovely day out if the weather is fine."

"If the sea is calm, you mean," said Nigel with a grin.

"Don't," begged Sir George, whose memories of war-time troop ships were not altogether pleasant. His friendship with Rear Admiral Leighton was never more at risk than on those occasions when the Buzzard chose to indulge in over-graphic reminiscence.

"Sorry, Dad," said Nigel at once, and addressed his mother. "All right, you're on. He which hath no stomach to this trip," he misquoted gaily, "let him not bother getting his passport made." In a school production of *Henry V* the main role had alternated between Colveden, N.P.R., and his best friend Simkins Major. "We'll ask Jack Crabbe to run a coach trip, shall we? Collect a few kindred spirits and leave the farm to its fate for a few hours. And to Dad's tender care," he added. "Even if it *is* only an hour or so, on a good day. 'The further off from England,' remember, 'the nearer is to France'—oh, I say. Gosh." And Nigel, astounded by his hitherto unsuspected mnemonic brilliance, fell silent.

Sir George thought of brandy, neat, double, for medicinal

purposes only. Lady Colveden forgot telephone boxes and village rivalries and Horace Jowett's stamp collection, and drifted into a gentle daydream of pavement tables with gay parasols, of red wine, sunshine, and paper-thin crepes.

What Nigel thought about is not recorded.

For those without their own transport there are two ways of reaching Plummergen: hire car (or taxi) and bus. Brettenden being the nearest town with a railway station to Plummergen, it is from Brettenden that aged and asthmatic Mr. Baxter's equally aged and asthmatic taxi will (when working) convey the innocent traveller who has arrived, courtesy of British Rail, within six miles of his ultimate destination in (relative) safety to that same destination. Contrariwise the experienced and twice-shy arrival, once bitten by the Baxter taxi service, prefers to wait for the bus, which is both cheaper than Baxter and less likely to break down.

The bus, however, is unfortunately not a regular option, running only three days out of seven—and of those three only one day can be attributed to the official timetable, the other two coming courtesy of the Crabbes, a public-spirited family who own Plummergen's garage-cum-repair-shop and filling station, and who run, as well as the twice-weekly bus, an excellent taxi service.

Although it was a bus day, the visitor who registered at the George and Dragon on the first day of June had arrived not by bus but driving a small, powerful sports car.

"Lovely bright blue, it is," Emmy Putts reported with wistful envy in her voice. Maureen, the George's part-time assistant waitress/receptionist, had savoured every minute of the phone call she made to her friend on Mr. Stillman's grocery counter. Maureen's Wayne owned a Kawasaki motorbike and wore black leather (about which Maureen in an unguarded moment had once confessed to having a Thing), and some of his mechanical enthusiasm had been transmitted to his sweetheart through a process similar to osmosis. Young Maureen's instinctive ability to hold what sounded like the right sort of conversation with Mr. Folland, owner of the bright blue sports car, had resulted in his promise that he might take her for a spin on one of her free afternoons.

"Not a mark on it, Maureen says," said Emmy, sighing. "All shiny with chrome, and badges, and real leather seats. And Mr. Folland's ever so good-looking, she says."

"Handsome is as handsome does," proclaimed Mrs. Skinner in hollow tones as Emmy sighed again. "You mark my words!"

A chorus of agreement promptly rippled around the post office, with Mrs. Newport's voice louder than the rest.

"And that's very true," she said sternly. "There's many an innocent girl gone weeping home after being taken in by appearances, Emmeline." Mrs. Newport, who was at best eight years older than Miss Putts, spoke with all the authority of a mother of four. "Never you mind Maureen, she's got Wayne to look after her, but shiny chrome and leather seats is neither here nor there—is it?" she demanded of the shop at large, and another ripple, louder than the first, heartily confirmed this point of view as well as drowning out Emmy's resentful sniff.

"What does anyone know about this Folland?" asked Mrs. Spice, who was trying to make up her mind between two brands of frozen pea in different-sized packs. "With strangers you can't be too careful."

"He's not here for the birds," said someone sagely. "Or if he is it's not feathered ones," she added with a meaningful look at Emmy. "Those twitchers, their minds don't work that way."

"Bright blue cars!" scoffed someone else, 'and everybody—except Emmy—sniggered. Experience had taught Plummergen that no serious bird-watcher (familiarly "twitcher") would ever display a tendency towards brightness in clothing or anything else. Dull green, brown, khaki, and fawn were far better for purposes of camouflage; and somehow the habit always seemed to spill over into all aspects of their lives.

"If it's not birds he might," someone suggested, "be another telly producer looking around."

"Or the films," breathed Miss Putts in hopeful ecstasy. Emmy and Maureen-from-the-George both harboured secret dreams of Discovery and subsequent Stardom. No amount of talking-to on the part of their elders could convince them that Things Like That Didn't Happen Anymore.

"Doris will soon find out," Mrs. Skinner said, and again her words were followed by a chorus of agreement. Doris, headwaitress/receptionist at the George and Dragon, was one of the best finder-outers in the village. The trouble was that she all too often claimed professional discretion and would refuse to say a word to anyone about her findings: but it had in the past been noted that once the ice of a visitor's identity had, as it were, been broken, it made the rest of the job much easier for other less scrupulous snoops.

In the end it was the less scrupulous Maureen who learned the truth about Mr. Folland—a truth she announced two days later in another gleeful telephone call to the grocery counter, making Emmy Putts green with envy. Mr. Folland was the travelling representative of a national children's charity umbrella organisation, whose interest had been drawn to Plummergen by reports of the late Horace Jowett's miserly beneficence. It was Mr. Folland's own car; and he didn't charge running costs to expenses when other representatives, who drove cheaper models, did because he didn't like to take advantage of people's good nature, and money donated to charity ought to be used entirely for charity. Mr. Folland recognised Maureen as a girl who knew a lot about cars, and would be happy to take her for a spin one day. . . .

He was; he did; and Maureen gloated for nearly a week. But then Mr. Folland bought stamps at the post office and met Emmy Putts. And offered to take her, also, for a spin— an offer Emmy had been only too happy to accept. . . .

Which might explain why Emmeline Putts grinned and smirked her way around the groceries on the day following her afternoon off. Maureen might have been Mr. Folland's initial choice for a travelling companion—but Maureen (Emmy was prepared to swear) hadn't done what Emmy had done. Been where she had been. If she had, Emmy knew, she wouldn't have been able to resist talking about it. Emmy prided herself on being able to keep her own counsel. Young Miss Putts, born and bred and hitherto likely to die in Plummergen, had on her afternoon off been Seeing Life. Living Dangerously. Getting (and Emmy grinned again) seriously One Up on her friend Maureen from the George and Dragon . . .

She just hoped nobody else in Plummergen ever got to know about it.

CHAPTER 2

As for Seeing Life and Living Dangerously . . . Miss Emily Dorothea Seeton, that most modest and unassuming of English maiden ladies, believes that—having almost eight years ago retired from teaching in London to her cottage in the country—she pursues an existence both conventional and quiet, without a hint of excitement and meriting no more than the most casual mention in anyone's general conversation. . . .

Miss Seeton's modest belief is wrong. She may not realise it, but she and her doings have been the main topics of conversation at (on occasion) the highest level; and they are seldom far from the thoughts of those who know her best. Her old headmistress always said that Seeton could cause more havoc in half an hour with her umbrella than the rest of the staff combined could achieve in a week: others since Mrs. Benn have spoken with yet greater force.

Of their opinion Miss Seeton remains blissfully ignorant; innocent. Miss Seeton has the happy faculty of being, not so much blind to the facts (she might be drawing her pension, but her Drawings of another sort are very much in demand) as in every instance able to interpret these facts to suit herself. While Miss Seeton's unique way of Seeing has caused her to be retained by Scotland Yard as an official art consultant—to Miss Seeton alone, when others are confused, the truth behind appearances is plain—in her own case, whatever the facts might suggest, she is always sure there has been some sort of misunderstanding. She persists in regarding herself as an ordinary gentlewoman of a certain age living an ordinary, uneventful, private life in a peaceful village in Kent. Any little hiccup she might encounter in life's normally smooth path is obviously nothing to do with her: it is a troublesome coincidence, that is all, and no amount of evidence to the contrary will persuade Miss Seeton otherwise.

Miss Seeton's many friends are in an unspoken conspiracy to keep the little teacher in this state of blissful ignorance. They see no point in trying to open her eyes: she is happy as she is; and they are happy for her. Some go so far as to be fiercely protective against any who would try to disillusion her. Among the fiercest of her protectors are those domestic dragons the Bloomers, who were inherited by Miss Seeton from her Cousin Flora along with Sweetbriars, her dear cottage. Stan Bloomer, a local farmhand, tended old Mrs. Bannet's garden and looked after the hens; Martha, his Cockney wife, kept Flora Bannet's house as well mopped and dusted as any house could be. Old Mrs. Bannet was as good as family to the childless couple, and Miss Seeton was only too thankful to be accepted as an honorary Bloomer when circumstance so directed.

The Bloomers have a pleasant, low-roofed cottage bright with paint and neat of garden on the far side of The Street from Miss Seeton's home, which stands on the corner where the main street narrows and divides at its southern end. The lane where the Bloomers live continues south over the canal to head across the marsh. The wider road meanders from its original lazy westward bent through various ill-signposted byways until it reaches Brettenden, a town six miles to the north and Plummergen's closest neighbour—apart, that is, from Murreystone, deadly rival long beyond Time Immemorial. This time has been defined by statute as being before the reign of the first Richard (who died in 1199); and

Plummergen will neither forget, nor forgive, the fact that when the Danes invaded at the end of the ninth century the village defence was unsupported by its nearest neighbours. Nor did the outbreak of civil war in the seventeenth century in any way lessen the rivalry, for Murreystone supported Protector Cromwell while Plummergen held out loyally for Charles.

Yet these and similar bygone skirmishes seemed likely to be far outdone during the current campaigning period. Not only was there the Best-Kept Village Competition to occupy the combative mind, but the much-publicised death and generous bequest of old Horace Jowett had inspired a frenzy of fund-raising and assorted good works that had charity organisations throughout the southeast blinking with astonished gratitude. Plummergen's Grand Lawnmower Race was countered by Ferret Bingo from Murreystone, in which the old custom of putting ferrets down rabbit holes was adapted for gambling purposes by means of a barrel with seven numbered pipes leading out of it. Plummergen, gleefully (and rightly) suspecting a London-based charity's ability to understand that ferrets—like all the weasel family—are born to go down dark holes and enjoy the going, avoided the charge of cruelty to animals by racing sponsored plastic ducks along the Royal Military Canal. Murreystone drew up elaborate scale plans of a suitable field and played Cowpat Roulette, the winner having to guess on which numbered square the next bovine blessing would descend. Plummergen played the "small is beautiful" card by arranging a Sponsored Snail Sprint from one side of a Ping-Pong table to the other. Murreystone's anglers at once sacrificed their best maggots in a parallel venture. . . .

Headmaster Mr. Jessyp, having press-ganged Sir George Colveden and Admiral Leighton to Do Their Bit, booked the village hall for the evening of Saturday 13th June, when they were to present a talk on "Kent at War," with contributions welcomed from the floor and a hefty entrance fee. Murreystone's History Society announced that on the same night it would open its doors to non-members for a debate on "Oliver Cromwell: Saint or Sinner?" Nigel Colveden and his Young Farmer colleagues talked of racing sheep with garden-gnome jockeys tied to their backs; the Royal Society for the Prevention of Cruelty to Animals approved the sheep, but vetoed the gnomes on grounds of comfort. Those village ladies whose knitting needles were not occupied with six-inch squares for Oxfam blankets set at once to work on dolls with long legs, short hair, and peaked caps. . . .

"Anyway," said Martha Bloomer to Miss Seeton, "if it's soft toys they want in such a hurry, why don't they just pop into Brettenden and buy a dozen teddy bears?"

"I suppose," said Miss Seeton, after considering for a few moments, "they wish to spend as little as possible on—on running expenses, in order that more money may go towards the children's wheelchairs."

A week after his arrival in the blue sports car, central coordination of local fund-raising efforts had been handed thankfully over to Benjamin Folland, self-styled representative of national charity umbrella group The Golden Brolly, by Plummergen's Charity Committee, chairman Sir George Colveden, Justice of the Peace—who during that week had used his contacts in the police to have the *bona fides* of Mr. Folland, and his connection with The Golden Brolly, verified. The Golden Brolly soon vouched for Mr. Folland, and reported that this year's chosen beneficiary was a charity supplying electrically powered wheelchairs for children crippled from birth, disease, or injury. . . .

"Poor little mites," interposed Martha now.

Miss Seeton sighed and nodded. "Those of us who enjoy good health are fortunate indeed," she said, and Martha did not disagree. "Of course," continued her employer, "as one grows older the occasional twinge is only to be expected, and I am only too thankful that I found out in time and could start to learn—my knees, that is—about yoga, which has been of quite remarkable benefit—but I do appreciate that there are others in far worse case, and some of them so very much younger. . . ." She sighed again and shook her head. "For children never to have known the pleasures of walking—running—skipping rope—climbing trees . . . How I wish I could do more, but I fear . . ."

Her third sigh echoed another from Martha; and yet Mrs. Bloomer's sole concern was for the lot of the crippled children, while—though their plight was not forgotten—Miss Seeton was at the same time lamenting her own sad inadequacies. In Martha's presence she was more conscious of these than at other times, for Mrs. Bloomer's fame as a seamstress equalled her renown as a paragon of domestic hygiene, and her skill as a *tricoteuse* was not far behind. Miss Seeton might be skilled with pencil, paint, and sketching block, but in the Company of Dorcas she knew herself to be among the lowest of the low. She could sew as fine a seam as Curly Locks in the nursery rhyme, but that was no more than setting down dainty stitches in a neat row, which anyone (or so Miss Seeton thought) with even a moderately accurate eye should be able to achieve, and after a lifetime teaching art she hoped that her eye was as accurate as any. . . .

She sighed again, then brightened. "I must remember to take my milk bottle tops to the post office when I go out this afternoon," she said, smiling. "Once, I recall, when there was a collection at Mrs. Benn's for the cottage hospital, some of the younger pupils from the preparatory section were convinced that the tops were to be melted down for use in clinical thermometers. Poor Mrs. Thorley, the science teacher, had the greatest difficulty persuading them that the silver paper used for milk bottle tops was in fact aluminium, while the silver in thermometers was, or rather is, mercury."

Martha chuckled. "It's a bit like the War over again, isn't it, dear?" With her feather duster she indicated the harmless *Times* over which, until Mrs. Bloomer's arrival, Miss Seeton had been poring. "Everything being saved, I mean," she went on as Miss Seeton with a murmur acknowledged the similarity. "The amount of old books and papers our street threw out for pulp you'd never credit, not to mention all the iron railings gone from the park for years after. And everyone's saucepans collected to make aeroplanes, not that they've gone as far as that this time—though I wouldn't care to bet on it if the idea's once put in their heads, what with Murreystone and everything." Martha waved her duster again. Miss Seeton stifled a sneeze. "You mark my words," warned Mrs. Bloomer. "If you wake up one morning and find your front fence has taken a walk, you won't have to look very far for it."

"I trust," said Miss Seeton with a twinkle, "that they manage to restrain themselves. Enthusiasm, you know, is all very well, Martha dear—indeed, in most instances it is to be commended—but one should always temper enthusiasm with common sense." She became serious. "Although I have not sponsored Nigel and his team to finish ahead of time or to shift more hay bales than the others—I feel, you see, that a lump sum given unconditionally is so much more efficient—but when it appears that this energy is being expended not so much for charitable purposes as in order to—to outdo a rival village . . ."

"Yes, but it means even more wheelchairs for the kiddies," said Martha. "Which can't be bad, now can it? Mind you, they say Ned Potter's trying to talk Charley Mountfitchet into organising a darts match with the Murreystone pub. Can you imagine anything so daft?"

Miss Seeton (whose memories—like Martha's—of some previous Plummergen-Murreystone encounters was vivid) could well imagine such a thing. She sighed. "But no doubt Constable Potter feels confident of his ability to keep the situation under control," she said. "He is, after all, an expert—although in hot weather tempers are likely to be— well, shorter than in the winter. . . ."

Then, resolutely banishing all thoughts of conflict from her mind, she turned back to *The Times*. "There is such an interesting piece in today's paper, Martha dear. A lake, you see, that is being built, or perhaps I should say excavated, in France. At the Château de—de Balivernes.'' Miss Seeton, whose linguistic talents were on a par with her knitting, stumbled a little over the correct pronunciation, but as Martha was likely to speak even less French than her employer, she was too tactful to apologise for her accent. ''A re-creation,'' she went on, ''of Monet's celebrated garden at Giverny, with an exact replica of the bridge, and the surface covered by lilies, with trees and flowering shrubs all around. . . .''

''Looks nice,'' said Martha, peeping over Miss Seeton's shoulder at the artist's impression. ''I could quite fancy a sit-down under one of them trees,'' she added wistfully. ''With a bit of a picnic to come, and perhaps a quick paddle first on account of my feet don't like the heat any more than the rest of me. I'll take the weight off them for a few minutes if you don't mind, dear—but I'll make us a cup of tea first, and we'll have a bite of my new chocolate cake I brought over special for you to try.''

Martha always apologised in advance when bringing a new recipe for Miss Seeton's approval. The apology was always unnecessary, but Martha was taking no risks. Her reputation as a maker of cakes was well deserved and jealously guarded. ''Five eggs there are in this one,'' she told Miss Seeton as she led the way into the kitchen. ''Five ounces of chocolate, five of ground almonds, and three of butter in the icing alone.'' She imparted this information with such pride that Miss Seeton, who in a general way was not overfond of rich food, sent up a silent prayer that dear Martha would not be too offended if asked to cut only a small slice.

''There,'' said Mrs. Bloomer, pointing in triumph at the dark, gleaming, luscious cake in the middle of the kitchen table. ''Never mind talking about the War, dear, pinch and scrape and everything rationed, one egg a week if you were lucky—and powdered, more often than not. How could a body take a pride in their cooking with that? Only an ounce of cocoa to six of flour! No, I like my cakes to taste of what they're meant to, and my mother the same before me.''

"But we were proud to make the sacrifice," Miss Seeton reminded her gently with a hint of sadness in her voice as she recalled many far more grievous sacrifices than those inflicted by the rationing scheme.

"We were lucky to get away with it," returned Martha. "Those first couple of years before the Yanks, bless 'em, were on our side—well, I was only a girl, but I wouldn't want to go through that lot again. I mean, think of 1940!''

Miss Seeton, thinking, nodded and sighed.

Martha took the sigh for an invitation to continue her lament even as she busied herself hunting out plates and knives while her employer boiled a kettle already filled and waiting: the prudent habits of those who had survived the bombing of London and the city's intermittent water supply were not easily lost.

"The Battle of Britain right through the summer," Martha reminisced as she worked, "and then the Blitz all through the winter. And then after all those years when we'd started to hope the worst was over, along come them horrible doodlebugs. I can still hear the way those engines used to sound, like a—like a wicked great fist punching through the air, it was—and then that awful quiet when they cut out and you hoped it was falling a long way off—horrible, they were.''

"Indeed, yes," murmured Miss Seeton. While every day of the duration had held its own hideous dangers, her closest shave with death had been when her mother had insisted the two of them should sleep in the cellar of their Hampstead home rather than in their beds, though the sirens had not yet sounded. The morning light had revealed gaping holes in the ceiling and floor of Emily's room where the water tank had crushed Emily's bed to matchwood. The vibration from a stick of bombs dropped the full length of the road, demolishing every house on the opposite side, had shaken the tank from its perch on the attic rafters and turned it into a torrent of destruction. . . .

Miss Seeton shivered. Her mother had never been able to explain why she had been so very insistent they sleep in the cellar that particular night. . . .

"And then," said Martha, eyeing her flawless chocolate icing one final time before regretfully seizing the knife, "there was the rockets, them V2 horrors. Worst of the lot, they were, with nobody ever knowing where they were going to land." She snorted. "Trying to tell us it was a gas main gone—but they couldn't fool the East End! Terrible times, they were, terrible. Like that one in Deptford, dear. New Cross—do you remember?"

"Woolworth's," said Miss Seeton in a near whisper. She did not forget: nobody who had lived through that time could forget. New Cross Woolworth's had been Britain's worst V2 incident. The rocket had erupted, howling, out of a clear November sky to extinguish the lives of almost a hundred and seventy people, many of them children—so many, thought Miss Seeton, feeling her eyes prick with tears, for it had been one of the first days for years that anything like ice cream had been on sale. One young shopgirl had been blown to relative safety through a door, but she was the only survivor. There was not another soul left alive in New Cross Woolworth's. Or even in one piece.

Miss Seeton shivered. "A terrible time indeed," she said. "And fortunately long over. Such suffering . . ."

"We'd have given him a good run for his money if he'd ever landed, I don't doubt." Martha, who had been hovering over the cake, thoughtfully contemplated the knife's sharp blade. "But he couldn't get across the Channel, thank the Lord, and we were spared."

In her heart Miss Seeton echoed the thanksgiving, but she resolved to lighten the mood. It had become too sombre for such a beautiful summer afternoon, thirty years beyond the hideous times being evoked: an oblique change of subject would, she thought, be best. "And if the tunnel had already been built," she said with a forced smile, "I'm sure you would have been guarding the entrance with the rest of us,

Martha dear. It seems strange to think that after so many centuries there will at last be a permanent link between England and France.''

''Catch me ever going in that Chunnel of theirs,'' said Martha, seizing on the fresh topic with such enthusiasm Miss Seeton suspected she, too, had been growing depressed. ''I don't hold with the idea of so much water above me, I really don't.'' She plunged the knife into the cake and began to slice. ''And if it springs a leak,'' she went on, ''you don't stand the ghost of a chance, do you?''

''From what I have read in the paper,'' said Miss Seeton, trying to recall recent popular science and engineering articles, ''the tunnel will be lined—with concrete, I believe.''

''Now, it stands to reason, Miss Emily.'' Martha wagged the knife at her employer. ''If there's white chalk cliffs this side and there's chalk the other side in France—as anyone can see on a clear day—then it'll be chalk the rest of the way between. And who knows what happens to chalk when it gets wet?''

''I am rather afraid I skipped over what might be called the heavier technical passages—but,'' ventured Miss Seeton, ''I am sure nobody would dream of digging a tunnel if they thought it was at all likely to leak.''

''That's as may be,'' said Mrs. Bloomer stoutly. ''But I'll be sticking to the ferry and the fresh air, and so will Stan.'' She edged a generous slice of chocolate cake on a rosebud plate, and Miss Seeton's heart sank as it became clear it was for herself. ''This one's for you, dear,'' said Mrs. Bloomer, beaming. ''And another for me, and we'll see what you think. . . .''

To cover a potentially awkward moment, she reverted to her previous topic of conversation. ''Not that we take that many trips across, mind you,'' she said as she stirred the tea. ''But when we do, it's going to be on the ferry. You get life jackets in a ferry—and duty-free shops—and you can walk about to look at things—and there are other boats close by to rescue you. You stand a sporting chance on the water, but miles under the ground in a tunnel . . .''

''The safety measures are of the highest,'' Miss Seeton began trying to tell her.

But Martha remained unconvinced.

''Emmeline Putts!'' said Mrs. Stillman, rapping on the grocery counter to catch the young assistant's wandering attention. ''If you don't wipe that silly grin off your face and get on with serving Mrs. Flax, you'll be sorry you ever asked for that afternoon off. And I'll be even sorrier I gave it to you,'' she added grimly. Those who annoyed the village's Wise Woman didn't believe—not really—she could do them any harm . . . but there was no sense in taking risks.

Emmy muttered something Mrs. Stillman thought it wiser not to hear, and tossed her head (the muslin cap wavered but stayed firm) in a way she thought hinted at Mystery and Experience.

''Emmy!'' said Mrs. Stillman in a third-time-of-asking voice. ''Mrs. Flax is wanting cheese, and you're grinning again. Stop it this minute, do you hear?''

Sighing, Emmy picked up the cheese wire. Her daydreams faded into reality. A truly Mysterious Woman—Mata Hari, say—would have slaughtered spies with such a weapon, and here she was going to cut half a pound of cheddar. . . .

''Last bus of the day,'' someone said as the wire sliced crookedly through the dark yellow mass and Mrs. Flax prepared to argue that it looked a couple of ounces over.

The shopping gossips began drifting to the front of the post office, closer to the window and the open door. The bus could be heard approaching in the distance, and there was a moral obligation on those within sight of the stop to make sure who got on—although at this time of day it was unlikely that anyone would—and who got off.

''I didn't know Mrs. Blaine had gone into Brettenden,'' said someone in an aggrieved tone as a plump female form descended the steps, turned, and waited with her back to the

shop for the driver to hand her down a large brown paper
parcel tied with string.

"I thought she and Miss Nuttel," agreed someone else,
"were set to go picking dandelion heads along the canal for
wine. Remember Miss Nuttel came in this morning for that
special sugar and Mrs. Stillman had to go out the back for
it on account of Emmy not listening?"

Emmy tossed her head and smiled her Woman of Mystery
smile, making everyone long to box her ears.

"They'll have stopped the bus at the bottom o' The Street
and got on there," someone said, sounding peeved and intrigued in equal measure. It was irksome not to know what
was happening—but the possibilities for speculation were
delightful. Only those, after all, with Something to Hide
would be so devious as to hail and board the Brettenden bus
where nobody in the village could see what they were doing.

"They'll have gone into Brettenden for summat they
knew they couldn't get here," said someone else. It was a
fair guess. But what had Miss Nuttel and Mrs. Blaine—
known to Plummergen wits on account of their rampant veg-
etarianism as the Nuts—not been able to buy in any of the
local shops for which they (apparently) should recall so
pressing a need in the middle of the dandelion harvest?

And where—the other half of that normally inseparable
partnership—was Miss Nuttel?

As Mrs. Blaine was seen to thank the driver and the bus
pulled away, people began to mutter, shifting uneasily on
their feet and pressing close to the window. Mrs. Blaine—
quite alone—was walking to the kerb and checking for traffic. Mrs. Blaine, unescorted, was peering over the top of her
bulky parcel—was checking for traffic up and down The
Street—was crossing The Street in the direction of her plate-
glass-windowed home . . .

. . . Was lost to view as the pyramid of baked bean tins
Mr. Stillman had erected only that morning rendered her
plump shape, through the mysteries of parallax, invisible.

"Miss Nuttel's down by the canal still, I daresay," someone said, not sure whether she believed it or not.

"She'll have gone back to have the tea ready for when the Hot Cross Bun came home," said someone else. It was a disappointingly mundane solution to an otherwise fascinating little problem. All eyes, drawn by some superstitious and invisible cord, turned to Mrs. Flax.

The Wise Woman could be trusted not to disappoint. She raised her choppy finger to her lips and looked grave. "If it weren't so dreadful a chance," she said, "I'd not say a word—but it seems to me Ned Potter did really ought to go knocking on the Nuts' front door if Miss Nuttel's not seen over the next day or so. You all know what a mood those two have been in of late with the weather, and this morning no different when 'twas just the one of 'em we saw in here. It's police business, no question, when anybody goes missing—think o' that man who cut up his wife and six kiddies with the kitchen knife and left the pieces all along the motorway. Brown paper parcels," concluded Mrs. Flax darkly, "can hide a multitude o' sins. . . ."

CHAPTER 3

Nobody could seriously suppose that Miss Nuttel, having been lured (out of sight of witnesses) on the Brettenden bus by Mrs. Blaine, had at her destination been lured farther to a sinister and disunited doom by means of an axe, knife, or hacksaw purchased by her friend from the town's well-stocked ironmonger. Nobody could seriously suppose it—but there was no real harm in wondering and having some fun. The Nuts, after all, had been in a bit of an odd mood over the last few days. . . .

It had started with the mosquito. Mrs. Blaine, tossing on a sleepless bed, had been bitten at midnight by a bloodthirsty insect her vegetarian principles made it difficult for her to squash. We pass over (without saying how she finally resolved them) her impassioned struggles of conscience to the next morning, when she informed Miss Nuttel in no uncertain terms that while the summer continued and one was forced to keep the upstairs windows open, mosquito nets over the beds could only be a good idea.

Miss Nuttel (who hadn't been bitten, but who had spent half the night rushing to Bunny's room with poultices and herbal infusions) yawned and said she supposed Bunny hadn't had such a bad idea. A trip next day to Brettenden secured at cheaper-than-Plummergen prices muslin, tape, and a fresh reel of white cotton thread. Mrs. Blaine measured everything again, found the manipulation of muslin thirty-six inches wide for the protection of beds six and a half feet long more complicated than she had expected, and complained loud and long that if Eric hadn't left so many Do It Yourself books piled all over the dining room table (without, to add insult to injury, ever Doing It!) she would have room to see what she was about.

Another trip to Brettenden at the earliest opportunity secured three lengths of high-density fibreboard and six brackets. Miss Nuttel sawed wood, drilled holes, and drove Mrs. Blaine to distraction as she muttered at herself for having forgotten to buy screws. Mrs. Blaine drove the handle of her sewing machine as if it were a mincer and Miss Nuttel inside. Miss Nuttel's DIY books teetered on the edge of the table in their unruly heap until angry vibration tipped them to the floor.

"There!" said Mrs. Blaine. "What did I tell you? There simply isn't room to move in here!"

Miss Nuttel, thin-lipped, said nothing.

The shelves went up on brackets held by screws too short for the task assigned them. The books, lifted tenderly from the floor, went on the shelves.

In the middle of the night shelves, screws, brackets, and books came down at once with a crash.

On this occasion Miss Nuttel said rather a lot, and so did Mrs. Blaine. The honours were more or less even, for both women were equally sleepless and tired; but it was left to Mrs. Blaine to have the last word.

"I shan't," she complained, "get a wink of sleep for the rest of the night, I know I shan't! I'm sure I'm going to have one of my heads. It's simply too much—and in such awful weather, too. I'll be a wreck tomorrow!"

She detoured via the bathroom to take a roll of cottonwool from the cupboard. "Earplugs," she snapped as Miss Nuttel's eyes widened. "I don't want to be disturbed."

She was stamping her way up to bed until she remembered that the incipient headache must make every sound insufferable. Regretting the lost opportunity to slam her door in Eric's face, she could only close it—which she very firmly did; and she was not seen again by Miss Nuttel until well into the following afternoon.

"Heard you moving upstairs," was Miss Nuttel's greeting. "Have some chamomile tea? Just made some for myself," she added in case Mrs. Blaine should think the squabble truly over and forgotten.

Mrs. Blaine put a plump hand to her forehead. "It might help," she conceded bravely. Miss Nuttel looked at her over the top of her own mug, sipped once, put the mug down, and poured just-boiled water into a sinister green teapot, stirring the mixture viciously. Metal clinked on earthenware, and Mrs. Blaine winced.

There was silence while the process of infusion took place. Mrs. Blaine cast meaningful glances at the kitchen clock but said nothing. When she finally did speak:

"It's stewed," she said, and made a face. "And far too weak. You should have put in another pinch when you knew I would want some."

"Not made of money," returned Miss Nuttel, then realised the shakiness of this argument—the Nuts grew most of their own herbs—and hurried on. "Despite what some people think. Had a complete stranger on the phone just before lunch, and the operator asked me to accept a reversed charge call. Seemed very put out when I said no. Just before lunch," she reiterated. "Peak rate. And," she reminded Bunny grimly, "a complete stranger. Fine thing if I'd said yes."

Mrs. Blaine's button-black eyes brightened even as she silently regretted the cotton-wool earplugs that had caused her to miss the fun. "You might have found out what it was all about first and *then* hung up," she said wistfully. She cared nothing now for tea, stewed or otherwise. Here was a far more fruitful field for speculation and comment. "It might not have taken more than half a minute. Didn't the operator give you any idea what they wanted?"

"Didn't ask," Miss Nuttel told her. "Just said no, we'd never heard of the woman, and never mind her saying we'd be sorry we didn't accept it, we wouldn't." She stuck her nose into her mug to draw a refreshing draught in celebration of her firmness of purpose. "Probably trying to sell us double glazing," she added. "Don't need it—can't afford it. And a member of the aristocracy ought to know better."

Bright eyes gleamed. All trace of the mysterious and long-lived headache was gone. "Oh, Eric—not Lady Colveden!" cried Mrs. Blaine with glee. "Do you mean Sir George can't make the farm pay any longer with Nigel so much more in charge than he used to be? I always said"—Mrs. Blaine gloated over Miss Nuttel's attempted denial—"that these young men straight from college always think they know more than they do—and now you see I was right." ("He's not," Miss Nuttel tried to interpose, but Bunny ignored her.)

"They're probably going bankrupt," said Mrs. Blaine. "If they do, I wonder who will buy the house? And what about the furniture? They have some too lovely pieces it would be a crying shame to miss. What a pity the dining-room table is so big, even with all the leaves taken out—but we could always bid for the oak bookcase from the study." Speculation and its pleasures made the offer of this olive branch far less painful than Bunny might have expected. "I'm sure it must have been Lady Colveden," she concluded. "It's not as if we know anyone else among the aristocracy. Using a false identity, of course. What was she calling herself?"

"Noble," said Miss Nuttel. "You could be right, Bunny." Olive branches worked in two directions. "Hadn't thought before—but it makes sense. A nod's as good as a wink, after all. Noble. Aristocracy. And 'Ada' is close enough to 'Lady,' now you point it out—"

"What?" shrieked Mrs. Blaine. "You mean you refused a call from *Ada Noble*?"

"Told you I did," said Miss Nuttel. Mrs. Blaine slammed her mug on the table with such force that in circumstances less fraught it would have induced a new headache: but there was no time now for self-indulgence.

"My cousin Ada phoned, and you—you *refused to speak to her*?" cried Mrs. Blaine. "You had no right!"

"C-cousin?" echoed Miss Nuttel, considerably startled.

"There must be something terribly wrong at home for Ada to ring me here," said Mrs. Blaine, wringing her hands. "My favourite cousin, and married to the most frightful man—he drinks, you know, I'm sure I've told you about him—and Ada calling for help and *you refused*! How could you? Where is she? Anything could have happened to her by now!"

"Might have called the police," suggested Miss Nuttel, fearing the suggestion would only serve to fan the flames of Bunny's wrath. "If he was drinking," she enlarged as a hot and furious flash from the eyes of Mrs. Blaine would have reduced her, had such a thing been possible, to ashes on her chair. "As you . . . weren't available," she finished.

"You should have woken me!" cried Mrs. Blaine, forgetting her headache and the communications ban imposed by herself the previous night. "Poor Ada—and of course it's no use my phoning the house to ask. She wouldn't need to reverse the charges from home, so she must be somewhere else—a fugitive—in hiding—and you ignored her! It's simply too selfish of you, Erica Nuttel!"

"Hold on," protested Miss Nuttel faintly.

Mrs. Blaine ignored her. "My favourite cousin," she said, wringing her hands some more and thoroughly enjoying herself. "In trouble—frightened to death of that terrible alcoholic husband of hers, turning to me for help—blood is thicker than water, and it's only too true . . ."

The rest of her lamentation was lost on Miss Nuttel, who had—as Mrs. Blaine knew well—a profound dislike of the sanguinary, and who preferred to shut her ears rather than run the risk of worse occurring. A vegetarian diet did not, she had discovered, make it any less easy to faint than in the old omnivorous days.

"... who else to ask?" concluded Mrs. Blaine, and ceased the hand-wringing in order to leap from her chair and rush to the sitting room, where, in the bureau, her address book lived. Miss Nuttel drew several deep breaths and a mouthful of cold chamomile tea before feeling anything like herself. She was sorry to have upset Bunny, not to mention Ada (whose name, now that memory had been jogged, was vaguely familiar from Christmas cards), but was it altogether her fault? To blame her for refusing to accept the costs of a telephone call from who-knew-where and a complete (as far as she had then been concerned) stranger seemed ... unfair, to put it mildly. As for Ada's being Bunny's favourite cousin, Miss Nuttel took leave to doubt it. Favourites did not restrict themselves to Christmas: they remembered birthdays, too.

"Ha," said Miss Nuttel, much cheered by having come to this logical point in her deliberations. She pushed back her chair, rose to her feet, and went to pour the chilly rest of the chamomile tea down the sink. She would make another, fresher cup. Singular. Let Bunny make her own if she was going to be disagreeable!

From the sitting room the sound of exasperated rummaging showed that Mrs. Blaine was having difficulties finding the address book. Miss Nuttel had no idea whom she was going to phone—another member of the family, no doubt—but if it was before six o'clock and the cheaper cheap rate, things were likely to be awkward. Money was money—but better to say nothing, perhaps. Just this once. As Bunny seemed so upset. A drunken husband—when Bunny herself had found life with the unlamented Humphrey Blaine insupportable for similar (among other) reasons ...

"Salt in the wound," said Miss Nuttel sagely as she watched the kettle boil.

Above its merry whistle the telephone bell was heard.

Likewise Mrs. Blaine's voice. "*I'll* get it," she shouted from the sitting room. "It might be Ada again, and if you refuse her a second time, goodness knows what she might do!''

Miss Nuttel, spooning green leaves into the pot, uttered not a word. She heard silence as Mrs. Blaine picked up the receiver, and could hardly bear to pour water in case its bubble should drown out Bunny's side of the conversation.

''Yes,'' said Mrs. Blaine into the telephone in a louder than usual tone. Miss Nuttel sighed.

''Oh, yes!'' said Mrs. Blaine, increasing the volume so that Eric, by missing none of it, should be made to feel guilty. ''Yes, of course. By all means—please put her through—never mind the expense . . .'' This last was louder than ever. Miss Nuttel ground her teeth. ''Ada?'' cried Mrs. Blaine. ''Is that you? . . . Yes, I'm so sorry, too silly, a *mistake* . . .'' Miss Nuttel's teeth castanetted together as Mrs. Blaine's tone became shrill. ''Oh, you poor dear!'' cried Mrs. Blaine. ''Really? But then men can be such beasts. . . . Oh, yes, I sympathise, as you know. . . . Too dreadful for you . . . Yes, naturally . . . But of course, dear. Today—no, I positively insist, and so''—directing every syllable with vindictive accuracy into the kitchen—''does Eric. . . . Oh, very well. Tomorrow, then.'' For the briefest of moments a note of pique entered Mrs. Blaine's voice. ''You take the train from Charing Cross to Brettenden—''

Castanets gave way to a trumpet yodel as Eric yelped in surprise. Shock made her miss the next few words, and she surfaced in time to hear Mrs. Blaine positively insisting that Ada should take Mr. Baxter's taxi and (that dreadful phrase again) never mind the expense. ''For as long as you like,'' said Mrs. Blaine in conclusion. ''Honestly, Ada!''

Miss Nuttel tottered to the table and sat down.

The rest of the day had been a whirl of activity as Mrs. Blaine consulted cookery books and prepared the spare room on behalf of her imminent guest. Miss Nuttel (who felt that she should at least have been *asked* whether she was happy to have the unknown Ada visiting for an unspecified length of time) whirled herself outside to the garden, there to erad-

nocence of Miss Nuttel. "Which means," said Mrs. Blaine firmly, " we'll have plenty of time in the morning before it gets hot to go down to the canal and pick the dandelions there. Now the sheep have been gone for a couple of weeks it should be . . ."

Unwonted delicacy made her hesitate. "Safe," supplied Miss Nuttel crisply. "Fair enough." The honours, it seemed to her, were about equal now. If a quarrel lasted too long, it made life uncomfortable, and once this cousin arrived there was always the risk that she and Bunny might gang up together. Far better to give in. A little. But gracefully, of course.

"Check the recipe first. Make a list," she suggested, rising to her feet and heading for the shelf whereon were ranged Bunny's cherished cookery books. Mrs. Blaine's black eyes watched in a challenging silence, daring Eric to damage a cover or tear a page. Miss Nuttel, showing the greatest care, selected a volume and returned to the kitchen table.

"A gallon of dandelion heads," she read aloud. "Four pounds of Demerara sugar—"

"We've run out," snapped Mrs. Blaine. "Those whole-wheat biscuits you wanted used up the last, and I've been"—black eyes flashed—"*far too busy* to buy any more."

"It's after six," returned Miss Nuttel at once. "Every-where's shut. Time enough tomorrow morning." With a shrug she returned to her reading. "Half a pound of raisins. An orange. Root ginger—any left?"

"I'll lend you my string bag," said Mrs. Blaine, adopting a martyred tone. "Even if I slave all night, there's *simply too much* to do around the house for both of us to gad about the village from one shop to another wasting valuable time tomorrow."

"Right," said Miss Nuttel through her teeth as she banged the book shut. Talking of time, there was a limit to the amount of it a person could—would—should, for the sake

of self-respect—hold out an olive branch to someone who
clearly didn't want it. "String bag. And you can find a couple for the dandelions," she added as she headed towards
the hall. "Don't want to *waste any time* tomorrow, do we?"

Such might well have been the intention: but the intention
failed. The Nuts contrived to spend so long in overnight
sniping and breakfast bickering that they did not so much
waste as lose complete track of time. When the Demerara
sugar, fruit, and root ginger were finally dropped by a grim-
faced Miss Nuttel on the kitchen table, it was under the nose
of a salad-for-lunch-mixing Mrs. Blaine. Eric intercepted her
friend's pointed glance at the clock, muttered a remark
Bunny deemed it best to ignore, and began to snatch plates,
cutlery, and other paraphernalia from various drawers and
cupboards.

Miss Nuttel carved slices of Pressed Nut Loaf with an
action at which those of a nervous disposition might have
winced. With a cruelly clattering spoon Mrs. Blaine served
an unusually well-tossed salad from its bowl. Miss Nuttel
stabbed soya margarine out of what carnivores would call
the butter dish and applied it with force to a slice of bread
cut (by home baker Mrs. Blaine) an inch thicker at one end
than the other. Neither of the warring parties recalled until
lunch was under way that no liquid had been poured into
the glasses that had come ringing to the table. Both women
munched in a bitter, dry-mouthed silence. In silence the meal
ended. In comparative silence dishes were cleared, rinsed
under the tap, and put to one side until later. Mrs. Blaine
then retired to the downstairs lavatory, Miss Nuttel to the
bathroom. Each did her best not to let the other know that
she was running the cold tap for rather longer than required
by domestic hygiene.

Miss Nuttel reappeared looking smug, having pressed a
tooth glass into service. Mrs. Blaine, pink-cheeked and
breathless, emerged from the lavatory with a drip of water
on her chin and a large damp patch on the front of her

blouse. Miss Nuttel, biting her tongue, said nothing. Mrs. Blaine tossed her head, snatched up the fine string-net bags she had unearthed earlier, and made for the front door.

"Do hurry up," she commanded from the far end of the hall. "We want to pick the wretched things this afternoon, not next week!"

Miss Nuttel—who had been discreetly rummaging inside a drawer—slipped a pair of rubber gloves in her pocket and hurried to obey that command. Mustn't waste time looking for a second pair. If Bunny ended up with fingers all black and sticky . . .

Too bad.

It was a wearisome afternoon on the banks of the Royal Military Canal. Even the pleasures of squabbling soon lost their charm for the unhappy Nuts as they picked their sullen way among the dandelions. The sun blazed in triumph high above; the shade afforded by overhanging trees could be only moderately cooling when there was no breeze to speak of, and Miss Nuttel's dislike of wearing a hat—it made the top of the head even hotter, she maintained—inclined her to a sick giddiness she would not for worlds admit. The air was heavy with insects as well as with humidity and heat. Plump Mrs. Blaine began—despite her wide-brimmed straw—to glow with her exertions and brushed an absentminded hand across her brow.

Absentmindedness had much to answer for. Mrs. Blaine stamped to the canal edge and dipped her pocket handkerchief in the weed-green water in a vain attempt to scrub herself clean. Miss Nuttel said nothing, though Bunny's irritable splashing made her dream of long, cool glasses in a shady room. She resolved that once the dandelion bags were full, she would relent and suggest that they stop off at the bakery and enjoy one of Mrs. Wyght's celebrated ginger beer shandies. Ada Noble must surely have the sense to wait on the doorstep if there was nobody home when she knocked. . . .

•   •   •

A busy morning in the garden had been its own reward, but an afternoon's leisure—the heat—was a bonus. Miss Emily Seeton carried a posy of sweet-smelling flowers to her friend Miss Cecelia Wicks, by whom an automatic invitation to join her in a cup of tea was extended. Tea, biscuits, a few dainty cakes, and a considerable volume of amiable chatter ensued. The courtesies finally concluded, Miss Seeton offered to run any errand Miss Wicks might require, and was insistent that the posting of two letters and the purchase of a book of stamps was a small price to pay for such an enjoyable afternoon.

Miss Seeton, greeting her still-gardening neighbours with a nod and a smile, progressed happily and without hurry up The Street in the direction of Mr. Stillman's shop. She heard the distant rattle of the Brettenden bus and, as it approached, glanced across to see the plump and unmistakable form of Mrs. Blaine hovering near the driver, eager to be first off when the bus should stop.

Plump? But surely . . .

Miss Seeton blinked. The heat, no doubt. But surely hot weather made one lose, rather than gain, an appetite? And—with (or, as it might be, without) it—weight? Miss Seeton blushed for the personal nature of her musings. But surely, when she had last seen Mrs. Blaine—the day before yesterday, as she recalled—she had not been quite so . . . solid? Almost as if she were wearing more than one layer of clothes, which in this heat . . .

As Mrs. Blaine, now seen to be clutching a brown paper parcel, stepped down from the bus, Miss Seeton shook herself in gentle reproach. It was hardly her business how many clothes her neighbours might—or in such heat might not—choose to wear. Hurried movement in the windows of the post office behind the familiar plump figure hinted that others beside herself were somewhat . . . intrigued by Mrs. Blaine's apparent increase in girth as she waited in the shadow of the bus for it to depart. Miss Seeton shook herself again. One should be honest with oneself. She and the post-office shoppers were not so much intrigued as—well, displaying curiosity. Which, particularly in matters of so personal a nature as a lady's size, must rightly be deemed vulgar, if not discourteous. In the extreme. Which, when one could not call the lady in question anything more than a village acquaintance, was perhaps even more vulgar—discourteous—than if she had been a close friend, where such interest—Miss Seeton shook herself again—such curiosity could at least be taken in a—in a friendly spirit. Although still not to be condoned, of course. Whereas . . .

Her blush more pronounced than ever, Miss Seeton turned her head resolutely aside to savour the delightful summery scent of Admiral Leighton's roses. An optical illusion, no doubt. The shadow cast by the bus into the deeper shade of the post-office awning—the sunlight reflecting in silver shimmers as the bus then moved away . . .

Above the rattle of its departure Miss Seeton did not at first hear Mrs. Blaine making her way across the wide, empty Street towards the Lilikot front gate. When she did, she found herself in a dilemma. Would it seem, were she now to cross The Street herself in the opposite direction, all too obvious to Mrs. Blaine that Miss Seeton was . . . embarrassed at her most recent thoughts? On balance—and even though she had been on her way to the post office before the bus and Mrs. Blaine arrived—she thought it would. And it would likewise seem all too obvious if the admiral's roses were to engage her attention to the exclusion of everything else, when the approaching footsteps—slow, steady—the heat, of course—were now almost beside her.

Miss Seeton turned back, preparing to greet the newcomer with a courteous nod and a few polite words. Her head halfway inclined, she paused in mid-phrase to blink. She stared—coughed—rallied. She spoke again.

"Oh," said Miss Seeton. "Good gracious—I do beg your pardon for having—but I thought you were Mrs. Blaine—who lives here, you know—that is, of course you don't—but a quite remarkable likeness, I assure you. And I must again apologise—so many visitors, especially with the Best-Kept Village Competition—''

"And you must be Miss Seeton," broke in the plump woman who bore so remarkable a likeness to Mrs. Blaine. Her glance at the umbrella hooked in its accustomed manner over Miss Seeton's arm was eloquent. "My cousin has told me all about you," she added as Miss Seeton looked a little surprised.

"You are Mrs. Blaine's cousin?" Miss Seeton smiled. "A family likeness, of course," she said with a nod and another smile. "And, if you will permit the liberty, a close one. You are paying her a visit," she deduced. While no longer blessed with family herself, Miss Seeton had in the past known the pleasure of visiting her relations. "Then you must not let me detain you," she went on. "If you would excuse me . . ."

With a final nod and smile she moved past Mrs. Blaine's cousin and prepared to cross The Street to the post office.

CHAPTER 4

"An umbrella group," said Mr. Folland to the George's newest resident, Mrs. Raughton, who had wandered into the bar at the end of an afternoon's weary sightseeing and been invited by her fellow guest to name her poison. "A charity umbrella group, that's us—and thank you, Doris." Benjamin Folland received his tankard of ginger beer shandy with a wink that Doris, headwaitress/receptionist/barmaid at the George, might interpret how she chose. Mrs. Raughton had asked for a sweet sherry.

"That's why we call ourselves The Golden Brolly," continued Mr. Folland as he ushered Mrs. Raughton towards more comfortable seats and felt the eyes of an approving Doris on his back. Shandy, whether made with lemonade or ginger beer to an equal amount of best bitter, was a refreshing tipple for a summer day, its alcoholic content restrained. The George and Dragon didn't hold with those who got carried away by drink: and for a charity representative to be so conscious of his social responsibilities that he not only drank (on expenses, for he was chasing a prospective victim) cheaply but soberly made Doris more than ever favourably disposed towards Benjamin E. Folland, despite the real leather seats in his sports car that seemed to be having such an odd effect on Emmy Putts and young Maureen.

"The Golden Brolly coordinates people's golden deeds,"

explained Mr. Folland as he waited politely for Mrs. Raughton to settle herself. "You see, golden deeds very often—far too often—go unsung, Mrs. Raughton." At her smiling nod he sat beside her, first putting her sherry on the table within easy reach. "Unnoticed," he went on, having taken a thirsty sip from his mug. "Which is a shame. But there's much less room in this world for well-meaning amateurs than there used to be—and that's part of the trouble. This is 1974, not 1874. Dr. Barnado is—with all due respect to the good man's memory—years out of date. You can't just rely on good intentions, you need to get organised, you need to build up a profile—and you need money. Well, there's a limited amount of money around, with everyone after it, and the ones that make the most noise get the most notice taken of them—"

"And the most money," supplied Mrs. Raughton on cue, over the top of her sherry glass.

Benjamin Folland nodded. "That's right! They make the noise and they get the money, and I'm not for a minute saying they don't deserve it." Then he stabbed an emphatic forefinger in the air. Mrs. Raughton jumped. "But," said Benjamin, "who's to say the noisy ones are any more—or less—deserving than the charities that don't know how, maybe don't care, to make a noise?"

Mrs. Raughton pursed her lips and looked wise. "I can imagine," she offered, "that a lot of people might find the idea of publicity . . . distasteful, even in a good cause."

Benjamin grinned. "Especially the English," he said cheerfully. "The Scots, now, they're not half as stingy with their cash or their time or their own sweet selves as all those music-hall jokes would have us believe. If it's for a good cause and they're jollied along the right way, your average Scot will go on a sponsored haggis hunt or toss cabers into bowls of porridge till the highland cows come home, if you take my meaning. But your Englishman . . ."

Ben buried his nose deep in the tankard, giving Mrs. Raughton time to chuckle daintily at his little joke. "Your

Englishman's too . . . buttoned up," said Ben, emerging
from his shandy. "On the whole." He stabbed his finger in
the air again. "But not all of us, of course. I'm one of the
exceptions that proves the rule, see? I can make a noise on
behalf of the ones that want to and can't, or don't want to
but know they ought, or have been told they've got to by
someone else, like one of their major contributors."

"Big business," said Mrs. Raughton with a knowledgeable air. "I suppose the contributions are tax deductible, and
they want to be sure the effort is worth their while."

Ben grinned. "Couldn't have put it better myself, Mrs.
Raughton. Big business. And remember I said charity is big
business nowadays? So that's where I come in—as you
might say, to Plummergen, the same way I've gone to other
parts of the country on behalf of The Golden Brolly. The
other reps and I, we . . . ginger things up. Chivvy people
along. Get 'em interested—inspired—put new ideas in their
heads, and help 'em raise more money on behalf of the kiddies than they'd ever have dreamed they could in the small-
est village, let alone the towns. Even," he added rather
dryly, "the ones that don't like children."

"Oh, but surely—" began Mrs. Raughton, shocked.

"Not everyone's got your kind heart, Mrs. Raughton."
An admiring Doris watched from her place behind the bar
as Ben shuffled one of his by now familiar sponsorship
forms—that cheery yellow colour was a Golden Brolly
trademark—out of the briefcase that was never far from his
side.

"It's a sad fact," went on Ben with a sigh, "that there
are people—and we should feel sorry for them, Mrs. Raughton—who don't much care for kiddies. Sorry for them," he
reiterated, with a doleful shake of his head and another sigh
that was echoed by his companion, who was nodding above
her sherry and looked ready to burst into tears. Doris, who
had witnessed (and on only the second occasion succumbed
to) Mr. Folland's practised performance more than once in
the past ten days, made a silent bet with herself that Ben

would have his ballpoint pen under Mrs. Raughton's nose,
and her signature on a sponsorship form, within the next
two minutes.

"But sorrier for the children," said Ben, rallying. Mrs.
Raughton blinked, sniffed, and nodded again. "Poor crippled kids," said Mr. Folland in an earnest tone. "Good
health is a blessing we don't always appreciate, Mrs. Raughton, but for them . . . well, sometimes electric wheelchairs
are the first chance they've had in their lives to be anything
like normal children, poor mites. Playing and messing about
with their friends—races and ball games and able to go on
holiday with their families—like this, see?"

From a yellow folder that materialised from nowhere he
slid a sheaf of photographs—and his pen—across the table
for Mrs. Raughton's perusal. Doris mentally adjusted "two
minutes" to "three": Mr. Folland had let the sponsorship
form slip to the floor in the middle of his manoeuvring. It
was not until Mrs. Raughton's eye had been caught by the
topmost photo that he was able to retrieve it, in the knowledge (as Doris, from her own experience, also knew) that
there was almost nobody who could resist the sight of two
laughing childish faces—gap-toothed, freckled, cheeky—
above two frail bodies enthroned on cushioned and comfortable, yet efficient, metal-framed electric wheelchairs to
which small pennants in racing colours had been attached.
The photographer had waited for just the right amount of
breeze to snap the bright flags fluttering, the tousled hair
waving, and to give the impression that the race would begin
upon the instant the other wheelchairs just glimpsed over the
bright-eyed children's crooked shoulders had come up to the
starting line.

Mrs. Raughton proved (as Doris had suspected) no more
able to withstand the persuasive attack of Benjamin Folland
than the majority had been. After the heartwarming photos
of The Golden Brolly's most recent triumphs she was
handed a file of newspaper cuttings, all relating to one or
other of half a dozen respected children's charities on whose

behalf the Brolly (as Ben had begun explaining earlier) acted
as a central collection and distribution agency. The society's
latest annual report, complete with balance sheet, showed
that Mr. Folland's claims on his umbrella group's behalf
were not false. Letters of thanks, appreciation, and acknowledgement for the Brolly's fund-raising efforts were liberally
scattered throughout the report's neatly printed pages. The
names appended to many of these letters were of national
renown; the sums of money involved were more than generous.

"The only thing that puzzles me—" Mrs. Raughton began, and stopped. "I mean, a *national* organisation . . ." she
went on. "And I know you said . . ."

Ben, watching her as she puzzled, nodded. "Macspor-
ran," he said. "McTavish, Macdonald, MacDougal. You
want to know why so many of the children are Scottish,
don't you? That's easy." He fished inside his briefcase again
and produced another neatly printed brochure. "The year
before last," he said, brandishing the report with no little
pride and opening it to the middle page. Doris, polishing
glasses in the background, waited for the by now well-worn
joke.

She was not disappointed. "Mind you, Mrs. Raughton,"
Ben said with a grin, "while I can quote you some of the
names, please don't ask me to tell you their addresses, because I can't. You need double-jointed tonsils to do proper
justice to the Welsh language!" And he pointed to the open
page.

Mrs. Raughton, following his direction, looked and smiled
at the array of Llewellyns and Lloyds, of Madogs and Mor-
gans and Merediths who lived at Rhos This or Cwm That
or Llan the Other. "I quite understand," she said, smiling
again.

"The year before the year before last was easier," said
Ben, settling into his stride. "Unfortunately, that's one of
the reports I forgot to bring with me—but anyone'll tell you
we were in Cornwall in 1971, and you know the old saying:

'By Tre, Pol, and Pen ye shall know the Cornish men.' "
The listening Doris raised an empty glass to her lips in automatic sympathy with Mr. Folland's next punch line. "I
never," he assured Mrs. Raughton, "had to gargle once, the
whole time I was there!'

"Unlike Wales," said Mrs. Raughton, catching his drift.

"Exactly," he replied. "Exactly—and this year's going
to be easy, too. We concentrate on a different part of the
country in turn, you see. With all the publicity about old
man Jowett's bequest, we decided it was high time Kent was
on the receiving end of—of one of the Brolly's Blitzes, as
we call 'em." He hesitated and lowered his voice before
completing this sentence. "A bit tactless, in the circumstances," he whispered. "Given how badly this part of the
world fared in the War, as we're going to hear on Saturday
at the village hall—but that's our tactics, you see, all our
attention in one place, only kinder meant than Hitler. And
once we're done we move on, after a slap-bang finish that
has people seeing the results of all their hard work over the
past few weeks and giving The Golden Brolly a good send-
off and each of the charities we support a nice fat cheque.''

"And what," enquired Mrs. Raughton, her ears battered
by the torrent of words, "is the slap-bang finish for this part
of the world?"

"A Channel Tunnel Potato Race," Ben told her proudly.
"One of mine, this baby." He slid the yellow sponsorship
form under her hand with practised ease and rolled the pen
a little closer. "Not that we're using potatoes, of course, but
it's the same principle. Elimination heats in surrounding villages first—lawn mowers and grassboxes, tractors and bales
of hay—between you and me, we'll try to wangle it so that
as many groups as possible qualify for the finals—and
then—courtesy of the Chunnel Consortium—the Potato
Race, using genuine Chunnel spoil instead of spuds and with
the teams driving genuine Chunnel bulldozer-diggers—
Golden Brolly pays for the insurance, of course—instead of
their own tractors. Just in case of any hanky-panky.''

Mr. Folland waved amiably in the direction of the still-listening Doris. "I've heard fearful tales," he assured his table companion in thrilling accents, "of dirty tricks and nobbling on the part of certain rival villages that would set your hair on end, Mrs. Raughton. There's a place called Murreystone a few miles from here—"

"Ha!" cried Doris, on cue. Mr. Folland waved again and grinned at Mrs. Raughton.

"See what I mean?" he whispered as Doris emerged from behind the bar and marched across to join them.

By the time Plummergen's favourite Hebe had finished enumerating the many offences of Murreystone against her native hearth, Mrs. Raughton's name and address had joined the multitude on The Golden Brolly sponsorship form for Plummergen's entry in the Chunnel Potato Race, Mr. Folland saying that as a visitor she wouldn't know enough of the locals by name to sponsor any of them in their individual efforts. "Yet," he added with one of his grins. "But stick around long enough, and we'll get you again, just see if we don't!"

Then he ordered another round of drinks in celebration. This year's Brolly Blitz, he felt sure, would be a winner.

"I thought you might be interested, Ada," said Miss Nuttel, smiling the nearest to a smile that Mrs. Blaine had seen for several days. "With Bunny not up to it, I mean."

Bunny confirmed this lack of gusto in a muted whimper. Ada Noble patted her cousin on the hand and turned to smile at Miss Nuttel. "Poor Norah never could take the sun, you know, even when we were kids," she said. "Well, neither could I, though I'm not so bad now—but it's no surprise she's a bit under par, in the kitchen all morning and shopping in the afternoon when the weather's so hot. Hat or no hat," she added.

Miss Nuttel did not reply. Bunny had *positively insisted* she be left alone to keep the place running while Eric took Ada on a sightseeing tour—which Miss Nuttel could accept, as she knew Mrs. Blaine didn't much care for the sun. But to have lent Ada Noble her straw hat for the tour and then gone out shopping when there was no real need smacked more of deliberate martyrdom than anything else, and Miss Nuttel saw no good reason why Bunny should have a monopoly on martyrdom. . . .

Ada was still oozing sympathy. "The best thing for you, old girl," she told her cousin, "is peace and quiet and nobody disturbing you—and you know me, tongue hung in the middle, that's what they always used to say." She chuckled richly. "With me only been here a couple of days poor Erica would still feel obliged to make polite conversation, and I'd feel quite as obliged to answer"—she grinned at Miss Nuttel—"and Norah wouldn't have a minute's peace! You're sensible to get me out of the house so that she can have a proper rest—and this talk sounds fascinating, I must say. It would be a real pity to miss it, especially when it's for charity and all about this part of the world."

Miss Nuttel achieved another smile for Mrs. Noble. She had been annoyed with Mrs. Blaine, and doubtful about the wisdom of inviting a stranger to stay—but if Ada turned out to be this accommodating for the remainder of her visit, then Erica Nuttel, for one, wasn't going to argue with a guest who so obviously wanted to cause no bother to either of her hostesses. When, three days before, she had seen the two of them limping in weary silence through Lilikot's front gate, she had leaped up from the step where she'd been sitting and, without a word of complaint for the length of time she'd been locked out of the house with nobody at home, rushed to seize the bags of dandelions from the hands of not only her cousin (which was understandable) but her cousin's friend as well.

At first Miss Nuttel had been disposed to suspect such behaviour as mere favour-currying pretence, but on closer acquaintance Ada Noble did appear to be full of honest goodwill towards all. She smiled. She chuckled. She praised and admired; she argued cheerfully and without malice (there were some, thought Miss Nuttel, who might profit by Ada's example) and accepted the majority verdict of chamomile tea instead of rose hip with no more than a wink and a rueful sigh. She was, Miss Nuttel found herself thinking, her cousin moved up a notch, as it were. The improved, higher-powered model—except (Miss Nuttel mused the first night) that poor Bunny really had been having a bad time recently with the heat, and if Ada (who was quite as—well, there was no disputing it—*solidly built*) seemed livelier, it was only because she was putting a brave face on things. And because she'd been sitting still half the afternoon while her cousin had been hard at work in the canal-bank pasture picking dandelion heads for wine . . .

Those dandelion heads had rankled for several days, and now Miss Nuttel felt a (slight) twinge of conscience. "Poor old Bunny," she said aloud. "A nice quiet lie-down's what you need. Ada and I will go to the talk without you."

"And of course we'll pop your entrance fee in with ours so the charity won't miss out," added Mrs. Noble brightly. A flicker of irritation crossed her cousin's face, but in deference to her headache, Mrs. Blaine said nothing.

She said it, however, with such emphasis that the other two were overcome with guilt, and spent rather longer than Miss Nuttel would have liked settling the invalid comfortably before leaving for the village hall (newly furbished courtesy of Horace Jowett, misanthropist, deceased) and the talk. The Street was empty as they hurried on their way, and Miss Nuttel muttered that they would be lucky, at this rate, to find seats.

They were. The door of the hall stood open in the heat, and they could see that the room was almost full—and could hear that on the platform Sir George Colveden, nervous but resigned to his fund-raising fate, was already speaking. Miss Nuttel said something irritable under her breath, but Ada whispered that it was better late than never, and fed the triple entrance fee with relish into the collecting tin. Miss Nuttel winced as heads—not too many, but enough to raise a blush—turned to seek the cause of the disturbance, but Mrs. Noble, guessing that most of those who stared had mistaken her for Cousin Norah, smiled and waved apology as she supposed her cousin would do, and then crept after Miss Nuttel to a seat in the back row with the smile still firmly in place.

". . . nearest to Occupied France they called it Hellfire Corner," said Sir George as Miss Nuttel's attention focused itself at last. "Hardly surprising, when you think that on just one day in 1944 fifty shells fell in Dover and killed six people." He paused to clear his throat. "Yes. Fifty, I said, not fifteen, in case you weren't paying attention. Ahem. Yes. By the time the Canadians, God bless 'em, liberated Calais and captured the big guns in September 1944, nearly two and a quarter thousand shells had landed in poor old Dover since August 1940. Think of that." Thinking of it, he cleared his throat again. From the front row of seats Lady Colveden looked up to smile encouragement at the spouse who had faced Germans, Italians, and Japanese without flinching, but who now needed a stiff whisky to chat informally with his neighbours.

"Yes," said Sir George, consulting the cards on which he had scribbled the statistics compiled by Mr. Jessyp. "Two and a quarter thousand of the things, never mind the bombs and doodlebugs and rockets adding their blasted bit. Dover lost more than nine hundred buildings by the end of the War—and almost two hundred people." Sir George took a couple of deep breaths and blinked.

"Er—yes," he said. "A pretty grim business—but they couldn't keep a good town down. When Churchill visited Dover . . ." Sir George's voice faltered at the name of his hero. "When Churchill visited Dover and everyone rushed up to shake his hand, he told the policemen to let 'em through. 'These hands,' said Winston, " 'are worth shaking'—and, dammit, he was right!"

A burst of applause greeted these final words. Dropping his prompt cards and mopping his forehead, the baronet sat

down with a sigh of relief and closed his eyes, entirely forgetting his cue. It was left to master of ceremonies Martin
C. Jessyp, hiding a smile, to signal Admiral Leighton to take
up the story.

"Talking of Canadians," began the Buzzard, his ginger
beard alive with amusement, "I knew a splendid chap, told
he was too old for the Canadian Air Force, so he came over
here and joined the Wavy Navy—the Volunteer Reserve,"
he translated for the benefit of a younger, peacetime generation. "Gunboat captain. Never saw action for longer than
ten minutes at a time—things happen fast in battle—and you
learn fast, too. He lasted through more than a hundred fire-
fights because he learned how to duck when he saw the
tracer coming. D.S.C. (that's the Distinguished Service
Cross) and two bars—which means three times," he translated again. "A funny coincidence—he was court-martialled
three times, too. Reported himself once, as I recall." The
beard began wagging with laughter. "It was after he'd got
back from a trip when he'd had a British officer along for
the ride, and this chap outranked him. When things started
hotting up, the Royal Navy man started giving orders, so
my pal thumped him over the head with a number-six fire
extinguisher and stood on top of him for the rest of the
action, then turned himself in for mutiny once they were
safely back in port."

The mothers among his audience started to wish they had
left their offspring at home. Teenagers shifted on their chairs
and sniggered. The admiral shot them a darting look from
beneath his brows and carried on. "Talking of the Air
Force," he said, "there was a chap I knew so keen to do
his bit against the Nazis he lied through his teeth to get in.
Asked him if he could ride a horse: he said yes when he
didn't know one end from the other, and got away with it.
Then they asked him if he could drive, so he thought this
time he'd better own up and say he couldn't. Shoved him
in a car and told him to drive twice round the airfield. Didn't
hit anything, so they told him he could drive and that was

it, he was in. Splendid chap, name of Aaronson. Didn't . . ."
In deference to the age of some of his audience, the admiral
hesitated. "Didn't like what was happening to his family
and friends on the continent," he said at last. "So every
time he went on a bombing raid he took a brick wrapped in
the *Jewish Chronicle* and used to chuck it out of the cockpit
window when they were over Germany. . . ."

Major Howett, released from collecting-tin duty on the
door to add her pennyworth, told a moving story of how,
when nursing in a field hospital after D-Day, she had been
in the office between two wards, one full of wounded Allies
and the other full of Germans, when a young German boy
started to sing "Lili Marlene." The music floated through
the walls of the tent to reach the ears of the Tommies, who,
though knowing no German, joined in with the English
translation of the song and sang it to the end.

"Amazin'," said the major as Sir George blew his nose,
Benjamin Folland and Mr. Jessyp stared at their fingers, and
even the admiral coughed. "Here were these young lads,
ours and theirs, singin' away together as if they were a
choir—and not an hour before they'd all been doin' their
best to blow the other chaps' heads off. Makes you realise
what a terrible waste it is, when underneath everyone's the
same as everyone else. . . ."

Mr. Jessyp went farther back in time for his contribution
to the evening's entertainment. He spoke with eloquence of
the zeppelin threat during the First World War, when for the
first time in history the civilian populace had been in the
front line. Over a thousand people died in air raids during
that war supposed to end all end wars, and those who did
not believe in the pious supposition naturally feared that
more deaths would ensue the next time around.

"Interestingly," said Mr. Jessyp, "it wasn't Germany we
seem to have been afraid of then so much as France."

"Napoleon," growled the admiral, thinking of Nelson.

"Agincourt," offered Sir George Colveden at his side.

"Crécy," countered Mr. Jessyp before Major Howett

could mention Waterloo or Benjamin Folland he-had-no-idea-what. "Yes, Sir George and the admiral are right. We as a nation have had far more practice fighting the French than fighting almost any other nation—as the sound mirrors about which I'm going to tell you clearly show, because they're aligned more towards Paris than towards, say, Berlin as you might expect. . . ."

Mr. Jessyp went on to explain how during World War I it became possible to track the approach of enemy aircraft by using "elephant's ear-trumpets" mounted on motor vehicles that would turn to follow and "catch" the sound as it drew near. He told his audience to cup their hands behind their ears and say whether this action made it more, or less, easy to hear him talking. One look from the admiral, and even the teenagers agreed that it made it easier.

"Which is the same principle," said Mr. Jessyp, "as the acoustic mirrors." Later experiments by the Air Ministry and War Department (he continued) developed these trumpets into flat discs with microphones attached, which discs were in their turn developed in the 1920s into "sound mirrors," parabolic concrete dishes twenty or thirty feet in diameter, with microphones at the focal point to collect and amplify every sound and transmit it via a "periscope" to listening operators wearing first a primitive stethoscope, but latterly a set of earphones.

"The listeners," said Mr. Jessyp, "telephoned details of what they heard to a central point—Biggin Hill, which we all know from the Battle of Britain in the last war—where it was cross-referenced with information being received from other acoustic mirrors." The schoolmaster waxed pedagogic, explaining how it was theoretically possible, with an accurate cross reference and triangulation, to plot the direction, if not the speed, from which an aircraft was approaching.

"But theory," said Mr. Jessyp, "is one thing. Practice, as the sound-mirror boffins found out, is another. . . ."

He told how there had been erected, as well as the huge concrete bowls or dishes at various sites along the south and

east coasts of England, a monumental two-hundred-foot
long curved, concrete wall at Greatstone on the Kent coast
between Dungeness and New Romney. (A stirring among
the audience made him interject the advice that it was possible to see some of these mirrors still in place, and perhaps
a coach party might be made up to visit them one day. The
audience subsiding with nods of agreement, he went on.)

It was at the Greatstone site (he explained) that the sound
mirrors' weaknesses began to become apparent—weaknesses that arose partly from their strengths, because the mirrors, whether concave bowl or curved wall, worked (in some
ways) almost too well. Top brass attending a demonstration
was collectively deafened by the clop of a pony's hooves as
the milk cart passed along the road several hundred yards in
front of the mirror with harness jingling and bottles clanking.
On a windy day the rustling of marshland grass muffled and
distorted the sound of engines until aircraft were almost
within sight. Grazing sheep munched, rabbits hopped and
thumped—and, worst indignity of all, people wandered
across the vital "sound collection" area in front of the two-
hundred-foot wall and tried to picnic in its windshadow shelter.

"Why, you might ask," said Mr. Jessyp, "didn't they
build them right on the coast, where people were unlikely
to walk in front of them?"

"Waves," called someone from the audience, and everyone cheered as the schoolmaster confirmed the answer.

"But," he went on, "the most serious threat of all to the
success of the acoustic mirrors was the improvement in aircraft design. When the first mirror was constructed, the average speed of a bomber was eighty miles an hour, whereas
ten years later it was *two hundred and eighty* miles an hour.
Technology then was simply not geared to collecting, plotting, and triangulating the information fast enough—but
while the boffins were still trying to iron out the problems
with the dishes and bowls, there were other boffins at work
on something that would ultimately be far more successful:

Radio Direction Finding, R.D.F, that later became Radio Detection and Ranging—Radar. Without which,'' he said as he prepared to sit down, ''we might not have won the Battle of Britain.''

''Talking of the Battle of Britain,'' said Mr. Folland, who had recognised his cue and wasn't letting it escape, ''it was during the last war that this country got recycling down to a fine art. Aluminium saucepans went to make Spitfires, garden railings went to make tanks and guns and ammunition.'' Miss Seeton and Martha Bloomer, sitting together, exchanged quick smiles. ''Now, The Golden Brolly,'' said Mr. Folland with one of his characteristic finger stabs, ''doesn't want your saucepans or your garden railings—but we *do* want your stamps and your silver paper and your milk-bottle tops—and your money. Most of all, your money. The generosity of Plummergen has been—has been an example to the nation. I know I can rely on every one of you to sponsor your team in the many events that have been organised in the area over the next couple of weeks—but just in case there's anyone who hasn't signed up, I have some extra forms here and a spare collecting tin. . . .''

There was no doubt about it. He had.

While an outing to the acoustic mirrors on which he had lectured might or might not in due course take place, it was only a few days after his lecture that Mr. Jessyp found himself hurriedly arranging a day trip to France.

Like so many of Plummergen's current activities, the trip was inspired by the charitable frenzy into which the death of Horace Jowett and the arrival of Benjamin Folland had hurled its inhabitants. Mr. Folland having announced the climactic Potato Race with Bulldozers at Shakespeare Cliff, site of the Chunnel dig, Schoolmaster Jessyp began to ponder a production of one of the Bard's plays, ticket prices to be double the normal rate and the extra sum to go to the wheelchair fund. Mr. Folland, when the idea was proposed, thanked him, but pointed out that Golden Brolly Blitzes only lasted a month in each area, and he had already been at the George a fortnight, near enough. Did Mr. Jessyp feel that—with his teaching and other commitments—he could coax a worthwhile performance out of even the most dedicated thespians in little more than two weeks?

"A nice music-hall," suggested Mr. Folland. "With everyone who wants to do a turn bidding for the privilege. The squire, so I've heard, does a splendid auctioneer."

Mr. Jessyp was unable to deny that Sir George Colveden, whose toothbrush moustache could always be grown to waxing length in a good cause, made an excellent auctioneer, but it had taken some persuasion for him to agree to the village hall talk, and Mr. Jessyp never liked to push his volunteers too far. Mr. Jessyp, moreover, did not feel that Plummergen possessed sufficient talent of what he might call an *endurable* nature to make such an enterprise viable.

"The ones who'll bid the most," he predicted with an expressive shudder, "will be those who never get beyond the auditions when the Padders—the Plummergen Amateur Dramatic Society—put on a show. In this particular case we won't be able to turn them down, as it's for charity—but even for charity, Mr. Folland, there are some things no audience should be asked to suffer."

"Pity," said Mr. Folland. "But I know what you mean." He grinned. "I daresay they'd have all their friends sponsoring them for the longest poem or the funniest song, and us poor devils would have to sit through ninety-seven versions of 'The Green Eye of the Little Yellow God' or 'Abdul the Bulbul Emir' or something of the sort while they enjoy their—what's he say?—their one brief hour upon the stage. And the ones with ciné cameras will make a regular night of it, I shouldn't wonder, though I suppose we could charge them for the privilege."

" 'Yellow God,' " Mr. Jessyp corrected him absently. "No 'Little' . . ." He frowned. "Ciné cameras," he said aloud. "Shakespeare!"

"I thought it was," said Benjamin. "Strutting, eh?"

"No, no—I mean, yes, but no," said Mr. Jessyp. "You've given me a better idea, Mr. Folland. We won't act a Shakespeare play—you're right, we haven't the time—but we'll show a film in the village hall and charge double entrance. Shakespeare, of course. I'll telephone the agency on Monday to see what they have for hire—but we can spread the word now that there will be a film show on Wednesday night."

•   •   •

Mr. Jessyp was not displeased with the first available choice of *Henry V*. He felt it, indeed, peculiarly apposite, given that the digging at Shakespeare Cliff was to link those age-old foes, the English and the French. *Henry V* would serve as a reminder of times when cross-Channel *entente* had been far less *cordiale* while giving hope for the future, as well as being an educational treat for the children and a fine evening's entertainment for their parents.

To say that the village enjoyed itself is an understatement. Plummergen was never known to do things by halves. A minority, among whom were the Lilikot contingent, were surprised by the film's popularity and, arriving too late to find seats, refused to cram into the hall to stand at the back and went home in a huff. But many were only too willing to stand, and at the thrilling parts of the action stamped their feet quite as loudly as those sitting down, while their whistling was even louder. Without exception the children forgot to eat the sandwiches packed by their mothers as provision against the rigours of a late night. The hail of arrows was greeted with view-halloos that made the rafters ring. The downhill charge on horseback had people whooping their encouragement to drown the music, and the news of the slaughtered luggage boys brought a salvo of hisses and boos from even the most sober of the audience. When Montjoy, Herald of France, confessed the day lost, more cheers and yells brought flakes of plaster from the ceiling. After Henry wooed and won his Kate and the final credits rolled, the cry arose for a second showing even before the lights had gone up.

Mr. Jessyp hurried to rewind the spools as those with seats yielded place to those who had not, though some (but politely) refused to budge, saying they would gladly pay to see it all again. The representative of The Golden Brolly beamed on them and did the rounds with a collecting tin. Mr. Jessyp nodded to Major Howett, on duty at the central light switch.

"Silence in the ranks, there!" she cried, and clicked the main switch down as people cheered. The lights went out, the spool whirred, and the Chorus for the second time invoked a Muse of fire.

People were still quoting as they prepared to call it a night. " 'Once more into the breach, dear friends!' " cried Sir George Colveden, galloping down the path from the village hall with Admiral Leighton and Nigel on either side of him, Nigel supplying the remainder of the speech as his father ran out of steam.

" 'And gentlemen in England, now a-bed','' chanted Major Howett behind them, " 'Shall think themselves accurs'd they were not here, And hold their manhoods cheap—' Damn cheek, don't you think? Nothin' about women bein' every good at scrappin' as the men!''

"Every bit as good,'' agreed the admiral promptly while Lady Colveden in the decorous rear hid a smile. "Half a dozen like you in my squadron, Major, and I know we'd have had Jerry on the run as soon as we saw the whites of the devil's eyes!''

" 'Devils incarnate,' " offered Sir George, who thought it sounded familiar but wasn't entirely sure why.

" 'The devil would have him about women,' " gurgled Nigel.

Lady Colveden coughed as the rest of the crowd streamed past on its way to bed. Nigel, all innocence, turned to his mother. "Don't encourage them,'' warned her ladyship as Sir George, the admiral, and Major Howett blocked the end of the path, apparently preparing to go their separate ways.

"Me?'' Nigel contrived to look hurt at her suspicious mind. "As if I would. As if I needed to,'' he added as he heard the admiral speak the fatal words.

"How about a spot before we toddle off to Bedfordshire? You game, Colveden? Major? Nigel? Padre?'' This last as the Reverend Arthur Treeves, his sister Molly, and Benjamin Folland—acting as escorts to Mr. Jessyp and the takings—arrived with the keys of the locked and darkened hall in their responsible possession.

"Ah,'' said the Reverend Arthur, who could remember,

albeit hazily, previous occasions when he had accepted an invitation from "Buzzard" Leighton to join him and his cronies for a drink. "A—a spot?" The Reverend Arthur could sense his sister radiating disapproval at his side. Molly Treeves remembered those occasions as well. "It—it's a little late for me, I fear," the vicar said quickly. "Sermons to write, you know." He felt himself blush for this mendacity: it was only Wednesday. "But thank you for the invitation. Most kind," he added. "Most . . ."

"And we have to make sure Mr. Jessyp reaches home in one piece," supplied Molly as her brother stuttered into an awkward silence. "There aren't so many people around as there were five minutes ago."

"And the money," interposed Mr. Folland, "is a serious responsibility. I could give you a receipt for it now if you prefer, Mr. Jessyp, and place it in the hotel safe."

"Come home with me and we'll count it again," said Mr. Jessyp, who saw a certain merit in the scheme.

"Talking of home . . ." said Lady Colveden, and prepared to take her leave, telling Nigel as she departed that she held him fully responsible for the state in which his father appeared the following day.

"I'll see you home," offered Nigel hastily.

"Don't be so feeble," said his mother. "There may not be as many people around as there were five minutes ago, but there are still more than enough. It's a lovely night for a stroll, and I intend to enjoy it. Molly and the vicar have asked me in for coffee—and I'll have some waiting at home for the two of you," she added. "Strong, black coffee."

"I really don't mind seeing you home," insisted Nigel, but his mother laughed at him.

"Run along, my son, and learn by horrid example if you are unable to set a good one. Don't make too much noise coming in. George—have fun."

"He will," muttered Nigel, prophet of doom. "He will!"

•   •   •

Lady Colveden was down to breakfast long before either of her menfolk. Having reached the toast-and-marmalade stage, she was perusing the daily paper's "Court and Social" columns, sighing quietly over the betrothal announcements and wondering if Nigel would ever find the right girl, when the creak of a guilty door announced the arrival of the very object of her maternal speculation.

"Good afternoon," she greeted him cheerily.

Nigel groaned.

"Coffee?" enquired his mother with a nod towards the pot. "It's fresh, though terribly wasteful, and you hardly deserve it, either of you. I noticed you didn't drink what I left you last night."

"You mean this morning," said Nigel, staggering to his place and collapsing on the chair.

"Coffee," said Lady Colveden, hurriedly pouring. She was not a cruel woman. "Strong and black, as recommended by the best medical authorities."

Nigel groaned again, and his mother thought she caught a reference to Dr. Knight.

"You'd better let me sugar it for you, too," she went on, busily stirring. "And what about your father? Assuming, of course, that the anonymous lump snarling at me from under the bedclothes *is* your father. I can't *imagine* you would bring a complete stranger home and put him to bed beside me, but if that's what you did, I should hate him to see me in my dressing gown."

"It's perfectly respectable," protested Nigel, who had taken in only half of what she was saying. He seized the coffee cup with grateful hands and drank. He shuddered, closed his eyes, and groaned again as the caffeine began to work. "Ouch," he said.

"Are you alive yet?" asked her ladyship.

"No," said Nigel.

"Then I'll leave the corpse in front of the funeral baked meats while I take this upstairs," said his mother, poised with another cup in her hand. She stopped. "Goodness, what

a Shakespearean time we're having of it! But I rather think
it was Hamlet, not Henry, who said that.''

"Don't,'' begged Nigel as he groped for his coffee again.
"If you only knew . . .''

"It's probably as well I don't.'' Then Meg Colveden set
her husband's cup on the table and faced her son squarely.
"Or maybe it isn't. Perhaps you'd better tell me.''

Nigel reached across and took his father's coffee from
under his mother's nose. "My need is greater than his,'' he
told her. "And I hope that wasn't Shakespeare,'' he added
as she uttered only a faint protest and watched him drink.
"I never,'' said Nigel, "want to hear that name again.''

"Shakespeare? A little difficult to avoid our national bard,
I should think,'' observed Lady Colveden. "Why?''

"It only encourages them,'' came the glum rejoinder.
"We all seem to have done the wretched play at school.
Everyone was quoting bits at everyone else—even Colonel
Windup, who materialised out of nowhere the way he in-
variably does when there's any drink around. . . .''

"Nigel,'' said his mother. "But I do know what you
mean. Poor old man,'' she added kindly.

"Save your sympathy for Dad,'' Nigel told her as he put
out a feeble hand for cold toast and the butter dish.

Lady Colveden stared. "For George? He was moaning in
quite his usual style when I came down. He sounded no
worse than he normally does the day after he's been drinking
with the admiral. What's happened?''

"To skip the dull preliminaries,'' said Nigel, "assume the
lapse of a considerable period of time and the consumption
of—of considerable quantities of alcohol.''

Lady Colveden indicated that she had, warily, made this
assumption.

"Then,'' said Nigel with relish, "they started to imitate
the action of the tiger.''

"The tiger,'' reiterated her ladyship.

"Yes,'' said Nigel with even greater relish. "All over the
house, at top speed—the silly chumps.''

Lady Colveden looked at him. "You don't, I notice, seem to be including yourself among the chumpish ranks."

Nigel had the grace to blush. "Oh, well." He grinned. "But I was a good generation younger than anyone else there. My physical coordination's far better, so it wasn't such a risk for me."

"Risk?" His mother seized upon the vital word. "Nigel, *what* has happened to your father? I insist that you tell me before I find out for myself and the shock makes me do something I might later come to regret."

"I," said Nigel, "already regret it. It's my own fault. You told me to keep an eye on him—and now we're going to be one man short on the farm at the busiest time of year because he's sprained his perishing wrist. The right one, what's more," he enlarged above her startled little cry. "I had a pretty grim job helping him into his pyjamas with that whacking great bandage on his arm."

The faint anxiety—Nigel was generally reliable, but she knew what the admiral's parties could be like—faded from Lady Colveden's expressive eyes. "Major Howett, of course," she said, relieved.

"Dr. Knight," her son corrected her with a grin. "When the Howitzer didn't sign on for the late-night shift, he came steaming down from the nursing home to look for her." Nigel glanced at his mother. "Odd, don't you think? I mean, he could have phoned. He knows the Buzzard never misses the chance to push the boat out. He might have guessed she'd be there—but he came along in person to fetch her and ended up joining in the singsong instead."

"Singsong," repeated Lady Colveden faintly. "Oh, dear."

" 'Oh, dear' indeed," said Nigel. "You know how warm it was last night. They had all the upstairs windows open at Lilikot. . . ."

Lady Colveden stifled an unladylike giggle. Nigel's chortle was even less restrained.

"I should think they were hard at it with with the

dictionary this morning,'' he said as he sobered. ''I mean, I know education's supposed to be a wonderful thing and all that, but 'Colonel Bogey' was the final straw, to judge by the way the windows suddenly started banging. I'm amazed the glass didn't fall out.''

'' 'Colonel Bogey,' '' echoed his mother.

''Blame that on the Bard as well,'' said Nigel. ''I told you they were quoting chunks of *Henry* at one another—and somebody came up with the ''Tennis balls, my liege' bit from when he's making up his mind to invade, and then—''

''Yes,'' said his mother rather sharply.

Nigel's eyes opened wide. ''Mother! I'm shocked.''

''Don't be silly, Nigel. I remember the War very well.''

''And I,'' returned her son, ''remember you taking me to see *The Bridge on the River Kwai* at the local fleapit. I wondered at the time why you wouldn't let Dad come, too.'' He began to hum the well-known theme tune, conducting with the butter knife. ''*Dah*-da, di dada dum dum *dah* . . .''

''Nigel,'' said his mother.

''. . . *Goer*ing has two—but ve-ry small,'' sang Nigel, his eyes on his mother's face. ''*Himm*ler—has something sim'lar—And poor old Goebbels—has n—''

''Nigel!'' cried his mother, and Nigel subsided. ''I shall make some more coffee,'' she said. ''For me. And if you want hot toast you can do it yourself. Really!''

But as her ladyship busied herself in the kitchen, her undutiful son could hear her clearly through the hatch. She was humming ''Colonel Bogey.'' Memories of the War were easily woken in those who had survived it.

The war that now seemed to have caught the attention of Plummergen's small fry had been fought far more than thirty years ago. The day after the film, scenes from *Henry V* were reenacted with much infant enthusiasm in the playground before school began—at the morning, midday, and afternoon breaks—and even on the way home, despite the heat of the midsummer sun. Questions were asked in class. Royal pedigrees and family trees were drawn up as Mr. Jessyp and Miss Maynard (who taught the younger children) did their best to explain early fifteenth-century history and politics. Maps of Europe were consulted. The children became more vocal and definite in their demands.

On Thursday evening, having spent some time on the telephone, Mr. Jessyp knocked at Miss Seeton's door.

"Come and join me in the garden," Miss Seeton invited as she welcomed the schoolmaster with a smile. "It's a shame to sit indoors when the weather is so fine."

"I only hope it stays fine," said Mr. Jessyp, following her through the cottage to the blossom-scented air of the garden. "No wind," he enlarged as he settled himself on a chair and accepted a tumbler of cool raspberry vinegar from a large jug covered with a bead-edged crochet circle to keep out the numerous winged insects of the evening.

Miss Seeton studied the topmost branches of the apple trees at the less sheltered end of the garden. Even they were not moving. "There is," she remarked, "no breeze at present, certainly—of course, with the English climate one can never be certain for long."

"Ah," said Mr. Jessyp, peering at Miss Seeton over the top of his glass. "The English climate—yes. England . . . This is most refreshing, Miss Seeton. Your own fruit, might I enquire?"

Miss Seeton beamed. "It is Stan who should receive the compliment," she said, paying tribute to her tame gardener. "But in his absence I will accept it gladly on his behalf. And dear Cousin Flora's, too, for it was in one of her old commonplace books I found the receipt, as she called it."

"So very English," murmured Mr. Jessyp, with a faint sigh as he turned his eyes to the heavens. "Miss Seeton, I will come straight to the point. Would you—in your capacity as a part-time teacher—be willing to accompany the school on a day trip to France on Saturday?"

Miss Seeton blinked at him.

"Not alone, I hasten to add," he went on, running a finger round the inside of his collar. "Miss Maynard and I will be there, too, of course. And, given the popularity of the suggestion with the children, I imagine some of their parents might well wish to join the party." He coughed. "In one way I feel it's a case of the more the merrier, but in the interests of . . . Well, let's just say I would prefer there to be three, as it were, official representatives of the teaching profession rather than two." He took a deep breath. "At least one of whom," he added sadly, "is not exactly the best sailor in the world—and Miss Maynard, poor soul, tells me she is inclined to the same weakness."

"Oh, dear," said Miss Seeton, who had been blessed with a sound travelling stomach and had seldom suffered from motion sickness. "The Channel can be so . . . uncertain, can't it?"

"Don't," begged Mr. Jessyp, turning pale. Miss Seeton was reminded of nothing so much as Lady Colveden's description of Sir George on the morning after the night before chez Admiral Leighton. "I hate even thinking about it," said the schoolmaster with a shudder. "But the children seem so very keen—and you know how important it is to encourage them in their enthusiasms. . . ."

"Indeed I do," said Miss Seeton. She twinkled at him. "Sir Laurence Olivier," she ventured, "has a lot to answer for, has he not?"

Mr. Jessyp agreed that the consequences of showing *Henry V* had been more far-reaching than he had anticipated. The boost to Golden Brolly funds was one thing, but that juvenile Plummergen should display so overwhelming an interest in the Plantagenet claim to the throne of France was quite another. "They really want to *know*," he said, much gratified. "They want to understand! They were disappointed when I explained that Agincourt itself was of very little interest, merely an empty field, but even that didn't stop them saying they still wanted to go"—he gulped—"to France. Even Calais would be better than nothing, they said.

And in the circumstances—as I was the one who started all this . . .''

"You and Sir Laurence," Miss Seeton reminded him with another twinkle.

Her smile seemed to cheer him. The thought of a Channel crossing did not sit lightly on the shoulders of Martin C. Jessyp, but at least he could laugh now about the situation into which he had impelled himself, though he suspected that he would not be so cheerful once he was on the high seas.

"Guilty as charged, the pair of us," he said. "Would you be willing to share some of the guilt, Miss Seeton?"

Miss Seeton expressed herself more than willing. It was two years since her last trip across the Channel—she begged his pardon as Mr. Jessyp turned pale again—and it would be a pleasure to renew her acquaintance with Calais if with nowhere else. But—as the children were so interested in matters French—it would perhaps be a shame not to take them farther afield, should this be possible. She couldn't help but be reminded, in the continuing hot weather, of the Monet garden being re-created in the grounds of his château by the Comte de Balivernes. She was not entirely sure how near to Calais or Agincourt the château might be, but if— again she begged Mr. Jessyp's pardon—an educational excuse (as one might say) were needed for the trip . . .

"Miss Seeton, you're brilliant!" Mr. Jessyp raised his glass of raspberry vinegar in an admiring toast. "They'll know nothing about Monet and care less for his garden, I'm sure, but if it's war heroes they want, then the Comte de Balivernes is their man. I've read quite a bit about him. He was in the Maquis—organised a network single-handed— was captured, but escaped and made his way to England, then went back with fresh recruits—played a vital part in the preparations for D-Day—Croix de Guerre, Légion d'Honneur, you name it, he's got it. They'll be thrilled to have even the chance of bumping into a chap like that, especially when I tell them his wife was a member of the Resistance, too.''

Miss Seeton nodded. "I recall something of the story," she said slowly. Her interest had been more in the garden, but the articles describing the re-creation had not neglected the human-interest aspect, either. "From Edinburgh, was she not? The historical links between France and Scotland are of long standing, of course."

Mr. Jessyp's turn to nod. "And she was one of the young women who went back with him on his second attempt to— to cause havoc among the occupying forces." In deference to his hostess he did not say what he had at first intended.

Miss Seeton sighed. "And she died so young," she said. "Such a tragic ending to a—a truly gallant romance. To have survived all the deprivations of living hand to mouth in the wild—to wait so long for a much-wanted child and then to die giving birth . . ."

"We won't tell the youngsters that," said Mr. Jessyp quickly. "We want them to enjoy their day out." He smiled, a little weakly. "I've a feeling they're going to enjoy it a good deal more than I will—or Miss Maynard!"

To which Miss Seeton could find no suitable reply.

As the sun went down, Mr. Jessyp, having thoroughly enjoyed a second glass of raspberry vinegar, took his reluctant leave. In the marginally cooler air Miss Seeton pottered about the garden for a while, pulling up the occasional weed, snipping off a dead rose head or two, watering the raspberry canes to ensure a good crop of fruit to turn into cordial for next year's summer. She settled the hens in the fowl house, tidied the garden chairs and table under their green plastic sheet, and went indoors to prepare for bed.

She did not neglect her yoga routine, hot and somewhat tiring though the weather was. She spread her plaid rug on the bedroom floor and addressed herself to the warm-up exercises before undertaking the routine of the day, her knees neither clicking nor creaking as she bowed and bent, stretched and curled, and tied herself in the knots that were, after seven years, so easy and comfortable, even if when she had first opened the pages of *Yoga and Younger Every Day* she would have supposed the normal human body to be incapable of such contortions.

The *normal* human body. Those who, unlike herself, were naturally double-jointed would have been less . . . daunted at the start than she had been, she supposed: and yet here she was now, balanced with her hands palm down, her bottom a good six inches off the rug, and her legs wrapped forward over her elbows, giving her an excellent view of ten well-manicured toes. Miss Seeton counted one hundred calm and quiet breaths, then spread her fingers a little more, tipped her head slightly up, and unfolded herself out of the *Kakasana*, or Crow Posture, into a simple headstand. She held the pose for another count of one hundred, overbalanced gently downwards, and lay flat on her back with her hands, palm up, at her sides and her eyes closed.

This favourite *Savasana,* or Dead Pose, was intended to relax and refresh. Tonight it failed to work as well as it sometimes did. Mr. Jessyp's plans for the school outing to France drifted in and out of Miss Seeton's consciousness, mingled with her hopes that the party would, after all, be able to visit the Monet garden . . . so delightfully cool . . . *Flaming June* . . . the celebrated painting by Sir Frederic Leighton . . . the languorous model, draped in her classical dress of orange gauze, sleeping in an attitude surely only a practitioner of yoga could hope to emulate . . . the rising moon, glistening on the wine-dark sea behind her head . . . Admiral Leighton . . . dear Sir George and his reminiscences of war . . . France . . . Balivernes . . . Monet's lilies . . . midsummer heat . . . flame-coloured gauze and moonlit waters . . . dangerous moonlight . . . flames . . . the war . . .

Miss Seeton awoke with a start. She shivered. Such a vivid—disturbing—yet thankfully fading memory . . .

Lady Colveden's lively tale of how Sir George came by his sprained wrist had been censored only a little in the tell-

ing, and that was more to spare Lady Colveden's blushes
than Miss Seeton's. Those who have lived through the Blitz
and heard beleaguered London's forthright views on the enemy are not easily shocked. Miss Seeton might not be able
to hold much of a tune, but she knew "Colonel Bogey." In
wartime London it had been impossible to avoid him.

The War. Miss Seeton rolled over to her side, tipped on
her tummy, and rose to her feet before folding the rug away
and making final preparations for bed. After so many years
one could still not forget, although one should hope, or at
least try, to forgive. It was thirty years since the lights went
on again in blacked-out London; when a trip to France could
once more be mooted as a pleasure rather than a grim necessity. The last shell to fall on front-line Britain, she recalled, had landed in Dover thirty years ago, all but a matter
of weeks—and in a matter of days—hours, almost—she
would be in Dover preparing to travel to France with no
worries beyond whether Mr. Jessyp would suffer as much
in the crossing as he feared he might.

And Miss Maynard another sufferer, poor thing. Miss Seeton hoped that those of the children's parents who elected
to come would have stomachs as strong as she believed her
own to be, although the Channel could be so very uncertain,
and it would be foolish to rely on willpower alone. There
were such things as tablets—first used, she remembered, in
the D-Day landings, for seasick soldiers would have been
no use as fighting men. Dear Sir George. Perhaps—as the
sprain must mean he was unable to help on the farm—he
and Lady Colveden might care to join the party. "The more
the merrier," Mr. Jessyp had said. But she must be careful
not to say "merry" when Sir George was listening. Nigel—
or so she had been given to understand—had teased his father dreadfully about old soldiers and their less-than-cast-
iron heads for drink, which—as far as she knew, from what
Miss Treeves had told her of the vicar's experiences at one
of the admiral's parties—was not entirely Sir George's fault.
During the War so many had learned to drink as if there

were no tomorrow because, all too often, there had not been. . . .

Miss Seeton fell asleep at last, but her dreams were far from peaceful. When she woke next morning, the ghosts of those dreams still swimming in her head, she found herself hurrying to her sketchbook. Only when she had exorcised her ghosts did she feel able to close the book and resume her daily routine, her mind no longer restless as it had been the night before.

The flames, the destruction, and the bomb she had drawn with such swift clarity lay out of sight, hidden—muffled— stifled and impotent between the covers of her sketchbook.

Hidden . . . and waiting.

CHAPTER 6

As all Plummergen had observed, the atmosphere in Lilikot had been under increasing strain since the arrival of the hot weather; the arrival of Ada Noble had served to defuse the situation slightly, but only slightly. Two (said Plummergen in knowing accents) was company. Three, sooner or later, was a crowd. A third party could act as a buffer in any quarrel . . . for a while. But it couldn't—wouldn't—last, because human nature didn't work that way. Plummergen waited in gleeful expectation for the explosion. Plummergen thought it knew when someone's nose was out of joint. Mrs. Blaine had taken to staying at home and using the heat as an excuse for not going out and about with Miss Nuttel as she used to do: Cousin Ada had started to go out and about in Mrs. Blaine's place—and, to Plummergen's amusement, in Mrs. Blaine's straw hat.

What Plummergen didn't realise was that Mrs. Blaine's dislike of the heat—and her subsequent ill temper—was genuine. Her staying indoors was no excuse, but a physical necessity for one so plump and out of condition. Ada was quite as plump as her cousin, but having lived in London (where it was impossible to drive and retain one's sanity), she was in far better condition from running after buses and racing other passengers for taxis. She had also spent many hours in recent weeks walking aimlessly around town just to get herself out of the house and away from Algernon while she thought things through. Having made the decision to end her marriage, she had packed what she could carry, crammed on as many extra clothes as possible, and left.

Now Ada Noble revelled in the non-London air and the wide, free horizons of the marsh. She was only too happy to help Norah (when allowed by that cousinly martyr) with the housework, or Erica with shopping and the garden: all she asked was that until her financial situation was resolved she could be permitted to stay, borrowing where necessary from Cousin Norah anything—except money—for which she might have a short-term need. Mrs. Blaine, after a few days, agreed that as they were the same size there was little difficulty in lending poor Ada her clothes. . . .

"Only what's washable and drip-dry, thanks," said Ada, accepting the offer with a smile. "I don't want to be a nuisance, and once the weather breaks . . ."

"Wish it would," growled Miss Nuttel, brooding on the garden and rubbing the small of her back. Ada had, without complaint, helped her carry watering can after can from the kitchen tap or the outside pump to the most important vegetable beds, but the flowers of which Bunny was so fond were having to fend for themselves. Who in her right mind wanted to end up crippled for the sake of a bunch of sweet peas when the edible variety were struggling to survive? Ada had proposed an ingenious siphon system for the upstairs bathroom, and if it didn't rain in the next few days, they would visit Brettenden to buy top-grade hose pipe—it had been so long since they'd last used the hose that it had perished—and a funnel. The water butt had been empty for over a fortnight now, and the Meteorological Office saw no relief on the immediate horizon.

"Let's think positive," said Ada as Mrs. Blaine sighed in silent regret for her lost sweet peas. The pop of their drying pods—in drought-desperation they had seeded early—made sitting outside in the evening an uncomfortable experience. "The admiral tells me it should be a splendid year for honey," said Ada cheerfully. "Bees like the sun."

"The admiral," echoed Miss Nuttel, for once ignoring the chance to complain about her neighbour's bees. "Been chatting to him, have you?"

"We had a few words over the fence this morning," said Ada. "While you and Norah were sorting out the shopping list." Mrs. Blaine frowned, and Miss Nuttel shook her head. Mrs. Noble looked surprised by their reaction. "He seems a decent sort of chap," she said. "In spite of—well, that business the other night. Can't blame a man if his guests get a little out of hand."

Miss Nuttel snorted. Mrs. Blaine tittered. Mrs. Noble shrugged. "Oh, well," she said. "Live and let live—as long as he doesn't make a habit of it, that is. But he's got a good sense of humour. Jolly Jack Tar, and so on."

Miss Nuttel glanced sideways at Mrs. Blaine. "Jolly Jack Tar," she said slowly. "Didn't . . . happen to say if he was going to France, did he?"

"He said he wasn't," said Ada promptly. "Sorry, Erica, but you're on your own. If an admiral of the fleet doesn't fancy the idea of a Channel crossing, then I think Norah and I are entitled to feel the same way!"

Lilikot, arriving late and refusing to stand, had perforce missed the momentous screening of *Henry V*—but its aftermath had been both unavoidable and inharmonious. Miss Nuttel, learning that the trip to France was open to all, was keen to go. Mrs. Blaine was adamant that nothing would persuade her to set foot on a Channel ferry again. She and Humphrey had gone abroad for their honeymoon, and . . .

Ada Noble, doing her best to accommodate herself to the needs of both her hostesses, tried to remain neutral in the discussions, but in the end, cornered by Miss Nuttel, she confessed that seasickness was a family trait and she couldn't agree more with Norah that the only place to be was on dry land. If they'd been *flying* to France, she wouldn't have minded any more than Norah would—but a ferry trip . . .

"If it's the duty-free you want," she said, "why not ask a friend to buy it on your behalf? Not everyone uses their allowance, you know. Cigarettes and—and so forth."

"We don't smoke," said Miss Nuttel.

"We make our own wine," said Mrs. Blaine. They looked at each other. Harmony was restored. . . .

Temporarily.

Miss Nuttel had resigned herself to not going to France, but at some cost to her peace of mind. She was able to rationalise her staying at home only by telling herself that if she left them alone together for the day, Bunny and Ada would be able to gang up on her during her absence. That they hadn't yet shown any inclination to gang up on her was neither here nor there. Blood was thicker than water. Miss Nuttel's subsequent brooding had not made for happiness in the home. It wasn't as if she could even tell the other two *why* she brooded. That would be to let them know she was worried—which she kept assuring herself she wasn't—because Bunny wasn't like that. She hoped. Norah Blaine two-faced and scheming? Plotting against her best friend of thirteen years? Never!

She hoped.

But she'd heard Plummergen's whispers and she couldn't help wondering. Two was company: three was a crowd. Erica Nuttel had no intention of being the crowded third—but how to prevent it? On her first evening in Plummergen, Ada had set out to charm Bunny's friend Eric and succeeded. Bunny started sulking, and her cousin hurried to make amends, but she'd done so in such a way that Miss Nuttel hadn't felt neglected. Miss Nuttel *liked* Ada Noble. The woman walked an emotional tightrope—and walked it, on the whole, with remarkable skill. Miss Nuttel liked her . . . but so did Bunny, who felt herself to have a prior claim and could make her annoyance all too clear if she felt that claim was being ignored.

"I shall go to the shops once I've finished all this," she announced, slipping a rinsed breakfast plate into the rack on the draining board. "Before it gets too hot for walking, even if . . ." Her sigh, weary shrug, and drooping shoulders suggested it would take so long to finish the dishes that the heat was bound to be intolerable by the time it came to shop.

"I'll pop across for you now, if you like," said Ada promptly. Miss Nuttel, poring over a seed catalogue brought in that morning's post, had not been minded to chat, and Ada—whose cheery offer to dry and put away the washer-upper had gracelessly refused—was at a loose end. "Give me the list, old girl."

"You'll have to wait. My hands are wet," returned Mrs. Blaine, determined to feel hard-done-by somehow.

"Bag in the hall," said Miss Nuttel, for whom the charms of the catalogue had faded at the sharpness of Bunny's tone. "I'll write the list," she added as Ada departed bagwards. "You tell me."

Mrs. Blaine sloshed washing-up water round the bowl with her worn string mop-on-a-stick and tossed her head.

"You're sure to get it all wrong," she told her friend of thirteen years. "Besides, Ada won't be able to read your writing—I'm sure I never can."

"Oh, I'll manage," said Ada, reappearing with the string bag in her hand. "Or Erica can come with me to translate," she added. As Miss Nuttel glanced at her she winked and made sure the high-denomination treasury note she slipped into the leather purse inside the bag did not go unnoticed. "Time I paid my way," she explained.

"Nonsense!" cried Mrs. Blaine, who, busy with the dishes, had missed the byplay. "You're a visitor, Ada—although it's too unfair to expect *anyone* to have to walk miles up and down the village carrying bags full of shopping in such *dreadful* weather."

"Post office right across The Street," objected Miss Nuttel, who had just realised what this was all about. Miss Nuttel held strong views on pollution in general and on the internal combustion engine in particular. Every few months Bunny (concerning whose ecological dedication Miss Nuttel sometimes couldn't help wondering) dropped artful hints as to how much easier their life might be if they had a car. Every few months Eric, disregarding the hints, delivered a pithy lecture about the merits of the tandem bicycle, or advised her friend to think of the generations yet unborn to whom they, the keepers of the conservational flame, must be responsible.

"I won't melt," said Ada now with a laugh that set her chins—she had quite as many as Mrs. Blaine—quivering. "And I'll have your hat, old girl, so don't worry about me. If it's too hot, I'll make two or three journeys instead of trying to do everything all in one go."

Miss Nuttel, for whom Norah Blaine's martyr act—some of her heat collapse had been caused by her insistence on doing *everything all in one go*—could wear a little thin, nodded. "Sensible," she said with an emphasis that made Mrs. Blaine toss her head again. "Many hands, though," she went on, addressing Ada. "I'll come, too. Won't hurt the garden to leave it. You tell me, Bunny."

But Mrs. Blaine ignored the pencil poised over the waiting inside-out envelope, and sloshed the dishwater all the harder. Miss Nuttel hesitated—looked at Cousin Ada with the string bag ready for action—and announced to the world at large that she prided herself on her memory, and if what she couldn't remember mattered That Much, then someone else could go and Buy It Afterwards. Mrs. Blaine retorted that Eric knew very well she would if she could, but she couldn't in the heat . . . and she retired to bed with a headache.

The excursion to France began early on Saturday morning. Crabbe's Garage provided the bus (a fifty-seater coach) and the driver (Jack Crabbe, complete with reference books and crossword grids to occupy him during his spare moments). The children's parents provided the picnic meals, as you couldn't be sure with foreign food, and they didn't want to end up having to eat snails, did they? The Colvedens, Miss Seeton, and a few other adults more adventurous than their peers packed a handful of emergency rations and agreed to dine on whatever might be available, in the interests of Anglo-French relations.

Mr. Jessyp held a whispered conversation with Miss Maynard, who passed him a packet of ginger nuts when she hoped nobody was looking. Miss Seeton, whose quick eyes missed little, thought it tactful to say nothing of Cousin Flora's own remedy for motion sickness, discovered in the commonplace book but (as far as Miss Seeton knew) never tried—and (she suspected) rightly so. There was much to be said in favour of the ginger-nut regime. In moments of crisis it would surely be easier for sufferers to crunch hard, round, spicy sweet biscuits on the storm-tossed deck of a ferry than to sip from a flask filled with an infusion of valerian root, scullcap, mistletoe, gentian, and cayenne pepper in milk. Apart from the risk that the flask might bump in the swell and chip the drinker's teeth, Cousin Flora's hint that milk should be included to make the mixture more palatable made the attractions of the ginger biscuits even greater.

Fortunately for all concerned the crossing from Dover to Calais was tranquil. The sky was blue, the sun was bright, the breeze was merely brisk; the only hint that there might be bad weather ahead lay in the antics of the few cotton-wool clouds that could be seen high in the heavens, scurrying and bouncing in a manner suggestive of children let loose on a trampoline. Miss Seeton observed Mr. Jessyp's anxious scanning of the heavens, and heard him tell himself sternly that there was no sense in meeting trouble halfway.

Sir George, who had spent some of his war in France, insisted that their first halt should be at the memorial near the Calais public gardens, where he stood in silence for a long, respectful minute shared amid the civic rush by those of the Plummergen party who had their own respects to pay. A trip to the Calais museum induced silence even among the children, who, when told the reason for the pockmarks and scars on the concrete walls, were loud in their denunciation of the Nazi firing squads and in their praise for the heroes of the Resistance.

"Perhaps we'll meet the Comte when we arrive at Balivernes," said Mr. Jessyp as he shepherded the party in the direction of the shops, where the adults wanted coffee and the children ice cream before they boarded the bus again. Those who had learned a little French used phrase books and sign language to buy postcards (and stamps) to send home to taunt those villagers who had been unable to come. Miss Seeton, thinking (in quite another way) of Martha and Stan, selected a pavement café scene in which a merry crowd of drinkers sat round a yellow-clothed table under a scarlet awning, while in the background a more serious group, their faces in shadow, played cards and smoked cigarettes. It was a scene far removed from all the wartime horror the visit to the memorial had revived. . . .

But thirty years had passed. The people of France were now free, as indeed were the people of Germany—or those in the west, at least. The sky was blue, the sun was bright, and the bus rumbled its way out of Calais with everyone in high spirits: some a little higher than others. Sir George, pleading pain in his bandaged wrist, had been allowed by his wife to enjoy one (small) glass of brandy while the rest drank coffee or (the more daring) red wine. There was an air of festivity on board as the children, conducted by Miss Maynard, warbled "Sur le Pont D'Avignon." Lady Colveden with a freezing look silenced Sir George's muted suggestion of "Mademoiselle from Armentières," and stifled the very idea of "Colonel Bogey"; Miss Seeton hurriedly proposed "Frère Jacques," which, having been led by Miss Maynard, Mr. Jessyp, and Miss Seeton herself, was followed by other round tunes, including "London's Burning."

Sir George shot Lady Colveden a triumphant look. "No getting away from it, you see," he whispered. "Different Fire of London, of course, but—"

"Whatever do you mean?" asked his wife, still brooding

on the mademoiselle, the colonel, and the wisdom of having allowed her spouse that solitary cognac.

"The War, Meg," said Sir George, leaning back on his seat with a sigh. "The War."

The Château de Balivernes was an impressive stone edifice, set in elegant and spacious grounds where, their teachers silently gave thanks, the children could run about and make (within reason) as much noise as they liked. Despite the singsong and the—heavily censored—stories told by Sir George and others, Plummergen's Junior Mixed Infants had found the last part of the journey from Calais rather dull. Agincourt had indeed been no more than a large, empty field with nothing to see, and they had been almost glad to get back on the bus—but sitting still is hard when you are not yet twelve years old. Scenery has no charms when all you can do is watch it pass you by. Youthful legs, bare inside shorts or frilly skirts, prickled on the velveteen seats and made their owners restless as the sun rose higher in the sky, and despite the air conditioning, the coach became stuffy. Boys pulled girls' hair. Girls squealed, stuck out their tongues at boys, or kicked their neighbours on the ankle. Jack Crabbe at the wheel threatened to turn the coach right round and head back to the ferry, but even this threat did not quell the fractious small fry for long.

"Soon be there, thank the Lord," said Sir George as he spotted a signpost. "I think," he added. "Never could get the hang of this metric nonsense."

"Isn't it something like divide by five and multiply by eight to turn kilometres into miles?" Lady Colveden shook her head. "Or do I mean multiply by eight and divide by five? Or is that nautical miles? The admiral would know."

"Don't," begged her husband, casting an anxious glance out of the window at the cloud-scudding sky. "The Buzzard ought to have come, too," he grumbled. "Told us if it was a good day to travel or not."

"I don't suppose his opinion would have made the

slightest difference," said Lady Colveden briskly. "Everyone was so set on this trip it would have taken a hurricane to stop them. Us," she felt obliged to append as her loving spouse favoured her with a knowing look. "Well," she protested, "what else could we—you—have usefully done, if we hadn't come today? You could hardly help the admiral chase swarms of bees around the village with your arm in a sling, though I've no doubt you would have tried something equally silly if I hadn't made you come with me. It isn't often I insist on a day out—but be reasonable, George."

Sir George muttered something about dry land, subsiding as Jack flicked the indicator and the bus slowed for the turn into the pillared gateway of the Château de Balivernes. Mr. Jessyp in the front seat—elected spokesman by every single adult in the group—thumbed his phrase book, took a deep breath, and prepared to make a fool of himself in the interests of his pupils.

"Er—*bonjour*," he said in a very English accent to the gnarled old gentleman who materialised in the now-open door of the coach. "Er—*nous voulons visiter le château, s'il vous plaît. C'est possible aujourd'hui?*"

"*Oui, c'est possible,*" agreed the gnarled one, mounting the steps and casting a knowledgeable eye the length of the coach. His face cracked in a beaming smile. "*Les enfants!*"

"*Oui,*" said Mr. Jessyp, wondering how he asked for half-price tickets. "*Une école,*" he said.

The gnarled one burst out laughing. "*Vraiment? Tous?*" He stabbed a withered finger in the direction of the most definitely non-school-age Sir George, and emitted a swift stream of syllables out of which only the word *moustache* could be distinguished. "*Une école!*" cried the gnarled one, bent double with mirth. "*Tous!*"

By the time everything was sorted out to everyone's satisfaction, the adults were as eager to be off the bus as were the children. Mr. Jessyp, mopping his brow and clutching his phrase book, left following the map to Miss Maynard. She turned to Miss Seeton for advice, knowing the expertise of the older woman's eye. Miss Seeton, sighing quietly for the Monet garden, suggested a route to the picnic area that the gnarled one, eavesdropping amiably in the background, confirmed with nods and further beams.

"Lunch first," decreed Mr. Jessyp, watching—hearing— the children run ahead in the direction indicated. "Then a short rest for digestion, and *then* the tour of the château."

"It will be so much cooler out of the afternoon sun," Miss Seeton agreed, as none of the other adults seemed inclined to speak. "Indoors, that is, for with the high ceilings and large rooms . . ."

"We wouldn't want anyone going down with sunstroke," said Lady Colveden with a quiet smile as she watched her husband surreptitiously mop what Nigel called his bald patch and its indignant owner "well, perhaps just a little on the thin side." From a handbag that was almost as big as Miss Seeton's (the art teacher, of course, had brought her small sketching block and pencils with her) Sir George's helpmeet produced his rolled panama hat, which she handed to her absentminded spouse with another smile.

Sir George accepted the hat with becoming gratitude and brightened at once. He strode off to join Mr. Jessyp at the van of the adult part of the procession, and the two of them soon organised everyone into spreading rugs, opening foil-wrapped and greaseproof-papered packages, and displaying the samples of food and drink bought earlier in Calais. Nobody (said Sir George) was obliged to try anything if they didn't want to, but when in Rome . . .

This, too, needed sorting out, the children clamouring to know why they had been taken to Italy when they'd been told they were going to France. Sir George, wishing he'd kept his mouth shut, huffed through his moustache, drained a glass of *vin rouge ordinaire,* and fanned himself awkwardly with his hat. Miss Seeton met his gaze with a twinkle.

"Mr. Jessyp was right," she said with a pleased nod for the schoolmaster bent over his phrase book with an air of studious triumph. "The children are so very enthusiastic, aren't they? Which is always to be encouraged, especially in the young."

Sir George supposed that this was so, and poured himself some more red wine. Lady Colveden, without a word but in a manner that spoke louder than words, handed him a crusty slice of bread and a hunk of cheese. Sir George put down his glass obediently and ate.

Under the trees the cooling shade rippled and danced in a gentle, sunlight-sparkling breeze. The air was clear, the food was good, the company (in general) was enjoying itself, though there were one or two encounters with creepy-crawlies and insects that had some of the children squealing and their parents, where present, threatening to box their ears. As if French mosquitoes could bite worse than English ones! No, they wouldn't get malaria, because they didn't have it in this part of France—did they? This last with a silent appeal to Sir George, who was known to have travelled widely on the continent.

Miss Seeton—watching, listening, answering questions when she was able—thought of mosquitoes, and malaria, and water. She consumed her modest picnic, ventured a polite cough, and interrupted Mr. Jessyp's studies to murmur that she could really eat no more. It was so hot. If, with everyone else still eating, she could be spared for perhaps a quarter of an hour to visit the Monet garden . . . ?

It had been agreed among the adults that few—if any—of the children were likely to show much interest in the artistic side of the Giverny re-creation, which (as it was still in progress) ran the serious risk of being something of a building site. All three teachers were adamant that youthful Plummergen and expensive excavation and earthmoving equipment were best far kept apart.

"Does anyone want to go with Miss Seeton to look at the famous gardens?" asked Mr. Jessyp, as arranged. As expected, when offered the chance everyone refused it. With a quiet smile of thanks Miss Seeton rose nimbly to her feet—not a click, not a creak from her knees—and walked away, patting into position the cherry-trimmed straw that had been tipped slightly askew by a drooping branch.

CHAPTER 7

In the lazy summer sun Miss Seeton found herself walking far less briskly than she would have walked at home. Her feet in their sensible shoes crushed browning grass on which no rain had fallen for days, and raised little puffs of dust that turned to stifling haze in the heavy air. *Flaming June.* Miss Seeton thought of the contorted girl in the fiery dress, and pondered the refreshing contrast of lilies floating on dappled water under shady trees. In her mind's eye she saw the wooden bridge—familiar from a score of paintings—with its graceful arch and the double handrail supported on plain squared timbers. . . .

And then she caught her breath as, rounding a corner, she found the very bridge mirrored in the weed-rippling lake in front of her.

But that was not all she found. On the far side of the lake—although it was really no more than a large pond—squatted a bulldozer, a huge mechanical hulk of a dull blue shade patterned with orange-brown streaks of sunbaked mud. Near the bulldozer, lounging in the shade of a chestnut tree, were three men, none of whom wore shirts and all of whom were fine, muscular specimens tanned to the colour of (Miss Seeton hid a patriotic smile) English oak. They had obviously stopped work for a siesta, or whatever the French equivalent might be. The glint of glass here and there on the grass beside the resting workmen suggested that the siesta had not been undertaken without liquid refreshment.

Miss Seeton's smile faded. She frowned. It had seemed, when reading her newspaper on the other side of the Channel, a modest and not unreasonable ambition to wish to visit the Monet garden—but now that she was there in person . . . Did she, in fact, intrude? Ought she perhaps to beat a quiet retreat before the lounging men should notice the intrusion? The old man at the gate had said nothing about the lake being forbidden until the work was finished . . . although as it had been Mr. Jessyp to whom he had spoken there might have been a—a certain lack of communication. . . .

Miss Seeton, uncertain, hesitated. The three suntanned musclemen continued to lounge. From across the lake drifted the sound of a loud, contented snore.

Miss Seeton made up her mind. If the men were having a break from their work—a break more than deserved, in such heat—they could surely have no objection to the presence of a stranger for a few moments, always provided that this presence was discreet. Miss Seeton was by birth an English gentlewoman. No gentlewoman draws deliberate attention to herself or is purposefully indiscreet. Miss Seeton, moving discreetly, walked a little way round the edge of the lake so that the bulldozer stood between herself and the sleeping workmen, and took her sketchbook from her bag. The view of the bridge might not be quite as fine as that from the point where she had first been standing, but . . .

"But, madame, if you will excuse me, you should surely be drawing from another spot than this," came a voice from behind her that made Miss Seeton's pencil skitter across the page. "*Mon Dieu,* a thousand pardons for startling you!" the voice went on quickly. It was a mellow, musical, masculine voice. For such a voice as this Maurice Chevalier himself would have killed. Miss Seeton turned hurriedly to meet its owner's gaze.

"The view of the bridge," the musical voice continued,

as its owner bowed to Miss Seeton, "would be finer, would it not, were you to move just a little way around the edge of the lake?"

Blushing, Miss Seeton began to explain that her wish not to disturb anyone. . . .

"Those lazy fellows?" The voice belonged to a tall, grey-haired man in his sixties, who held himself with an upright carriage and had laughter—and something else—in his dark brown eyes. "My dear madame," he said with another bow, "you are too considerate. You have my assurance that they will sleep until sundown unless the rains begin to fall—and there is, as you see, not a cloud in the sky. The sun," he continued with an expressive wave of one slim brown hand, "casts a clear reflection upon the water, does it not? You are an artist, as one sees from the drawing in which you were engrossed as I interrupted you. For this interruption I again apologise, but I felt most strongly that the opportunity was not to be lost, for from just over there"—and the slim brown hand pointed—"you would observe, Madame Artiste, how the curve of the bridge above meets that of its shadow below in a—in a form . . ."

For the first time the speaker's fluency deserted him. With an apologetic laugh and an expressive movement of his hands he described perfectly the shape that Miss Seeton, had she remained in her first position, would have seen.

"Lenticular," supplied Miss Seeton, her pencil moving in sympathy to draw the shape on the paper. "Like a lens, or the shape of a simple leaf—as opposed to a compound leaf, that is."

"Lenticular," repeated the grey-haired man, tasting the word as he spoke it and ignoring the compound complication. "Lenticular—yes. Like a lens—and a leaf—but like a lentil also, is this not so? For they are very similar in shape—in outline—when seen from the edge, and the Latin root is, I believe, the same."

Miss Seeton, still doodling leaf and edgeways lentil shapes, murmured that she also believed this to be the case.

"And by a strange coincidence," she went on, adding stalks to the shapes and turning what had been a simple sketch of the lake into an exotic shrub, "I was thinking only just now, as I drew—or perhaps it is not so strange—that Monet and several others of the Impressionist school were burdened—if one may call it that—with poor eyesight." She finished the stalks, enlarged one or two into branches and stems, and in deference to her new acquaintance's etymological remark added a sprawling and elaborate root system to the base of the shrub. "And of course," she added, "it might be that they regarded short sight as a—as a positive benefit, without which their vision of the world would have been far different, and we would be the poorer."

"Degas," offered the grey-haired man as he admired the visionary plant now appearing before him, "wore the most remarkable of spectacles, this is true, with one eye blocked altogether completely, and the other with a lens that was no more than a slit."

"Like the blackout on car headlights during the War," agreed Miss Seeton absently. The grey-haired man sighed. Miss Seeton recalled the tumultuous history of France during the years of war, occupation, collaboration, and resistance, and hurried to make amends. "Cézanne and Renoir," she said as she applied the final strokes, "needed glasses quite as much as did Monet, but like him they were adamant that they would not wear them." She held out her completed sketch at arm's length, and narrowed her eyes at the page. She laughed. "Good gracious," she said. "I must have been thinking of something else."

"It is my fault for having interrupted you," said the grey-haired man quickly. "But a most interesting treatment, madame. Were I to achieve the growth of so rare a plant in my garden, I feel sure that it would be visited by many more than those who, like yourself, are of artistic bent and wish to see Monet's lilies brought again to life. Forgive my curiosity, but you are perhaps interested in gardens also?"

Miss Seeton, about to explain that despite her reliance on

that invaluable tome *Greenfinger Points the Way,* dear Stan trusted her to do little more than weed and potter, realised what the grey-haired man had just said. "Your garden?" she echoed. "Then—I do beg your pardon—but you must be . . ."

Overcome by embarrassment identical to that suffered by Mr. Jessyp when attempting to speak French, Miss Seeton came to a flustered halt.

The grey-haired man smiled and bowed. "Jean-Louis de Balivernes, madame, at your service. And you are . . ."

"Emily Seeton." Miss Seeton gasped as the intricacies of etiquette loomed suddenly before her. Should one, or should one not, curtsey? She was, after all, English, not French, but the French were renowned for their good manners, and when one was on foreign soil . . . And did a French count count, so to speak, as royalty? When France was, after all, a republic. . . . And she did not curtsey to dear Sir George or Lady Colveden—perhaps a slight bob . . .

"Oh," said Miss Seeton faintly as the hand in which she did not hold her sketchbook was politely acquired by Monsieur le Comte and raised as politely to his lips.

"Enchanté, chère mademoiselle," he said after stealing a quick look at her ringless fingers. "Emily Seeton," he repeated, releasing her hand. "A charming name, and so very English. My dear wife was of your island race, although a Scot, not an Englishwoman. Unmistakable," he added with another smile. "As soon as I saw you, I knew. I would no more have addressed you in French than I would in— German," he concluded, stumbling over the word. The War could never be far from the memories of those who had lived through it.

"I'm afraid," said Miss Seeton, "that my command of the French language is very poor—er—monsieur." She had no idea how a count should be addressed. She stole a look at him and saw that the smile still lingered in his eyes: she had not offended him, then. "Monsieur le Comte," she ventured, and thought herself very daring.

"Mademoiselle," returned the count, bowing. "But your sketch," he went on, reaching out for her block and tucking her free hand under his arm. "You permit that I escort you to the most favourable position? And, with your further permission, I may watch you at work? Or would this be too much of a distraction?"

"Er—no, indeed," said Miss Seeton, her cheeks a little pink as he adjusted his long-legged stride to keep gentle pace with her. "I fear, though, that my poor efforts—the genius of Monet—a personal memento of our visit, nothing more . . ."

"Our visit?" The comte nodded, as if confirming what he had already guessed. "Ah, you are with the English school, Miss Seeton." He laughed again. "The English school that, so the astonished Gaston tells me, is full of pupils so old in years that they wear the moustaches! He amused himself very much with this, I have to tell you, and those who guide around the interior of the château will also see the joke. It is not only the English, Miss Seeton, who have a—a robust sense of humour."

Miss Seeton, whose own sense of humour was far from robust, nodded and smiled without speaking. She was still accustoming herself to the escort of so distinguished a gentleman—she silently begged his pardon, a nobleman—when she could not help but feel her presence to be something of an intrusion. She had meant to be away from the Plummergen party for no more than a quarter of an hour: she suspected her absence had already extended far beyond the allotted time—but the undoubted pleasures of conversation with one whose appreciation of the Impressionist genius—if, that was to say, he had not found her conversation tiresomely ignorant—although this did not (and Miss Seeton felt her cheeks turn pink again) appear to be the case . . .

"Here, Miss Seeton." The Comte de Balivernes had come to a halt in exactly the spot Miss Seeton would, if left to her own devices, have chosen, were it not for the sight of the sleeping workmen, who might, should they wake, regard her with some annoyance. "The bridge, and the—the lens-like reflection." He smiled at her. "My memory for English all too often escapes me. You will remind me, please."

"Lenticular," said Miss Seeton, taking the chance of his gesturing towards the bridge to snatch a look at the watch on his wrist. She stifled a gasp.

"Something is wrong?" The Comte de Balivernes looked down at Miss Seeton in some concern. "You are unwell? The heat—we walked too fast?"

"Oh, no," said Miss Seeton quickly. "But—my friends— they will be wondering—I had no idea how late . . ."

Once more she blushed. How rude to suggest to this charming, courteous, and knowledgeable man that she was— well—keeping track of the time. But . . .

"Miss Seeton, I cannot allow you to depart without your sketch of the bridge," said the comte firmly. "Mine was the fault, the reason that you were delayed in your intention, and so I return with you now to explain—to plead your cause—should any of your party have it in mind to administer a rebuke. Not," he added, setting her hand once more on his arm and patting it as he began to walk, "that any would dare. We will soon be here again, and you shall sketch in perfect liberty. Only the most brave would contest the will of Jean-Louis de Balivernes—and, with all due respect to your countrymen, that means a Frenchman. A Frenchman would fight a duel to defend your honour." Miss Seeton, who was starting to think he might be serious, was relieved to hear him chuckle. She looked up at him with a dawning twinkle in her eye. He twinkled back at her. "What do you say, Miss Seeton?" he cried, gesturing with his free hand. "Shall I challenge the leader of your party to fight me with swords in the gallery under the portraits of my ancestors?"

Miss Seeton—the courteous guest will always follow the conversational lead of the host—considered the problem as the two of them made their way towards the picnic area and the château beyond it. She had to confess that although Mr.

Jessyp was undoubtedly the best French speaker of the party, and thus the most likely of them all to understand a challenge—which she assumed the comte would deliver in his own language—she had some doubts as to the schoolmaster's ability to fight with a sword.

"Pistols, then," said the comte. "The decision is made, Miss Seeton. This Monsieur . . . Jasper? Ah, *pardon,* Jessyp. He shall permit you to accompany me for the remainder of the visit, or he shall meet me at dawn to avenge the insult."

Miss Seeton pointed out that the party would be back in England by dawn, adding that she doubted whether Mr. Jessyp rose so early. The comte insisted that to stay in bed when one should be fighting a duel was an insult almost greater than the original. At this monstrous thought he began to walk more quickly, but as Miss Seeton pattered at his side he recollected his manners and, with an apologetic bow, slowed his steps again.

He never (he told her in solemn tones) forgot an insult—or a face. Let him speak but once with Monsieur Jessyp when the challenge was issued and he would know him instantly, were it a hundred years hence, as the man who preferred to sleep than to defend the honour of a countrywoman. The purchase of an alarm clock (said the comte) must become the most important matter in the mind of Monsieur Jessyp after the purchase of a suitable pistol, or the man would be branded a coward for all time.

Miss Seeton said that she was sure Mr. Jessyp owned at least one reliable alarm clock, otherwise he could never be sure of arriving on time at school. One had to teach the children by example, and early rising—except, that is, at dawn, when even the local farmers . . .

"Pissarro," broke in the comte, delighted. "*La Meule*—The Haystack. You know it? Another Impressionist painting, and for such a day an entirely suitable subject."

Miss Seeton agreed, but added that there was a great deal of sheep farming in her part of the world, and she did not immediately recollect any Impressionist sheep. Did the

comte? The comte regretted that he did not, but would Miss
Seeton accept a *Landscape with Cattle by a Stream* as being
in sympathy with her request?

"Daubigny," said Miss Seeton after a brief pause. "And
in sympathy with the Impressionists, too, even though he
was of an older generation. Especially Monet," she added.

"Indeed," said the comte, who was coming to regard
Miss Seeton with more and more approval. "And Pissarro,"
he said with a chuckle. "If not necessarily his haystacks."

"There is always standing corn," suggested Miss Seeton
with another twinkle, and waited.

It was the comte's turn to pause. "Sisley!" he cried at
last. "*Le Champ de Blé*—The Wheatfield!"

"Near—er—Argenteuil," supplied Miss Seeton as the
comte patted her hand in triumph. By this time she and he
were agreeing so well together that she felt almost no awk-
wardness about attempting a French accent.

"Bravo!" applauded the Comte de Balivernes, and might
have patted her hand again had they not turned a corner and
reached the picnic site. Every adult—the children were playing tag, to the ruin of their infant digestions—looked up
from the final postprandial tidying to greet Miss Seeton and
to stare, with a greater or lesser degree of curiosity, at her
unknown companion.

Sir George's stare was by far the most curious. Lady Colveden, realising his all too obvious interest, nudged him with
an unobtrusive elbow. Sir George shook the elbow away and
clambered to his feet. He pushed his panama hat to the back
of his head and marched across to Miss Seeton.

Miss Seeton found herself jerked almost off her feet as
the comte, her hand firmly tucked under his arm, stopped
dead in his tracks and then, with a muffled cry, began to
stride forwards.

"Good God!" cried Sir George. "It *is* old Fleabag!"

And everyone stared at the sight of Major-General Sir
George Colveden, KCB, DSO, JP, being hailed by the unknown with a hearty Gallic embrace and a kiss on both
cheeks.

CHAPTER 8

Sir George, a true-blue Englishman, had never been one to boast. Like many heroes, he seldom talked about his war—except to reminisce in ways that (as Nigel often said) made the listener "wonder how on earth we managed to win."

"Coincidence? Hah!" Sir George might say, if sufficiently mellow after someone else had told a story. "Nothing of the sort, with all due respect. Now, this chap—friend of mine—in the desert, it was—miles from nowhere, smack in the middle of the dunes—and what does he do but find a pair of climbing boots *just the right size* for him? Side by side in the sand like a pair of blasted bookends!"

The coincidence having been duly admired (and the question of whether the friend in fact wanted, or needed, a pair of climbing boots among the dunes having been ignored), Sir George might be encouraged to expand on the virtues of economic planning. "France, just after D-Day," he would say. "This chap—friend of mine—leading a party trying to capture the high ground. Didn't do such a bad job, at that. Plans made—went like clockwork, for once—enemy on the run inside ten minutes—and then, when they turned up at the inn—owner delighted to see them, of course—she told 'em lunch was on Jerry and they could have as much as they liked. Seems a group of their officers had ordered a meal and left before it was ready." And here Sir George would

stroke his moustache and grin a sideways grin. "She'd made
the blighters pay in advance," was the punch line, which
always brought the house down.

"Tell 'em what to do," Sir George might say, if pressed
by an appreciative audience to continue, "and they do it.
Did it. Difference between us and them, I suppose. What we
fought for. Freedom—the right to choose. Think for yourself." Then he would blush and change the subject. "Friend
of mine—amazing chap. Voice you could hear in the middle
of a twenty-five-pound barrage. Advance guard one day—
the machine gun jammed, so he had 'em fix a captured
German gun on the Jeep and used that instead. The biter bit,
eh? Then they got bogged down in sand. Gaggle of Italian
soldiers—hadn't surrendered yet—hanging around gawping.
M'friend just stood there and *told* the blighters to push it
free—and they dashed well did. Some people," Sir George
would conclude with pride, "obeyed orders—but some people . . . thought about things."

Lady Colveden spared a fleeting second for regret that
Nigel and Julia were absent from the scene as their father
accepted the kisses of this grey-haired stranger, returning the
compliment with a bellow of laughter and a series of clumsy
thumps on the back from a willing but unaccustomed left
hand. Regret soon turned to recollection—but unsuccess-
fully. As far as her ladyship could recall, there was not,
among the many "friends" who featured in Sir George's
store of reminiscence, anyone with the soubriquet of Fleabag. And then her ladyship, like Miss Seeton before her,
remembered the recent history of France . . . and guessed
that there were some things about her husband she was des-
tined never to know.

Although . . . she had to wonder . . . perhaps now might be
the time to try to find out a little more. . . .

"Come and meet m'wife," Sir George was urging, for
once in his life oblivious of the courtesies due to a lady.
Miss Seeton, forgotten in all the excitement, stood discreetly
in the background and beamed at this unexpected reunion

of old comrades. "Meg!" roared Sir George, dragging his willing captive by the sleeve while trampling underfoot the hat the embrace of this stranger had knocked from his head to the ground. "Meg," cried Sir George. "I want you to meet a friend of mine: Fleabag—very best of chaps, believe me. Knew him in the War. Pleased to see he made it after all. One or two pretty hairy moments, eh, Fleabag? Lots of good chaps gone—but here you are, large as life. Fleabag, this is m'wife Margaret. Everyone calls her Meg."

"Enchanté, madame." An elegant hand raised the hand of Lady Colveden to finely shaped lips, and a graceful bow allowed the stranger to introduce himself properly. "Jean-Louis de Balivernes, at your service."

"That your name?" cried Sir George, staring at him. "I never knew that. Jean-Louis. Well, well. Always thought of you as Fleabag."

Lady Colveden sighed. "Really, George," she chided her spouse gently. "Given that nobody in a civilised country could possibly be christened 'Fleabag,' it must have been an example of forces humour. From 'Jean-Louis' to 'Flea' isn't so farfetched, is it?"

Sir George stared, started laughing again, and as he laughed clapped his friend on the shoulder. Jean-Louis, pummelling Sir George quite as hard on his unbandaged arm, laughed, too.

Lady Colveden elected to frown, demanding to be enlightened as to the true explanation for the nickname. "I can't presume," she said, "on my husband's acquaintance to address a man as 'Fleabag' without knowing why. It sounds so rude."

"Ma chère Meg—if I may presume—it is a name by which I have not been called for many years." Jean-Louis looked with affection upon Sir George. "Indeed, until this moment I had almost entirely forgotten it." That hint of something darker than laughter that Miss Seeton had already glimpsed was back in his eyes—and then was gone. "I never forget a face, but there are some things . . . a foolish

episode—the youthful bravado of a hothead who might by his actions have caused more harm to his friends than to the enemy—"

"Nonsense," interrupted Sir George cheerfully. "Anyone could have told you they'd want it kept quiet, just as they did. Made 'em look such blasted—sorry, m'dear—fools."

For the first time the baronet noticed that a sizeable group of Plummergen worthies had been making its way towards the reunion. Sir George smoothed his toothbrush moustache and clapped his friend on the shoulder again. "Old Fleabag here," he explained to the assembly, "this was before I knew him, broke into the Jerry equivalent of the quartermaster's stores one night and put—oh, dear—itching powder in a whole batch of U-boat uniforms." Sir George began to laugh again. "Itching powder! Water's like gold in a submarine. Can't afford to waste the stuff *washing*, for heaven's sake. Everyone hopping and scratching about the place—not a hope in hell of aiming a torpedo or laying a mine—sleepless nights—days even worse—back to port for fumigation—bug chaps can't find anything—medics think it might be some sort of plague—quarantine . . ."

At this point Sir George gave himself up entirely to laughter, in which everyone who had heard the story joined. Jean-Louis blushed beneath his tan at the cries of "well done!" and "good for you!" that accompanied the clapping of enthusiastic hands. Lady Colveden and Miss Seeton added their own amused applause, while Sir George struggled to wipe the tears from his eyes with a handkerchief clutched in his left hand.

"Mon cher Georges," said Jean-Louis, "you are injured. To come through the War without a scratch, and to meet now, here, with your arm in a bandage—how is this?"

"Don't ask," Lady Colveden told him quickly. "You can blame that on the War, too. Men," she added, but for once Sir George did not rise to the bait.

He was too busy gazing at his old friend. "Your name's Balivernes," he said slowly. "That what you said?"

"Yes, it is." Jean-Louis bowed again.

"Then," said Sir George, trying to work it out, "you're the chap who owns this place?"

"Yes, I am," said his old friend Fleabag. "Jean-Louis, Comte de Balivernes—but the title is of no account, among friends. I am happy to welcome you to my home, and only sorry that my daughter Louise is not here, for she would be delighted, I know, to meet one of whom I have told her— a little," he added, as Sir George's face showed his consternation. "We do not tell the ones who were not there the whole story, do we, *mon vieux*?"

"No, good God, we don't," agreed Sir George with a fervour that surprised everyone except his wife—who nevertheless promised herself a quiet talk with her husband when the opportunity should arise.

"You have a daughter? So have we," said Lady Colveden aloud, with a dazzling smile for the handsome comte. "Julia—she's married, and they have a daughter, Janie, the dearest little girl in the world."

The comte murmured that the lovely Meg did not seem of an age to be a grandmother; indeed, it was hard to believe that she was even a mother.

"Oh, you'd believe it soon enough if you saw Nigel," returned her ladyship with a twinkle. "Our son is blessed with good heredity, Jean-Louis. He gets his hair from my side of the family, not his father's—which reminds me, George. Where's your hat? On a day like this you'll be peeling in five minutes if you don't take proper care."

"Here it is," said Miss Seeton, who had gathered up the trampled panama after Sir George's passage and spent several minutes trying to push it into shape. "A trifle battered, I fear, but still serviceable."

"Miss Seeton!" The horrified Jean-Louis de Balivernes was all apology. To have so basely ignored—abandoned— her on recognising his friend! Even the passage of thirty years was insufficient excuse! He abased himself before her—he begged her pardon—he would devote himself most humbly to her and to none other for the rest of the afternoon. . . .

At first Miss Seeton did her best to deflect some of the Frenchman's flowery gallantries. Cyrano de Bergerac (apart from the nose) and D'Artagnan might have been his brothers, and she was somewhat overpowered; but then she caught a wink from Sir George and realised that the comte was enjoying the scene in which he had chosen to play the lead quite as much as his audience. Yes, he was playing a part—as, she suspected, he had done on many previous occasions. But thirty years before it might have been his life, or the lives of others, that depended on the skill of his performance. . . .

". . . back to the lake," said the Comte de Balivernes, taking Miss Seeton by the arm. "I wish, with Miss Seeton's permission, to watch her interpret on paper my own interpretation of Monet's celebrated garden. You, *cher Georges,* and Madame Meg, will tour the château with the rest of your party, and then we will meet for drinks, and you shall give me your address so that we may not lose touch for another thirty years. Is this agreed?"

It was agreed. Perhaps only Miss Seeton noticed the quick smile of satisfaction that gleamed in Lady Colveden's expressive eyes before she suppressed it: and Miss Seeton would have considered it an impertinence on her part even to think of guessing what that gleam might signify.

Sir George, had he noticed it, would have told his wife sharply to stop matchmaking when Nigel hadn't even seen the girl, and for all they knew she was keeping company with one of the most eligible bachelors in France; but Sir George was far too busy reminding his old friend Fleabag of the time the back tyres had disappeared from a Nazi staff car with a drowsy driver, and how they had reappeared in a shoe shop the following day as the soles of a pair of boots, with the serial numbers clearly visible on the treads.

• • •

Jean-Louis, Comte de Balivernes, was every bit as hospitable as might be expected of any friend of Sir George Colveden. It was two hours later than originally planned that the Plummergen bus rumbled out through the great gateway on the return trip to Calais, with the schoolchildren enchanted at the (censored) stories Monsieur le Comte had narrated as he showed them around parts of the château the public did not generally see. Miss Seeton, while secretly regretting her now lost opportunity to sketch the Monet garden, had felt too embarrassed to accept the count's offer of his personal escort for the rest of the afternoon. Jean-Louis, with a sweeping gesture, had promptly dismissed the regular guide and taken the party around his family home as if his life depended on their enjoyment of the treat. While duly acknowledging his three decades' friendship with Sir George, it was to Miss Emily Seeton that his closest attention was devoted. When Miss Seeton smiled, he smiled. Those pictures that she seemed to admire were pointed out with pride. When she appeared bemused at any part of his narrative, he redoubled his efforts to find the exact phrase to explain what he was trying to say.

"Old Fleabag's almost as bad as Nigel," muttered Sir George, nudging his wife in the ribs when nobody was looking. "Seemed very taken with Miss Seeton, didn't he?"

"And why not?" retorted the wife of his bosom. "They're both so interested in art, for one thing. And of course he's a widower," she added thoughtfully.

"With a daughter," said Sir George, with another nudge. "You can't fool me, m'dear."

Lady Colveden blushed. "Don't be silly," she told her husband. "Just because I've invited them to spend a long weekend with us certainly doesn't mean I'm . . . interfering in their private lives. For all we know, Louise is engaged to be married and Jean-Louis has a string of mistresses."

"Shouldn't think that would worry Miss Seeton," said Sir George, waving his free hand. "Broad-minded little soul. Artistic. Bohemian type—must have known hundreds in her time, and never turned a hair. Remember when she danced in that Parisian revue? And old Fleabag's French. Different approach to ours. Wouldn't suit me,'' he was quick to emphasise as his wife uttered an exasperated cry. "But then, who's to say they could make a match of it? Can't see Miss Seeton happy living in France—not really. Far too . . . English,'' concluded Sir George, with the triumphant air of one making an earth-shattering discovery.

Although Lady Colveden agreed with her husband, she was disinclined to tell him so. Nigel had inherited more than his thick, wavy brown hair from his mother: there was a decidedly romantic streak in young Galahad Colveden, and it did not come entirely from his warrior sire. As the bus wound its way through the country lanes of France, Meg Colveden mused on matrimony, and the single state, and the advantages (or otherwise) of either condition to those who had experienced it for any length of time.

"Ugh!'' The bus took a corner rather more speedily than Sir George, with his bandage-impaired sense of balance, liked. He slipped sideways on the seat and, unable to grab in time for support from the seat in front, bumped into his wife and drove the breath from her ribs. "Sorry, m'dear,'' he said as he righted himself.

"Sorry, everyone,'' said Jack Crabbe, switching on the driver's microphone and slowing the bus for a moment or two. "It's just—well, I don't like the look of the weather up yonder, so I was going maybe faster than I ought to've done on these roads—but we've a ferry to catch, and we don't want to leave it too late.''

"No harm done,'' Mr. Jessyp assured him. The schoolmaster was still basking in the compliments paid him by Monsieur le Comte for the purity of his accent, and if Jack had been going at twice the speed, he would have been reluctant to chide him. Everyone knew that Jack Crabbe—son, grandson, and great-grandson of skilled mechanical men—was one of the safest drivers in Kent. Mr. Jessyp, in his turn, knew there was no need to feel concern in Crabbe's capable hands, even though those hands were steering a wheel in another country than Kent, and on the wrong side of the road. . . .

But Jack was not the only one to have spotted the clouds up ahead. Even as the last straggler had been climbing into the bus at the château, a sinister breeze was trickling its way around people's legs and necks, and sending shivers down their spines. Leaves on the topmost branches of nearby trees skittered in a wild dance of semaphore warning before subsiding into a calm that seemed somehow even more sinister. Sir George, who until the moment of departure had been brimming over with the thrill of his reunion with Fleabag de Balivernes, ran an uneasy finger round the inside of his collar and gazed at the sky with worried eyes.

"Glad I listened to the Buzzard," he muttered as he settled in his seat beside her ladyship. "But it's a dashed good thing old Fleabag topped up our emergency supplies." He patted the pocket in which his trusty hip flask rested. Its contents had been broached, and drained, within five minutes of the Grand Reunion, and in all the excitement it had taken Sir George some time to start having doubts about the wisdom of this action. But Jean-Louis had been a more than generous host. Not only did he refill the silver flask to the brim with five-star cognac, but he insisted that Lady Colveden should take home an unbroached bottle for medicinal purposes. Miss Seeton likewise had been pressed to accept some brandy as a token of the comte's high esteem, although at her hesitation—the courteous guest does not argue with the host, but she didn't drink spirits and it would be a shocking waste, she could tell from the look on Sir George's face, to use it on the Christmas pudding—he promptly changed tack, urging her to take instead three bottles of the château's own vintage white, which he thought might better suit her palate.

Sir George patted his pocket again, discreetly, and did his best to smother a sigh. Not that he wanted to put ideas in people's heads, of course, but anyone with half an eye could

see the weather was getting up. He had the personal guar-
antee of Rear Admiral Bernard "Buzzard" Leighton that the
cure for seasickness was a double measure of neat brandy
followed no more than eight minutes later by a repeat dose,
but he had never tried it out before. He hoped his friend was
right. He'd heard Miss Seeton and Miss Maynard murmuring together about ginger biscuits and the wisdom of keeping
the children on deck in the fresh air. . . .

Sir George loosened his collar again, and sat back to
watch the scenery unwind on the other side of the glass. He
wished with all his heart that it could be English countryside,
not French, through which he was travelling.

Of quite the same opinion as the unhappy baronet, the
three in charge of the school party had determined that the
best thing to do would be to say nothing about the likely
roughness of the crossing to come and trust to the natural
resilience of Plummergen's Junior Mixed Infants to bring
them through. The adults accompanying them must (it was
tacitly agreed) fend for themselves. Miss Seeton, Miss Maynard, and Mr. Jessyp heard the merry chatter of youthful
voices all around them. The introduction to a genuine hero
of the War (Sir George, with whom the village was already
acquainted, rated low in heroic glamour) had been a thrilling
bonus to the day's entertainment, and young Plummergen
liked to savour its pleasures. Miss Seeton, Miss Maynard,
and Mr. Jessyp thought what a pity it would be to have those
merry voices raised in queasy lamentation, and each crossed
mental fingers in the hope that the Channel might, after all,
be kind.

By the time they reached Calais not even the most opti-
mistic among them could expect any kindness. Though more
than an hour remained until sunset, the sky was darkening
fast. Great grey clouds barrelled out of the west, barged into
the slower, lower-lying clouds in front of them, and bludg-
eoned them into shreds that exploded in a thousand different
directions at once, the shrapnel of the storm. There was no
rain as yet, but the windscreen of the bus was spattered with

water that was salt, not fresh, ripped from the heaving seas
by a ruthless wind.

The bus was directed by a grim-faced official to its place
in the large concrete expanse that was the waiting area, last
in the queue that was last in a rank of queues of coaches,
lorries, and cars. Even before the brakes were properly applied, other vehicles were queueing up behind.

"Busy tonight," observed Jack Crabbe, who knew what
he was talking about. Crabbe's Garage had supplied more
than one touring bus to Francophile citizens of Kent, though
not for some while to a party from Plummergen. "A sight
more folk on foot than usual, too." He lowered his voice to
address Mr. Jessyp in the courier seat beside him. "If you
ask me, half this lot'll be from the hovercraft. They'll have
had to cancel the sailings on account of this weather, see if
I'm not right."

Mr. Jessyp gulped. "I'd rather not," was all he said; but
his heart sank within him as he realised that he probably
would.

The first queue of the rank, at a signal from a second
grim-faced official—was it only the weather that worried
them, or something else?—began moving in single file over
the concrete towards the loading ramp that was the shining
tongue of the Ferry Giant, whose huge metal maw stood
open to engulf the hapless humans about to discover his
strength and fury as he contended with the cruel Channel
Goddess. The steady rumble of engines in low gear acquired,
as each vehicle bounced its way up the ramp, a counterpoint
of rhythmic clanging that made Miss Seeton think of black-
smith Dan Eggleden at work in his forge. From the ferry's
funnel a puff of smoke erupted to give weight to her fancy—
and to be instantly dispersed by a vicious snarl of wind.

And now it was the turn of Jack Crabbe to drive up the
ramp. Passengers on the seaward side of the bus saw the
raging whitecapped waves boiling their way to shore between the massive arms of the harbour mouth . . . and shuddered.

• • •

A normal Channel crossing at the narrowest point will take on average an hour—perhaps (depending on the tides and the weather) an hour and a half.

Three hours after the sailing from Calais, a glitter of lights from the top of the famous white cliffs welcomed the ferry back to Dover.

"Nearly home!" cried Sir George, pointing. Those of the party who could still speak raised a ragged cheer. "That's the castle," continued the baronet, his voice loud above the howl of the wind and the thud of the ferry engines. "You children must ask Mr. Jessyp to arrange a trip there one day. A fascinating place . . ." And it was only at this point that the baronet's unwonted eloquence faltered, for the first time in three hours. Nine minutes after his first swig of brandy he had blazed into sudden life that had then not flickered once throughout the protracted torment of the crossing. Loyally assisted by the tuneless Miss Seeton and one or two others with strong stomachs, he led Plummergen in community singing, tempering the selection of songs to the innocence of the majority and, when carried away by the atmosphere into forgetting his audience, devising impromptu words for the less respectable ditties so that nobody—had they felt well enough to do so—should blush.

For variety he told jokes and shaggy-dog stories, bullied those who were not speechless with nausea into following his example, and raised the ferry's canopy roof with what he insisted would be the biggest sneeze in the world. Dividing Plummergen, like Gaul, in three, he named one part Russia, one part Prussia, and one part Austria. Using the hip flask as a baton, he induced everyone to shout the national identities in unison, at which even Mr. Jessyp was seen to smile.

"It's . . . very old," said Sir George now of the castle. "Bits, anyway," he added. "A Roman tower, I remember that—and—and . . ."

He scratched his head and studied the pale faces turned

towards him. He remembered the reason for his unaccustomed centre-staging, and thought of how in future the necessity might be avoided. Under the influence of brandy, it was a perfectly logical thought. "Tunnels," he said as the ferry heaved and pitched beneath his feet. "Hundreds of them—regular labyrinth—people wandered off, lost and died—built in the time of Napoleon—prisoners of war, you know. *Our* war, it was all very hush-hush down there. We've still no real idea what went on, though no doubt one day we'll be told—like the sound mirrors, and so forth. I'm sure we'd never have ended up with radar if the boffins hadn't tried the mirrors first. Official Secrets Act, of course." Sir George stroked his moustache and gazed proudly up at the silhouette of the castle. "They said, y'know, that Hitler planned to have his first meal on English soil in Dover Castle. Damned cheek. We settled his hash. . . ." He blew his nose, and coughed. "Dashed useful, y'know," he went on hurriedly. "When you're expecting an invasion at any minute, there are far worse places to be than in a castle on top of a cliff that's riddled with tunnels so old nobody has a map of them, believe me."

None could argue with Sir George about the usefulness of tunnels. As the ferry staggered the final few yards towards its berth, Martin C. Jessyp was heard to remark weakly that, as far as he was concerned, the more tunnels in the world the better.

Especially under the Channel.

CHAPTER 9

At Sir George's earnest recommendation Jack Crabbe brought the bus to a halt as soon as they were safely out of Dover so that the still-pale party might experience the restorative powers of a clifftop stroll in good, fresh, English air from which all clouds had been blown by a westerly wind that was now dying down, leaving the sky velvet black and speckled with stars where the midnight moon did not drown them. Mr. Jessyp (after a surreptitious and substantial swig of brandy) and Sir George marshalled the adults into line; Miss Maynard, with the kindly help of her ladyship and Miss Seeton, assembled the children two by two.

"Best foot forward!" cried Major-General Sir George Colveden. "No straggling in the ranks! By the right, everyone—quiiiiick march!" And, whistling "Colonel Bogey," he urged his company on.

To those who have lived in a rural area for any length of time, the carrying of a flashlight about the person is almost second nature. Miss Seeton fastened hers to the tip of her umbrella and led the parade from the front; Lady Colveden supported Miss Maynard (who had refused the offer of brandy in case her mother came to hear of it) at the rear. Sir George and Mr. Jessyp (also whistling, albeit feebly) were escorts on the flank.

The Folkestone Road was too far from the cliff edge to

allow anyone to look down on the Chunnel excavations,
even had it been broad daylight; but it was well understood
that, not a million miles from the remedial march, work was
in progress on an engineering project likely to prove of the
greatest benefit to mankind—especially that percentage of it
prone to seasickness. When Plummergen, feeling rather less
queasy but extremely tired, was marched back to the bus,
there was general agreement that the day the tunnel opened
for business would deserve its place in history.

Jack Crabbe gentled his vehicle every inch of the way,
but by the time they were finally home, even Sir George was
starting to feel the strain. Anxious parents whose offspring
had gone without them on the excursion to foreign parts
began clamouring for answers before the doors were open
or the first passengers had set more than a nose tip outside.

"For heaven's sake!" cried the exasperated baronet as the
clamour continued and even children hitherto philosophic
about their woes began to wail. "What's an hour or two—
or three, dammit? Nobody's hurt—nobody's ill, unless you
count feeding the fishes—nobody's dead. Everyone's back
here safe and sound, as you could see for your silly selves
if you'd only stop milling about making such a dashed
racket a man can't hear himself think."

Sir George drew himself to his full height, glaring into
the darkness at the upturned faces of his fellow villagers.
"Nothing," he announced in parade-ground tones that
should reach every house in The Street, "has gone wrong—
operation went like clockwork—everyone had a splendid
time—and the sooner you all get home to bed the better!"

With this reprimand ringing in their ears the citizens of
Plummergen dispersed. Swift footsteps and shrill voices
mingled as parents dragged their excited children out of
range of Sir George's prolonged mutterings, many of which
were couched in military terms unfit for an infant audience.
The reunion with Fleabag de Balivernes, the brandy, and the
opportunity for reminiscence had ripened the major-
general's speech to a level last achieved thirty years before.

Lady Colveden, who had earlier regretted the absence of Nigel and Julia, was only too thankful for that absence now.

"Dear Sir George," murmured Miss Seeton as she headed south beside her ladyship, with the baronet striding out in front, "has been on top form today, hasn't he? One might almost believe he thought the inconvenience of a sprained wrist worthwhile."

"He may not think so tomorrow," returned Sir George's spouse with a grim chuckle. "For one thing, he'll have a shocking head. I've never known him to talk so much, or for so long, in all the years since we were married." She paused to consider the accuracy of this observation. "I've never known him to talk so much, full stop," she amended. "Even at our wedding he could only mumble a few words and sit down to let the poor best man try to respond to the Toast to the Bridesmaids George had forgotten to make!"

Miss Seeton expressed discreet mirth at the story, while regretting the embarrassment poor Sir George must have felt.

Lady Colveden emitted another grim chuckle. "He'll be even more embarrassed tomorrow when I tell him just how many windows were open and lights were on while he was pontificating—and that's just here in Plummergen. When he has time to look back on today's performance on the ferry, bless him, he'll want to curl up in a corner and hide until he thinks everyone has forgotten."

"Which they won't," said Miss Seeton warmly. "Why, Sir George should be proud of himself. Had it not been for his efforts at—at distraction and entertainment . . ."

"Hmmm," said Lady Colveden, glancing back up The Street towards the bus stop. Some of the windows standing open during her husband's exasperated pontification had belonged to Lilikot. Her ladyship recalled Nigel's report of Admiral Leighton's singsong and the casement-slamming horror of the Nuts. She then recalled that nobody from Lilikot had done more than exchange icy nods with anyone from Rytham Hall since the night of that singsong. . . .

"It's an ill wind," said Lady Colveden cheerfully. Then

she giggled. "If it isn't indelicate of me to say so after the crossing we've just had, that is."

Miss Seeton stifled a yawn. "It has certainly been a—a tiring day," she said.

"I shall have nightmares about brown paper bags for weeks." Lady Colveden seemed little daunted by the prospect. "And once the word gets round—you know how much everyone gossips—poor George is going to be teased quite dreadfully, even by people who weren't there. Especially by Nigel," she added, becoming thoughtful.

Miss Seeton knew that her ladyship was right. As there was nothing useful to be said, she said nothing.

"He's promised to bring his daughter for a visit sometime soon," said Lady Colveden after a pause, completing a train of thought that was entirely logical both to herself and to Miss Seeton. "She's an attractive girl, isn't she?"

"She photographs very well," agreed Miss Seeton at once. "As, of course, does dear Nigel." She wondered why she had said that. "Her bones," she went on quickly. "And such lovely hair, with those expressive dark eyes—so very like her father—but there is still something of her mother, as far as I could tell from the snapshot. Which must be a—a rather mournful, while naturally pleasing, reminder for the count whenever he looks at her."

"I suppose so," said her ladyship, still thinking. Miss Seeton was, indeed, very English—too English to be happy living in France—but it seemed a shame not to encourage a little romance for the summer—a romance that would harm nobody and might, perhaps, find a more lasting echo in the younger generation. . . .

But then all thoughts of romance were shattered by Sir George, who suddenly struck up "Colonel Bogey" again.

At full volume.

And this time he wasn't whistling.

The day after Miss Nuttel's lost excursion to France, Mrs. Blaine came down to breakfast with another headache. On a normal morning she would have stayed, silent and bravely suffering, in bed, but the opportunity for complaint was simply too good to be missed.

"Morning," Miss Nuttel greeted her as she groped her way into the kitchen and staggered towards a chair.

"You look rough, old girl," was the greeting from Ada.

Mrs. Blaine, pale of face, confirmed in feeble accents that she felt rough. "But of course it's hardly surprising," she went on in a slightly stronger voice, directing her remarks to Miss Nuttel as well. "You know how sensitive I am to noise and . . . unpleasantness." There was no harm in reminding certain people that certain other people had every right, on occasion, to feel aggrieved at the way they were treated, even if the previous evening and subsequent night had been occasions entirely different in kind. "You," said Mrs. Blaine in tones the less sensitive might have thought accusing, "have always been so *strong,* Eric. So *confident*— and you, too, Ada. You cope with things as they are—you don't realise what it is to have an *imagination.*"

Miss Nuttel wondered about protesting, Mrs. Noble about laughing, but by now Mrs. Blaine was in full flight, and they could do nothing to bring her back to earth. "I'm sure," she quavered with a hand to her aching brow, "I can't have had a wink of sleep last night, first of all worrying about those *dreadful bees,* and then that shocking rumpus up and down The Street—and such language!"

Ada coughed. "I've *said* I'll buy you a new hat," she reminded her cousin: and she did not remind her as gently as she might have done a few days earlier. Norah's Wilting Blossom act could be a little wearing, even for her family, and Ada had now been more than a week under the same roof. "Mind you," she added, "if the admiral offers to stump up the cost, I won't say no—but it really was my fault for being so absentminded, especially when it wasn't my hat and I had no business to be so careless."

"Isn't anyone's hat now," said Miss Nuttel, who had

gone outside to check. "Blown to pieces last night—what they left of it."

"I suppose they'd chewed holes in it even before he came and smoked them out, or whatever he did," said Mrs. Blaine, who had retired to her room and locked both door and windows the instant the sinister buzzing had been heard in the back garden the previous evening. With Miss Nuttel as terrified of bees as her friend, it had been left to Ada to peer out of the kitchen window and announce that Mrs. Blaine's straw hat, which she had inadvertently forgotten to bring indoors, had been invaded by a black, seething mass she could only assume had come from the admiral's hives.

"Don't let them in!" screamed Mrs. Blaine, muffled by planking.

"Use the phone!" cried Miss Nuttel from behind her bedroom door.

Ada regretted the chance to become further acquainted with her next-door neighbour, but as she had no idea how dangerous the swarming bees might be, she decided to follow instructions and telephone him rather than risk death by stinging. The admiral did not answer the phone. Ada rang again. Still there was no answer. Miss Nuttel and Mrs. Blaine, duly consulted, were adamant that she should not open the house to the invaders—even at the front when the bees were at the back. Mrs. Noble settled to a long, lonely vigil at the sitting-room window before the admiral hove into view on his return from Saturday night at the George and Dragon. Ada listened for the bang of his front door and telephoned again.

After the problem had been explained, the admiral, all apology, was round within minutes wearing his broad-brimmed hat, his beekeeper's veil, and his gloves. In one hand he held a basket, in the other a smoke puffer; a powerful torch was tucked under his arm. Mrs. Noble, now at the kitchen window, watched him apply smoke to the seething hat and tip the quietened contents into the basket. He glanced towards the kitchen, saw Mrs. Noble in silhouette against electric light, and waved his thanks as he vanished in the direction of his hives.

It took Ada some time to persuade Miss Nuttel and Mrs. Blaine that the danger, such as it had been, was past. They emerged from their rooms pale of face, quivering, and crying for chamomile tea, which she had brewed in anticipation. It was agreed that everyone would sleep late next morning, and that while it was just about permissible to open windows at the front, it would be far too risky to open those at the back—just in case.

This lack of a through draught had been another reason for everyone's tetchiness on the morning after the missed excursion to France: and not the last reason.

"It was certainly noisy, wasn't it?" said Ada as she took a fresh spoon of chamomile from the tin. "I had no idea the hooligan element was so active in this quiet little village of yours, Norah."

"Hooligans? Ha!" said Miss Nuttel as Mrs. Blaine's lips parted to allow a similarly scornful (though weak) exclamation to escape her. "Some people pride themselves on being important figures in the community—responsible position—supposed to set an example—"

Mrs. Blaine achieved another exclamation. Having heard and seen the kettle safely on the boil, she made it stronger than her previous attempt.

"—but they say," went on Miss Nuttel, "blue blood's the worst—and it's true. Carry on as if they own the place— walk all over everyone else—treat them like dirt—don't give tuppence for their rights—"

"Or feelings," supplied Mrs. Blaine as Miss Nuttel drew breath. "I had the most frightful nightmares after it was all over—not," she added hastily, "that it *was* over for *positively hours*—and until I recognised Crabbe's bus I was *terrified* it was those ghastly motorbike thugs from Ashford running riot the way they did before—"

"Choppers," supplied Miss Nuttel as it was Bunny's turn to breathe. The kettle was bubbling now, and it took more of an effort to speak above it. "Knuckle-dusters," enlarged Miss Nuttel for the edification of Cousin Ada. "Chains—knives—that sort of thing. Nasty fight a year or so back. In prison, most of them. Good thing."

"But not *all* of them, Eric," objected Bunny, who wanted to relish her sleepless terror without the facts diminishing the fun. "That class of person always comes from a large family, and of course they teach one another their criminal habits. And with all that noise in The Street, is it any wonder I thought we were being invaded again?"

Miss Nuttel, after a moment, conceded that Bunny might have a point, though if she had looked out of the window—

"I *told* you," said Mrs. Blaine somewhat waspishly, "that I recognised the bus—what a disgraceful way to behave in front of those children!—otherwise of course I would have come down to telephone the police. But when I saw it was Sir George Colveden, of all people, creating such a scene—and his wife is one of the school governors—I knew the only thing to do was ignore him. So I did."

"Drunk," suggested Ada as chamomile began to infuse.

"Drunk?" Mrs. Blaine considered the suggestion. "Yes, that could be it. He was certainly . . . forceful, and the last time he was anything like as—as eloquent . . ." Her cheeks lost the pallor of insomnia beneath a blush of pure embarrassment, and she fell silent.

"The admiral's party," said Miss Nuttel after a long and thoughtful pause.

Mrs. Noble remembered the admiral's party, and the talk at the village hall. "So it *was* Sir George who was singing 'Colonel Bogey' all the way down The Street," she said as she stirred the tea and removed the spoon. Mrs. Blaine, worried about her weight, was taking her tea unsweetened. "I had a feeling the voice was familiar."

"And the words," snapped Miss Nuttel as Mrs. Blaine blushed even more and buried her nose in welcome chamomile steam.

"Drink," said Ada, "brings out the very worst in men,

as I should know—and you, too, of course, Norah."

"Duty-free, I expect," said Miss Nuttel, who had never cared even for the thought of Humphrey Blaine. It was the first remark that popped into her head, but an unfortunate one. No sooner did she remind herself of the fun she might have missed the day before—and if she, Erica Nuttel, had been in that party, it would have arrived home at a civilised hour and with everybody stone-cold sober—than a creeping sense of injustice began to work upon her soul. Here was Bunny, being waited on hand and foot with a headache that was no more than each of them in the house had a right to suffer, grumbling about noise and nightmares and drunken carousal when it was all her own fault for making out she couldn't face a Channel crossing—when, with a little effort and willpower, she could easily have done so. If she'd wanted. But no, she had preferred to stay at home with Ada Noble, plotting. . . .

Miss Nuttel chose to overlook the inconvenient fact that she, too, had stayed at home with Ada. There had been little opportunity for plotting when the three of them had been tripping over one another's feet all day, getting hotter and crosser by the minute when a cool sea breeze would have been just the job. . . .

"Duty-free," said Miss Nuttel, sounding annoyed.

"I thought you only drank homemade, Erica." Ada heard the annoyance but failed to understand its cause. "That's what you said, I'm sure. Do you mean you did ask someone to bring you something back after all?"

"Wish I had," said Miss Nuttel, who really believed she did. She heard Mrs. Blaine draw in a startled breath, and felt pleased. Bunny enjoyed the little luxuries of life: soap, perfume, bath salts, talc. Now she knew—but too late— what her selfishness had done. "Wish I had," said Miss Nuttel, almost gleeful. "Too late now."

Barely one minute later Mrs. Blaine and her headache were on their way back to bed. Ada was tactfully moving unused plates around the kitchen shelves, and Miss Nuttel,

in the garden, was hacking with a savage knife at a plant
that had done her no especial harm. The short-term burst of
domestic harmony, induced by the shared experience of the
previous night, was gone.

Two was company: three was a crowd.

Miss Nuttel severed an unwary deadhead from its stem,
and stamped it into the ground. Things just hadn't been the
same since Bunny—without so much as a by-your-leave—
had invited her cousin to stay. Before Ada's arrival there
was none of this nonsense about being seasick: Miss Nuttel
knew that Bunny would have been as keen to visit France
as anyone could have wished. Admittedly, Ada was trying
to save on expenses, and the cost of the trip might well be
beyond her—Miss Nuttel had some sympathy with this point
of view—but there was no need for Bunny to go to such
selfish lengths to save her cousin's face. Or was it that Norah
couldn't bear to leave dear Ada all by herself for the day?

If it was, Miss Nuttel suspected that Bunny's reasons were
less to do with a reluctance to leave a stranger alone in the
house than with a burst of cousinly zeal. Blood, so Bunny
kept saying (when she *knew* how it upset Miss Nuttel!) was
thicker than water. Miss Nuttel waited in dread for the moment she was taken quietly to one side to be asked whether
she didn't think it would be only generous if poor Cousin
Ada could share their home on a more permanent basis. . . .

Three was a crowd . . . *and would be.*

Would not—must not—be!

Miss Nuttel felt that a quick—anonymous—telephone call
to Algernon Noble, telling him where his wife was and sug-
gesting that he came to remove her, might not be such a bad
idea. She was sure he could not be as . . . unpleasant as Ada
insisted: exaggeration was obviously a family failing. Gentlemen (and Bunny had always said that the Lindlys never
married beneath them) did not mistreat their wives, even
when drunk. Sir George, for all his ripe language and—and
hearty ways, had never laid a finger on Lady Colveden . . .
as far as anyone knew.

Miss Nuttel paused to consider the likelihood that Sir George was indeed a closet wife-beater, but her heart wasn't in it. She sighed. How life had changed—and not for the better—since Ada had come to stay! How Bunny, in more normal circumstances, would have relished the chance to speculate on the Rytham Hall ménage—whereas now, Miss Nuttel felt sure, she would say it was only upsetting Ada to be reminded of the husband from whom she had fled.

Fled from a house—with a telephone number—that Miss Nuttel knew must be in Bunny's address book. Once she and Ada were out of the house . . . If only she didn't have to wait too long: her patience was running out. . . .

Far too risky to call from the box at the end of The Street. That vandalised pane had still not been replaced, and anyone might hear what she was saying.

Especially—with the windows of her cottage overlooking the telephone box—That Woman.

Miss Seeton.

CHAPTER 10

On a desk in a modest office on the umpteenth floor of New Scotland Yard the telephone rang at one minute past nine on Monday morning. The sound was greeted with a muttered oath by Chief Superintendent Delphick, engrossed in the contents of a folder of thick and all too complex documents on which he made frequent pencilled notes as he cross-referenced from one file to another and, more frequently than he would like, back again.

The telephone continued to ring. Delphick continued to ignore it. After counting ten rings, the only other occupant of the room picked up his party-line receiver and warily greeted the importunate caller.

"Ranger?" barked the caller. The mighty Detective Sergeant Bob Ranger, six-foot-seven and seventeen stone, leaped on his chair at this assault on his eardrums. Floorboards vibrated right across the room. Delphick, resolutely preoccupied, did not look up even when his pencils rattled in their jam-jar holder. "Where's the Oracle?" demanded Sir Hubert Everleigh. "Hiding?"

"Er—working, sir," said the sergeant. At his final word the Oracle muttered a second oath, though he kept his head over his papers and would not catch Bob's pleading eye. "We're, uh, rather busy at the moment, sir," said Bob. "If you remember. That forgery case—"

"Never mind forgery cases, Ranger," snapped Sir Heavily. Bob moved the earpiece several inches from his ear. "You young men," said Sir Hubert, "have no idea what being busy means. I know he's there. Tell him to pick up the phone and—no, tell him I want him. Upstairs in my office, five minutes. No argument—and in the circumstances I suppose it wouldn't do any harm for you to come, too. Five minutes, please." And without waiting for a reply, London's Assistant Commissioner (Crime) broke the connection.

"Sir," said Bob as Delphick did not look up.

"Sir," said Bob, more loudly.

"I heard you the first time," said the Oracle, head down and pencil busy.

"Did you hear the Ass. Comm., too, sir?" enquired Ranger, whose eardrums had not quite stopped ringing.

"No," lied his superior officer, the man who was meant to lead by example.

Bob coughed. "He, uh, did say five minutes, sir," he ventured after ninety seconds had passed.

Delphick threw down his pencil and roundly cursed all assistant commissioners who couldn't leave a hardworking detective to get on with the business of detection.

"Yes, sir," said Bob as he ran out of steam. "But it's only a couple of minutes to go, now. Hadn't we better be making tracks?"

Delphick shoved the chair away from his desk and rose reluctantly to his feet. "I have an uneasy feeling about all this, Sergeant Ranger. Sterling character though you undoubtedly are—even if your skills of obfuscation leave something to be desired—the higher echelons of Scotland Yard are not normally so eager to hobnob with Other Ranks unless the matter is one that requires a particular expertise." He watched the startled realisation beginning to dawn on his sergeant's face. "Quite so, Bob," said Chief Superintendent Delphick.

"Not for nothing," he went on as the two made their way

from the office, "have I acquired the soubriquet of Oracle. My oracular powers tell me now that no common or garden conundrum is about to be presented to us, Sergeant Ranger." They were at the lift. The chief superintendent pressed the relevant button. "Moreover," he went on as the doors thudded open, "given Sir Hubert's insistence on your accompanying me—after you, Sergeant—I would venture to suggest that this conundrum will, not far from its heart, have much to do with the county of Kent."

The last words were almost lost as the doors thumped together and the lift began to rise, but it did not matter. "Yes, sir," said Bob. Although Delphick's use of *insistence* had been overdoing it a bit, his sergeant knew very well what he meant.

Sir Hubert was waiting for them in his office and directed them to their seats with a brisk wave. "The Channel Tunnel," he said. "What are your thoughts on it?"

Delphick, at whom this remark had been fired, blinked. Bob's jaw dropped and was hurriedly replaced. Life was full of surprises. What on or under earth had the Chunnel got to do with—

"I must confess," replied the Oracle, "that I've hardly wast—that is, spared the time to think about it, sir." He coughed. "I have of late," he said carefully, "as you know, been rather more concerned with the number of forged stamps currently flooding the capital, and with the resultant loss to Her Majesty's Exchequer." Sir Hubert gestured irritably. Delphick inclined his head to hide a smile.

"The Channel Tunnel," he offered after a pause, "is a considerable challenge both to those of a civil-engineering bent and to those with financial investment in mind—as has been all too clearly shown by recent events, although I take it that was not the import of your question, sir. Had you any particular direction for my, ah, thoughts in mind?"

Sir Hubert breathed heavily for a few moments, and Bob tried to stifle a snort. They didn't call the Ass. Comm. "Sir Heavily" just on account of his name. "Yes," said Sir Hubert Everleigh after a few moments. "Security."

"Security?" reiterated Delphick. "Well, sir, if you mean the roof of the blessed thing is liable to collapse without warning, then—"

"I don't," he was curtly informed. "You're a policeman, Delphick, not a navvy. If my concern was with the—the mechanics of the digging, I would ask someone who knew about pneumatic drills. As it is not, I ask you."

"About Channel Tunnel security," murmured Delphick. "By which I infer that you don't mean the constructional so much as the, ah, physical security."

"Yes," said the Assistant Commissioner (Crime).

Delphick frowned. "Terrorists," he said. "Smugglers. Rabies. Military invasion. How am I doing so far, sir?"

"The new builders—the Chunnel Consortium, they call themselves—want to talk to someone from the Yard," said Sir Hubert, without answering him directly. "You are the obvious choice, Chief Superintendent Delphick. I should like you to pass the relevant files on your stamp case to Superintendent Borden of Fraud and then report as soon as possible, with such of your officers as you think necessary, to their head office. In Ashford," he added as Delphick was about to protest that he saw no reason why he of all Yarders should be the obvious choice.

Sir Hubert's mention of Ashford, and the emphasis he had placed on those two innocuous syllables, gave Delphick the clue. Relieved that his oracular powers had not been as far out of tune as he'd begun to suspect, he nodded. "Ashford," he repeated, "in Kent, I assume. As opposed to Ashford in Devonshire, Ashford in Derbyshire, or Ashford in Middlesex?"

"Your assumption," said Sir Hubert, "is correct."

Delphick nodded again. "There is," he said, "no point in my remarking—with the greatest respect, naturally, sir— that I have no *particular or specialist knowledge* of such matters as smuggling, terrorism, or pest control, I suppose?"

"Your supposition," Sir Hubert told him, "is correct."

He coughed. "The contents of your personal file, Chief Superintendent Delphick, are not unknown to me."

"No, sir," said Delphick. He glanced at Bob, who was doing his seventeen-stone best to appear unobtrusive on the chair at his side. "The same, ah, consideration," went on the chief superintendent, "applies with equal . . . let us say force in the case of my sergeant here, no doubt."

"Let us, indeed," said Sir Hubert. "No doubt at all—oh, dammit, you know perfectly well why you've been lumbered, both of you. Any fool can cope with a forgery case—your face, Chief Superintendent, is perhaps more expressive than you realise—"

"Sir," interposed Delphick with equal courtesy.

"—but," pressed on the Assistant Commissioner, "it takes a man—or two—an entire battalion, on occasion—with what you would doubtless call *particular and specialist knowledge* of a certain spinster of a parish not a million miles from the Chunnel mouth to cope with anything . . . out of the ordinary that might run even the slightest risk of occurring in the county of Kent."

There followed a lengthy pause. Sir Hubert drummed his fingers on the desk; Delphick was determined not to crack. Circumstances, however, conspired against him.

"You have something to contribute to this discussion, Sergeant?" he at last enquired with chilling politeness as Bob choked back a splutter.

Sir Hubert's gaze fell upon the hapless young giant, and there was a wild moment when Bob would have been prepared to swear he saw the Old Man wink at him. He decided afterwards that he must have imagined it. "Sorry, sir," he said once he had finished choking. His face was hot, and his tie felt tight about his neck. "I mean—nothing to say, sir."

"Good," said Delphick. "Perhaps," he went on, turning with resignation back to Sir Hubert, "if you could give me—us—an idea of what exactly is required of us?"

"There's going to be some sort of terminal at Ashford," he was informed with an airy wave of Sir Hubert's hand.

Now that the Oracle was willing to carry the can, the Assistant Commissioner, it was clear, had more important matters on his mind. "You'll have to find out exactly what's what for yourselves. It will mean having to liaise not only with the contractors but also with the authorities at Ashford. . . ."

"Which means Superintendent Brinton," supplied Delphick as Sir Heavily shot him a meaningful look. "Of course."

"Of course," echoed the Assistant Commissioner (Crime). "Scotland Yard is not . . . vindictive, Chief Superintendent. If that's the word I want," he added with a frown. "What I mean is that we shouldn't want you—or anyone else—to . . . take it personally. . . ."

"Or, as you say, sir, anyone else," agreed Delphick with another glance at Bob, who was spluttering again. "I would, however, and with the utmost respect, remind you that Dover, where the digging is under way, and—and Plummergen are twenty-five miles apart even as the crow flies, and ten or more miles farther by road."

"Not far enough," said Sir Hubert quickly. "Neither for my peace of mind, nor for that of anyone else." He favoured Detective Sergeant Ranger with an appraising look. "Well," conceded the Ass. Comm. as Bob—to his own eternal astonishment—returned that look with interest, "perhaps I am being a touch unfair to . . . a certain party of our mutual acquaintance, gentlemen." He coughed. "Overreacting, it might be said—but the basic arguments hold. *Someone* is required to discuss Chunnel security with the contractors, and as it has to be someone with knowledge of the area, that means an Ashford man, senior among the suitable men being Superintendent Brinton. And as these new builder chaps now insist—rightly, in my opinion—on a Yard involvement as well, the logical person is yourself, Delphick, given that you and Brinton have worked together before."

"Quite so, sir," said Delphick as Sir Heavily waited for a response. Bob managed to make not a sound.

In lieu of drumming them, Sir Hubert locked his restless fingers in an unsteady steeple. "And," he went on, "with Plummergen—as you have reminded me—not thirty miles from Dover, it makes yet more sense from what one might call the insurance point of view to be prepared to include Sergeant Ranger here as someone who, heaven help him, has chosen to adopt Miss Seeton as an honorary aunt. I may be hoping for miracles, but between the three of you it should in theory be possible to keep her and her umbrella under control."

This was too much for the loyal Bob. "She's never been anywhere near the Channel Tunnel!" he protested, and when two pairs of high-ranking eyes focused on him was unabashed. "And as far as I know she's no intention of going there," he continued, only a little less hotly. "Why should she? The whole village is far too busy making money for charity for them to want to go and look at a—a dirty great hole in the ground, and even if they did . . ."

Then he came to his belated senses and subsided, with a horrified gulp and a blush.

Delphick's expression was unreadable. Sir Hubert, after a heart-stopping moment, smiled, albeit thinly. "Quite so," he said, adopting the same dry tone the Oracle himself had used. "Then, with the sergeant's permission, I believe we may consider the matter settled." Sir Hubert turned from the blushing Bob to his superior. "Mr. Delphick, you will pass all working files on the stamp forgeries to Mr. Borden, after which you will arrange to visit Ashford"—he glanced at Bob—"with, as I said before, such of your officers as you think necessary . . ."

Bob could have sworn there was a gleam in Sir Heavily's eye. But he must have been wrong. . . .

". . . in order," the Ass. Comm. continued, "to liaise with Mr. Brinton and the Chunnel people. That will be all, thank you, gentlemen. Good day to you both."

There was nothing more to be said. Delphick and Ranger accordingly said it, murmuring their farewells and taking their leave. Bob risked a quick look back as he closed the door, and thought he saw the Assistant Commissioner's shoulders heaving as he bent his head over his desk. He'd have been half willing to swear the Old Man was laughing. . . .

"You made a pretty spectacle of yourself in there," was the Oracle's observation as they walked towards the lift.

Bob, who had been desperately framing an apology, still had no idea how to start. "Sir—I—"

Delphick raised a hand. "Don't bother," he said. "You couldn't possibly excuse yourself, so don't even try." Was the Oracle laughing, too? Once again Bob couldn't be sure, but . . . "Tell me instead," invited the chief superintendent, "why Miss Seeton and her friends are showing this unexpected interest in matters charitable."

Thankfully, Bob cleared his throat, fiddled with the knot of his tie, and began. "Well, sir, I thought you must have read about it in the papers, but anyway a bloke called Horace Jowett died in Plummergen last month, and . . ."

The Monday after Plummergen's trip to France there occurred the sort of storm compared with which the Channel wind had been a murmuring zephyr. The rain came in horizontal stair rods, lashed against windows that, where they did not break, would have no need of washing for a while. The lightning flashed, the thunder boomed and bawled, and farmers agonised over the harvest they had lost and the beasts that would be panic-stricken in the flooded, clamorous fields.

Nobody slept a wink that night: but life had to go on. Maureen-from-the-George's Wayne, steering his careful way between the puddles, arrived from Brettenden only ten minutes later than the usual hour for collecting his young lady for the motorbike drive to work—to be told by her yawning mother the girl was still in bed. Would he like to come in for a cup of tea?

Wayne (whose own approach to steady employment was

that you shouldn't push your luck) hesitated and then refused
the offer, saying he must be going. With a roar of his Kawasaki engine, he went.

With the result that for the first time in her life poor Maureen *walked* the weary distance from one end of Plummergen to the pub at the other—where Doris had given up all
hope of seeing her. As Maureen tumbled, breathless and
gasping, through the door to collapse on a convenient bench,
the headwaitress glared at her from behind the desk.

"If you're dying, young Maureen, don't do it here. I've
more to worry about this morning than bodies in Reception.
There's been twice the work for me and Mr. Mountfitchet
with you not here when you ought to have been."

Maureen mumbled something about the storm, and how
tired she felt this morning, and how her eyes hurt and her
head ached and her feet had the most awful blisters. . . .

Doris dismissed these complaints with scorn. Were not
she and Charley Mountfitchet—and everyone else in the village—every bit as tired as Maureen? That storm hadn't just
been over the council houses, she would have Maureen
know. Being tired was no excuse. Blisters could be put right
with a sterilised needle and some sticking plaster. If Maureen wanted her full wages this week, which in the opinion
of Doris she didn't deserve, then she had best get down to
Hoovering the carpets and the rest of the tidying she ought
to have finished an hour or more ago.

The bang and the flash ten minutes after she started her
apathetic pushing of the vacuum cleaner made Maureen
move faster than she had in years.

She hadn't screamed so loudly in years, either.

Miss Seeton was more than surprised to find Martha
Bloomer on the step when she went to fetch the morning
milk, which had arrived much later than usual on account
of the floods in the dairy yard and the resultant shorted bat-
teries in most of the delivery floats.

"You're just in time for a cup of tea, Martha dear," her

friend and employer greeted the newcomer. "Last night's storm curdled all that I had left, even though it was in the refrigerator and—but do please come in," urged Miss Seeton with a swift change of tack as she remembered that Martha was terrified of thunder. "We'll call it elevenses, even if it is rather past the hour—but I think we may all be excused a little tardiness after last night, and—and it isn't one of your days, is it?" she enquired hastily as she led the way along the passage to the kitchen, blushing to think that this further reminder of the storm and subsequent muddled memories was quite as tactless as—

"No," said Martha, who sometimes knew Miss Seeton's mind as well as she knew her own. "No, that's all right, dear, it's not the wrong day, it's just I came to say ta for the postcard from France, Bert brought it dead on the usual time—I could hardly believe my ears when it popped through the letter box—and do you mind if I use your kettle to steam off the stamp for the kiddies' wheelchairs? Our electric's not back on yet, even if yours is."

"Good gracious," said Miss Seeton, impressed at the speed of the card's arrival and the dedication of Postman Bert. She wondered if he had worn gumboots to walk from his van up people's paths: although the rain had now stopped, everywhere was still very wet, after the storm—which it seemed had caused more damage than she had realised. "You say you have no electricity? That must be a great inconvenience. And with your house being just the other side of the road—which of course would explain, if there was a power cut last night, why my milk turned sour even inside the fridge—but it seems odd that yours should still be off when mine is not."

Martha shrugged. "Could be worse," she said. "All the houses right from the vicarage to the canal are out our side of the road, with water getting into the main, though they say the men will be here by dinnertime—which I take leave to believe when I see it, knowing what workmen are like—but at least we've still got the phones to call for 'em to come and sort it out. Over at the George there's not a phone in the place, all on account of young Maureen Hoovering clean across the cable where it comes in by the door and scaring herself into a blue fit, the daft creature.''

Miss Seeton frowned. "Hysterics, you mean?" she asked a little sadly; and she sighed as Martha confirmed this. It had always struck Miss Seeton that a little less nightlife, some regular exercise, and a modicum of common sense could do wonders for young Maureen, although of course it was hardly her place to say so.

"Don't see why not," said the loyal Martha. "With you knowing more about youngsters than most in this village, they ought to be grateful for your advice." She grinned. "I'd not wish to commit myself as to the common sense, but Doris tells me Maureen's tried the exercise, at any rate. She was still in bed when Wayne turned up on his bike to take her to work, and he wouldn't wait—and I can't say I blame him, the lazy little madam—and the fuss she kicked up about her feet when she got to the George Doris says you'd never believe. Had to speak to her real sharp, Doris did, before she'd even think of starting work, and grumbling the whole time once she had."

Miss Seeton looked shocked. "Surely, Martha dear, you don't suspect Maureen of—of deliberately sabotaging the telephone system?" Miss Seeton herself would have not the faintest idea of how to go about such sabotage; and, while she knew that modern youth understood far more about matters technological than older generations, Maureen's inability to absorb new ideas—any ideas—was a village byword.

"If she did," Martha told her with another grin, "she got a box on the ear for her pains—and her wages docked, Doris says, which she's been dying to do for years and this time she'd had enough and wouldn't let Charley talk her out of it the way he always does with him feeling sorry for the girl and saying we were all young once." Martha snorted. "When *I* was young, there was a war on—and if I'd been half as dozy as Maureen I'd've been dead. Common sense?

There's one as wouldn't have the sense to get into the shelter if she could see the bombs dropping all around her.''

Miss Seeton thought that even Maureen—

Miss Seeton recalled a long-ago acquaintance of statistical bent who had calculated (to his own satisfaction) the odds against being hit by either a bomb, a chunk of masonry, or a piece of shrapnel. A long-ago and *late* acquaintance, Miss Seeton added with a sigh as Martha rolled her eyes. An acquaintance who, scorning even the wearing of a tin hat, had braved the firestorm with a borrowed umbrella—

''Not one of mine, I am thankful to say,'' Miss Seeton hurried to explain. ''It was some time after it happened that I heard of his death, and of course if he had asked me I should have refused, and although one hesitates to interfere, I hope I would have done my best to persuade him not to act in quite so foolish a manner, even if his view that one should not—should not bend the knee to Hitler was one with which, naturally, we all agreed. And everyone was happy to lend and borrow and to help one another during the War— but really—an umbrella, in an air raid.'' Miss Seeton, for once in her life, found it hard to adopt a charitable point of view. ''As you say, Martha dear, there are some people for whom the words *common sense* appear to have no meaning whatsoever—and he was, as I recall, an extremely talented young sculptor—if perhaps not entirely to my taste—which makes his loss even more regrettable.''

Martha nodded. ''Kettle's ready,'' she said happily. ''We'll make ourselves that cuppa first and use what's left for the stamp, if that's all right by you.''

It was. Miss Seeton poured boiling water into the teapot, swirled it round, tipped it away, dropped in—stifling a sigh—three heaped spoonfuls—Martha preferred her tea mouse-trot strong, while Miss Seeton knew she could always weaken hers with extra water—and then, having filled the pot and replaced the lid, went back to the kettle to watch with interest as Martha held the business side of the postcard from France over the steaming spout.

"Lucky you used one of your pencils, dear." Progress was slow, and Martha was inspecting the curling corners of the card and wishing the corners of the stamp would do the same. "If this'd been written in ink it would have run all over the show by now."

"The French," said Miss Seeton after a further period of unsuccessful steaming, "do seem to use particularly—well, forceful glue on their stamps."

"Don't they just," agreed Martha, poking a tentative fingernail under one edge of the stamp and finding that all it did was wrinkle.

"I accept, Martha dear, that this is for charity," said Miss Seeton when the tea had been poured and the stamp still adhered to its postcard base, "but perhaps—as things seem to be going wrong . . ."

Miss Seeton fell silent. After a moment a thoughtful pucker appeared upon her brow.

"Never say die," chirped Mrs. Bloomer, busy at the kettle and for once less understanding of her employer than she liked to think herself. Miss Seeton continued to gaze at the stubborn stamp in thoughtful silence.

Martha let out an exclamation and threw the postcard on the table. "If you was to hand me a pair of scissors right now," she said, "I'd—I'd chop the whole blessed corner off the dratted thing—if it wasn't that I like the picture so much—and let the charity people do the job instead, except that it seems daft to be beaten by a silly little bit of paper, especially in a good cause like wheelchairs for the poor crippled kiddies—but we've never had any of this bother with sensible English stamps," concluded the breathless and patriotic cockney.

"N-no . . . May I?" Without waiting for an answer Miss Seeton took up the postcard and examined it carefully. That thoughtful pucker remained upon her brow as she gazed in turn at the bright café awning and the cheerful diners, at the stamp, at the message she had written in coloured pencil . . . and at the stamp again.

"If," she said slowly, "it is the picture that you find particularly attractive, Martha dear, I would be more than happy to copy it for you. A crayon sketch, perhaps, or pastels—and then, with your permission, I would soak the card in a dish of warm water, rather than steam it, to remove the stamp, as I have heard the children say they sometimes do, in cases of this sort." Miss Seeton looked again at the dining party, reversed the card, and contemplated the stamp.

"Of course," she went on, turning the card over and over in her hands, "although soaking would probably remove it as you wish—except that until I have tried the experiment I cannot *promise* it will succeed—we may be reasonably sure that it will spoil the card. Even if it had a calendered finish on both sides—as of course it does not, for nobody could expect to write a useful message on a shiny surface— it would certainly not be waterproof. Rather like the bowl my dear mother had—and Cousin Flora, too, of course—for washing the best china. Or rather, not."

Only at this memory did Miss Seeton smile, and Martha smiled, too. She well recalled the small papier-mâché basin to which Mrs. Bannet had remained loyal despite the advent of plastic, and how it had taken Miss Seeton's tactful present of a dark blue bowl one Christmas to persuade the old lady—with a little help from Martha—that it might at last be time to retire the trusty workhorse that had for so many years preserved her delicate porcelain and glass against the risk of breakage in an earthenware sink.

"And didn't you get a bargain, dear?" said Martha with a wave towards the kitchen window and the garden beyond. "Mrs. Bannet would keep worrying you'd paid over the odds for it, but I told her straight: 'Charity begins at home,' I said, 'and if Miss Emily is willing to spend her money on you, that's her affair, so you just be grateful and don't hurt her feelings and let me use that bowl for the fine china,' I said, so of course she did. And thankful I was you gave it to her, dear, so chipped as the other one was getting and me afraid one day it would fall to pieces in my hands. And even if yours is too faded now to look smart in here, Stan says there's nothing like it for washing his flowerpots at the end of the season so's they can all be put away clean for next year.''

"Yes," said Miss Seeton absently. She was subjecting the postcard to further study. "A bargain . . .''

Martha recognised the signs of artistic inspiration, and realised that although she hadn't accepted Miss Seeton's kindly offer in so many words, the postcard copy was already under way. "Then I'll finish my tea and leave you to it, shall I?" she said, blowing gently on what was left in the cup and with true heroism restraining herself from checking the pot to see how much was left. "I'm sure you'll do a lovely picture for me, dear, and thank you very much. Ta-ta for now, and thanks for the cuppa!''

"Goodbye," said Miss Seeton. "Charity begins at home," she added in a murmur; but Martha had gone, and the murmur went unanswered.

Miss Seeton carried the postcard with her into the sitting room, where she opened the bureau in which she kept much of her sketching gear and removed a block, her crayons and pastels, and an eraser. She hesitated, frowned, and went back for the tin in which she kept her stamp money. For a second time she hesitated, then set the tin at a convenient point on the sitting room table, propped the postcard against it, stopped it slipping by using the eraser as a brake, and arranged herself on a chair with the open block in front of her and the crayons close to hand.

She stared at the jolly faces of the drinkers outside the café with the scarlet awning, and considered the more sober faces of the men behind them at another table, playing cards. Outside the awning orange shadows fell across the drinkers' table where the sun, shining through glasses of red wine, made patterns on the yellow cloth. The yellow cloth of the card players' table under the awning was even more darkly orange; the card players' glasses of wine were brown in the crimson light, and the shadows they cast were very nearly black.

Miss Seeton blinked, shook her head, and looked at the clock. She picked up the card, turned it over, and looked again at the stamp. She read her pencil message to Martha and Stan, and wondered why she was making such heavy weather of a mere copying job. . . .

"Charity begins at home," she told herself sternly, and reached for a scarlet crayon.

CHAPTER 11

The cheese plant had been a Reception focal point since it first outgrew its six-inch starter pot many years before. With the tender loving care of Charley Mountfitchet and Doris, it had grown into a fine specimen, whose leaves must be washed with milk at least once a week to maintain their rich green sheen, and into whose compost liquid fertiliser of exactly the right chemical balance must be poured in measured doses if its roots were not to wither and die.

Doris was on her knees beside the desk giving the pot its regular quarter turn—the light must fall on all sides equally, or the stem would grow lopsided—when Benjamin Folland bustled down the stairs and marched across to her.

"My telephone isn't working," he complained. "I've just been trying to dial an outside number, and nothing happens—and when I tried to call Reception, there was nothing but silence. What is going on?"

Doris creaked her way up from her knees—one day, she promised herself, she really would ask Miss Seeton how she did it—to apologise. She explained Maureen's part in the communications catastrophe and said that Mr. Folland wasn't to worry, steps had been taken and the girl would have her wages docked as a result, though she was surprised that Mr. Folland hadn't heard all the ... fuss when the ... accident happened.

"I was busy in my room with paperwork," said Benjamin, who had eaten a quick breakfast and vanished back upstairs while Charley in the kitchen was still trying to decide how the new toaster—normally the responsibility of Doris, who was waiting at table in Maureen's absence—worked. "I have to give a progress report to Golden Brolly headquarters," Mr. Folland went on as Doris tried to apologise again. "When are the repairs likely to be finished?"

"Ah," said Doris, who could gladly have boxed Maureen's ears again if the girl hadn't been banished to an upstairs corridor under strict instruction to apply lavender polish to the woodwork and not to come back down until the tin was empty. "Yes. Well, I'm sorry, but what with the storm last night there's been a lot of overhead lines gone down, they said, and the repair people are so short of men they've even had to borrow from the private lot who deal with phones like ours, and . . ."

"And you don't know," supplied Benjamin neatly as Doris blundered to a halt.

"No," said Doris grimly, thinking of Maureen. "We don't—and I'm sorry for it—but there'll be a reduction in your bill when the time comes to settle, you can be sure of that. And if you need a phone in a hurry, why, there's always the call box on the corner by the bakery, just across The Street—and you could pop into Mrs. Wyght's afterwards for some sticky buns," she added in the voice of the serpent. "Very popular, the sticky buns."

"Sticky buns," echoed Mr. Folland, with a rueful pat for the trouser belt that over the past three weeks had been let out by a notch, and was on the point of being let out again. While *cuisine* at the George and Dragon was hardly *haute,* it was undoubtedly good, substantial, traditional fare, and Benjamin had proved himself a noted trencherman. "I think not, Doris, thank you—although . . ." This time it was his pockets rather than his plumping tummy that he patted. "Um, yes. I do seem to be a little short of loose change for the phone," he said slowly. "I suppose you don't keep the odd coin or two in your desk for just such an emergency?''

Doris shook her head and explained that Mr. Mountfitchet didn't hold with putting temptation in people's way, the number of strangers that came in and out of the place with it being the best pub for miles. There might (she went on) be ten bob or so's worth in her handbag she could let him have, but—

"Oh, no," broke in Benjamin on cue. "My report always takes quite a time, and ten shillings—fifty pence, I mean—I'll never get used to this decimal currency—won't go far. If it wasn't so expensive, I'd reverse the charges, but I don't think I can waste charity funds on—but never mind. And thanks for the offer." He squared his shoulders. "It's got to be the bakery, then," he said. "But before, rather than after. And of course I can hardly go in and ask for change without buying something, can I?"

"Indeed you can't," responded Doris at once, properly shocked. "Of course you'll have to buy something, otherwise it'd be taking advantage of her good nature. How about some sticky buns?"

Mr. Folland thanked her for the suggestion and retreated upstairs for his notes and the weekly report. Doris, grinning, resumed flowerpot duty, and two minutes later waved her milky cloth in salute as Mr. Folland bustled his way from the bottom of the stairs across Reception and out through the main door in the direction of the telephone box on the corner—with a detour via the sticky buns and a pocketful of loose change.

The next time Doris looked up was when her attention was diverted from her study of the hotel register by the clump of feet, accompanied by a series of sniffs, descending the stairs. She didn't really need to look up: she knew who it was—only a martyred Maureen could make a walk on quality carpet sound like hobnailed boots on concrete—but she was understandably curious. Maureen was supposed to be polishing panels, newel posts, and banisters on the top landing. Never in her young life had she been known to work so hard that she finished a job, unsupervised, in even double the time it would take anyone else.

"Well?" demanded Doris as Maureen clumped and sniffed her way past the cheese plant in the direction of the door. As Doris snapped that one word Maureen desisted from her percussive locomotion and turned to face the face above the registration desk. "Well?" demanded Doris again as Maureen stared blankly. "If you're looking for something else to do, there's—"

"I haven't done the banisters yet," Maureen told her. "Not all of 'em, that is," she added as the eyes of Doris narrowed dangerously, and it was obvious—even to Maureen—that awkward questions about her presence in Reception were about to be asked. "I just wanted a closer look, that's all. No harm in that, is there?"

"Isn't there?" countered Doris. "Closer look at what, may I ask? You're paid to work, my girl, not go around looking at things, whatever they might be."

"The sign was in the way," mumbled Maureen. She sighed. "And she's probably stopped by now." She put a hand to her mouth and yawned. "Might as well make a cup of tea," she said with a yearning look towards the door that separated the public from the private half of the hotel.

"Who's *she*—the cat's mother? And what *sign*?" Doris had always known that Maureen was a little . . . lacking. Now she started to wonder if the girl suffered from delusions. There was nobody else on the top floor of the hotel: Mrs. Raughton and the other guests were gone for the day, sightseeing or bird-watching or otherwise about their business. So Maureen was seeing visions—or might it be ghosts? Either way, it was better not to encourage her. "You're talking nonsense, Maureen," said Doris crisply. "Pull yourself together and get back to work this minute."

"Daft old biddy," replied Maureen behind another yawn.

Doris rose from her chair and marched round to give her junior's ears the buffet of a lifetime. Then she saw the glint in the girl's eye, and paused. She had often wondered

whether Maureen could really be as stupid as she
seemed. . . .

"That daft cousin of Mrs. Blaine's," amplified Maureen,
a mere whisker from retribution and yet unaware of the fact.

Or . . . was she?

"Thought it was Mrs. Blaine, at first," continued Maureen blithely as Doris fixed her with an awful look. "Or
Miss Seeton," she added. "From high up you don't get the
proper view, see? Standing there with her umbrella wide
open when it's not even raining! You've got to wonder why,
haven't you?"

"No," said Doris, breathing hard as she thrust twitching
fingers in the pockets of her dress. "What Miss Seeton or
anyone else does is nothing to do with you, umbrellas or
otherwise, young Maureen, when you're meant to be working—and even when you're not," she added. Doris did not
approve of gossip, as anyone with half her wits about her
ought to have known. "Besides," she went on, "who's to
say Mrs. Noble wasn't worried by some of them pigeons
from the trees by the church—or feeling the sun on her head
when she's forgot her hat—or—"

"Sun's shining," agreed Maureen, nodding towards the
open door through which a yellow gleam was visible. "But
the wind's not blowing," she added in tones that suggested
this fact displeased her. Her next words explained why. "If
there'd been a wind the sign would've swung, so's I could
see what she was up to—"

"Which," Doris reminded her, "is nothing to do with
you! And never you mind your sniffing, my girl—and you
can forget a cup of tea, too. I want that oak upstairs so's I
can see my face in it—and if you look at me like that again,
young Maureen, you'll feel the back of my hand, believe
me. If there's a hundred umbrellas outside the George—
inside out, upside down, or flying through the air—I don't
want to hear another peep from you until that tin of polish
is empty, understand?"

To which, as Maureen's rebellious burst dwindled into her

accustomed apathy, there could be only one response. Clumping (and, defiantly, sniffing) Maureen made her way back up the stairs to the top corridor, leaving Ada Noble—if it had indeed been Mrs. Blaine's cousin and not Mrs. Blaine herself of whom she had failed to "get the proper view"—to whatever devices she, and her umbrella, might choose to call their own.

The June sunshine had brought on Plummergen's gardens quite wonderfully. It is true that the lawns of properties at the northern end of The Street had started to look a little brown, but those towards the south, where the Royal Military Canal wound its way along the edge of the marsh, were as green as ever; and even among the brown there was the emerald exception that proved the rule. Not for the first time, it was Miss Nuttel's pleasure to gloat over Lilikot's fresh water supply, even though she had her suspicions that it was starting to fail. A hand pump and well—Bunny had wanted to add a bucket and a trio of gnomes with fishing rods, but after an experimental gnome with a wheelbarrow had been kidnapped (to return with a placard of ribald legend tied about his neck) Miss Nuttel was adamant in her refusal—might not be able to support a hose, even if they had one; but they could fill a watering can as many times in an evening as muscle and sinew would permit, and with Ada Noble's noble—Miss Nuttel grinned—help, the muscle power had doubled.

Since the arrival of Mrs. Noble, Admiral Leighton, from his vantage point next door in Ararat Cottage, had noticed that Miss Nuttel and her guest were spending longer than usual in the pumping, carrying, and pouring of well water on Lilikot's lawn, fruit bushes, and vegetable patch. He also noticed that the flower beds had rather less attention than they might in normal circumstances have expected—but it was none of his business, and he said nothing. He wondered, however, if Mrs. Blaine had noticed. He suspected she might well have done. Mrs. Blaine was, he knew, particularly fond of flowers, and the retired sea dog couldn't help calculating that the amount of water poured on the flower beds was decreasing daily in direct proportion to the length of Mrs. Noble's stay.

"Women," observed the Buzzard in a murmur to his bees; and the bees, happy now that they had swarmed and been given new accommodation, murmured back at him.

Ada Noble seemed a most unlikely source of discord in what had hitherto been a happy home. Yes, the Nuts had had their squabbles: what dwellers under the same roof did not? Mrs. Blaine was given to headaches and sulks and hot flashes of temper that had earned her the nickname of the Hot Cross Bun. Miss Nuttel's habitually abbreviating tongue could wax cruelly sarcastic if she found herself provoked. Admiral Leighton thought it a pity that one or other of the original pair couldn't relieve her feelings by a damn good curse or by throwing something, but it was too hot to throw things—women had no eye for throwing anyway—and it took a man with naval experience to know the right sort of oath, which he was da-dashed if he was going to teach 'em. But it was no wonder Mrs. Blaine had spent so much of the past few weeks indoors with, he'd heard people in the post office saying, a headache.

"Ought to see a doctor if this goes on," muttered the admiral, who knew very well why seeing a doctor would make no difference. He couldn't abide a sulky woman. His sister Bernice hadn't subjected him to moods and tantrums when they were living together: if she had she'd be a spinster still, instead of married to her Brylcreem Boy widower. "Ha! The Air Force," said Admiral Leighton as he watched the bees bumble their unaerodynamic way from the hive to the flowers and back again. "What do *they* know about flying?"

He'd heard rumours that the absent Noble husband was a serviceman of some sort, although if other rumours were true—the admiral tried not to listen, but the post-office door was always open in this hot weather, and the women were so used to clacking together they often said more than they ought when a nonclacker appeared on the scene—he could not (the admiral thought) be a navy man. The Royal Navy might drink, but it did not mistreat its wives and sweethearts. Was not one of the traditional wardroom toasts to those very ladies?

"Seems like a lady," the admiral told his bees, who did not contradict him. "Decent about that hat. Unlike some. Really must remember to do something about it," he added. Mrs. Noble had met with more of his approval than her bee-hysterical hostesses, appearing to be indeed the soul of tact, discretion, and modest, not overfriendly, friendliness. What she was like within the four walls of Lilikot he had no idea, but when she saw her neighbour over the fence, she would nod and greet him cheerily. When she met him in The Street or in the shops, she would pass the time of day without pushing her company upon him, crusty old bachelor that he was. She was forever taking herself off on bus tours out of her hostesses' way and bringing back—he'd seen her himself—little treats, she called them, to tempt a failing Nutty appetite when Mrs. Blaine was trapped indoors with her head and Miss Nuttel was too busy in the garden to take time out on Bunny's ailing behalf.

"Almost too good to be true," concluded the admiral. If Miss Nuttel had heard him she would have voiced another sentiment entirely.

The strain was beginning to tell on Ada, too. Algernon might have been a drinker and—the Noble jaw clenched in reminiscence—inclined to violence, but at least once it was over for the moment it was—well—over. His temper flared up and fell down like a rocket, but if she kept her wits about her, which she did, she knew at least when the touchpaper had been lit. It wasn't easy to gauge what might happen next in such an atmosphere of simmering irritation; there was the perpetual risk of eruption any minute into a very nasty emotional storm—and it was strange. She didn't remember that Norah, as a child, had been so . . . difficult. She wondered how Erica put up with her—until she had to wonder, when that sarcastic tongue snapped and snarled, how poor Norah could put up with Miss Nuttel.

Only in moments of abstraction, soon dismissed, did it occur to Ada that it might be her fault the two friends were agreeing less and less easily than they once had. Her subconscious would not allow her to accept any of the blame for the growing rift in the Lilikot lute: Ada had decided there would be far worse places than Plummergen to settle once her matrimonial problems were resolved, and where else in the village but Lilikot could she think of making her home? To begin with, anyway. Norah was always saying that blood was thicker than water. Ada did not realise how much less often her cousin said this than she had a fortnight ago: she was sure Norah would be mortally offended if Cousin Ada went and lived in another house—even supposing another house came on the market at the right time and price, which seemed unlikely, to judge from the checks she had made in estate agents' windows during her frequent bus trips. Of course, there was always the chance she might marry again, but—

Ada dismissed Admiral Leighton firmly from her thoughts. Plenty of time for all that later, once Algernon was—well—settled, if he ever was, which sometimes she felt was an impossibility. The last telephone conversation had been bad-tempered, to say the least, when she refused to tell him where she was and said her solicitor would handle everything in the future—but then she had to make allowances, even for Algernon. It was hot in London, she was sure: far worse than Plummergen, which was quite hot enough. She blamed the heat for everyone's moods. Once there came a nice cool spell things would become easier again, she was sure; and in the meantime, while she remained at Lilikot, it was up to her to make things easier where and when she could.

Ada Noble strolled into the George and Dragon just before the hour when the dining room began to fill for lunch.

"Is there a table free?" she enquired of Doris, who had long since given up all hope of Maureen's achieving a polished surface on the upstairs oak and had donned her headwaitress outfit under muted but significant protest. Her feet were giving her gyp in this heat. She would have loved the chance to sit down behind the desk in Reception and simply check people in and out—but Charley Mountfitchet relied on Doris, and she wasn't going to let him down while he was in the kitchen, struggling with the cooker.

"A table?" Doris achieved a smile even as she rubbed one aching instep against the other. "Of course there is, with most of the guests out and about on such a lovely day—and then we'd always find room for a friend, Mrs. Noble."

Ada's heart leaped within her. *A friend!* Why, it was the very next thing to being a local! "Then—a table for one, please, Doris." She produced the Christian name with pride. "And—could I have a drink first?"

Doris looked at her for a moment. Then, slowly, a grin manifested itself upon her honest features. "I daresay you need one," she said slowly. "And would you like to see the menu—or will you have a nice plain steak for your dinner?" She paused to read the expression on Ada's face. "Or," she went on, "do you fancy a mushroom omelette?"

She was still grinning. An answering grin lightened the face of Ada Noble. "Oh, yes," she whispered ecstatically. "Steak! But . . ."

"But not by itself," supplied Doris promptly. "Salad, of course, on a day like this." She took care to ignore Ada's neatly furled umbrella. Nobody thought anything of Miss Seeton's carrying a brolly with her in all weathers, and she supposed Mrs. Noble ought to be permitted the same liberty if, as seemed probable, she was to make her home in Plummergen. "With a few onions," Doris went on. "Fried crispy brown and sweet in the fat." She paused, watching Ada lick her lips. "And a bit of liver—two or three rashers of bacon—some sausages, maybe . . ."

"Oh!" cried Ada. "Oh, yes, please!" Then she blushed.

"You—you won't tell my cousin or Miss Nuttel, will you?" she begged. "I should hate them to think—that is, they've been so very—so very hospitable, but it *has* been something of a strain. . . ."

"I can imagine," said Doris, who could. She ran her right forefinger in a slicing motion across her throat and winked. "Not a word," she promised, "to a soul, Mrs. Noble. Not if they was to send in a whole team of wild horses."

"Thank you," whispered Ada, and winked back.

Ushering the way into the dining room, Doris stopped so suddenly that Ada almost bumped into her. "Oh, dear." The waitress greeted the man at the only occupied table. "Oh, dear, I'm sorry, Mr. Folland, but I didn't think to see you eating in today. You're usually out and about by now."

"It took far longer than I expected to make my telephone call," returned Benjamin with more than a hint of waspishness. "Every time the pips went—"

He broke off as Ada's bulk emerged from the shadow cast by the slighter form of Doris. "Oh, well," he muttered, and tried to sound philosophical. "I *suppose* it couldn't be helped—but I really can't afford to waste any more time today." This warning was issued, no doubt, in case Doris should plan to sit with her feet up doing nothing for the rest of the afternoon. "The menu, please, and quickly," he said. "How soon will lunch be ready?"

Doris thought of Maureen upstairs and of Charley alone in the kitchen. "It all depends what you'd like," she said, pointing Ada in the vague direction of a table as she fished a pad and pencil from her apron pocket. "Mrs. Noble's having liver and bacon and a nice thick steak with—oh. Oh, dear, I'm sorry, Mrs. Noble." If it wasn't bad enough to have made the poor man stand for hours feeding coins into a telephone box, now she'd gone and let slip—

"I'm sorry, Mrs. Noble," said Doris, and blushed.

"No harm done," said Ada cheerfully as she settled herself at the table next to his. "It's Mr. Folland, isn't it? The gentleman from the wheelchair people? Well, I'd trust anyone who works for charity quite as much as I'd trust myself. You won't spill the—the b-beans, will you?''

''Er—no,'' said Benjamin, puzzled by the quick exchange of looks between Ada and Doris. Mr. Folland had only once shopped in the post office and hadn't heard the gossips. He had no idea that even the most oblique reference to a vegetarian lifestyle would invariably arouse Plummergen's mirth. ''No,'' he said. ''But as for liver and bacon and steak—on a hot day like this . . .''

He was less circumspect than Doris in the matter of the Noble umbrella. He stared at it for a moment or two as it hung on the back of a chair and then reiterated: ''On a hot day like this,'' and shook his head. ''I'll have a ham salad, thank you, with two hard-boiled eggs and some grated cheese. Steak,'' he added under his breath as Doris bustled through the swing doors into the kitchen. ''Steak!''

''It takes all sorts, Mr. Folland,'' Ada told him as he sat and stared at her again. She was feeling perkier by the minute now that she was out of the sun, and someone new to talk to was always interesting. ''I've never met anyone from a charity before,'' she said chattily. ''Apart from people at the door selling flags, that is, or in the street with collecting tins. Do tell me how your particular end of the business works!''

Mr. Folland was more relieved than he could say when the advent of his ham salad and Ada's steak silenced her for a while. She was brimming over with questions that courtesy made him answer—but courtesy required also that neither party should speak with a mouth even partly full of food, and while salad could be eaten cold, steak most emphatically should not. Had Benjamin—who had never seen the cousins together—realised that Ada Noble was a blood relation of the thirteen-years resident Mrs. Blaine, he would not have been surprised in the least that the plump woman at the neighbouring table was proving herself as expert in the information-and-surmising stakes as anyone in the village, although she had been there no more than a matter of days.

Benjamin bolted his last mouthful of egg and lettuce, pushed the chewy bits of ham to the edge of his plate, and hurried from the dining room before Doris could return to offer him sweet or coffee, leaving Ada to revel in meat-juice gravy and the rich dark redness of a fillet steak, medium-rare, and the promise of pudding—with cream—still to come.

CHAPTER 12

The cooking pans were rinsed, waiting with the plates and cutlery in the dishwasher for Lady Colveden to add the last few items and switch on. "They'll be here in a couple of hours," she said, glancing at the kitchen clock. "Nigel, do hurry up with your coffee."

"Are you trying to give me indigestion?" Nigel's head appeared through the hatch in the wake of his arm and hand, the latter brandishing an empty cup precariously on its saucer. "Catch!"

"Nigel," said her ladyship with a frown.

Nigel grinned as she took the cup and saucer from him and put them in the machine. "Be fair, Mother darling," he said. "Suppose I *had* thrown it and you'd dropped it— would it have mattered? It's hardly a family heirloom. We're saving the Spode for old Fleabag, aren't we?"

"Nigel," said her ladyship again.

"For Jean-Louis, Comte de Balivernes," amended the unrepentant Nigel. "And his daughter, Mademoiselle Louise," he added, watching his mother's expression.

Her ladyship's plans had been laid with more than usual skill. She ignored him to frown again. "I can't help wondering," she said slowly, "whether your father was right to insist they stay here."

"What? Ugh." Nigel's head had shot up in surprise and

connected painfully with the top of the hatch. "That hurt." He retreated into the dining room, where his mother found him rubbing his scalp and muttering.

"You'll live," she told him cheerfully as she began to rummage in the sideboard for the largest tablecloth and assorted decorative finery. "But just in case you don't, my son, shouldn't you be out in the fields now—making up for all the time we'll have to lose at your funeral?"

Nigel stared. "That bump's making me hallucinate," he said. "If you can have a hallucination of the ears, that is. I could have sworn I heard you having second thoughts about asking our visitors to—well—visit."

"I didn't say that," said his mother. "Or maybe I did," she amended as Nigel tapped his forehead with his finger and rolled his eyes. "What I meant was that perhaps we really should have fallen in with Jean-Louis' original suggestion that they should stay at the George, rather than making so much fuss about their coming to the hall."

"But—good heavens, we're hardly short of space here," protested Nigel. "It's not as if they'd be in sleeping bags on the drawing-room floor, is it? Why shouldn't they be allowed under the same roof as us? Is Jean-Louis some kind of secret axe maniac liable to murder us all in our beds? Because if he is, I call it a bit thick to send him off to the George to massacre everyone there instead. The war has a lot to answer for, if you ask me."

"Nobody did," said Lady Colveden crossly. "Don't be silly, Nigel, and try to use your imagination. How do you suppose Jean-Louis knew anything about the George in the first place?"

Nigel shrugged. "Haven't the foggiest. You told him?"

"Miss Seeton told him," said her ladyship in triumph. "But if you breathe one word, Nigel—"

Nigel rocked back on his heels and gaped at his mother. "Miss Seeton told him? You don't mean—"

"Miss Seeton," said Lady Colveden with dignity, "shares an interest in art with Jean-Louis, among other things. I know they found a great deal to talk about during our tour of the château—and afterwards. He told me on the phone how they had discussed the curious coincidence that his wartime friend—your father, Nigel—should share the name of the village's only hotel, which is a short walk from this house and *just across the road from where she lives.*"

"I was right!" Nigel stifled a guffaw that would have had the lustres ringing in the chandelier. "You *are* trying to matchmake, Mother—and talk about using my imagination— I'm trying to imagine Miss Seeton as a French countess!"

This time the guffaw could not be stifled. The chandelier danced and rang on its triple chain above his head. . . .

Nigel was so busy laughing he completely missed the smile of satisfaction that curved his mother's lips. Her son, she knew, would be so preoccupied with the romance (or otherwise) between the Comte de Balivernes and Miss Emily Seeton that Mademoiselle Louise, the lovely girl in the photograph, was going to hit him like the proverbial ton of bricks. Lady Colveden's smile grew broader. Louise, even if her mother had been a Scot, had been raised in France. The French thought in metric units. *Like the proverbial kilogramme of bricks,* she amended silently as she listened to Nigel's laughter.

Events continued to fall out according to Lady Colveden's grand design. She had dismissed Sir George straight after lunch with orders to shave, a task that took him twice as long as normal with his wrist in bandages. Nigel's suggestion that his father might care to grow a beard for the nonce was sternly suppressed.

"You should have taken more care this morning, George," said the wife of the baronet's bosom. "I can accept whiskers in an emergency—if you're extra busy on the farm, for instance. But a visitor you haven't seen for thirty years is not an emergency."

"And his daughter," put in Nigel as his father passed a rueful hand across his chin.

Sir George brightened. "Pretty girl," he said. "You're right, Meg. Can't beat the good old cutthroat. An electric razor's not the same. I'll give it another buzz."

"Are you sure you wouldn't like me—" began Nigel, and was answered with a horrified groan. He wasn't surprised. He had made the offer before and hadn't expected to have it accepted this time, either. Sir George had made very plain his views on letting his son and heir, a safety-razor man, anywhere near the jugular vein of his sire with a blade in whose use he was not expert.

"Nigel, there's no need for you to wait for your father to come down," said her ladyship now, counting napkins with an abstracted air. "I'm surprised Len hasn't come looking for you. It's not like you to leave him with all the work."

Nigel was stung that his mother felt him to be imposing on the young farm manager's good nature. "I'm going," he said quickly. "I'm going—but I just wanted to check you were happy about driving to Dover."

"Perhaps you should send out a search party if I'm not back by midnight," said Lady Colveden. "Thirty-five miles across country in bright sunshine—I can understand that you'd be worried about my going so far with only a crippled husband to protect me from the wolves—"

"Wild boar, you mean," interposed Nigel, grinning.

Her ladyship looked up from the damask napery. "Haven't they recaptured them all yet?"

Nigel shook his head. "Not according to the gossip at Young Farmers the other night. If you ask me, those beasts are on the other side of the fence for good. We'll have our own local colony once they start breeding."

"They're very shy, aren't they?" Lady Colveden giggled. "You know what I mean. But I remember the *Beacon* interview with the farmer when he was starting up, and as long as you leave them alone they'll do their best to leave *you*—and talking of leaving, Nigel . . ."

"I'm going," said Nigel again, this time with a little more conviction. He had reached the dining-room door, which was a move in the right direction. "Well—if you're sure you can manage . . ."

"Nigel, please!" His mother allowed exasperation to enter her voice. "Apart from anything else, you have no idea what he—what either of them—looks like."

"She's a pretty girl with dark hair, in her twenties," said Nigel promptly.

"I suppose she is," replied her ladyship with a marked lack of interest. "But—"

"And she'll be with her father, who by inference is a bloke about the same age as Dad, and you said he was tall. They won't be too difficult to find."

"You're right," said his mother. "They won't. Your father and I will find them very easily, thank you."

"I could stand there with a placard saying 'Colveden,' " said Nigel, but caught his mother's eye and ducked out of the door before she could scold him again about slackness.

When Lady Colveden was sure her son was safely out of the way, she chuckled to herself. She was still chuckling when her husband trotted down the stairs with his newly razored chin.

"How's that?" he enquired.

"Much better," said her ladyship after a cursory glance. Sir George favoured his wife with a shrewd look. "Wasn't too bad in the first place, m'dear. Own up. Trying to get me out of the way, weren't you?"

Wide eyes turned, all injured innocence, to meet a knowing twinkle. "I have no idea what you mean," said Lady Colveden, on her dignity. "It's time we were going. You know I'm not keen on driving round and round car parks looking for a space at the last minute."

"Know a sight more than that," said Sir George, but the remark was ignored. "Ah, well." He sighed as they prepared to leave the house. "Boy would've cut a fine figure in the MG," he observed to nobody in particular as his wife unlocked the little Hillman, her dislike of driving the larger station wagon—luggage space notwithstanding—being well

known. "Red. Much more . . . dashing than blue," said Sir
George, musing on his Galahad son.

"George," protested Lady Colveden.

It was a very faint protest.

Nigel was expecting them back by teatime.

"It's a beautiful afternoon," said Lady Colveden, once
the greetings and introductions were over and the Hillman,
with four adults and two weekend bags inside, was making
its way from the ferry terminal. "As you've both survived
the crossing so well, would you like a quick tour before we
go back to Plummergen? George and I would love to show
you some of our adopted countryside at its best—just in case
it rains again tomorrow. We had a fearful storm the other
night, didn't we, George?"

"Pretty bad," said Sir George. "Flattened half the harvest." Meg—give her her due—was right. Never knew
when a storm like that might blow up again, not that anything of the sort was forecast for the weekend, as she knew
very well. Tour of the countryside, indeed. Still—no harm
in humouring her. Nothing wrong in arriving a little later
than expected. No harm making him wait to meet the girl.
Pretty girl. Lovely eyes. Smile like her father's . . .

"I believe," said Jean-Louis, "that we in Pas de Calais
had the remnants of this storm of yours ourselves. It was a
welcome home my daughter will not in a hurry forget—will
you, Louise?"

The merry laugh of Mademoiselle de Balivernes rippled
round the little car. "At first," she said, "I think it is Papa
arranging a display of fireworks in my honour, but a long
way off, only I was wrong." She shivered dramatically.
"Oh, how wrong! For as it comes—came—closer with such
noise and banging—and the rain, so heavy—I knew it was
more than even my clever father could achieve."

"Congratulations," said Sir George, nudging his friend in
the ribs. "Your daughter's a splendid girl. Does you proud.

I'd like to hear either of our two pay either of us a compliment to our faces."

"Ah, your children," said the count. "We shall not, I think, meet Julia on this occasion—but your son?"

"Nigel," said Lady Colveden, negotiating a bend in the road. "Oh, yes, you'll see him, but of course it's one of our busy times on the farm. Miss Seeton—you remember our friend the artist—has made some wonderful sketches of haystacks and things, and everyone working."

"But, yes, I remember Miss Seeton," said M. le Comte de Balivernes in a voice that made his daughter, in the front seat, stifle a giggle. "I told you, *ma chère* Meg, that I never forget a face, and I look forward to renewing our acquaintance. We may talk of the progress that has been made on the Monet garden, among other matters. That storm of which we spoke filled more of the lake than could a dozen of bulldozers in the same time."

Lady Colveden briefly regretted that Miss Seeton, who was no actress, had already promised to take tea that afternoon with Miss Cecelia Wicks. "We thought we might invite her to tea tomorrow," she said aloud. "Or supper, perhaps, and we could make an occasion out of it. Supper tonight is rather a plain affair, I'm afraid. We had no idea what the weather would be like, or—"

"Don't," begged Sir George, who, despite the infallible nature of the cognac cure, had no wish to be reminded of the recent occasion when that cure had been required.

"This is Shakespeare Cliff," said Lady Colveden as the Hillman purred along the road out of Dover. "The Channel Tunnel entrance is here, where they're having the final of the great bulldozer race on Saturday. Nigel's one of the team captains," she added casually. "He'll give himself that much time off work, but of course it means he has to work twice as hard beforehand to justify not being there for a whole afternoon."

"Conscientious," said Sir George proudly.

"An admirable example," agreed Jean-Louis politely.

"Nigel—he would be about my age, would he not?" asked Mademoiselle Louise diffidently. "And Julia, of course," she added. "I am sorry that we will not meet with her and her husband and little girl on this visit."

Lady Colveden made the right noises in reply, but inside she was one huge smile.

Her ladyship drove on. She showed her passengers the Martello Tower at Folkestone (Jean-Louis apologised for Napoléon; Lady Colveden said things could have been worse) and explained the significance of the Cinque Ports as they reached Hythe.

"Skulls," said Sir George with a dry chuckle, waving towards the ancient church on the hill. "Thousands of 'em, in the crypt. Thighbones, too."

"Another day, perhaps," said Lady Colveden as the Balivernes demanded an explanation and Sir George had to confess that nobody was quite sure why some twelve hundred skulls and eight thousand femurs were stacked in the basement of St. Leonard's, but grave clearance to accommodate victims of the plague was a possibility.

"Do let's think of something more cheerful," said Lady Colveden. "History is always so gloomy, that's the trouble. Saltwood Castle—back there—is where the knights who murdered Thomas à Becket had their last meeting before they killed him in front of the altar in Canterbury Cathedral. Lympne Castle—we'll pass it in a few minutes—isn't so violent, thank goodness. It's a private house now, but nowhere near as splendid as your château, Jean-Louis."

The comte uttered the deprecating denials required by courtesy, and Lady Colveden launched into her next set piece of tourist lore. "There's a windmill here," she said as they drew close to Woodchurch, "and a village green. And some wonderful stained glass, and one of the oldest brasses in the country, in the church. Would you like me to stop so that you can stretch your legs?"

They would; she did; and they did. Jean-Louis was much taken by the thirteenth-century stained glass, and wondered if it might be possible to take—not a photograph, which would be sacrilege, but a likeness in the form of a sketch or painting. Such fine workmanship; the artistic gift could be used in many ways, could it not?

"We could ask Miss Seeton tomorrow," said Lady Colveden; and once more, inside, she smiled.

There was no smile on the face of Nigel as he rushed out of the house at the sound of the Hillman's approach.

"For heaven's sake!" he cried to his mother through the open window. "Where have you been? I was starting to think the wolves really had . . ."

He stumbled to a halt. Lady Colveden had leaned back in the driver's seat to close her eyes after the strain of the journey. Beside her in the passenger seat Louise—as one does if a stranger draws near—leaned forward and slightly to the side for a closer look.

Their eyes met.

There was silence.

"Hello," croaked Nigel after an eternity. "I mean—*bonjour,* Louise."

"*Bonjour,* Nigel," said Mademoiselle de Balivernes.

"Let's all have a cup of tea, shall we?" Lady Colveden bustled everyone from the car into the house and left her son to bring the bags, asking him if he'd thought to put the kettle on because he might have known they'd all be thirsty after the drive.

Her ladyship observed with interest that, though Sir George and the count obeyed orders and were in the sitting room enjoying the summer perfumes wafting through the open windows, Louise had somehow contrived to evade the bustle and was even now arguing with Nigel over which of them would carry the smaller bag up the stairs.

"Très bon," murmured Lady Colveden to herself. And she smiled the widest smile of the day.

After tea Jean-Louis confessed that his legs were still in need of a little stretch. Was he correct in his thought that English licensing laws did not permit, as they did in Scotland and France, the all-day opening of *les hôtels*? Otherwise he would have been delighted to invite his old friend Georges to one of those Drinks that were the very heart of English culture, and a game of dominoes or darts. Ah—the *hôtel* had already opened at six? Then perhaps, if *chère* Meg would excuse them, he and Georges might . . . ?

"Don't be too long," said Lady Colveden, who could hear Nigel enthusing to Louise about birdlife on the banks of the canal and the wonderful view across the marsh. Lady Colveden had a strong suspicion she would dine alone that night. "Oh, George," she added as her husband took his panama from its peg in the hall. "As you're going right past the front door you might drop in and remind Miss Seeton she's coming to tea tomorrow, as I can't remind her myself."

Providence and Martha Bloomer might almost be said to have conspired in her ladyship's innocently romantic purpose. In honour of the visit of a genuine (albeit French) aristocrat—the Colvedens, being local, didn't count—the normal domestic whirlwind in which Mrs. Bloomer operated had whirled to even greater effect the day before the visit and, to quote Nigel, had "gone and done a Maureen" and put the Rytham Hall telephone out of order. In the flurry of preparation, nobody had arranged for the repairman to call. . . .

"Miss Seeton, tea tomorrow," repeated Sir George obediently. "Right. Fine."

"Fine," echoed Jean-Louis with a bow and a smile that suggested this was an understatement.

Lady Colveden's smile was carefully contained until the pair had departed, Sir George tipping the brim of his hat in farewell and—to her ladyship's annoyance—winking at Nigel and Louise, who luckily took no notice. Her ladyship felt more strongly than ever that she would dine alone that night. . . .

They were, in the end, a party not of two but three for the typical English Drink and the cribbage Sir George had hinted his old comrade might prefer to either dominoes or darts—the third member of the party being Miss Seeton.

Miss Seeton approved of bullies no more than did the two heroes of the War, who, as they drew near her front garden, heard her making her views very clear to Tibs, the enormous, vindictive tabby from the far end of the village. Tibs had stalked the whole mile in order to take on the bakery's four felines single-pawed, when they had done nothing to harm her beyond merely existing in the same geographical area. Miss Seeton, returning rather later than the usual hour—such a pleasant afternoon—from tea with Miss Wicks, had chivvied Tibs from the slaughter with the ferrule of a well-aimed umbrella. Miss Seeton being one of the few people in Plummergen who was not afraid of Tibs, the cat was prepared to afford the former teacher as much respect as any feline, superior as the race knows itself to be, can grant a human. This meant that she did not bolt (as Chippy and the rest had bolted) at Miss Seeton's approach, but sat and listened with narrowed eyes and twitching tail to the scolding her mentor tried to deliver. The instant the voice of Sir George broke into the scolding, she flicked back her ears and was gone.

'*Mon Dieu!*'' cried Jean-Louis as the tabby shape streaked past him up The Street. ''You did not warn me, *cher Georges,* that your little village had tigers as well as wild boar!'' He turned to Miss Seeton, who greeted him with a twinkle and assured him that Tibs was no tiger but the police house cat.

''Cat?'' Sir George snorted, then begged Miss Seeton's pardon, adding that Tibs had always struck him as—well, in the presence of a lady perhaps he'd better not say.

''Perhaps, indeed,'' said the count with a smile for Miss Seeton. ''You do not appear much troubled by your encounter with the wild beast, Miss Seeton, but I know well how you brave English—ah, I beg pardon of the memory of my dear wife—you brave *British* ladies struggle to conceal your feelings. You must allow us to escort you to the *hôtel* over the way, where a glass of fine cognac will soothe you.''

"Good idea," said Sir George before Miss Seeton could demur, as he felt sure her innate modesty would urge her to do. "Come and join us, Miss Seeton. Pleasure of your company. Intelligent conversation. Fleabag here'll have had quite enough of us Colvedens by the time he goes."

The comte smiled again with a roguish air that would have captivated a lesser woman. Even Miss Seeton found herself not immune to his undoubted charm. "But, of course, *mon vieux,*" said Jean-Louis de Balivernes. "Bored, as you say, to distraction. Was it not for such reasons that the excellent Meg has invited Miss Seeton to tea tomorrow?"

"Leaven for the lump," said Sir George with a chuckle for Miss Seeton's startled expression. "Dashed good thing, too—but always a pleasure, of course," he added quickly.

Miss Seeton knew what he meant and smiled. "It will indeed be a pleasure," she said warmly, before realising that this might be considered as ambiguous as Sir George's quick addition. She blushed. "I could," she offered, "bring my sketchbook, if you would be interested, monsieur, to see my recollections—interpretations—of Monet's garden. . . ." She paused and frowned. There was that *other* "interpretation"—her copy of Martha's postcard—that had turned out—well—not at all as she had expected. . . .

"Cheer up. m'dear." Sir George's tone was more urgent than encouraging. "Cheer up," He hadn't missed Miss Seeton's frown, which (though fleeting, for at his command she forced a smile) had given him an uncomfortable feeling. The little woman had looked that way more than once before, usually when Delphick had come charging down from the Yard to get her in one of her confounded Drawing moods—after which there was, all too often, hell—dash it—the deuce to pay. Bother Meg and her matchmaking. He should never have reminded Miss Seeton about the sketchbook. But she was smiling now, chatting away with old Fleabag as if there was nothing wrong. And maybe there was. Now it was his

turn to frown. Or wasn't. Dash it—*he* knew what he meant.
He knew what Miss Seeton's Drawing meant, too.

Trouble.

By the time Sir George surfaced from the depths of his uneasy musings, Miss Seeton had accepted the kind invitation
of Monsieur le Comte, although she had parlayed the brandy
he offered into a small glass of dry sherry.

"And I," said the count, offering Miss Seeton his arm,
"shall drink beer. English hops—ah, there is nothing in the
world to equal their richness and refreshment on a hot day,
although when we are in Scotland with the family of my
dear wife, I drink whisky, to keep out the cold."

Miss Seeton remarked that she had some acquaintances in
Scotland: the MacSporrans, Lord and Lady Glenclachan.
Were they by any chance friends of Monsieur de Balivernes?
They had a delightful baby daughter, Marguerite. She looked
forward to meeting the count's daughter Louise. . . .

Sir George, completely forgotten by his friends, strolled
behind them in the direction of the pub and reflected that
his wife might not have been so wrong, after all.

After they were settled at the table with their drinks, a
pack of cards, and the board, Jean-Louis insisted that unless
Miss Seeton aided him in the correct selection for playing
and discarding, he would never, but never, fathom the mysteries of cribbage. To peg as they played a score of fifteen
or thirty-one he could understand. With pairs he had no
problem. But "one for his nob" and "two for his heels"?
"Pairs royal"?

"Don't forget 'the lurch,' " warned Sir George, enjoying
himself immensely. "Scoring sixty-one before the other
chap reaches thirty-one," he explained as the comte threw
up his hands in a Gallic gesture of despair, and Miss Seeton
shook her head in gentle reproof at the mischievous baronet.

"This would," said Jean-Louis once play had begun, with
all of them making merry over Sir George's attempts to keep

the score left-handed, "be the origin of your expressive term 'pegged out,' perhaps?"

Sir George huffed through his moustache and admitted that he really couldn't say.

"I believe," said Miss Seeton, "that it is. And, as you say, so expressive a term for the very end of one's life."

"One may be restored to life by a stiff peg of whisky," said Jean-Louis, producing the colloquialism with pride.

"Nothing like scotch when you're feeling a peg too low," offered Sir George with a twinkle for Miss Seeton. "Come now, schoolma'am—how about that one?"

Miss Seeton, after a moment, twinkled back at him. "The reference," she said, "is, I believe, to the drinking habits of our Saxon ancestors, and St. Dunstan's attempts to deflect argument as to the amount any one drinker might drink from a shared bowl."

"God bless my soul," said Sir George. "Dashed clever, Miss Seeton—eh, Fleabag? All that reading, I suppose."

Jean-Louis inclined his head in acknowledgement of Miss Seeton's cleverness. Miss Seeton blushed as she murmured that really, when one was retired and had the time to find so many interesting books in the library . . .

"St. Dunstan," said the comte quickly, sensing his partner's unease at having attention focused upon her modest self. "He is not your patron saint, of course, but famous. An archbishop, was he not?"

"Of Canterbury," confirmed Miss Seeton as it was Sir George's turn to throw up his hands in a gesture of despair. Jean-Louis was all smiling encouragement. "The patron saint of goldsmiths," went on Miss Seeton, duly encouraged, "as opposed to blacksmiths, who have St. Clement— which is odd, since it is St. Dunstan who is said to have tethered the devil to the wall of his forge and nailed a horseshoe to his foot. And," she added as the count chuckled his appreciation of the legend, "to have seized his nose in red-hot pincers and made him promise never to tempt him again."

"Must have made Old Scratch's eyes water," said Sir George. "That why he's the Blind Home chap, Miss Seeton? St. Dunstan, I mean, not the devil," he added for the benefit of Jean-Louis. "Sorry, Fleabag. Can't expect a Frenchman to know about English charities."

Miss Seeton shifted restlessly on her chair. Jean-Louis was at once contrite. "We interrupt the game!" he cried in deference to Miss Seeton's feelings. "Silence, my friends, until the first of us has pegged out!"

The trio had acquired an interested and kindly audience by the time Sir George, who had done his best to cheat on his friend's behalf, was obliged to count the red peg, which was his, past the last eight holes to score nine and win the match. "Bad luck, old chap," he said to the white-pegged loser. "When it was your crib, too. Turn the cards and let's see if you'd have thrashed me if you'd gone first."

A clamour of voices from those who had been peering over the count's shoulder assured Sir George that he would indeed have been thrashed. Miss Seeton, consulted by the baronet with a lift of the eyebrow, nodded and smiled.

"It is, then, a matter of redeeming my honour," said the Frenchman at once. "But after a long day's travelling, it is too much to ask of any man that he should rise at dawn to fight a duel. We shall play another game, *cher Georges,* and this time it is I who will buy the drinks."

"Nonsense, m'dear fellow." Sir George had leaped up as the count was speaking. "I mean—dash it, you're my guest. Miss Seeton, another sherry? Same again for you, Fleabag?"

Jean-Louis began a spirited speech about the reciprocal duties of host and guest, but Sir George vanished into the crowd before he had uttered more than a dozen syllables. The count watched him go, and his lips curved in a smile that to Miss Seeton's knowledgeable eye was one of reminiscence. Like Lady Colveden, she couldn't help wondering how the paths of Major-General Sir George and Jean-Louis, hero of the Resistance, had first crossed: but again like Lady Colveden, she knew there were some subjects of conversation it was better, even after thirty years, to leave alone.

The smile faded. The face of the comte registered . . . surprise, thought Miss Seeton. Was Sir George buying the wrong drinks? Had he dropped the tray? Carrying it one-handed, resting on the crook of his sprained arm, was not easy—but she had heard no crash of broken glass, and there were enough people in the bar to offer assistance should he appear in need of it. Although it might look a little discourteous, she ventured a quick peek over her shoulder . . . to see Mrs. Raughton and Mr. Folland, who seemed to have come in together, being handed by Charley Mountfitchet those folded sheets of card that said *Menu* to all who saw them.

Miss Seeton remembered Lady Colveden, and the delicious supper she was sure to have prepared for her visitors, and how at least one of those visitors (Nigel's whereabouts with Louise remained unknown) was a quarter of a mile away from the house with (obviously) no thought of being back on time—and with her ladyship's husband . . . inciting (Miss Seeton decided was the apposite term) that visitor to the delay. She had to smile, even though she felt a little guilty about her part in what Nigel would no doubt call the rebellion. Dear Lady Colveden was always so understanding. But perhaps the count was—well—hungry? And politeness made him say nothing about it—and Sir George had bought another round of drinks—and perhaps she should plead a headache, which would be dishonest but in a good cause, the lesser of the two evils of blatant discourtesy and mild deception. . . .

Or perhaps she should just accept that all three of them were having a good time together and—well—Lady Colveden was a very understanding woman.

Miss Seeton smiled.

Miss Seeton blinked as the count, who was still looking thoughtful, jumped to his feet.

"Crisps," announced Sir George as Jean-Louis reached up for the elbow-resting tray before it should slip from the bandaged arm. "And those stick things with Marmite on 'em, and cheesy biscuits. Thought you might like to try some English pub food with your drink, Fleabag.''

"Ah, well," said Miss Seeton under her breath. Despite her previous musings, she did feel a little sorry for Lady Colveden, understanding though Sir George's wife—Nigel's mother—undoubtedly was. Miss Seeton had a very strong suspicion that her ladyship would dine alone that night.

Miss Seeton was absolutely right.

CHAPTER 13

Monsieur le Comte de Balivernes and his daughter crossed the Channel by ferry, and—the weather having been kind—had enjoyed their crossing.

The day after that crossing the weather was rather less than kind, although its unkindness did not matter to Chief Superintendent Delphick of Scotland Yard. The Oracle was safely out of reach of the wind-whipped waves, coming to the end of a guided tour of the Channel Tunnel dig.

Delphick's personal vanity made him secretly relieved that Sergeant Ranger was, for once, not with him. While always scrupulous in obeying the law, the Oracle couldn't help but wish the hard hat he sported as required by health and safety legislation had been a less virulent shade of orange. Bob (the Oracular sense suspected) would in normal circumstances have made discreetly merry over the discomfiture of his superior for some weeks had he observed him under the tunnel's fluorescent lighting.

Thank goodness the circumstances weren't normal, as Sir Hubert Everleigh had known. (Could there be anyone in Scotland Yard who didn't?) Bob was taking a long overdue day off to drive Anne to visit her parents in Plummergen. He had gravely explained that he didn't care to let her drive herself just now, despite her repeated insistence (conveyed in desperation to Delphick, who confessed himself unable to help) that she was flourishing in the early stages of what the expectant first-time father would keep calling a delicate state of health. Bob's boss guessed, from the daily bulletins, that the poor girl—her opinion as a trained nurse notwithstanding—was being cosseted to distraction. A change of scene would do the pair of them good.

". . . cubic yards of spoil an hour," his escort concluded at his side. "Which is a considerable achievement, eh?"

Delphick, musing on christening mugs and drinks all round and a vision of Bob with a fat cigar, hid his dismay at having allowed his attention to wander quite so far. The tunnel builders had proved, very early in the visit, to have covered (as reported the previous week after his own tour by Superintendent Brinton) to the highest degree of efficiency every conceivable security eventuality, with the regrettable result that the Oracle had functioned for most of the time on automatic pilot, relying on his trained eye to notice anything unsafe or untoward. Which it hadn't. For which he was thankful—and, now, a little embarrassed.

He took his tone from the note of triumph in the other man's voice. "Remarkable, if I may venture to correct you," he said politely. "As is the whole project, in fact." He chuckled. "I believe I've run out of adjectives—as everyone who has seen all this," he said with a sweeping gesture, "must have told you many times before."

"It's the sheer bloody scale of the thing," agreed another of the little group who had been deployed to escort the Scotland Yarder and explain whatever he wanted to know. "When people have talked about something like this for hundreds of years, to see the reality—so far beyond what anybody ever dreamed could be possible. . . ."

He laughed and gestured with as much sweep and force as Delphick. "Run out of words myself," he said, subsiding.

The little group of men chuckled in sympathy. The sound echoed strangely around the huge, high hollow of the otherwise silent dig—Delphick had asked that his tour (Brinton having reported being almost deafened by noise) should take place when no machinery or plant was running, save that essential for the support of life so far underground. Eager to do all they could to accommodate the Yard's security expert but anxious to keep working, the Consortium had agreed; and they cut it rather fine, for the last "dump" of the day had emerged in a relay of waggons from the Chunnel mouth at the very instant Delphick was walking into it. As he and his companions walked on, the lights buzzed, the fans hummed, the drainage pumps gurgled; and there was no other sound save that of voices, and the footsteps of the men in their steel-capped boots grating on the concrete floor, occasionally chinking as they caught against the metal rail of the track down which the mighty tunnelling mole, chewing its forward way through Channel chalk, sent back down its hollow middle the waggon loads of spoil and rubble to the entrance for disposal.

"I believe," said Delphick, who (thanks to Bob) knew very well but thought he should make conversation, "that you'll be giving the general public a few lessons in spoil disposal in a day or two's time, and also saving yourselves some work—a charity race on Saturday, I understand, with bulldozers shifting tons of the stuff for you."

The head engineer snorted. "Save ourselves work? We've ended up with even more—which we can well do without, when we're losing money at the same time. First," he explained, "we'll have to stop boring, in case we run over any of the spectators when we remove the spoil—which means a whole shift twiddling their thumbs for the sake of this blasted charity. Then we've had to build six absolutely identical 'hills' of spoil, which is a damned sight easier said than done, just for the teams to shift. You can see the things when we go back outside." He sounded so bitter that Delphick kept to himself his reflection that by the time they were back outside he, for one, would have seen more than enough chalk spoil, in hills or not, to last him a lifetime.

They walked on for a while, the head engineer muttering to himself about charities and bulldozers without expecting

any response beyond a sympathetic murmur Delphick felt
duty bound to utter every few yards. And then, merci-
fully . . .

"Well, Chief Superintendent, here is the monster!" The
head engineer grinned as the party drew near the looming
metal bulk that filled the entire twenty-foot diameter of the
dig. At first sight it was no more than a gigantic mechanical
ring with an apparently hollow middle: closer observation
showed the railway track continuing from the concrete floor
outside right through to the front, where there were portholes
and gears, wheels and hydraulic jacks about which (Delphick feared) his guide was all too eager to lecture him.

"Walk through that and out of the front door and you'll
be as far under the English Channel as anyone's ever been,"
said the head engineer. "The farther off from England, eh?
And France coming nearer by the day!" He coughed. Delphick braced himself for the clearly imminent explanation.

It came. "The cutting edges—blades, if you like—are
attached to the front section of the borer," he was told.
"Which is pushed forward and rotated so that the edges cut
the rock in front. A bit like a bacon slicer, as I said," he
added, although as this was one of his set pieces, he wasn't
going to miss the chance of saying it again. "Every yard we
move forward means another twenty trucks of spoil to be
cleared—after which we stop the cutters rotating, to give the
chaps with the sections of cast-iron hoops and the concrete
grout room to get to work. Once they've reinforced the area
in front, we can move the mole forward to catch up with
the rotating section and start the process again—but we've
stopped just now for a routine inspection before we fit the
cast-iron linings, and you're going to join us on that inspection, Mr. Delphick."

Delphick, still a little guilty at having allowed his thoughts
to wander, gave no indication by his reply that he had been
told the basic methods of Chunnel excavation more than
once that day. "I feel honoured," he said courteously, "to
be permitted to join you. Seldom is anyone offered the

chance to be part, as it were, of history in the making."

The head engineer regarded his guest with a thoughtful eye. "Chief Superintendent," he said at last, "would you care to do the honours with me?"

Delphick, looking startled, after a brief moment nodded in his turn. "I confess," he said with a smile, "that I'll be as ignorant of what I'm looking at as anyone can possibly be. Rock, I fear, is rock, as far as I'm concerned, although I am always interested to watch an expert at work."

The other engineers chuckled as they shuffled the papers on their clipboards, fished out pens, hammers, and measuring instruments; and prepared to follow their leader. Delphick, with a comical grin of self-mockery, did his best to clump his boots in the regular manner and raised another friendly laugh from his companions as he was ushered through the heavy metal door in the lower front of the mole and into the bare rock "cave" of recent excavation.

It was undoubtedly interesting to watch experts at work: but as what they were doing was (despite the head engineer's explanatory monologue) of a highly technical nature, Delphick found his attention wandering again as he tried to gaze with knowledgeable eyes upon either the rock in front of him or the curved side circumference against which ladders had been propped for engineers to climb. With the click of hammers, the whir of metal tape measures, and the hum of voices in his ears, the Oracle wondered how Bob and Anne were faring in Plummergen. He thought of their adopted aunt Miss Seeton and her likely delight at the news that there would be a little grandniece or nephew in the spring. He wondered how soon this news would spread to the rest of the village, and how many of the villagers would change from knitting squares for Oxfam blankets to knitting dainty matinée jackets, bootees, and lacy shawls.

He brooded again on the hints Bob had dropped about godfathers and wondered how much he would have to spend on a christening mug, and whether (as had once happened to a colleague who never quite recovered from the shock) he would be charged by the individual letter for having the infant's name engraved. He raised despairing eyes to heaven—to the roof of the tunnel, and thence again to its forward end—as he calculated the likely cost of "Andrew Robert" compared with "Annette Roberta Emily Knight," and stifled a groan . . .

He blinked. He must be seeing things: that christening mug was preying on his mind. He hadn't even been asked yet, not outright, although he could recognise a hint as well as the next chief superintendent. . . .

He blinked again and shook his head. He looked back to the outcrop (or whatever it was called) where he had first thought he'd seen . . . Yes, it was still there. That gleam of metal in the tunnel face—the engineers were working their way up and around, but they didn't seem so bothered by the front of the thing—was *not* his imagination.

He waited for a pause in the hammering before addressing the head engineer. "Excuse me," he ventured. "Didn't you say we were several hundred feet below the surface here?"

"That's right," said the head engineer.

"And the—the blades—the business end of the drilling mole is—are—made of—a special alloy?"

"Hadfield manganese steel with tungsten carbide inserts—toughest tunnelling alloy in the world," said the head engineer proudly. "That's why we're currently advancing at eighteen inches per hour. The biggest problem, as I said, is shifting the spoil fast enough so the mole doesn't get choked inside before the blokes with the shovels can load the waggons and get them clear."

"Yes," said Delphick slowly. "I remember. Well, so far from the shore it can't be a discarded drinks can—so is that a broken piece of blade? And . . ."

Delphick had pointed to the metallic gleam in the rock of the tunnel face. The rest of his words were lost in a growing clamour as the engineers, following his direction, began scrambling down their ladders in order to carry them across for closer examination of the gleam.

"Could be mica," offered someone climbing more slowly than the rest.

"Not in chalk," scoffed someone else.

"It isn't," said the head engineer, now arrived at the gleam and with his hard hat light switched on for closer examination. "It's metal," he reported. "One more turn of the screw would have freed enough to show us . . . The rest of you, get down. Stand back below, there!"

No sooner had he issued this command than he snatched the hammer from his tool belt, leaned up and slightly back, and struck the chalk near the gleaming metal with a skilful sideways blow. He struck again, still sideways, and a few chips of chalk crumbled to the tunnel floor.

"Once more should do it," he muttered, and hefted the hammer in his hand.

"Look out!" cried Delphick and the engineers in chorus. The head engineer automatically ducked, dropping his hammer as he gripped the ladder with both hands. There came more chips of chalk—a short cascade of pebbles—and a sudden downrush of heavier rocky shards from the crack that had appeared and spread like the web of some monstrous spider from the spot where the first blow of the hammer had fallen.

Coughing and spluttering, the men below began brushing dust from themselves. The head engineer ventured to look up, though he still gripped the ladder with white-knuckled hands.

"That was uncomfortable," he observed with classic British understatement. "I didn't enjoy that at all. I'll just— oh." The *quick look* he had been about to announce himself as taking before his descent to safety became a long, hard, horrified stare. "Oh," he said again, his voice as cold and shocked and shaken as any his companions had heard. "Oh, my great good God. I don't believe this."

There was something about the way he spoke—the way he stood frozen, his eyes drawn to the metal now exposed to the harsh electric light—that made the humming air of the tunnel turn to an icy blast about the shoulders and spines of the men waiting at the foot of the ladder. The man at the top bowed his head and drew in a series of long, shuddering breaths before, with one last horrified stare at the metal, he made his way to the ground.

"Out," was all he said as everyone demanded to be told what he had seen. "Now. Move it!"

His tone did not leave room for argument. He led the way, his face set and grey, his lips pressed close together. Delphick walked at his side and walked a little faster than the rest, moving out of earshot.

"I think I need to know," he said in a low tone as a glance behind him showed that they would not be overheard. "It . . . wasn't a piece of the blade, was it?"

"It's thirty years too old to be anything of ours," said the head engineer. "I never thought I'd ever . . . and if they had drilled the one more turn I mentioned, the whole thing would have been blown to kingdom come. . . ."

Delphick shot him a quick look. "I'm beginning to guess," he said. "A—a present from Germany?"

The head engineer shuddered. "The damned thing must have misfired somehow and dropped short of the mainland and burrowed its blasted way down from the seabed as far as . . . where we found it," he concluded with a vicious jerk of his head in the direction of the offending article. "Never in my born days did I think to be that close to one of those devils unless it was defused, in a museum. But for all I know, the thing's still live—I couldn't take any risks—and that's why we're getting out and stopping work until I can talk to someone from the Imperial War Museum."

"A present from Germany," Delphick repeated sadly. He would have much preferred his guess to have been wrong.

"It's from Germany, all right," said the head engineer. "It's been waiting for us to unwrap it for more than thirty years, and now we have. A present from Germany. It was the swastika on the fuse pocket that gave the game away."

• • •

"Oh, bless him—he's driving me mad, Aunt Em." Anne was with Miss Seeton in the kitchen, helping her hostess prepare the afternoon tea. Bob was in the garden in the apple-tree shade, under strict instruction to sit still and do nothing. This negativity to include . . .

"Fussing," said Anne with a chuckle that yet had a hint of irritation in it. "He *will fuss,* although I keep saying there's no need—but you know Bob. Anyone would think no one had ever had a baby before, the way he's carrying on. I'd hoped that Dad might talk some sense into him, but he's just as bad, and all Mother can do is talk about bonnets and bootees and shawls—though I suppose," she concluded with another chuckle, "that makes a change from Oxfam squares."

Miss Seeton, waiting for the kettle to come to the boil, twinkled at her across a loaded tea-tray. "I hope you won't take it personally, Anne dear, if—if any knitted item you receive as a gift from me is—well, not. Homemade, that is—or rather," she amended in the interests of accuracy, "not made by me. Even six-inch squares, which one would suppose ought to be simply achieved by increasing at the start of the line and then decreasing again, seem to turn out sadly . . . oblong when I try them. The tension, Martha tells me—but there it is. My talents lie in other directions than fancywork, I fear."

"Of course they do," said Anne at once. "Now, if you were to offer to make some sketches of the sprog once it's safely here, Bob and I certainly wouldn't say no. Besides," she went on as Miss Seeton blushed and beamed with pleasure, "I've made a bet with myself that as soon as the news gets out—which, knowing Plummergen, was about five seconds after we arrived—every other knitter in the village will change from squares to layettes, and we'll be snowed under with fleecy garments and hurt feelings. I gather from my parents that you've all been taking this charity business *very* seriously—and I can't think six-inch squares can be much fun in large numbers." Anne laughed. "I foresee," she said cheerfully, "an outbreak of sponsored matinée jacketing, with a bonus prize for the neatest buttonholes!"

"It will all be kindly meant," said Miss Seeton. "And of—of double benefit as well, for you and Bob will end up with, as it were, the practical results of so much activity, while The Golden Brolly will have increased funds for buying wheelchairs."

"I'm not complaining," Anne hurried to assure her. "I'm going to take it as an enormous compliment if we're anything like snowed under—the more the merrier, in fact. We've decided to accept whatever we're offered with a great big Thank You and then . . ." She glanced at Miss Seeton, who was listening with interest that was more than merely polite. "Well," Anne said, "we've talked it over—and I know you won't say anything—but there are many expectant mothers who come to the clinic who aren't as lucky as I am in their families and friends." Her voice was earnest now. "And I do think luck should be shared out: charity ought to begin at home, if you like. Bob agrees with me that it will be sensible—fair—to upset *everyone* equally, by only ever bringing the baby here in clothes we've bought ourselves, or made in the immediate family—because the others will have been shared out back in Bromley." She smiled at Miss Seeton. "So please don't feel in the least guilty about not knitting anything for us, Aunt Em. We would far rather have a Raphael Ranger cherub from you to keep than a cot blanket we're never going to use."

Miss Seeton gazed at her young friend with admiration. "I think that's a perfectly splendid idea," she said. "And naturally I will say nothing to anyone—but as for cherubs, my dear, if you will excuse me, that could be why they are so anxious about you." She blushed, this time with evident embarrassment. "Dear Bob," she explained as Anne regarded her doubtfully, "is so very . . ."

"Unlike a cherub?" supplied Anne with a grin as her elderly friend mislaid the tactful phrase.

Miss Seeton blushed still more. "Large," she amended

bravely. "While you, my dear, are—well . . ."

"Not," said Anne, not even as big as her hostess, who was five-foot nothing in her stockinged toes and weighed seven stone soaking wet. "The law of averages," said Mrs. Robert Ranger, qualified nurse, "is going to have a field day with this one—but don't look so worried or you'll set Bob off again when we take the tea things out. I keep telling him there are such things as caesareans, if the worst comes to the worst, and there's no particular reason why it should. Medical science has moved on in the past century or so. This is 1974, not 1914."

"Or 1944," said Miss Seeton, seizing with relief upon the opportunity to turn the conversation. One's practical knowledge of such matters was limited—but the contrasting skeletal structures of her adopted niece and nephew, of whom she was so fond and on whose behalf she was bound, despite Anne's courageous talk of medical advances, to worry . . .

"As you say," she said firmly, "the village has been taking all this charity activity seriously indeed. One cannot help but be reminded of the recycling and make-do-and-mend of the last war: an admirable spirit then, if perhaps not quite so . . . single-minded now. Or possibly," she added, "rather more so, and not necessarily the right spirit even if the—the end results must be as favourable as the knitting of baby clothes for you and Bob."

"You mean Murreystone," said Anne. "We've been getting almost daily reports over the past fortnight. It's all in a good cause, in theory—but theory's one thing. Practice is quite another. I know the crippled children will benefit from all this competition, but honestly. When even Nigel Colveden . . . Don't you think men can be silly sometimes?"

"Certainly not," said Bob from the kitchen door. He had done his best to settle to idleness outside, and failed to manage it. Suppose Aunt Em were to put too much cake on the plates? Politeness and Anne went together like—well, like Plummergen and Murreystone didn't. She'd insist on carrying the heavy tray out to the garden—she would strain her-self—he'd better hurry to offer his services before—

"Oh," said Bob, crestfallen, as he watched Miss Seeton unfold a small trolley with rubber-tyred wheels that had been hidden in a shaded corner. "Oh—yes. Well, uh, I can see you don't need any help from me. Shall I pop outside again and, uh, keep the deck chairs warm?"

"Indeed no," Miss Seeton told him promptly. "The wheels on this trolley—although Stan has always been so clever at patching it up—have always been a little inclined to stick on uneven ground, which I fear my lawn—although please don't tell him I said so—is not. Stan, I mean. Every square inch, that is to say. Cousin Flora, you see, seldom took more than a cup of tea and a plate outside in later years, and indoors, of course, one has the wooden one. It needs a steady eye and a strong hand to guide it all the way across the lawn to the trees, which is why I generally take tea, when I have visitors, on the patio, but with the sun so bright it seemed the perfect opportunity, if dear Bob has no objection."

"Of course he hasn't," said Anne before Bob could reply. "It'll get him in practice for pushing a pram."

Bob turned proudly pink as he seized the trolley handle in his mighty grasp. "Prams are fine by me," he observed. "Prams're about my level of technology. But how about Nigel and his pals and those earthmoving monsters they're going to race up and down the Chunnel, or whatever it is you were telling us about? Potato races? Tea trolleys and prams is nothing compared to tractors and bulldozers. Now, *there's* a case where it's practice makes perfect."

"If they live so long," interposed Anne with a chuckle. "Is it true Murreystone have already tried to nobble them in the pub during a darts match?"

Miss Seeton, sighing faintly, said that she had heard something from Martha (via Stan) to this effect. She hoped that people would be—well, restrained in their response, but she rather feared . . .

"Of course you do," said Anne as the trolley bounced and jangled its dainty way across the lawn and she walked with Miss Seeton in its wake. "So do I. Remember when Murreystone set the cart horse drunk and it broke Dan Eggleden's arm just before the cricket match? That sort of thing isn't easily forgotten, Aunt Em."

"No," said Miss Seeton, who thought village rivalry historically interesting, but in modern reality rather foolish.

"Plummergen and Murreystone?" said Bob, catching the end of the conversation as the other two arrived under the apple tree. "It'll be out-and-out war," he predicted, and Miss Seeton sighed again.

CHAPTER 14

Sworn to secrecy, the public relations people went into over-drive inventing the right story to leak to the media to account for the unaccountable—the halting of the Channel Tunnel project for the second time that year. Failure on the first occasion had occurred when the original contractors ran out of money and the Chunnel Consortium stepped in with a financial rescue package. But while the dig was delayed—again!—for the foreseeable future, the reason for that delay had to be concealed. For a second failure to occur so soon after the first would be worse than disastrous to the very concept of a Channel Tunnel, no matter who was in charge of the project now.

"Better to let the public think there's a fault in the digger than that the whole damn tunnel might be riddled with holes," decreed the chairman of the Consortium when the true nature of the metal gleam at the rock face was discussed at a Restricted-Personnel Top-Security Hush-Hush No-Minutes meeting held behind firmly closed doors.

"The firm who made the machine won't like that," warned the horrified head of the PR department. "It's bad for business if we give people the impression they sold sub-standard equipment, when we know perfectly well they didn't. There's nothing wrong with the digger at all except that it's gone and unearthed a highly inconvenient Nazi souvenir—and the manufacturers can't be blamed for that."

The Consortium's legal eagle had turned pale. "They could sue for libel!" he objected, emerging from a clause-by-clause study of the government contract to see whether (a) suspension of digging due to enemy action—and this thirty years after the event!—was an acceptable reason for delay, and (b) whether such delay would be covered by the new Consortium's company insurance.

"Libel," he repeated, mopping his brow with a handkerchief but, despite the heat, more than glad the doors were shut. "Libel," he said again with a gulp. "And—they would win. They only have to let their engineers examine the thing—which they'd be perfectly within their rights to insist on doing—and if we refused them an examination, it would look more than suspicious—and then, when they found nothing wrong with it . . ."

"Perhaps," suggested the chairman, "by the time they came to examine it there might be something wrong with it."

The legal eagle turned from pale to ghastly white. His face and his handkerchief were a perfect match. "Don't," he begged, shuddering. "Don't even joke about it."

"I wasn't—" began the chairman.

"Ha, *ha*, HA!" interrupted the PR person in a burst of hearty and deafening laughter. Walls, he knew, could have ears despite the very best endeavours. Not every locked door was soundproof. . . . "Good joke, sir," he enunciated for the benefit of any industrial spies. "But perhaps . . . in bad taste, don't you think?" And he leaned under the table to kick the chairman sharply on the ankle.

"Ugh," said the chairman. "Oh. Yes. Ha, ha—but bad taste, yes. Right. So—er—what do you suggest?"

"The digger's fine," said the Eagle hurriedly as the PR person frowned. "But might some of the—the outer diggings have encountered some—some hitherto unsuspected geological anomaly that means the—the produce of the digger can't be efficiently removed for a few weeks?"

"A tricky problem with spoil-dumping," translated the PR person as the chairman looked blank. "And we believe it's more sensible to stop moving the stuff about until we've found a better way of doing it—yes, that might work. . . ."

"But what about the geological survey?" demanded the chairman, who, slow though he might be to absorb a new idea, was always eager (once such absorption had been made) to flaunt his greater understanding of affairs. "Won't the people who carried out the survey be just as likely as the digger lot to sue if we start to blame them for not telling us—our predecessors—the place was a—a seething mass of geological anomalies?"

"No," said the PR person. "They didn't use an outside firm, they used their own geologists, most of whom came to work for us after the buyout. They'll be so worried about losing their jobs a second time they won't say a word, even if the story doesn't really hold water." He caught the eye of the chairman, who was glaring like a basilisk. "Sorry," he mumbled. "Tactless. Sorry."

"There's always some high-minded fool willing to risk his job on a matter of principle," said the chairman in a voice of bitter experience. "Better make it clear anyone who doesn't like the sound of the official line can easily be made redundant."

"We can't do that," protested the Eagle, who was coming rapidly to the conclusion that he should have stuck with his student hobby of deep-sea diving and gone to work on a North Sea oil rig rather than opting for what he had innocently supposed would be safety on—or rather under—dry land. "If they weren't made redundant months ago when the survey was finished, why should we need to do it now? It's going to look bad when they all sue us for unfair dismissal."

"Relocation," said the chairman airily. "Say we'll send 'em to the Arctic if they don't behave themselves. Tell 'em we're planning a tunnel from Greenland to Iceland or somewhere—ferry routes, icebergs, that general idea."

"I suppose we could think of *something*," said the Eagle, looking hopefully at the PR person.

Who had in his turn turned pale. "You mean I'd have to sell the story *inside the company*?" he almost yelped. "But I—I don't know the first thing about the Arctic! I could never make it sound convincing!"

Fortunately for the safety of the PR person's job the chairman did not spot the flaw in this argument. He was too busy savouring his alternative proposal. "Make it equatorial Africa, then," he said. "A tunnel under some jungle full of man-eating tigers the conservation lobby won't let anyone move. Easy."

"There aren't any tigers in—" the PR person began to object, and then caught on. He hoped. "Oh, yes—jolly good, sir!" he cried. "Ha, ha, ha!"

"Ha, ha," echoed the Eagle kindly.

The chairman nodded at both of them. "Leave the details to you," he said. It was an order, not a statement of intent. "Nobody's fault—one of those things—that's the party line. Just *don't* let it come out that there's a Nazi rocket ready to go bang if the digger moves another half inch forward—which reminds me. Why hasn't the boffin's report been submitted yet? If we're going to have to call a halt to digging at the tunnel face—there must be *something* we can keep doing outside to stop rumours spreading—we'd appreciate the ghost of an idea how long it's likely to be! Time," he pointed out, "is money. It's not five minutes since the last Chunnel group gave up for financial reasons. We don't want to be the second, thank you very much."

"No," said the PR person, horrified.

"No," agreed the legal eagle, shaken.

"Right," said the chairman, reaching for the internal telephone and then hesitating. In the security-conscious absence of his secretary, he was unsure how to work it. "*You* ask," he commanded, pushing the telephone across the table towards the PR person. "Update from the engineering department—forget his name—"

"I know it," interposed the PR person brightly, but he was ignored.

"The head chap," the chairman went on. "He was there at the time—told me all about it. And I told *him* to find me some historical boffin who knows about rockets, and find him fast. Time's money, I said, and there's got to be a way of making the thing safe—soonest."

"And don't forget," his deputy reminded him quietly, "we have those charity people racing with our bulldozers at the tunnel entrance tomorrow. As you'll be there to present the prizes, we don't want anyone wandering off into the workings, thinking it's safe just because we've stopped boring for the day." And that observation, he thought, could raise more than his salary.

As the PR person obediently dialled, the chairman sighed. "Talk about suing," he said, with an eye on the legal eagle. "I would dearly love to blame the man from Scotland Yard for what's happened . . . except that I suppose if he *hadn't* spotted the blasted thing, it would have gone off while the digger was working. A nose cone full of thirty-year-old explosive is going to be unstable at the best of times," he went on, paraphrasing the preliminary verbal report presented by the head engineer. "Which," he added, raising his voice above the PR person's conversation with the telephone, "having sat around rotting under the sea after drilling miles through solid rock, you can't say it is. And then—well, never mind the immediate . . . inconvenience of it all. If that rocket had gone off, it would have been the end of the Channel Tunnel project—in our lifetimes, at least. The sooner the boffin comes up with the goods, the happier I—and the rest of the Board—*and* the shareholders will be. Right?"

"Right," said the PR person, and handed him the phone.

"I picked this down by the canal," said Ada, offering Mrs. Blaine a generous handful of greenery. "I *think* it's watercress—isn't it? Would it do for tonight's salad?" Mrs. Noble was suffering belated pangs of guilt over Tuesday's carnivorous carousal at the George and lived in dread that one or other of her hostesses would, the promises of Doris notwithstanding, get to hear about it.

Mrs. Blaine hesitated. "Down by the canal," she repeated slowly. "What do you think, Eric?"

"No," said Miss Nuttel very firmly. "Thanks, but—no, thanks, Ada. Liver fluke."

Ada blinked. "It—it looks like watercress," she said. "Of course, I appreciate that you and Norah know far more than I about such matters—but when I think of the dinner parties we used to have in London, I would almost be prepared to swear that's what it was."

"Sheep," said Miss Nuttel, and made a face.

"It's the National Trust," enlarged Mrs. Blaine as Ada blinked again. "They rent out the banks of the canal for grazing, and of course no matter how careful the farmers are, there's the risk the sheep will have liver fluke, which is the most appalling parasite. The horrid things positively lurk inside any hollow stems just waiting to infect whoever eats them. It's too revolting."

"Ugh," was Ada's not unexpected response.

Miss Nuttel nodded to her. "Do for compost," she said kindly as she scooped up the rejected vegetation from the worktop where Bunny had dropped it. "Waste not, want not."

"Didn't you notice the sheep when you were out for your walk?" enquired Mrs. Blaine, busy chopping parsley as Ada watched Miss Nuttel return her prize to the great outdoors. "Unless they've moved again—they brought them back a day or so ago—I don't see how you can have missed them."

"I didn't," said Ada. She brightened. "As you say, I couldn't possibly miss them—and I'll tell you what else I didn't miss."

At this point, naturally, she paused. After the right number of seconds had elapsed, Mrs. Blaine, just as naturally, asked to know what she had seen.

"Nigel Colveden—with a girl," said Ada Noble.

"Nothing new," said Miss Nuttel, returning from her trip to the compost heap. "More unusual if he'd been alone."

"True," said Mrs. Blaine, waving her chopping knife with a didactic motion. "It's high time that young man settled down, though I suppose he thinks as the son of a baronet he needn't hurry."

"Droit du seigneur," said Miss Nuttel in what she hoped was a French accent.

"That's it!" cried Ada. "That's why I noticed, because this girl wasn't a bit like any of the others you've told me about. She was . . . foreign."

"French," deduced Miss Nuttel, pleased that her accent hadn't been as bad as she'd feared.

"Yes," said Ada. "I heard them talking—not that I was listening, of course, but a canal bank doesn't allow a lot of room for passing people when you're trying to avoid all those sheep."

"She must be the daughter of that count they have staying with them." Mrs. Blaine pursed her lips. "If," she added darkly, "he *is* a count—which I very much doubt."

"Said in the post office people met him at the château," said Miss Nuttel. It had only been when the ladies of Lilikot realised how, by Certain People's refusal to travel on a cross-Channel ferry, they had missed their chance to meet a genuine aristocrat—the Colvedens, being local, didn't count—that all three had become united in their regret at having missed the excursion to France, despite the various discomforts suffered on the return journey.

"Anyone," said Mrs. Blaine, darker than ever, "can buy a house in the country and give himself the airs to go with it. Look at the Colvedens, Eric. It's not as if they *inherited* Rytham Hall, is it?"

As Eric conceded this point, Ada chimed in loyally, "And the French don't hold with titles, do they? Or they shouldn't if they have an ounce of principle, considering they had a—a revolution and everything."

"Napoleon," said Miss Nuttel.

"Well, yes," said Ada. "But he was even more foreign than the French, wasn't he? The Corsican Tyrant. He had to *bribe* people with titles not to betray him! You can't call it a *proper* aristocracy when it's—it's invented for such a selfish reason."

"He'll be one of those, then," decided Mrs. Blaine with no further ado. "An imitation aristocrat. I'm surprised at the Colvedens for being taken in by him."

"Met in the War," Miss Nuttel reminded her. It had been the talk of the post office for almost a week. ".Fleabane."

"Er—excuse me, Erica. Fleabag, I think," said Ada.

"I think so, too," came from Mrs. Blaine.

Miss Nuttel snorted. "Tells you a lot, whichever it is," she said, every bit as dark as Mrs. Blaine had been a few minutes earlier. "As bad as liver flukes," she added, with another nod for Ada. "Or bees." It was plain from the second snort she now emitted that Miss Nuttel was trying to make a joke.

Ada achieved a shudder quite as good as any Mrs. Blaine might in similar circumstances have contrived. "I'm still so sorry about your hat, Norah," she said. "Remember, with tomorrow being a bus day, we simply must go into Brettenden and you must take me to the milliner's you mentioned and I'll treat you to a new one."

"Monica Mary," said Mrs. Blaine eagerly. "Well, really, Ada, her prices are out of this world—but so are her hats, and if you're sure . . ."

"Not your fault," said Miss Nuttel. "Not your bees."

Ada was anxious to stay on good terms with the admiral. "Of course it's my fault," she said. "I should never have been so silly and forgetful. If I'd remembered to bring Norah's hat in from the garden—but there, I didn't, and I won't have anyone saying I don't pay my debts. First thing tomorrow, Norah, we'll be on that bus to Brettenden!"

But when Friday morning came, it was only Miss Nuttel who was on the Brettenden bus. Another mosquito had found its midnight way through the open window of Mrs.

Blaine's room. With Ada in the room next door, Norah had felt honour bound to set an example of nonviolence. She listened to the insect's whine for what felt like several hours—and almost was—and came down to breakfast next morning white-faced, with a splitting headache she blamed partly on nightmares about wildlife in the tropics, but mostly on lack of sleep.

"Please," she begged as Miss Nuttel clinked a careless knife against earthenware. "The noise—it's too frightful! I shall simply have to go back to bed."

"Cotton wool in your ears, that's the ticket," Ada told her as Miss Nuttel spread hydrogenated olive oil with great care on bread whose crumbs pattered on the plate and made Mrs. Blaine wince all the more.

"What about Brettenden?" enquired Miss Nuttel. "Don't want to miss that."

"Yes, I do," said Mrs. Blaine in a feeble voice, her hand to her forehead. "I'm sorry, Ada. I simply can't—but you go with Eric." She did not add *and enjoy yourselves* as Miss Nuttel was half expecting. Miss Nuttel gave her friend a long, thoughtful stare.

"I wouldn't dream of it, old thing," said Cousin Ada, as anyone with sympathy for family ties must do.

Miss Nuttel continued to study the white, weary face of Mrs. Blaine. If Bunny was passing up the chance of a Monica Mary creation, she must feel really ill. "Don't like to leave you alone," she said slowly. "But—shopping to be done. Hats can wait—the market can't." She brightened. "More than one bus today, mind you. Could be back in a couple of hours."

"Not me," said Ada promptly. "I'm staying with Norah. I'm sure she shouldn't be left alone—she looks dreadful— and if I knew my way about I'd offer to go to the market while you stayed with her to make tea and so forth just the way she likes it." She reached across to pat Mrs. Blaine's plump hand. "But I'm sorry, old thing, I'll do my best but . . . I can't promise you'll like it, because my bump of

direction is nonexistent. I always end up having to ask my
way at least twice, and when you're in a hurry . . . And I'm
sure, Erica, you'd prefer to make your own selection even
if you wrote me out a list.''

Miss Nuttel nodded. "Kind of you to offer," she said,
"but—well, you're right. Better for me to go, if Bunny's
agreeable.''

"Of course she is," said Ada. "Aren't you, Norah?"

"Don't worry about me," said Mrs. Blaine faintly; and
with her hand to her head she groped her way out of the
kitchen back up the stairs to bed.

Miss Nuttel, with Ada's help, contrived a shopping list,
after which contriving—and before Miss Nuttel caught the
bus—Ada popped across to the post office for some more
chamomile tea bags and a small packet of cotton-wool puffs,
Miss Nuttel promising to buy a more-value-for-money
jumbo pack in Brettenden. Miss Nuttel then departed bar-
gainwards, whereupon Ada trotted upstairs, tapped on Mrs.
Blaine's door, and when she heard no answering voice
peeped inside. With the curtains closed it was difficult to be
sure—but it did seem that Mrs. Blaine had taken her
cousin's advice and was lying down with her ears blocked
against whatever racket or rumpus might occur to delay her
recovery.

CHAPTER 15

The discussion with, and about, Mrs. Blaine meant that Miss Nuttel did not catch the early bus. By the time she was aboard the second bus of the day, the sun was already high. The windows were wide open, but across the marsh no welcome breeze was blowing. The main topic of conversation during the six-mile journey to Brettenden was Turkish baths, though a minority of shoppers opted to discuss barbecues and gridirons and the state of their feet after being kept waiting at the stop for the bus to come.

Miss Nuttel kept silent—too much effort to talk—but secretly thought it providential that a headache had kept Mrs. Blaine at home. Bunny disliked the heat and would have grumbled (Miss Nuttel knew well) the entire day had she been well enough to do so. Miss Nuttel pursed her thin lips. Ada Noble was every bit as . . . full in the figure as Bunny, but *she* wasn't always complaining. *Ailing.* Miss Nuttel very much approved of those who put a brave face on things. Odd how different members of the same family behaved in similar situations . . .

It was while she was examining the relative merits of two wicker baskets that Miss Nuttel realised how right Mrs. Blaine had been to pay heed to the warnings of Providence. Peering at the handles to check whether they were lapped or roped—and, if the latter, how many turns—Miss Nuttel found that she was squinting. Seeing spots before the eyes. Feeling slightly sick. Hearing out-of-focus bells in her ears. Swaying . . .

Miss Nuttel assured the stall-holder that she would be fine, tried to sound as if she meant it, and made her way from the market square in search of somewhere shady to sit down. Her knees shook. Her head pounded. The back of her neck was—ugh—clammy. Miss Nuttel gulped. She took a deep breath. She gave herself a silent scolding. Was she not (apart from her little weakness in the matter of blood) the strong one in the Lilikot partnership? What would Bunny say—do—if . . . ?

"Bunny," said Miss Nuttel out loud. Those within earshot glanced nervously at the madwoman talking to imaginary rabbits in Brettenden High Street. Perhaps (conceded Miss Nuttel as she mopped her brow) Bunny's insistence on wearing a hat in hot weather was not, after all, the self-indulgence Eric had always supposed it to be. Perhaps there might be a stall on the market that sold summer hats—

"No!" said Miss Nuttel in a voice that had those within earshot moving hurriedly away. No, she would not go back to the market—go back to have everyone stare at her and ask impertinent questions. (Both Nuts considered the asking of questions by any but themselves to be impertinence of the highest order.) She would . . . go to Monica Mary, where Plummergen only shopped for special occasions. Where she was most unlikely to see anyone she knew, as there were no special occasions on the village horizon. And where she would buy a hat . . . for Bunny!

Yes—Erica Nuttel would buy on Ada's behalf the hat promised as a replacement for that borrowed, bee-infested, storm-damaged straw. Promises had to be kept. Ada had stayed at home to take care of her cousin and spare Miss Nuttel the worry—it was the least Miss Nuttel could do to oblige one who was obliging her—the financial side could be settled later—a straw hat was more easily worn than carried—Miss Nuttel's honour and face would be saved. . . .

Honour was saved; faced was saved. Money was not.

Miss Monica Mary Brown didn't so much sell hats as creations, and creations never come cheap. Miss Nuttel, spoiled for choice, gritted her teeth and agonised over that choice for what felt like hours. . . .

And was. When she emerged at last into the afternoon glare (from which her eyes were shielded by a perky-brimmed straw trimmed with neat ribbon bows and a sunflower), it was to the realisation that the Plummergen bus had gone, and there wouldn't be another for an hour and a half. Miss Nuttel felt her arms growing longer with the weight of her shopping. She wished she had not come to Brettenden alone. She thought of Mrs. Blaine . . . and she thought of Ada Noble. And the watercress.

"Sheep!" cried Miss Nuttel, at which cry another group of people chose to beat a hasty retreat from her immediate vicinity. "And lambs," she added with a philosophical shrug. She braced herself against the heat blasting up from the pavement, sighed, and headed for the railway station, where, in the taxi rank, she found Mr. Baxter with his car.

After the shock of the Monica Mary experience Miss Nuttel had gained her second wind. When she saw that the elderly taxi driver had nodded off to sleep in the sunshine, she thumped on the bonnet with a decisive hand and watched impassively as Mr. Baxter coughed himself awake.

"Brattle, please," said Miss Nuttel, climbing into the passenger seat. "Post office," she enlarged. "Stamps." During her walk across town she'd had time to plan. If they took the direct route to Plummergen, everyone would see her driving down The Street in a taxi (Lilikot was, after all, opposite the post office) and would start to wonder why—when *why* was none of their business—and to ask impertinent questions, a risk Erica Nuttel would do much to avoid. And then Bunny (headache permitting) would talk about the housekeeping money, which was *her* business. Miss Nuttel thought she could rely on Ada's happily refunding the purchase price of the hat, but she doubted that even in her most

compliant mood Mrs. Noble would agree to the cost of a
taxi when a mere ninety-minute wait would have resulted in
efficient use of the unused half of a return ticket. How alike
(Miss Nuttel reflected wryly) members of the same family
were in similar situations. It wasn't as if she could claim to
be worried about Bunny's migraine, as to admit to worry
would be an insult to the nursing skills of Ada. If family
likeness was all it seemed, then the subsequent sulks would
be more than anyone should have to tolerate in such weather.
Miss Nuttel sighed. This shopping expedition was turning
out to be one of the most expensive of her life. . . .

And was to prove one of the most circumnavigatory. At
Brattle post office Miss Nuttel confessed to having changed
her mind, and asked to be taken instead to Warehorne, which
was bigger. At Warehorne she explained that it was really
Snargate she had meant, and at Snargate she decided that
her true destination was the canal bridge at the southern end
of Plummergen.

Where nobody would see her arriving . . .

At the canal bridge Mr. Baxter drew up as requested, with
an air of silent amazement that his passenger hadn't changed
her mind yet again. Miss Nuttel thanked him, paid him, and
in relief that so far was so good tipped him rather more
heavily than she had intended. Mr. Baxter pocketed the coins
and gave her one final curious look before rattling off, leaving his passenger with almost a mile to walk. Uphill.

With her feet, back, and shopping-encumbered arms aching, she thankfully commenced the weary northward trudge
across the bridge, past the church and the pub and the
houses—if anyone saw her now, they would have no idea
where she had been—and (for she was fundamentally an
honest woman) as far as the post office, where the door stood
open to welcome her, and she walked in.

"A regular scorcher today, Miss Nuttel," came the cheery
greeting from Mrs. Skinner. "Hardly the weather for walking far—specially by yourself. A body could collapse with
heatstroke. . . ."

Courtesy required that Miss Nuttel should reply, but she gave as little away as she could. All she wanted was to be home with the shopping packed away and her weary feet in a bowl of hot, salty water. She bought the stamps she didn't really need, had it wormed out of her that Mrs. Blaine was in bed with a migraine, began to worry again, and hurried as fast as her feet would carry her out of the post office and across The Street to Lilikot.

Admiral Leighton's inquisitive bee sent her scurrying up the front path through a haze of whining insects, which made her reflect even more on the sufferings of Mrs. Blaine. Poor old Bunny. A dreadful head and a miserable day, all because of one wretched mosquito she'd been too tenderhearted to squash in the middle of the night. Erica Nuttel wondered whether she, in similar circumstances, would have as much self-control, and suspected she wouldn't. Good for Bunny. She took her hat off to her! *Her* hat. Miss Nuttel, even while stricken with anxiety, achieved a thin smile. She hoped Bunny would approve of her choice. Poor old Bunny—but at least she'd had the chance for a decent rest. She might be feeling better now. Might be downstairs in the kitchen this minute with the kettle on the boil . . .

Miss Nuttel drew several deep breaths as she stood on trembling legs in the cooler air of the hall before—after a quick glance in the direction of the stairs—hurrying kettle and chamomile-teawards. She pushed open the kitchen door. Golden sunlight filled the room and cast dark, sharp-edged shadows on the floor. Miss Nuttel heard the whine of insects—saw the buzzing business of bluebottles—about a shadow that, dark as it was, seemed to sprawl without shape in a corner of the room. . . .

"Bunny!" cried Miss Nuttel, and fainted.

CHAPTER 16

"Dates from the war—no doubt about it." The professor was as delighted as any man Delphick had seen in his life—even Bob when he announced that Anne was pregnant. "No doubt at all," reiterated the man with the luxuriant moustaches and egg-shaped head that would have reminded those who loved mystery fiction of a certain celebrated Belgian.

As Bob sat discreetly silent in his corner of the office, Delphick, while acknowledging the ballistics expertise of Professor Moustache, ventured to express polite surprise that there should have been any doubt in the matter. He himself (he pointed out) had only to hear from the head engineer of the ugly broken-armed crosses adorning what was visible of the device to be confident that it was neither British nor French in origin.

"It might," said the professor, twirling his moustache, "have been a modern replica."

Bob's jaw dropped. Delphick's did the same, but he was quick to pull himself together. "A—a modern replica?" the chief superintendent echoed faintly. "But what possible purpose could anyone be served by firing fake Nazi rockets into the Channel Tunnel dig?"

"Commercial sabotage," said Professor Moustache airily. "Big business—conspiracy—although," he added, "if it's conspiracies you want, you should try the groves of academe—but never mind that." He waggled a didactic finger under Delphick's startled nose. "One company has—has gone bust already, remember." He offered the colloquialism with a wink. "Who was I to say, sight unseen, that this wasn't . . . another lot trying something of the same sort?"

Delphick prepared to lecture this innocent scholar on the laws of libel. "I sincerely hope," he began, "that you didn't put that suggestion in your report to the Chunnel Consortium, Professor. The previous company's failure was due to financial difficulties, pure and simple. There has been no suggestion that the new Consortium indulged in any . . . sharp practice whatsoever, and if—"

"No, no, no!" The professor waved his arms in the air. "Of course I didn't mean—dear, dear—when I used the word *modern* I meant in relative terms only, you know. That is, dating from after the war—but not necessarily of *recent* date." In his turn he prepared to lecture. "Think, Chief Superintendent." He had completely forgotten the sergeant taking notes out of sight in the corner. "How many times," demanded Professor Moustache, "has a scheme to link England and France by tunnel been mooted, eh? Even . . . been started? There was one attempt in the 1880s—another in the 1920s—both cancelled. Engineering problems—unfavourable political climate—it must have seemed fated to fail. England is an island nation and always will be. That's what everyone thought. . . .

"But"—and here the professor waggled another finger— "the project currently under way, although not *physically* started until this year, had its origins in the late 1950s, when holidaying on the continent was becoming popular as currency restrictions were lifted. Flying was still a comparatively expensive means of transport, you will recall. Large sums of money had been invested in the Channel ferry routes—and then Her Majesty's Government announced yet another proposal for a tunnel that would, in the minds of the ferry people, be bound in time to take away the greater part of their ever-growing business!"

"Good heavens," murmured Delphick, not daring to meet his sergeant's eye.

Professor Moustache ignored him. "I thought it entirely credible," he went on, "that in the 1950s there might have been those in the ferry industry who lacked the confidence that history would repeat itself a third time—as, indeed, they would have been right in doing—but never mind that. For all I knew before my inspection of the site, there could have been hundreds of these—these rocket depth charges, as we may call them—dropped secretly from ferries passing over what was likely to be the chosen route for the Chunnel with the intent that should digging ever reach thus far, the subsequent explosion would serve as sabotage of a—a most decided nature. Most decided," he repeated, twirling his moustache as Delphick could only stare, marvelling at the tortuous hoops through which the human mind, if sufficiently ingenious, could make itself jump.

"However," said the professor, "once I had visited the site I realised that my misgivings as to the—the probity of the 1950s ferry companies had been unfounded. Only the most detailed knowledge of wartime rocketry could have contrived the—the devilry that has been uncovered, and there is now only one person in the country with such knowledge." Once more he twirled his moustaches, completing the gesture with a bow. "Myself, Chief Superintendent." He smiled. "And I knew very well that I had done no such contriving. The rocket was therefore no depth-charge imitation, but a genuine V4."

"A V4?" Delphick frowned. "I've never heard . . ."

"I told you only one person in the country would have known about it," the professor reminded him with a hint of smugness. "One person still living, that is. Immediately after the war there were perhaps three rocketry experts whose expertise would have allowed them to recognise—but never mind that. Now there remains only myself." He bowed again. "To recognise the thing for what it is—and perhaps to know how to deal with it."

"Then you know," said Delphick in some relief.

"No," said the professor. "I'm afraid I don't."

"But—" began the chief superintendent in protest.

"But I believe," said the professor loudly, "that I know how to find out how to deal with it." As Delphick shot him a warning look he once more went into lecturing mode. "You have to remember the atmosphere towards the end of the war in Europe," he said firmly. "The V1 and V2 had almost played their part—and a vicious part it was. Did you know, Chief Superintendent, that a hundred and fifty people died in Kent alone from V1 attack—that more than fourteen hundred V1s fell in the county, with another thousand shot down over the Channel? As for the V2, it flew so fast there was no time even to think of shooting it down. With a V2 you were on your own, with nothing but hope." He coughed. "The thing was forty-five feet long and carried a one-ton warhead—but the V2 was very small beer beside the V3, the multistage rocket with the side-boosters, launched underground, that was in preparation in the hidden tunnels of France." He coughed again. "Then there was talk of the A10—the modified V2 with the finned warhead that would detach in the stratosphere and glide as far as America—"

"What?" cried Bob before he could stop himself.

Professor Moustache turned to him. "Dear me, yes," he said. "An ingenious mind must have dreamed up that particular nasty—a rocket fired from Europe and able to cross the Atlantic! The amount of explosive it could carry would, of course, have been small, and the subsequent damage would have been as nothing to what we in Britain suffered for so many years. But the propaganda value of a long-range rocket would have been, I assure you, immense."

"I believe you," said Delphick when a horrified Bob could only stutter.

"But never mind that," said the professor. "What I was trying to explain was that while the A10 was still at the theoretical, drawing-board stage there was a final, secret, desperate attempt to create the ultimate *practical* weapon, the V4—a rocket that could travel from the farthest reaches of occupied Europe—virtually the Russian border—to batter this country, if not America, into submission. No part of the British Isles would have been out of its range. Its invention was unknown to all but the most fanatical of Hitler's officers—and of course to the poor devils of slave workers forced to labour on it, none of whom lived to tell their story.''

Once more he coughed, and there was silence for a moment until he cleared his throat. "As if any of them," he went on, "could have given away any secrets! They would have been too busy trying to keep body and soul together to concern themselves with the technical details of what they were forced to build, even if some brave souls in the V1 factories did manage to sabotage the direction finders—but the V1 technology was so *simple*. The V4 was a more sophisticated evil. Nothing could be done to stop it—but of course that didn't matter to the Nazis. By the time the Allies reached that hellish camp, there was nobody left alive. The slaves had been forced to dig their own graves before . . .''

"Yes," said Delphick, his voice husky.

There was another silence. "Yes," said the professor. "Well. These Nazis, as I said, were fanatics—the most fanatical of the lot. The officers had watched their men . . . despatch the slave labourers and then had—had turned upon those same men and killed them all, throwing their bodies into the same graves before committing mass suicide—but not''—and he waggled his finger again—"before they had fired one of the only two V4 rockets ever completed.''

"Ah," said Delphick, sitting forward.

"Quite so," said Professor Moustache. "Experimental— fired in a hurry by people with . . . other things on their minds . . . It's no wonder it fell short, and let us be thankful that it did. Had it reached the land—had it exploded as intended . . .''

"And we've inherited the problem," Delphick said dryly.

"You mentioned two rockets, Professor. What happened to the other? Could we use it for . . . purposes of comparison?"

Moustaches shook his head. "Such was the revulsion felt by the Allies when they entered the charnel house that had been the rocket site that they dismantled the remaining V4 that day. Only later, when they were a little recovered, did they think to search for plans, drawings, test results, photographs—but all had been destroyed by the Nazis. We, in common with the other Allied powers, were entitled to whatever knowledge they had obtained, the hope being that we should turn their evil into good and make the sacrifices of the thousands who died perhaps a little easier to justify. The landings on the moon," he said sadly, "would have been impossible without the work begun by Hitler's scientists, you know. Sometimes I wonder if—but never mind that.

"It's ironic," he went on in a stronger voice, "that when Wernher von Braun—the rocketry expert—surrendered to the Americans, they had never heard of Peenemünde or the factory there. They sent all his papers to the nearest Russian headquarters, and by the time we learned what had happened, it was too late. Years of research—work carried out using slaves—were lost and had to be reduplicated at enormous expense that . . . seems to make a mockery of the thousands who died. The plans for the V4 will have been handed over to the Russians with the rest of them. Over the years there has been some duplication of the work—diagrams, sketches, photostats of people's notes and memories—and the Americans have done the best they can to rectify their original unfortunate mistake. Which means, in short," said Professor Moustache, "that we will have to go to the American archives for help in this. And I fear it may take a little time."

Almost the last people in Plummergen to know what had happened in the Lilikot kitchen were the Colvedens, their Balivernes guests, and Miss Seeton. The Rytham Hall telephone was still (thanks to Martha) out of order, life having been so peaceful without "the bally thing always interrupting" (this from Sir George) that nobody had been in any particular hurry to instruct the repairmen to call. . . .

Indeed, when Jean-Louis, Comte de Balivernes, had raised the question of a box of chocolates for Miss Emily Seeton, spinster of the parish and teatime guest for the second day running, Lady Colveden had been unable to phone the post office to ask what they had in stock. Jean-Louis was forced to walk the mile from Rytham Hall to find out, and her ladyship had been glad to see the back of him. He had fidgeted about the place and distracted her all morning, and restless men made her nervous. She kept waiting for the crash as he dropped something valuable, or tripped down the stairs and broke his neck.

It was only when Jean-Louis offered—almost forced—his escort on her homeward journey to Miss Emily Seeton, spinster of the parish who had come to tea and stayed (at the comte's courteous urging) to supper, that news of the Lilikot murder finally broke.

It was Superintendent Brinton who broke it. As the tall and elegant Jean-Louis—with little Miss Seeton on one arm and her sketchbook under the other—rounded the bend before the bend in Marsh Road that gave a clear view of the church, the pub, and the space outside Sweetbriars, he looked over the intervening hedgerow and stopped in his tracks. Miss Seeton, perforce, stopped, too.

"You have, it seems, a visitor, my dear Miss Seeton," the comte reported as he moved on again at a slower—delaying?—pace. "A man." Did the pause—faint as it was—hint at a touch of jealousy? "He is a man tall and bulky—ah, pardon, burly, I should say—and of an expression most intense." Certainly some emotion, whether jealousy or another, was making the fluent Jean-Louis forget his English. "Impatient," he said. "Urgent. He strides up and down beside his car—it is a make I do not know—and consults with his watch. And scowls."

The scowl was the clincher. "That sounds not unlike Su-

perintendent Brinton,'' said Miss Seeton. "A—a friend."
Innate diffidence made her hesitate to claim the superintendent as the colleague he assuredly was (Scotland Yard, after
all, paid her that monthly retainer) when, she supposed, he
must at this time in the evening be paying a purely social
call. She stifled a sigh. *She hoped.* There had been times in
the past when a visit from Mr. Brinton—or from dear Mr.
Delphick—had been rather more serious than social. . . .

"Ah," said Jean-Louis. "A friend." Miss Seeton's sigh
and innocent hesitation could be taken two ways. It was the
fiery Gallic temperament that made him take the wrong one.
"This friend—he is of long standing, might one enquire?"

"Indeed, yes," said Miss Seeton with an enthusiasm that
did not please her companion. "We must have known each
other nearly eight years—since I first came to live in Plummergen, you know, although he comes from Ashford."

"Ah," said Jean-Louis again. "Ashford. This is a town
far from here? An easy journey?"

"It's only fifteen miles," said Miss Seeton. "Which is
easier when one has a car, since by bus it means changing
at Brettenden—but it doesn't seem far when you do. Or
even, as the countryside is so picturesque, when you don't.
Have a car, I mean, as you travel more slowly in a bus."

"A car," said Jean-Louis. He was rapidly coming to the
conclusion that he had made a grave error in allowing his
dislike of driving on what was (to any but a Briton) the
wrong side of the road to encourage him to leave his trusty
Peugeot at home. But then—would Miss Seeton, given the
choice, prefer an honest Peugeot to the—the car owned by
this burly English Brinton?

Jean-Louis stopped in his tracks again, and again Miss
Seeton had to stop, too. Only now had the light of memory
penetrated the fog of aristocratic jealousy. "*Superintendent*
Brinton," said the Comte de Balivernes. "My dear Miss
Seeton, I sincerely hope that there is nothing wrong—but it
would come as no surprise to me if there were. . . ."

He began to march the remaining few yards at such a pace

Miss Seeton had to trot to keep up with him. She was mildly intrigued by the misgiving in his voice, but supposed that anyone, on learning that an acquaintance was being visited by the police, might feel some justifiable concern as to the reason for the visit—at least until the social nature of the call had been made clear.

If, indeed, it *was* a social call.

"Miss Seeton!" Brinton had turned in his impatient up-and-down striding beside the car to recognise, in some relief, the smaller of the two who now approached him. "Miss Seeton, I'm glad to see you," he said as he covered the distance between them in a few hasty steps. "And your sketchbook?" he added in a lower tone, with a speaking glance for the parcel tucked under the count's free arm.

"My sketchbook," repeated Miss Seeton, a little sadly. All at once the pleasant afternoon—and evening—had lost their charm. She knew, or at least had a fair idea, what the superintendent was trying to convey.

"Then d'you think," Brinton continued, "you could spare me a few minutes? In—er—private," he added, with an apologetic nod for Miss Seeton's distinguished escort.

"Er—Superintendent." Miss Seeton's manners were never so correct as when she knew that this was *not* a social call. Something inside her whispered that she was merely putting off the evil hour, but she chose to ignore it. "That is—may I introduce Monsieur le Comte de Balivernes? He and his daughter Louise are staying at Rytham Hall for a few days. Superintendent Brinton is in charge of the Ashford force, monsieur."

"Er—monsieur," said Brinton with another nod that was less apologetic, more man-to-man. Any friend of Sir George Colveden, French or English, was bound to have common sense (he told himself). Was bound to see that when professional duty called, there was no time to mess around with flowery compliments. "You'll excuse me, I hope, if I take Miss Seeton inside for a little chat," he went on. Jean-Louis's knowledge of colloquial English was good enough

for him to flinch at the policeman's use of the word *inside,*
but he realised just in time what was meant, and said nothing. "I hope," Brinton went on, "you hadn't got anything
planned for the next half hour or so, MissEss?"

Her official name. Miss Seeton stifled a sigh. She had
been right: this was no social call. Now it was her turn to
apologise to Jean-Louis. Over supper *chez* Colveden she had
proposed that they should glance through one or two of her
books of old prints with a view to another garden idea in
the style of Monet for the château grounds, but that pleasure
would have to be deferred. She could tell from the superintendent's tone that he was anxious—and in a hurry—so
much of a hurry that he had come to call on her alone.

"Mr. Foxon is not with you, I see," said Miss Seeton.

"No," said Brinton. "Not . . . exactly—but he's busy.
Might come along a bit later, though. When you and I have
had our little chat."

"If you wish a—a chaperon, Miss Seeton, believe me that
I am yours to command," said Jean-Louis, placing his hand
on his heart and bowing. Miss Seeton glanced in Brinton's
direction, thanked the count, and assured him that the offer,
while much appreciated, was not needed.

"I hope this means there is nothing seriously wrong,"
persisted Jean-Louis, who suspected there was and did not
care to think of Miss Seeton involved in it. Whatever *it*
might be. He remembered, only too well, the dealings of his
late wife with the police—with the Gestapo—not that this
English superintendent, simmering with anger as he clearly
was, could be as evil as the Gestapo in their cruelty—but
the gentle sex should have no dealings with uniforms unless
in time of war—which this was not.

Brinton shrugged and moved closer. "You'll know soon
enough," he said, "so there's no reason why I shouldn't tell
you when half the village knows already, and what they
don't know they'll invent—but there's been murder done at
Lilikot, Miss Seeton, and I'd like your . . . advice."

The meaning of that pause was plain to two of the three

who heard it. The third, baffled, but accepting that Miss
Seeton—despite her evident dismay—remained serene in
the face of catastrophe, bowed once more.

"Murder," said Jean-Louis de Balivernes thoughtfully.
"A truly terrible crime, although . . . But what is this—this
Lilikot, might one enquire?"

Brinton jerked his thumb over his shoulder. "Half a mile
or so from here, opposite the post office," he said. "Look
for all the fuss and the crowds gawping outside, and there
you are."

Miss Seeton, busy with her own thoughts, did not follow
this direction, but Jean-Louis glanced northwards up the
gentle curve of The Street to see the blue flashing lights of
police cars reflected from houses and walls, and to hear—
when he listened—the distant murmurings of an excited
crowd. He sighed. "It is," he said, "a tragedy, that even in
so delightful a spot as this English Eden the snake will always find itself—but if you, Superintendent, are here to
grant your protection to Miss Seeton, then I will take my
leave and return to Rytham Hall." With a bow and a flourish
he entrusted his precious charge to Brinton's care. "And of
course," he went on, "I must not forget your sketchbook,
Miss Seeton. Ah—you are a connoisseur of art, Superintendent?" This last because, as the comte bowed a third time
and proffered the book to its owner, Brinton's hand shot out
instinctively to grab it.

"I, uh, know what I like," muttered Brinton, taking a
backward step as Miss Seeton, blinking, came to herself and
received the book with a smile of thanks for Jean-Louis before recollection of the superintendent's purpose in seeking
her company once more clouded her eyes.

The count did not miss that clouding. "You are certain—
you are sure," he insisted, "that you wish for no—no companion at this time, Miss Seeton?"

"Quite sure—thank you," said Miss Seeton. She stopped
herself just in time from saying *I'm afraid*. "Superintendent
Brinton and I—and his colleague, Mr. Foxon—are—are

friends of many years' standing.'' Even at such a moment she could not help twinkling a little as she went on: ''Indeed, Mr. Foxon and I once spent the night together—in the most respectable manner,'' she was quick to add as the count's jaw dropped. ''In church,'' she amplified, ''when they were holding a Black Mass—such nonsense! But I beg your pardon, Mr. Brinton, you wished to—to ask my advice.'' Better to use the superintendent's own phrase than to risk the implication that one was being—Miss Seeton blushed—consulted, which (even if it *was* the term used, more than once, by dear Chief Superintendent Delphick) sounded so—well—conceited in one whose talent was really very undistinguished. Yet Scotland Yard paid a monthly retainer for sketches as and when required, and since it seemed that sketches were Mr. Brinton's purpose in coming here this evening—

''Lilikot!'' exclaimed Miss Seeton, who had been trying not to think about it and, with her consciousness otherwise preoccupied, now found that it had sneaked in without her notice. ''Superintendent, who . . . ?''

CHAPTER 17

Superintendent Brinton had been thankful to see the back of Jean-Louis. Had things been otherwise, it would have tickled his fancy (though he would've been terrified young Foxon'd find out and send him up something rotten) to have a French count—a war hero with a château, no less!—think him a rival for the favours of Miss Emily Dorothea Seeton. Every blush, every falter in her speech—which to Brinton, who understood her, made perfect sense—had registered with the count—who didn't—and (the superintendent could tell) had set the old green-eyed monster on the warpath. He hoped one or other of the Colvedens would put him, Monsieur le Comte, straight about his, Brinton's, intentions before too long. He rather liked the idea of Miss Seeton being courted by anyone, let alone a foreigner, and wondered if Miss Wicks, who told fortunes, had read in the cards that her friend was about to meet a tall, dark-eyed, handsome stranger. . . .

Miss Seeton coughed politely. Brinton, who had drifted into what a lesser man might have called a trance, but what for Brinton was an honest doze, snapped upright on the easy chair in Miss Seeton's sitting room and gazed expectantly at his hostess.

"Well?" he said. "What have you got?"

Miss Seeton hesitated. "I have finished," she admitted,

"but although, naturally, I hope . . . yet I fear it will be of little help to you, Superintendent. As a likeness it is—well—good, which I'm not sure is what you wanted. It is—it is *no more than* a likeness, you see, and of course she resembles—resembled, that is—oh, dear—her cousin quite closely—the build, you know, and the facial structure, not that anyone would confuse them if you saw them together, although during the recent hot weather, which I gather from Martha that Mrs. Blaine so much disliked, you seldom did—but I fear that it is only this—this superficial likeness I have managed to capture, since, as I told you, I didn't know her particularly well, except to pass the time of day." Miss Seeton paused. "And I confess that neither Miss Nuttel nor Mrs. Blaine have ever been more than village acquaintances," she said, just as that pause was growing awkward.

Brinton interpreted the remark as a gentlewoman's way of saying she couldn't stand the sight of the individuals in question. Well, he didn't blame her for that. He couldn't stand the Nuts—didn't know anyone who could. He mumbled something noncommittal, and continued to study the portrait she had handed him.

"So I have—that is, had—no idea of her as a—as a personality," Miss Seeton struggled to explain. "Which—that is to say—it *is* what you wanted to know, isn't it?"

"It might help," said Brinton. He looked up from Miss Seeton's likeness of the late Ada Noble to find her worried gaze—make that *guilty,* he thought—upon him. "Yes," he went on, letting his attention drift from Miss Seeton's face—still worried, trying to hide the guilt—to her hands. For which *still* was definitely *not* the word. The Oracle'd put him on to this one years ago. When she's restless, when she fidgets and twitches her fingers and tries not to let you know that's what she's doing, *then* you know you're in with a chance. Fifty to one she's drawn something she feels embarrassed about, and she only feels embarrassed about the special Drawings she does—the ones for which we pay her. The ones the right sort of interpretation often helps to put us on the road to solving whatever mystery's got us poor coppers flummoxed . . .

Brinton went back to looking at the likeness of Ada, but from the corner of his eye he watched Miss Seeton's fingers. They danced on her lap—she twined them together—he heard a faint sigh—perhaps a "poor Mrs. Noble," said very softly—and then the fingers were still.

"I can see the family likeness all right." Brinton held the portrait at arm's length, closed one eye, and tilted his head. He chuckled. "Reminds me a bit of Queen Victoria, except that on stamps and coins she's in profile—" He broke off. He had seen Miss Seeton's fingers leap in a sudden twitch from her lap. "When she was an old lady, of course," he continued as if he had noticed nothing. "Not young, with her hair up and that long neck—remember the Bun Pennies we sometimes got in our change before all this decimal rubbish came in?" He did not wait for Miss Seeton to reply—to lose whatever vein of thought into which he had inadvertently tapped. "I mean when the old girl was little and dumpy—though Mrs. Blaine won't thank me to hear me say so, and I hope you won't let on."

"No, indeed," said Miss Seeton absently. On her lap her fingers lay entwined and motionless.

"Mind you, she might be pleased to think *I* think she has a—an aristocratic profile," offered Brinton with a chuckle, and his eye on those motionless fingers. "Which I don't. I'd say the cousin, poor woman, must have looked slightly the more aristocratic of the two—but it was difficult to tell, the state she was in when we found her, or rather Miss Nuttel did and passed out cold, for which I can't blame her, while Mrs. Blaine found both of 'em and went into hysterics— and I don't blame *her*, either. It was Admiral Leighton who heard the kerfuffle and raised the alarm. You can always trust the Royal Navy to do the sensible thing."

"Y-yes, indeed," said Miss Seeton, sounding almost back in focus. Brinton stifled a curse. He was losing it, whatever it was—losing *her*. Dammit. He wished Foxon would hurry up and finish all the scene-of-crime stuff at Lilikot and come down here—the lad had a way with him, especially with the ladies, and Miss Seeton was a favourite of his. And he of hers. He might coax what they wanted out of her . . . if only they knew what it was. The one thing Brinton knew was that it *wasn't* what she'd given him. Any competent artist could have produced what he was holding: neat, crisp, clear. In focus. *Out of focus.* There'd been that wobble in her voice—now what . . . ?

"The Royal Navy," he repeated softly. "Queen Victoria," he ventured. Miss Seeton's hands stayed still. "Aristocratic profile," he offered, and Miss Seeton's hands twitched.

"Miss Seeton, you've been holding out on me," the superintendent told her. She blinked at him. He held out his hand and spoke sternly. "Let me see your *other* sketchbook, please."

Once more Miss Seeton blinked. Really, although they were such very different people—except, of course, that both were tall, but Mr. Brinton was far more—well—solid in appearance, though one would not call him overweight as poor Queen Victoria had been—there were times when he and dear Mr. Delphick behaved—spoke—in exactly the same way. Their professional training, she supposed. "But how did you know—" she began, then shook herself. How silly. The professional training again, of course. Obediently she rose from her chair and trotted across to the bureau, from which she removed the sketchbook in which she had doodled, among other things, the first attempts at the copy of her French postcard for which Martha Bloomer had asked.

Brinton leafed through the book, studying each picture for only a few seconds before moving on to the next. There was—well—*something* about the special Drawings MissEss produced when she was in full flight. When she was most useful to him and his colleagues. He couldn't say what it was, any more than he could say what he liked in the way of . . . call it ordinary art—but he knew it when he saw it, and he hadn't seen it yet. He continued to leaf, holding the book open where Miss Seeton was bound to look at each page as it was turned, half his attention on the pictures and half—just in case on this one occasion he *didn't* know it when he saw it—on Miss Seeton.

Miss Seeton caught her breath. Someone not alert to the possibility would have missed it.

Brinton had been alert. "This one," he said, stabbing at the copy of Martha's picture of the card players and the café. "What's so special about it, Miss Seeton?"

"I—I'm afraid I don't know," she said. "It—there's another on the next page that's much better. Much more like what I was trying to copy."

"This one," Brinton told her firmly. If she was unhappy with it and not with the next one, this one suited him fine. "What were you trying to copy? And why?"

Miss Seeton described Plummergen's day trip to France, the tour of Calais, the postcards home, and the general teasing—kindly meant, of course—when they arrived, because by then everyone in the village knew what a rough crossing the party had endured—and if Mr. Brinton thought this an exaggerated term, she could assure him it was not, although Sir George had followed the dear admiral's advice and set a splendid example with the brandy....

"Aha," said Brinton. "The old duty-free, eh? What did *you* buy, Miss Seeton? Apart from postcards, that is." Get her talking—relaxed—and it would come.... Wouldn't it?

"Why, nothing," she said. "Because of the inconvenience of carrying it, when I drink very little—and no matter how careful one tries to be, there is always the risk the bottles might break. Except stamps, of course," she added in the interests of accuracy. "But it was in his flask," she went on after a pause, "not duty-free—the comte refilled it for him. And he very kindly gave me three bottles, which I hope was within the allowance...."

Brinton nodded, though if he had been asked to say what he'd just agreed to, he couldn't have done so to save his life. There had been an unmistakeable twitch as Miss Seeton finished speaking. "Try again," he commanded. "Here's the book—your crayons—and while you're at it I'll slip out to the hall, if I may, and use the phone. I want to know what's happening at Lilikot."

"Poor Mrs. Noble," said Miss Seeton automatically.

"You hang on to that thought," instructed Brinton as he hurried to the door. On the threshold he paused to snatch a quick look back at her. She was twiddling a crayon between her fingers. Frowning. Getting down to work in that queer, quick, not-thinking-about-it way he *knew* meant Business . . .

But when he returned with the intelligence that Foxon would be another half hour at least, Brinton was stumped. Miss Seeton meekly yielded her sketch and retreated to the kitchen to make a cup of tea. She had drawn Ada Noble— or was it, this time, Mrs. Blaine? Had the killer killed the wrong woman?—in head-and-shoulders profile. A decidedly nonaristocratic profile inside a frame that wasn't quite a conventional frame. Yes, it was oblong—portrait-shaped—but it was white, rather than gold leaf or moulded wood as most portrait frames seemed to be. And the outside edge all the way round had been . . . nibbled, as if by the teeth of a neat and well-trained mouse. Perforated. And in one corner there was a shape that looked like numbers—letters—a sum of money. . . .

"Good Lord," said Brinton. "It's a postage stamp. But why should she be so het up about that?"

He made a note to check, when he could, with the Nuts how many letters their guest had received during her stay, and who had sent them. This was no time to pretend those two women weren't the biggest gossips—and snoops—in the village, which was saying a great deal (from what he knew of Plummergen) but which happened to be true. Even if Ada had destroyed all her correspondence once she'd answered it, he would bet all Lombard Street to a China orange her hostesses could recite chapter and verse of every letter, if he leaned on them hard enough.

When he could. Both Nuts were currently in Dr. Knight's nursing home, heavily sedated, which in one way was a good thing, but from his point of view was a nuisance. Ada had only been in the place five minutes. Who would know more about her than her cousin and her friend? What the village would say was almost certain to be guesswork. Had she had either the time or the opportunity to annoy someone so badly they'd kill her rather than, say, slap a libel suit on her? *Had* she been as fearful a gossip as her cousin? (He'd have to ask the post-office crowd about that and risk the guesswork. Miss Seeton would be no help—she'd already said she barely knew the woman.)

Was it a case of mistaken identity? The enemies of Mrs. Blaine might be numbered in their hundreds, he supposed, except that *enemies* was a strong word for someone so cordially disliked by most of her neighbours as PC Potter—from his own experience of Mrs. Blaine—told him she was. Experience also told him that when nobody cared very much about you in the positive sense, they were seldom bothered enough to care about you in the negative sense, either. Certainly not bothered enough to kill you.

"It *must* be letters," Brinton decided. "Potter would have reported a rash of anonymous letters, so it can't be that. Or a parcel, perhaps. Something illegal. *Something* that's come through the post ... if she *has* drawn her as a stamp—but it looks like a stamp to me. . . ."

He brightened. Tomorrow the Oracle would be down from London to supervise security arrangements for the Channel Tunnel Bulldozer (or whatever they'd decided to use) Race.

He'd show Miss Seeton's picture to Chief Superintendent Delphick. *He'd* know what it meant, if anyone did.

On the evening of the murder there was considerable debate in Plummergen as to whether or not it was necessary to cancel the village team's appearance in Saturday's—the next

day's—Potato Race with Bulldozers. Mrs. Blaine and Miss
Nuttel, the persons most closely concerned, were in the care
of Dr. Knight and unavailable for consultation. Algernon
Noble (when Brinton asked the London police to call on
Ada's estranged husband) proved similarly incommunicado,
being away from home and with his neighbours having no
idea when he would be back.

The telephonically deprived Rytham Hall was likewise incommunicado, but as soon as the comte had brought the
tragic news, Sir George ripped the bandage from his wrist
and drove off, a little jerkily, in the station wagon to consult
with schoolmaster Martin Jessyp, Admiral Leighton, and
other local worthies. He slipped into the George (without
buying a drink) for a quiet word with Benjamin Folland,
who clutched wildly at the yellow sponsorship forms and
babbled about phoning headquarters—except that it was after hours—for advice; and ended up at the vicarage, where
he had a another quiet word, this time with Molly Treeves.
Miss Treeves did a brisk and thorough job of persuading her
brother that an emergency meeting must be convened first
thing next morning when the matter could be properly
thrashed out, and Sir George came back to the hall in a glow
of satisfaction at a job well done.

"The entry will stand, of course," said Lady Colveden
as she gave her wavy brown hair its regulation hundred
brush strokes before bed. "I know you all have to talk about
it for the look of the thing, but it isn't as if any of us really
knew the poor woman—and it *is* for charity." She glanced
in the mirror at her husband, who was frowning at the book
on his bedside table. "Anyway," she went on brightly, "we
all know how proud the vicar was when he won the Lawnmower Race. He's sure to want to—to maintain our stan-
dards of competition, isn't he?"

Sir George had stopped frowning. "Cynic," he remarked
affectionately, chuckling as he slipped between the sheets
and picked up Henty's *With Cortés in Mexico*. He had borrowed this treasure earlier that night from Admiral Leighton

and, until his wife had set him straight, had been doubtful as to the propriety of reading light fiction before dropping off to sleep. But, as Meg had said, it wasn't as if they'd known the poor woman. . . .

Before her husband lost himself among the Spaniards, Lady Colveden said quickly: "Jean-Louis was absolutely fascinated to learn about Miss Seeton—about how important she is to the police, I mean. He asked me all sorts of questions. He seems very taken with her." She waited. Sir George muttered something she couldn't hear. "And . . . Nigel seems to be getting on awfully well with Louise," she went on. "I'm so glad they were out of the house and had time to enjoy their evening before they heard what happened at Lilikot. Isn't she a lovely girl?"

Sir George muttered something about *too plump for his taste* that Lady Colveden took a moment or two to translate. He wasn't thinking about the lovely and elegant Louise at all: he was thinking of Ada Noble.

Or of Mrs. Blaine. "George, suppose she was murdered by mistake," said Lady Colveden. It was an obvious possibility, given the family likeness. "Suppose whoever it is comes back and tries to murder Mrs. Blaine? The police can't guard her every minute of the day. Do you think you should offer to teach her a few unarmed combat tricks?"

Horrified, Sir George emerged from his Henty—and it wasn't to mutter. "What?" he almost yelped. "Good God! Ask Fleabag," he appended in a quieter voice as her ladyship shushed him frantically. "Cheese-wire merchant, y'know. And very good at it, as I recall."

"But the Nuts are vegetarian," said Lady Colveden without thinking, then giggled. It sounded so silly.

"Quite," said Sir George, diving back into Henty before she could say anything else.

Her ladyship, very wisely, said nothing.

But as she thought of Jean-Louis she thought of how insistent he had been, earlier that day, on buying Miss Seeton a box of chocolates—on buying them from the post office—which stood almost directly opposite Lilikot. . . .

CHAPTER 18

Lady Colveden said nothing of her suspicions to Sir George either that night (when they seemed plausible) or next morning (when they seemed ridiculous). All she said was *I told you so*—to which her husband responded with another affectionate chuckle. He had returned from the vicarage meeting to confirm that Plummergen would (as predicted) not be withdrawing from the Grand Bulldozer Race. The Reverend Arthur Treeves had (said Sir George) orated with eloquence on the subject of healthy competition and man's eternal striving for self-improvement, while at the same time deploring the state of affairs between Plummergen and Murreystone that would, the vicar knew only too well, cause the latter to gloat unbearably over the former should Plummergen fail to compete. The Reverend Arthur saw no need to encourage the already short emotional fuses to burn even faster. Let whatever light they shed (he concluded) shine as a good deed in a sinful world—when it was, after all, for charity.

"No fuss, though," Sir George told the group assembled around the kitchen table. "No flags, brass bands, and so forth. Bad taste, in the circumstances."

"Just as long as we get to race," said Nigel, who drove a better tractor than almost anyone in the Young Farmers and hoped to impress Louise with a win. "Talking of which, now I know it's on, I'd better get going. Coming, Louise?"

The young couple—even Sir George was starting to think of them in that way—said their good-byes and hurried out of the door. The Chunnel Consortium had arranged for all competitors to have a full morning's practice before the race proper began, and while those used to driving tractors must have an advantage over those without that skill, there was every need for Nigel and his fellow racers to get in as much practice as they could.

"I imagine Mr. Folland isn't pleased," was Lady Colveden's comment as they heard the MG roar into the distance. "The Chunnel's over thirty miles from here. Of course we should . . . pay our respects—even though we hardly knew her—but there's surely no need to be quite so respectful. And won't there be cancellation fees? If The Golden Brolly has to pay for a brass band whether it uses it or not, it would be a fearful waste of money to—oh." She saw her husband's grin and the smile of Jean-Louis. "Yes, of course. You mean we have black armbands and crêpe while everyone else wears their best hats and has fun."

"Another hat?" said Sir George with a comical lift of one eyebrow. His wife's Freudian slips in the matter of their son's romances never failed to amuse him. Only known the girl a couple of days, and here was Meg busy measuring Nigel for a morning suit and—

"Good God!" The baronet fell back on his chair. "You mean *I'll* have to wear *a top hat*?"

"George," warned his wife, who knew him rather better than he realised. "Jean-Louis, please take no notice. Feel free to wear whatever you want this afternoon, and I apologise for this family's sense of humour." She shot the count a dazzling smile. "I was joking about the armbands, just in case you wondered."

Jean-Louis bowed across his coffee cup and returned her ladyship's smile, with interest. Meg Colveden wondered how Miss Seeton could resist him. If, indeed, that was what she would do if the question was ever popped.

Always assuming that Jean-Louis, Comte de Balivernes, did not turn out to be the killer of Ada Noble . . .

Crabbe's Garage thought it wise to obtain police permission for the removal of so many potential murder suspects from the village for the whole afternoon, with the Dover ferry and the hovercraft no more than a couple of miles from where they would be going. It was Jack and his father, Very Young Crabbe, who drove the two fifty-seater coaches in which most of attending Plummergen elected to travel to the Channel Tunnel dig. Benjamin Folland, organiser of the main event, had left several hours earlier in his sports car, disappointing both Maureen-from-the-George and Emmy Putts by failing to offer either of them a lift. Charley Mountfitchet and Doris, and the Stillmans (who agreed to shut the post office early for once) were a poor substitute for one who, professing ignorance of local history, had taken his young passengers (as neither girl had yet dared confess to her friend) to Murreystone for the biggest thrill of their lives. Each girl had secretly hoped for just such another—perhaps an even greater—thrill, and was understandably annoyed that she wasn't going to have it after all.

Sir George drove the admiral, the count, and the vicar in his shooting brake, while Lady Colveden's blue Hillman carried Miss Treeves and Miss Seeton. The village travelled in a muted but hopeful mood. It wouldn't do to make too much of a fuss with the Nuts doped to the eyeballs and someone dead, but they weren't going to let Murreystone know they were feeling a bit down, even if they hadn't got flags to wave—except the younger generation, to whom exemption had been granted on the grounds that the whole affair was for the benefit of children—in this case crippled children—and it didn't seem right to upset them when they'd hardly known the poor woman, after all.

There were uniformed and efficient stewards on duty at the gates to guide newly arrived vehicles to a safe parking area. The Chunnel Consortium, conscious that it must at all costs avoid a PR disaster, wanted to ensure that nobody who had no business being there would go anywhere near the mouth of the tunnel and the Nazi menace that lurked within. As far as the general public was concerned, the greatest menace they were likely to encounter was the Murreystone bus, which, directed by a steward with no local knowledge, pulled up beside Very Young Crabbe's coach and disgorged few woman, but a disproportionately large number of healthy-looking, muscular men.

"Farming community," said Sir George to Jean-Louis as they strolled across the car park in search of Lady Colveden and her friends, who had been directed to the end of a new double row and were several hundred yards away. "All of 'em used to tractors, of course, like Nigel—and most of 'em pretty tough specimens. Hay bales, sacks, and so on. Hope there won't be trouble if they do better than us."

"Or if you—we," amended Jean-Louis with a smile, "do better than they?"

"Ah," said Sir George. "Well, yes. Probably will, too. More of us than them—but of course we play fair, and when it comes to Murreystone . . ."

"They do not play the game," said Jean-Louis as his wartime comrade, now a magistrate, tried to find an accurate but nonslanderous way of putting it. "They cheat."

"They would if they could," agreed Sir George, casting judicial caution to the winds: but the wind soon dropped as he recalled conscience, in the form of the vicar, walking with the admiral close behind them. "Not that we *let* the blighters, of course, so they can't. And they don't." Sir George glanced back and saw how slowly the Reverend Arthur walked on the uneven ground. He coughed and let the wind blow free once more. "They try damned hard, though."

"They are dishonest," said Jean-Louis. He frowned. "And yet you still compete with them. Why is this?"

"Nothing proved, old chap. And because we make damned sure they can't get up to mischief, we won't *get* the proof, more's the pity." Again Sir George recalled the pres-

ence of the Reverend Arthur Treeves. "But there—innocent
until proved guilty, it's the only way. Can't have everyone
blaming everyone else on suspicion. That's . . . anarchy.
Lynch law. Damnable."

"Not English," said Jean-Louis, smiling; and Sir George
agreed that, by Jove, it wasn't.

"Miss Seeton," observed the count after they had walked
some yards farther, "is very English, is she not?"

"None more so," agreed Sir George. "Nice little woman.
A lot of common sense. Good at her job, too. They think a
lot of her at the Yard."

"As also do you," said Jean-Louis. And again Sir George
agreed with the sentiment expressed.

The gentlemen found the sensibly shod ladies threading
their passage through the parked cars in search of them. Sir
George's helpmeet greeted her spouse by waving her copy
of the sketch map each driver had been given on arrival at
the Chunnel site. "Isn't it a splendid turnout?" she cried as
the two parties converged. "This car park must be half-full
already—and it's the Overspill, according to the map, and
still filling up. And just look at the crowds over there by the
spoil heaps, if that's what they are. I should think The
Golden Brolly must be absolutely delighted."

Miss Seeton, blushing as the eyes of Jean-Louis turned in
her direction, hurried to correct the not illogical, but nevertheless somewhat awkward, misunderstanding. In a clear
voice she reminded her ladyship that Mr. Folland had travelled widely, with great energy and enthusiasm, during his
few weeks' stay in Kent. The number of sponsors he had
drummed up (if that was the phrase) for today's and numerous earlier events was quite remarkable. If the charity
was delighted, it should also be appreciative of its representative's sterling efforts towards increasing (as she believed
the term to be) its public profile. . . .

Miss Seeton faltered—stopped speaking—frowned.

Her friends knew well that the very idea of publicity
(which, when applied to herself, Miss Seeton found distaste-

ful) made her uncomfortable, even while her common sense acknowledged that there were those for whom self-promotion was essential. Lady Colveden, fearing that Jean-Louis might make some tactless reference to Scotland Yard, hurried into the conversational breach with an exhortation to her husband that they should decide the best vantage point from which to view that area of the ground in which the Plummergen team was expected to compete.

"We don't want to waste time on the funfair and stalls and all the rest of it," her ladyship decided. "That is—well, *I* don't—and we mustn't forget that Miss Seeton has promised Nigel a sketch of him being first across the line. If he is," she added. "But I do think he stands a good chance, even if I am his mother."

"Ha!" said Miss Treeves darkly. "We can only hope that the scorekeepers, linesmen, whatever they're called, have been carefully chosen. That they haven't been . . . nobbled."

"My dear," protested the vicar, shocked.

"You don't know Murreystone," said his sister. "After all these years you ought to, but you don't."

"I should think," broke in her ladyship before a sibling squabble could develop, "that with everyone standing around counting, even Murreystone would find it hard to cheat on the number of buckets they've shifted. Assuming they start with the piles of earth the same size," she added.

"Quite," said Miss Treeves.

"Folland says they'll be tossing coins for who starts where," interposed Sir George pacifically, before resuming his friendly argument with the admiral (more accustomed to reading charts of the high seas, while the major-general was happier on—and with maps of—terra firma) about the best place to stand. At last they all began moving out of the overspill car park. Jean-Louis and Miss Seeton found themselves walking in an amicable silence side by side. The count was quick to offer Miss Seeton his arm when her foot bumped against an uneven patch of ground, and she thanked him with a nod and an absent smile.

Lady Colveden watched her husband stride on ahead, still arguing with the admiral, while Miss Treeves took the arm of the vicar in a gesture her ladyship suspected had less to do with Molly's fear that she might trip than that her brother, musing on charitable impulses, might do so.

"Potato races," Miss Treeves remarked as they walked, "always used to be great favourites at the church fête. I wonder why we stopped having them? Perhaps we could think about reinstating them next year, Arthur."

"You must explain to me, Miss Seeton," said Jean-Louis as he helped her around a lump of dried mud. "In this race they are to use potatoes? Why should one for such a purpose need something so large as a bulldozer?"

Miss Seeton emerged from whatever thoughts had pre-occupied her. "I'm so sorry," she said. "You were asking about potato races? They are, I believe, a very English concept."

"As one would expect," replied the count, who would have bowed had the terrain permitted such gallantry.

Miss Seeton smiled, and this time it reached her eyes, which were no longer clouded in thought. "Potato races," she explained, "are a way for children to let off steam without one's having to allow them too far out of one's sight, which when they are in high spirits can be inadvisable. Or," she added, "as in this particular case, adults, although where Murreystone is concerned—but that," she said firmly, "is not what you were asking."

She stifled a sigh and pressed on with her explanation. "There are many different versions, but at our school we would line up the children, each beside a heap of perhaps a dozen potatoes—the same number for all—and tell them to carry just one potato at a time to the opposite end of the field, where there would be an empty bucket into which they must drop it before running back for another. When there were no potatoes left and the bucket was full, they had to carry it with them when they raced for home, and of course

the first to cross the finishing line—which was originally the
starting line—was the winner.''

"Ah,'' said the count, who had decided less than halfway
through the preamble that it would probably make more
sense when he saw it happening.

"The elimination heats for this event,'' Miss Seeton continued, ''were run in the individual villages, first using lawn
mowers and grass boxes, and then tractors and bales of hay,
which is where dear Nigel scored so highly that he is to
drive last of his team, the rest of whom will take it in turns
according to their position at the end of the original heat.
There is to be only one race here today, you see, even
though there are funfair attractions for the children, as bulldozers move rather slowly, and it will take time for all the
earth to be shifted from one end of the competition ground
to the other. And it will be in that final race for the line that
Nigel's driving skills will be of greatest use. Or so he told
me,'' she added. ''I must confess that I didn't quite understand it all—but I do understand that it is during the final
race for the line that Murreystone are most likely to—well—
to try something.''

"They will cheat,'' said Jean-Louis. "Except that one
must not say so, I am informed by *le cher Georges*.''

Miss Seeton glanced ahead to where a uniformed steward
stood by a gate ready to direct lost souls to the starting line,
and murmured of magistrates and the laws of libel. Or was
it slander? But—well—inadvisable, even though on many
previous occasions that she herself could recall . . .

"I thought,'' said Jean-Louis, ''that nothing—that is, that
they are innocent until proved guilty, so Georges told me.
And he was very strict in the telling,'' he finished with a
laugh. ''Your English law—I must watch my step, must I
not?''

At which point he contrived to trip—with an elegant,
sidestepping motion—over a tussock of grass, and Miss Seeton's laughter mingled with his own.

The steward at the gate was ready—indeed, eager—to

direct them. He managed to upset both the admiral and the major-general by pointing out what they should have realised themselves, namely that until they'd had the toss for which team raced from which heap of spoil, there was no particular sense in choosing to stand anywhere in preference to anywhere else. "Which means the first thing you'll want is to watch the toss," the Plummergen party was told. "There's been already been some argument about that, so I've heard. A six-way toss, that's not something you do every day of the week, and some people are saying it's too easy to fiddle the results if you're so minded."

"Oh, dear," said Lady Colveden. The original plan had been for lots to be drawn from a top hat (which had made Sir George groan), but it had been argued that this was unfair. The second suggestion had been for dice to be thrown, until someone pointed out that dice could be loaded. Tossing a coin had seemed the most equitable solution, until . . .

"Murreystone," said Miss Treeves.

"We don't know that," said Sir George quickly.

"It was one of the Romney Marsh villages," volunteered the steward, who had long since grown bored with the life of a mere signpost and made no secret now of the fact that he would cheerfully listen to any remark uttered within earshot. "And that *was* the name, as I recall. Reminded me of my aunt Myrtle, rest her soul, on account of her second husband, her first having passed beyond when he tumbled off the cliff at Beachy Head, being a bloke by the name of Tony—"

"Right. Thanks," broke in Sir George, nervous lest his troops should be trapped by this chatty mentor and be unable to make their escape until everything was over. "We'll just head for the crowds, shall we? Follow our noses and—and take what comes—so come along!"

And he led his party, with a rush, safely through the gate and on to where the noise and bustle and bunting showed that a major charity event was about to begin.

CHAPTER 19

Among the excited throng it was not hard for Jean-Louis to separate himself and Miss Seeton from the others. The mechanics of a six-way toss—especially when one of the six parties involved saw fit to dispute every flip of the coin and the ensuing calculations—took time, and the former war hero seemed to have little patience for such trivialities when there was a lady to entertain.

His wartime experiences had left the count with an eye every bit as quick as Miss Seeton's, and despite the grimness of some of those experiences, he remained a good twelve inches taller than she. "While we wait," he said, "you will prepare your first sketch, Miss Seeton—and I, with your permission, will keep watch and prevent any from interrupting you." He made a swift gesture towards the crowd that milled about them, and then began to withdraw, addressing his fair companion in accents rather lower than his normal clarion tones. "I have observed a slight rise in the surrounding earthworks from which, or so I think, there may be obtained the clearest view of the . . . racetrack, *ma chère* Miss Seeton. If that is the word," he added ambiguously.

"No matter the eventual choice of position," he continued as he made a passage through the crowd, "Nigel and the rest of the team will be visible—as will everyone else." He paused. "As also will Louise," he finished with a smile.

"For Louise is a girl of great beauty, even if as a father I may be thought prejudiced in her favour, and she is always of notice to those about her."

"No, indeed," Miss Seeton assured him, and then blushed. That hadn't been quite what—"I mean," she amended, "that though you are, not unnaturally, inclined to—to favour her, she is, undoubtedly, a very lovely girl, and it comes as no surprise that people will admire her."

"She reminds me so much of her mother," he said with a sigh. "Others may say no, it is I whom she resembles, but in her looks, certainly, it is clear to me, for I never forget a face, and there is an air—a carriage . . ." He frowned and then pulled himself together. "But also in her—her spirit, if that is the word. Her . . . soul, perhaps—and you, if I may, Miss Seeton, have something of the same quality—a simplicity—a directness—I cannot find the word, but there is no . . . intrigue, only honesty—and Nigel," he concluded, twinkling as Miss Seeton accepted the compliment with a modest blush, "will be a lucky young man, I think, for she seems as—as taken with him as he, most evidently, is with her."

"Nigel is a very charming, good-natured, and honourable young man," said Miss Seeton at once. "I hope—indeed, I am sure—they will be very happy together."

"I shall be lonely once she is gone," said Jean-Louis.

It was a remark—almost an afterthought—Miss Seeton deemed it only courteous to ignore. The count (she decided) had his mind on other things as he helped her to balance on a mound of earth—really, one's practice of yoga proved its worth in the most surprising circumstances—and waited for her to remove her sketchbook from her bag. One could hardly pay attention to, or take seriously—even should one wish to do so—the absent-minded murmurs of a man obviously concerned for his daughter's safety in a crowd of such size.

"I think you need have no fears for your daughter's safety in such a crowd," said Miss Seeton as her pencil began to dance across the page, capturing in swift, keen strokes all the tension of that unmistakable moment just before the start of an event, when plans and preparations are in the past and nothing more can be done except leave the matter to Fate. "Nigel, I know, will take good care of her until it is his turn to race, by which time the others in the Plummergen team will have done so, and they will be able to look after her until he comes back."

"And the wicked Murreystone?" enquired the count, with one of his infectious laughs.

Miss Seeton met his gaze and smiled. "It is true there is sometimes a little . . . liveliness during village encounters," she admitted, "but it is mostly the young men—and at night," she was quick to add, "rather than during the day." The count had stiffened at her words and was staring into the distance. Oh, dear. It had been less than tactful to mention the young men when Louise, as far as anyone knew, was right in the middle of a group of them. Which must be why the count was still staring—looking worried . . .

Miss Seeton followed his gaze. She did not immediately recognise Louise among the Plummergen contingent, but as the young men involved were all tall, this was no great surprise. She saw the top of what she thought was Nigel's head, and guessed the girl would not be far away. She saw Benjamin Folland scribbling on a clipboard—one of the calculations for the six-way toss, she supposed—and as the result was announced she heard the crowd shout, then saw it surge and divide as everyone moved off to the designated place—and Louise went with the rest of Plummergen towards spoil heap number five.

She heard the count beside her catch his breath. She wondered why. She looked beyond Louise to see—

"Oh, dear," said Miss Seeton. Murreystone, grim-faced, was being directed towards spoil heap number four.

"Indeed," said Jean-Louis.

They stood in silence for a while, watching. Benjamin Folland and his Golden Brolly colleagues consulted in a final quick huddle with those who, from their attire, were Chunnel

Consortium personnel, and then a man Miss Seeton did not know was handed a megaphone.

He introduced himself as the Consortium's chairman and delivered an efficient, morale-boosting speech about friendship with France, improved trade relations, and transport for the future. He coughed, as if waiting for applause. He was about to lower the megaphone when the PR person at his side kicked him on the ankle—Miss Seeton on her earthworks had a clear view of this *lèse-majesté*—and after another cough he appended a (brief) coda concerning the worthiness of the Crippled Children's Wheelchair Charity and the generosity of all who had sponsored the racing drivers in both local and final heats of the Bulldozer Race—which he proposed to start by firing a blank-charged pistol on a count of three.

The crack of the pistol was followed by a roar from the crowd that drowned out the rush of feet as six men pounded from the Le Mans–style starting line towards the six waiting bulldozers. The first man in the driver's seat switched on the engine. The other five soon thundered into life. The race was on.

Six bulldozers driven by those whose previous experience has been with tractors—even if there has been a morning of intensive coaching on the part of the bulldozer owners—move with neither fluency nor grace. The watching crowd of sponsors and others was kept well back from the arena as the mighty caterpillar tracks began trundling the mechanical monsters with their upheld buckets in clumsy semicircles to scoop the first bucket of spoil. Beside each heap the five men yet to race stood with shovels at the ready, poised to help fill the buckets faster than their unskilled comrade could achieve alone. On each bulldozer a skilled driver rode pillion, ready to take over the controls if any machine—or its driver—looked like running amok. The Chunnel Consortium was taking no risks with this particular public-relations exercise.

The roar of the crowd, once the bulldozers were moving,

was as nothing to the thunder of those six great engines in low gear. Miss Seeton saw one machine stop, stalled, and saw Murreystone gesture wildly—the jeers were inaudible—for it had been heading for spoil heap number five. There were some moments of frantic activity, and the adjudicator's motorbike pulled up alongside to give impartial advice. Plummergen, with a jerk and a judder, was on the move again, and Miss Seeton saw Murreystone complain (as she supposed) to the judges—who were Benjamin Folland (whose sojourn at the George might be deemed to render his neutrality doubtful) and his London colleagues.

"Good gracious!" Miss Seeton's exclamation passed unheard amid the clamour of several thousand throats in full cry. Only Jean-Louis glanced up at her, and—although he had not made out her words—wondered why she smiled and waved and looked so very pleased.

Miss Seeton felt his gaze and stopped waving to point with her pencil into the milling crowd. "A friend," she mouthed, adding boldly: *"Un ami."*

The count followed the pencil's pointing line and nodded. He prided himself on never forgetting a face: and he had seen that face before—in Plummergen, when he had been doubtful—no, jealous, he would confess it—of the owner's acquaintance with Miss Seeton. Now, however, that it had been explained to him how Miss Seeton was the colleague—the Umbrella—of the English police about whom one had heard in the newspapers . . .

"You must allow me to escort you, Miss Seeton," said the count, offering his arm. Miss Seeton saw the gesture, but could not hear the words. She shook her head and smiled a polite refusal. Had she not promised dear Nigel a sketch of his triumphant crossing of the line?

Then she blinked. She stared. Superintendent Brinton, a bulky man, had moved aside to reveal the well-known figure of Chief Superintendent Delphick—who was staring at what she instinctively knew for that drawing the superintendent had taken away with him after the murder of poor Mrs. Noble.

Now Miss Seeton's conscience was torn. It was all too clear to her that Mr. Delphick must have come down from Scotland Yard at Mr. Brinton's personal request because of her foolish—unhelpful—sketch of Mrs. Noble as a—she blushed—as a postage stamp. Mr. Brinton, Miss Seeton knew, was as capable an officer as any. For him to have summoned Mr. Delphick, who had praised—who had understood—her pictures in the past, all that way . . . to have taken him from his own, equally important, work just to look at her ridiculous doodle must mean that she—that her sketch—had confused rather than helped, as Mr. Brinton had hoped—had told her—would be the case.

Professional etiquette demanded that she should go at once to explain—to apologise—to her friends—to her colleagues. . . .

And yet—there was her promise to Nigel Colveden.

Miss Seeton's eye gauged the amount of spoil remaining at the near end of each track and compared it with the amount at the far end. They were not, she decided, even halfway there. Nigel's turn to drive was yet to come, and at the present rate of progress she suspected it would take the teams at least a double innings, if that was the word, for each driver before the nearer heap had been entirely removed to the new dump. There should, she thought, be ample time for her apology—perhaps time to draw another sketch that Mr. Brinton might find more helpful—before Nigel's first turn at the bulldozer controls. And certainly before his second.

Jean-Louis de Balivernes felt a tap on his shoulder. He glanced up at Miss Seeton and saw her smile. She handed him her sketchbook, on a fresh page of which she had scribbled her grateful acceptance of his escort through the crowd to the two policemen: she had even drawn a quick likeness of each man, in case among the thousands at the scene they should contrive to move from the spot where she had seen them. The count studied the faces, followed Miss Seeton's pointing pencil, saw the likenesses in real life, and knew them instantly. There was too much noise for him to waste his time in talking. He bowed, smiled back at his companion, and helped her gently down from her mound of earth to lead her to her friends.

The two figures—demonstrably the long and the short of it—made an intriguing sight as they threaded their way through the crowd. The count was tall, distinguished, and carried himself with an air that was far too elegant to be English. Miss Seeton was short, neatly but plainly dressed— apart from a rather remarkable hat—and distinguished only by the bulky handbag and the gold-handled, black silk umbrella she carried over the arm that was not tucked under the escorting arm of Monsieur le Comte de Balivernes. Heads turned as the unusual twosome passed. Pickpockets and sneak thieves on the lookout for likely targets soon recognised in Jean-Louis someone as alert as themselves, and decided to leave his wallet—and Miss Seeton's all too tempting handbag—where they were.

Brinton and Delphick, having contrived a "casual" meeting intended to raise no alarm among an innocent crowd bent only on pleasure, had moved away from the worst of the noise to a spot where they could hear themselves think, and where, coincidentally, Jean-Louis had no difficulty in seeing them. He deftly changed direction and headed after them, his eyes still scanning the surrounding crowd with a vigilance the passage of thirty years had not dimmed.

Miss Seeton felt his arm tense, and even above the noise of the crowd and the bulldozers she would have been prepared to affirm she heard him catch his breath. Before she could stop and signal her willingness to continue alone, however, he had relaxed again, although a sideways glance showed her that he was frowning. Worried about his daughter, no doubt. For Murreystone to have drawn the station next to Plummergen had been somewhat . . . unfortunate. . . .

"Miss Seeton!" Brinton's cheerful boom was muted by

the surrounding racket to a rumble, but at least (Miss Seeton realised in some relief) it *was* cheerful. He wasn't exactly smiling—Mr. Brinton seldom smiled—or she seldom *saw him* smile, she supposed she should say, as more often than not when she saw him it was on official business, and a policeman's lot was not a happy one—but he didn't look *annoyed* at her arrival. Perhaps Mr. Delphick had been able to help him with the picture, after all. . . .

"Miss Seeton!" Delphick's firm baritone was likewise muted, almost an undertone, but Miss Seeton had sharp eyes, and it was no more difficult for her to lip-read than it was for Jean-Louis—who had been in no doubt that these were the men he sought, for he never forget a face, and Miss Seeton's sketches had brought the pair to life.

"Mr. Delphick. Mr. Brinton." Miss Seeton, in whom years of teaching had developed the facility of voice projection to a nicety, had wondered briefly about such projection but decided against it. Her friends knew she was there: she saw no reason to draw further attention to herself. As she and the count drew closer she smiled (a little hesitantly) in greeting; and after the greeting felt obliged to fulfil the courtesies before getting down to business.

"May I," she said, "introduce Monsieur le Comte de Balivernes? Chief Superintendent Delphick of Scotland Yard—and Superintendent Brinton you already know, monsieur."

The gentlemen acknowledged one another with nods and what appeared to be polite murmurs, although Brinton shot the count a quick, knowing look and seemed about to speak until Delphick shook his head.

"Miss Seeton," said the Oracle, "I observe that you have your handbag—one of your more amply proportioned models—on your arm. May I hazard a guess that your sketchbook is inside?"

Miss Seeton, about to launch into her planned apology, was so startled by the question that she confirmed his guess at once, explaining that she had promised dear Nigel—

"Then I should like to see it, please," he broke in, and held out his hand in the long-familiar gesture that could not be disobeyed. Miss Seeton obediently opened her bag and removed the book. Jean-Louis took it from her and, with a bow, passed it to the policeman who seemed so eager to study its contents.

Miss Seeton, blushing, began the long-familiar apologia. Delphick had to hide a smile as he heard her babble of *a few rough impressions, merely ideas and suggestions for the finished drawing.* . . . He could have quoted the speech by heart, and had the matter not been so urgent might have done so—but Brinton was peering over his shoulder and muttering in his ear. A murder investigation was no place for whimsy.

Delphick had been turning the pages at intervals of no more than a few seconds, scanning Miss Seeton's mere ideas and moving on when they yielded no more than the impressions she had claimed for them. He had started at the back, where her most recent sketches were, and smiled as he saw himself and Brinton, and read Miss Seeton's writing underneath. But he didn't want reality or likeness—he wanted the offbeat, the bizarre, an indication that she had been Seeing in that strange way of hers, that she had looked beyond reality to the ultimate truth and—

"Ah!" The exclamation was low, but deeply satisfied. "I thought so," said Delphick. "If that's Nigel Colveden and a bulldozer . . . Miss Seeton, who is this?"

"Good gracious," said Miss Seeton. "I had no idea that I had—I mean, it must have been because I saw him from the corner of my eye while I was—but you are right, that is most certainly not Nigel."

CHAPTER 20

"Excuse me," came the unexpected voice of Jean-Louis. The heads of Delphick, Brinton, and Miss Seeton turned as one. "It may," said the count, "be perhaps not so much that you saw the—gentleman—under debate, Miss Seeton, as that I saw him, and with your sensitive eye you . . . noticed my notice, as one might say."

Delphick shot him a look every bit as quick and knowing as Brinton's earlier effort. "You had particular reason to notice this man, monsieur?" he enquired. "May I ask what?"

Jean-Louis bowed. "Chief Superintendent, you may, for while my old comrade Georges the magistrate cannot be far away, he is not at hand to remind me of your English laws of slander—and it is true that I have no definite cause to suspect—to accuse—this man, only that it is a coincidence most remarkable that I should see him first in Scotland, when visiting the family of my dear wife, and then to see him once more in Kent . . ." His face was grave. "It is perhaps that I am too suspicious, messieurs, but such suspicion one does not easily forget. Just as I do not forget a face, so do I not forget the time of war, when to see someone again many miles from the first encounter was so often a sign— an indication—of . . . mischief."

"He could say the same about you," put in Brinton with another of those knowing looks.

Jean-Louis bowed again. "Had he recognised me, this he might well have said, but I think he did not—has not—for there are few with my facility to remember a face, except Miss Seeton here, whose eye is as quick as my own."

Miss Seeton blushed again, but her modest murmurs were drowned out by the noise of the crowd and the bulldozers as Delphick demanded:

"You would be prepared to swear this was the same man?"

Jean-Louis took the sketchbook from the Oracle and contemplated in silence the features of the man Miss Seeton had portrayed in close-up, holding a pen in one hand and, in the other, a clipboard on which there was a long list of what appeared to be names and addresses.

"I would swear," replied the count after no more than a ten-second pause. "Should this be necessary," he added, as if Justice of the Peace Sir George were hovering at his shoulder whispering of *reasonable doubt,* and *innocent until proved guilty.*

"Then it's over to you, Miss Seeton," said Delphick. "Why, when you were supposed to be concentrating on Plummergen's efforts in the Bulldozer Race, should you bother to draw this man who has no connection with the village?"

"Oh, but he has," said Miss Seeton, just before Brinton and Jean-Louis (who had realised his original explanation left something to be desired) also confirmed the fact. The two men looked at each other, grinned, and left the lady to explain. Miss Seeton said:

"He has been staying at the George for the past few weeks. His name is Folland, and he is one of the organisers of the race—one of the judges, too. He must have been . . . in the way when I was looking for Nigel and the others."

"When I," interposed Jean-Louis, "was looking for my daughter." The count had had Miss Seeton's unique talents described in some detail by Lady Colveden. "You have," he said gently, "good eyesight, Miss Seeton, but assuredly no better than mine—and *I* was not able to see what this man had on his clipboard beyond a sheet of paper. Yet you show writing that to me very much resembles names and addresses. Why should this be?"

"I—I suppose," said Miss Seeton, looking to Delphick and Brinton and receiving no instruction to be silent, "it must be because of the sponsorship forms he always carries around with him—for people to sign, you know, and promise money in a—a sliding scale, so much per bucket of earth or bale of hay, or how fast they complete the task."

Brinton looked at Delphick. Delphick looked at Brinton. The latter shrugged. "That's the way it's normally done," he said. "Nothing unusual about it that I can see."

"But Miss Seeton can," said Delphick. He frowned. "Why the postage stamp, Miss Seeton?" He held out the sketch of Ada Noble in profile in a perforated frame.

"I—I'm not sure," said Miss Seeton. "But when Horace Jowett died—the Sothenhams auction, you know—and the children, of course, have been soaking them off envelopes and postcards, just as everyone has been saving silver paper and milk bottle tops—for charity—which is why Martha asked for a copy of—"

Both Delphick and Brinton recognised that sudden guilty start—or rather, stop—and the unhappy lowering of Miss Seeton's gaze to her hands, clasped about the golden crook of her black silk umbrella with her handbag over her arm.

"Martha," prompted Delphick. "A copy of what?"

"A—a postcard I sent her from France," said Miss Seeton. "She didn't want to cut it or soak it, but the stamp wouldn't come off and I promised I would copy it before she added it to the collection Mr. Folland . . ."

"Ah," said Delphick as she fell silent. "Mr. Folland strikes again. There's a little too much coincidence here, I think." He turned to Brinton. "What do you make of him?"

"He hasn't got an alibi for the murder," said Brinton,

"but the same's true of half the village, including monsieur here. I'd no reason to suspect him more than anyone else— my money was on the estranged husband, to be honest, once your Mets lot said he'd done a vanishing act."

"Talking of vanishing acts," Delphick said, "where is Mr. Folland right now?"

"Talking with his colleagues," said Jean-Louis at once. "These men," he went on, "I do not recognise—even though they have had their faces towards us when they think we are not looking."

"They are, I believe, from the charity's headquarters in London," offered Miss Seeton as Delphick and Brinton— with a startled *have they, indeed!*—turned to follow the count's discreet direction.

"The Golden Brolly," said Delphick thoughtfully, turning as discreetly back. "A logical title, reminiscent of golden deeds. An umbrella group for a number of charities dealing with sick and crippled children. An undoubtedly worthy cause, and yet . . ." He frowned again. "Miss Seeton, with your particular interest in umbrellas—especially golden ones—you don't seem entirely comfortable with the idea. Might I ask how much money you promised on behalf of Nigel and the others?"

"I—I didn't," she said, looking a little embarrassed and a little surprised. "Not as a sponsor, that is. He asked me, of course, but I found I preferred to give a lump sum unconditionally, as it was for such a good cause, so that whether or not they came in first, the wheelchair fund would benefit by the same amount."

"I see," said Delphick, who didn't, but who was starting to have the glimmerings of a theory. "Miss Seeton, has this coincidental Mr. Folland ever seen the umbrella I gave you?"

"I don't think so," she replied after a pause. "As you know, I keep it for best, which a film show in the village hall—so many feet to trip over it—or a talk on wartime recollections is—well—not."

"No," said Delphick. "No, I appreciate that: I remember what happened when you and young Foxon attended that ghastly Black Mass in Iverhurst church."

"And so do I," growled Brinton, who'd had to foot the bill for repairs—after which he had suggested she save Delphick's gift for safe and special occasions, such as tea at the vicarage, with friends.

"Are they still sneaking looks at us, monsieur?" asked the chief superintendent. Jean-Louis waited a moment and said that they were. "Then," said the Oracle, "let's give them something to look at. Miss Seeton, may I borrow your umbrella?"

Miss Seeton, somewhat surprised, handed it over. Dear Mr. Delphick—so good at his job, and such an original—but perhaps it was a touch of the sun, which was really rather hot just now, and (unlike herself) none of the gentlemen was wearing a hat. . . .

"A parasol, of course," said Miss Seeton; but nobody was listening. Chief Superintendent Delphick had regarded his black-silk, gold-crook-handled prize with affection for just two seconds before, with a flourish, opening it and holding it high above his head.

The immediate result was most gratifying.

The bulldozers were still thundering—the crowd was still roaring in support of the various teams—and the piles of earth at the starting line were almost gone. The drivers had obviously learned the knack of guiding heavy plant by lever instead of by wheel, and on their second runs had made considerably faster progress than on their first. It would not be long until the end heaps were ready and the dash for the finishing line would begin. The crowd swayed and surged to find a better viewing position. . . .

Benjamin Folland and his colleagues—who had shown so much covert interest in the deliberations of Superintendent Brinton (known to Mr. Folland, at least, as a policeman) and his friends—seemed to lose their heads as Chief Superintendent Delphick opened Miss Seeton's umbrella. They

stared—they exchanged swift words—they looked about
them and saw people—hundreds, thousands of people—
blocking their way wherever they looked. There was another
hurried colloquy between the three men, with Mr. Folland
appearing the most vocal—and all three then suddenly
leaped upon the driver of bulldozer number four—the Murreystone machine—and dragged off both driver and pillion
passenger. As Mr. Folland seized the controls his friends
leaped on behind and prepared to repel boarders as indignant
Murreystone, seeing their man grounded, charged from the
starting line with shovels at the ready.

The Chunnel security men did not at first realise what was
happening. Delphick, who did, at first tried shouting, but was
inaudible above the whoops and cheers of the crowd and
the diesel roar of five engines driven by practised amateurs—
and one engine driven by a man in an obvious panic.

"The fools!" cried Brinton as screams and shrieks of
warning began to mingle with the cheers. "Why didn't they
just make a run for it in the ordinary way? They'll flatten
someone with that thing if they're not careful!"

"They're hoping to break through the perimeter fence to
the road," said Delphick as he fumbled in his breast pocket.
"It's the only reason I can think of for their not losing themselves in the crowd—the most direct route to freedom."

"Ah," said Jean-Louis in the voice of experience. "When
there is more than one escaper, it is always more difficult to
arrange a subsequent rendezvous. Better to stay together
from the first if to meet later is an importance. . . ."

"He can't steer it," groaned Brinton. "He *will* kill someone—that ground's not level enough for running—all
they've got to do is trip. . . ."

"He *has* killed someone," amended Delphick as he withdrew from his pocket a walkie-talkie radio. "At least I'll
risk a sizeable wager that he has, if Miss Seeton's opinions
are anything to go by—"

"What?" gasped Miss Seeton, horrified.

"What?" bellowed Brinton, startled.

"Ah," murmured Jean-Louis, who never forgot a face. "It is, then, as I wondered. . . ."

"Never mind that now," said Delphick, fumbling with the controls and stifling a curse. "Hello? Hello? Is anyone listening, dammit?"

A crackle announced that someone was. Delphick informed the crackle in swift, crisp phrases that one of the bulldozers had been taken by unauthorised personnel, had broken out of the race arena, and must be stopped before innocent bystanders were harmed.

"Yes—we know—but we're on foot and we've a fight breaking out," the crackle told him. "We'll do what we can, though," it consoled him, and was gone.

"A fight?" echoed Delphick.

"Down there!" exclaimed Brinton, pointing.

"Oh, dear," said Miss Seeton. "Murreystone, I fear, and Plummergen."

She was right. Everyone knew that Benjamin Folland had been staying at the George and Dragon while he gingered up support for the various Golden Brolly-sponsored events and charity collections of stamps and silver paper. Murreystone had muttered from the start about his status as a judge, and when he was seen to spearhead an assault on what they were sure would have been the winning bulldozer, Plummergen's rival lost its collective head. To the roar of diesel and the applause of those race-watchers too far away to see what was happening, the clang of metal on metal was a discordant counterpoint—for when Plummergen found itself under attack, it did *not* turn the other cheek, but picked up its shovels and prepared to meet the foe.

The security men were sprinting for the arena, yelling into their walkie-talkies and gesturing to the crowd to stay back. The crowd, already trying to escape the erratic path of the fugitive bulldozer, heard—saw—instructions coming from all four corners of the compass at once, and scattered in a reckless explosion that left nowhere for the bulldozer to go. The perimeter fence was a million miles away across uneven ground thronged with running, jostling people. Only one route remained open—that which led over the spoil-waggons' "railway" track to the tunnel mouth—and beyond, to the edge of the cliff.

"There's no fence," said Delphick, who had checked this area for security purposes, "but they'll have to steer a damned straight line if they want to get out of this in one piece—and the way that man's driving, they won't make it!"

Benjamin Folland was ignoring the frantic gestures of his companions as he wrenched at the controls to bring the bull-dozer round with its head towards the tunnel and the cliff, and safety. Then, with a sudden fearful screech of metal, the bucket, its contents sprinkling as earthy rain on his upturned face, began to clang upwards and bang downwards in an uneasy rhythm as he struggled to steer, peering ahead when his line of sight was clear, desperately leaning to one side or the other as the bucket continued to rise and fall.

"He's jammed something, the fool," said Brinton. "He'll kill the lot of them!"

Delphick was feeling helpless in the face of imminent disaster. The cliff—it was more an outcrop of the higher cliffs above—was not as high as some in the region, but any fall in or from a moving vehicle is likely to cause damage (at least) to those who travel with it. They will probably end up under it, and a bulldozer weighs more than several tons. . . .

"Look!" cried Superintendent Brinton, as if everyone hadn't been looking. "He'll be over the track in a minute, and then—oh, no!"

A horrified gasp broke from Miss Seeton, although above the general clamour nobody could hear it. Jean-Louis found himself patting her hand. He had no idea when he had first seized it, and Miss Seeton was too preoccupied to raise any objection to the familiarity.

Benjamin Folland had indeed tried, with his bucket-impaired vision, to drive over the track, but *tried* was the operative word. With his still inefficient mastery of the controls he made the fundamental error common to all who have no knowledge of the safe way to cross tramlines and took the crossing at an oblique, rather than perpendicular, angle—and he approached it with caution instead of driving with boldness straight ahead.

The inevitable happened. The first caterpillar track cranked up and partly over—the bulldozer balanced, gears grinding, half on and half off—Folland threw himself like a madman at the controls, which were wrenched from his hands by one of the other two men—the bulldozer lurched, juddered, and as the bucket came down again fell with a resounding crash with the metal lines of the railway leading out of the Channel Tunnel jammed between its tracks.

Leading it *into* the tunnel.

Only Delphick among the watchers realised the possible danger—the *probable* danger—Folland was fighting with the other men now—nobody had proper control of the monster that was trundling, rumbling, vanishing towards and into the tunnel mouth and the digger at the far end and—

"Get back!" cried Delphick into the walkie-talkie. "Get everybody back—get them down!"

How fast does a bulldozer travel—five, ten miles an hour? It seemed an eternity to Delphick until someone could spare the time from suppressing the riot of village rivalry to respond and ask him why he was making such a request. His answer was curt and informative.

"Right," said the walkie-talkie, and said no more.

They waited—Delphick, Brinton, Miss Seeton, and Jean-Louis—in stunned silence, none of them taking their own advice, all of them standing, watching—waiting for something to happen—

A volley of shots rang out from below. The security guard had snatched the starting pistol from the hand of the PR person and was firing it in into the air. The sharpness of the sound penetrated even the bulldozer roar. Security guards in other parts of the field used their walkie-talkies to find out what was happening. Like wildfire the message was spread: *Get back from the tunnel! Get away! Lie down if you can't run!*

Even Murreystone and Plummergen cast aside their weapons and fled, their hands clasped over their heads, chivvying comrades and foes alike before them, out of the direct line of likely catastrophe—

Which struck with a dull and distant boom that burst on the eardrums and was followed by a storm of dust and rubble and choking cordite smoke that burst from the tunnel mouth with a plume of spray from the far side of the cliff . . . as the tunnel collapsed with a crash and a tumult of tumbling rock into the biggest heap of spoil for miles around.

CHAPTER 21

It was two days later. Superintendent Brinton had called to see how Miss Seeton (of whose nerves and common sense he had a high opinion, but of whose age he was aware) was recovering from her latest adventure. He was not greatly surprised to learn from Martha Bloomer, busy with beeswax polish and a soft lint-free cloth, that his quarry was not at home.

"That Frenchman's taken her for a walk by the canal," said Martha with a jealous sniff. "Off home later today, he is, and very keen to see it before he goes on account of it was built to stop Napoleon."

Brinton looked at his shoes, which gleamed in the way of well-cared-for leather. He grinned. Monsieur de Balivernes must be even keener on MissEss than he'd seemed on Saturday, the man being a snappy dresser and yet thinking nothing of a trudge through meadows in which there were flocks of sheep with all the attendant . . . inconveniences, thought Brinton with another grin.

"Invasion's not funny," said Martha sharply. "We were lucky he never came—neither of them," she added, thinking of a later attempt at invasion.

"We were certainly lucky on Saturday," said Brinton, his grin fading. "Apart from a few bumps and bruises and some

kiddies going into hysterics, there was nobody hurt at all—
except Folland and his pals, of course.''

"I'd say being blown up and dead and buried under a
million tons of chalk and seawater was a sight worse than
hurt," Martha told him. "Miss Emily didn't say much, but
I remember the War well enough, Mr. Brinton. That was
some Nazi devilry in there waiting for them, wasn't it?''

"If it was," said Brinton, choosing his words with care,
"they deserved it. Benjamin Folland killed Ada Noble, as
far as we can make out, and the other two were almost as
bad—crooks, the lot of 'em.''

"You mean The Golden Brolly's a—a fraud?'' cried Martha indignantly. "When we've been knitting and saving
stamps and silver paper and sponsoring races and swims and
even how many weeds you can pull up in half an hour—''

She paused for breath, which gave Brinton time to chip
in that The Golden Brolly *in itself* was an honest organisation. All the money raised for the charity—for the supply
of powered wheelchairs to crippled children—was used to
that end. The Charity Commissioners and Audit Committee
had investigated and found nothing wrong.

"But?'' said Martha.

"But," said Brinton, "if they'd looked at the sponsoring
side of the business, it would've been a different story. The
Oracle—Mr. Delphick—he got the idea when Miss Seeton
didn't seem keen to sign her name and address for the bloke,
just gave Nigel the money and told him to get on with it.
He—we—wondered why she was making so much fuss
about him knowing where she lived, and—''

"Miss Seeton doesn't make a fuss," protested Martha. "I
tell you, Mr. Brinton, you'll go a long way before you find
anyone as—as uncomplaining as her!''

"Yes, I know," said Brinton quickly. "What I meant was
that she kept Drawing—*you* know—all sorts of things that
led us back to the charity—postage stamps, when you'd
been collecting them—and sponsorship forms, when from
where she was standing she couldn't have seen them. It

made us take a closer look, and after the Oracle put out a few feelers to the Scottish police—we've Monsieur de Balivernes to thank for that particular lead—we realised what was going on.''

''And what was that?'' demanded Martha, who resented having to ask, when if only Miss Emily had been there she'd have heard the story straight out.

''Burglars,'' said Brinton. ''One of the most efficient schemes we've come across in years. Before they submitted the sponsorship forms to the Brolly accounts department—and remember, the contributions *always* matched the amounts pledged—very accurate, they were—Folland or one of the others would copy them so that they had a list of who lived at what address and how much they'd promised. Staying in one place for a few weeks using the Brolly Blitz as an excuse gave the blighters the chance to find out who was promising a lot because it was family, and who was doing it because they really had plenty of cash to throw around. And the ones with the most had burglars a month or so after the Brolly representative had moved on to another part of the country. . . .''

''Why,'' gasped Martha, ''that's—that's wicked! Taking advantage of people's good nature like that—they had *my* name and address on young Nigel's form! The cheek of it!''

''Yes,'' said Brinton. ''It'll take a while to round up the gang—there's a few in London the Oracle's seeing to—but they had quite a little network going. Oh, it was very clever. People like to give to charity, and of course children are always a safe bet. Starving refugees or cuddly animals *might* have done better, but they couldn't be sure. And nobody could ever point the finger and say they didn't get the right number of wheelchairs for the money raised, because they always did.''

''It's an ill wind,'' said Martha, who was frowning. ''But why,'' she enquired, ''did he kill Mrs. Noble? Far as I can see, she didn't have children herself and she hadn't sponsored anyone to do anything—at least, no more than the

Nuts did, saving stamps and silver paper and stuff like that.''

"Yes," said Brinton, "it's a puzzle. We'll never know for sure, but we think she somehow rumbled their little game—or they thought she did, which was just as dangerous for her as if she had. Remember that couple of days when the telephones at the George were out of order?''

"Maureen," said Martha, so startled by the apparent non sequitur that she answered in one word.

"Maureen," Brinton agreed. "And talk about coincidence! Folland had to keep in regular touch with charity headquarters, of course, and ten to one he let his gang there know how things were going on the names-and-addresses front at the same time. When we were interviewing at the George after Ada was killed, both Doris and young Maureen mentioned the woman had been spotted near the phone box on the corner when he was using it to make his report. My guess is that he was afraid she'd overheard something she shouldn't have done. There was a broken pane in the box, they tell me.''

"It's fixed now," said Martha absently. She was frowning again. "I still don't see why—''

"If she was anything like her cousin," said Brinton, "Ada Noble wouldn't have stood for any hanky-panky. If she thought there was anything fishy about the charity, she'd have said so—come right out with it and challenged him, or at least picked his brains good and proper—and he was a panicky sort of bloke. You were there on Saturday—did you see him on that bulldozer?''

Martha intimated that she had been too busy trying to prevent Stan joining in the Murreystone-Plummergen free-for-all to notice people on bulldozers until they were almost on top of her, at which point she certainly hadn't wasted time looking at them, she'd just got out of the way.

"Very wise, too," said Brinton. "But take it from me, he panicked easily. All it took was for the Oracle to open Miss Seeton's umbrella—and without prompting, too, as we hadn't made the connection then. Which is another coincidence,'' he concluded smugly. "The count's right, you know. They've got to mean *something*.''

Martha merely looked at him, waiting for the rest of it. Brinton grinned at her. "Well, you were there,'' he told her cheerfully. "Everyone else was, they tell me. The village hall—Mr. Jessyp and the others talking about the war—not *Henry V,* but the Hitler war—and the one before that as well. Sound mirrors, Mr. Jessyp mentioned. Making it easy to hear from a long way away—*and Ada Noble with her sun hat gone and a brolly open right outside the telephone box . . .*''

"Poor woman,'' said Martha after a respectful pause.

"A shocking waste,'' said Brinton. "The only possible consolation is that if he hadn't killed her, we might never have tumbled to his burglary scam—but then, what's being burgled, no matter how much they pinch, against a human life? And the lives of even three crooks is a pretty poor exchange, if you ask me—though I think we're well rid of the blighters. Folland took his time about bumping the poor woman off, if she saw him on Tuesday and he didn't kill her until the day before he was due to leave the village for good. Seems obvious to me he must have talked it over with the rest of the gang—which makes 'em equally guilty in my book. Pity we can't throw it at 'em,'' he added grimly. "Still, one way or another we got 'em. . . .''

"Thanks to Miss Emily,'' said the loyal Martha. "If she hadn't done those pictures for you, you wouldn't have known who it was, would you?''

"My money was on the husband,'' agreed Brinton. "Miss Seeton saved us a lot of bother, once I'd had the chance to show her stuff to the Oracle. Mind you, even he didn't get it right away. Opening her umbrella like that was just . . . bravado, you could call it. Experimenting. Wanting to know if The Golden Brolly lot really were watching us, and wondering what they'd do if they were, and why . . .''

"So now you know,'' said Martha.

"We do,'' said Brinton. "We think,'' he added.

"Thanks to Miss Seeton,'' she reminded him.

• • •

It was a pleasantly warm September day, with no more than half a dozen clouds in the whole blue arc of the sky and a breeze that was barely a sigh. The garden of Rytham Hall was a gorgeous riot of brown and copper, scarlet and crimson, purple and dark autumnal gold and every shade of green. On the lawn a group of ladies in Monica Mary hats mingled with gentlemen thankful they'd been spared the excesses of morning dress and with villagers in everyday attire who had just dropped in, at the Colvedens' invitation, to wish all the best to young Nigel, who next week was getting hitched at last and about time, too, even if he had to go all the way to Scotland to do it with his girlfriend's family living there, and they hoped the photographs came out well so that everyone could see them. A suggestion that Mr. Jessyp should hire a ciné camera and film the proceedings was being considered, the costs of hire, film, and travel (hitchhiking had been ruled out as undignified) to be met by door-to-door collection as Plummergen's contribution to the future happiness of the pair.

"I've counted four toast racks," said Lady Colveden to her daughter Julia, whose Janie was in a whirl of excitement at the idea of being a bridesmaid for Uncle Niggle. "Louise makes her own croissants, so what they'll do with the other three—you know Nigel can eat a whole rack by himself—I can't imagine."

"There are three electric toasters," said Julia. "Toby says we should give them a toasting fork to tease them, but I think they'll just have to work out a rota until everyone who's given them a duplicate of anything has had time to pop in and see it being used."

"Miss Seeton had the sense to ask what they'd like," her ladyship said wistfully. "I *told* everyone we had a list, but you know how people never pay attention."

"Sorry, Mother," said her ladyship's undutiful daughter. "What did you say?"

"If Toby doesn't beat you," said Lady Colveden sternly, "then I think I'll suggest that he does."

"That's no recipe for a happy marriage," said Julia at once. "And—talking of happy marriages . . ."

"Yes," said her ladyship, following Julia's gaze to the noble oak beneath whose shade two figures—one tall, one short; one male, one female—were strolling. "Yes," said her ladyship again. "They do seem to be getting on awfully well, don't they?"

Miss Seeton, chatting amiably with Monsieur le Comte de Balivernes, gave no impression to anyone watching that she had refused that gentleman's offer of matrimony not half an hour before. Such an idea, she told him, had never entered her head, even in her youth, and she was far too set in her ways by now. Too English to wish to live abroad. Happy as she was . . .

"It would," said the count, bending low over her hand, "make *me* very happy should you change your mind—and this you may yet do, for which I shall hope. And, should you *not* so change, then we may still be friends, may we not?"

"Indeed we may," said Miss Seeton. She had suspected all along—and now she was sure, from the cheerfulness of his response to her rejection—that his proposal had been the result of a—of an attack of gallantry, inspired by the obvious happiness of Nigel and Louise—and of dear Bob and his Anne, who was being fussed over and made to sit down when she had confided to Miss Seeton that she wanted to move among the crowd catching up with friends long unseen—and dear Sir George and Lady Colveden, of course, and Julia and her Toby—it was all, mused Miss Seeton, entirely *right,* and for one of a romantic temperament, which one could not deny was true of the French, a—an almost irresistible impulse. Which the count had not resisted, but to which she, being English, was—fortunately for Monsieur de Balivernes, for suppose she had said yes?—immune.

"We may be friends," said Miss Seeton firmly.

"We *are* friends," said the count with equal firmness; and he strolled up and down in the shade of the oak and talked of Monet, and the Impressionists, and Art, and the wonderful pictures in the Louvre, and the next time Miss Seeton came to France she must allow him to escort her as he would be interested to know whether her view of *La Gioconde,* the *Mona Lisa,* was the same as his own—namely, that when the painting had been stolen in the 1930s it had been replaced by a skilful forgery. . . .

"Can't stay away from crime, can you, Miss Seeton?" It was Detective Constable Foxon, resplendent in a yellow tie that failed to match his paisley shirt, who now addressed her. "Burglaries one minute, forgeries the next. You're a marvel—isn't she, sir?" This last to Jean-Louis, of whom Nigel had more than once spoken to his friend Foxon, who had an affection for his Art Consultant colleague and wanted to make sure she wasn't being led astray by a wrong 'un, though he supposed her instincts ought to tell her if he was and as they seemed pretty matey he guessed he wasn't, and if he was honest with himself he was just being nosey. . . .

"Miss Seeton is indeed a . . . marvellous lady," said Jean-Louis with a smile. "I am trying to persuade her not to leave it so long before her next visit to my country."

Miss Seeton blushed and smiled and murmured of the equinox and the likelihood that the Channel crossing would be . . . squally.

"Pity about the Chunnel," said Foxon. "I mean—a good idea and all that, but with the whole thing blown to kingdom come, who's to say when anyone'll risk putting the money together to try again?"

"Who, indeed?" said Jean-Louis politely. "And yet in ten, or twenty, or thirty years' time, perhaps, there will come forward someone with the vision and the—the technical expertise, if that is the word, to build—to excavate—a tunnel where it is far safer than this now destroyed site at Shakespeare Cliff."

"Twenty years is a long time to wait," said Foxon.

"It is," said Jean-Louis. He turned to Miss Seeton. "But there are some," he told her softly, "who do not mind waiting—if what is at the end of the wait is regarded as worth waiting for."

To Foxon's great surprise, Miss Emily Seeton blushed.

$\mathscr{A}$BOUT THE $\mathscr{A}$UTHOR

Hamilton Crane is the pseudonym of Sarah Jill Mason, who was born in England (Bishop's Stortford), went to university in Scotland (St. Andrews), and lived for a year in New Zealand (Rotorua) before returning to settle only twelve miles from where she started. She now lives about twenty miles outside London with a welding engineer, a materials engineer, a corrosion engineer, a husband—and a pair of schipperke dogs, making it a household of four including herself.

Bonjour, Miss Seeton is Hamilton Crane's thirteenth book in the series created by the late Heron Carvic.

Under her real name, Sarah J. Mason has so far written six mysteries starring Detective Superintendent Trewley and Detective Sergeant Stone of the Allingham police force.